LOSS

Victoria Hislop's fir̶ ̶ ̶ ̶ ̶ ̶ ̶ ̶ ̶ ̶ ̶ ̶ ̶ ̶ ̶ ̶ ̶ held the number o̶ ̶ ̶ ̶ ̶ ̶ ̶ ̶ ̶ ̶ ̶ ̶ .day *Times* paperback chart ̶ ̶ ̶ ̶ ̶ ̶ ̶ ̶ ̶ ̶ nsecutive weeks and has sold ̶ ̶ ̶ o million copies worldwide. Her second novel, *The Return*, was also a *Sunday Times* bestseller and her third, *The Thread* was shortlisted for a British Book Award. Her books have been translated into more than 30 languages.

A great fan of the short story, she has had her own published in magazines and newspapers, and her first collection, *The Last Dance*, has been widely acclaimed. She has also been a judge for several national competitions including the Costa Short Story Award.

THE
STORY

· ·

LOVE · LOSS · LIFE

THE STORY is an anthology in three parts: LOVE, LOSS and LIFE. It comprises one hundred pieces celebrating women writers working in the short story form.

The selection ranges from Willa Cather's story *Consequences,* to the inaugural winner of the Costa Short Story Award, Avril Joy's story, *Millie and Bird*. One hundred stories for the last hundred years.

Each story and themed volume is a personal selection by the bestselling author and champion of the short story, Victoria Hislop.

LOSS

Great short stories
by women chosen by
Victoria Hislop

HEAD
ZEUS

CONTENTS

Introduction

Extended Copyright

THE
STORY

······································

A GENERAL INTRODUCTION
TO LOVE, LIFE AND LOSS
BY VICTORIA HISLOP

······································

While gathering the short stories for the anthology in which this volume *Loss* originally appeared, I read some of the most brilliant and profound pieces of writing that I have ever come across.

The authors in the anthology range from a Nobel Prize winner, Doris Lessing, to the acknowledged queen of short stories, Alice Munro. There are Man Booker winners, Costa winners and Pulitzer winners. A few were born in the 19th century but the majority are more modern. Several of them are as yet unknown, others are household names, like Virginia Woolf. Many of the most vivid and passionate storytellers are young. And without doubt many of the most powerfully original are contemporary writers.

Apart from the writers all being female, the other guiding factor in the selection is that the stories have been written in English. The stories are varied and I am sure that no single reader will like them all. Perhaps I enjoyed certain stories because they meant something very personal to me. Others I think would be admired by any reader.

I discovered that it is possible for a short story (unlike a novel) to attain something close to perfection. Its brevity can mean that an author has the chance to produce a series of almost perfectly formed sentences, where every carefully chosen word contributes to its meaning. Occasionally the result is flawless, something a novel can never be.

Readers are allowed to be impatient with short stories. My own patience limit for a novel which I am not hugely enjoying may be three or four chapters. If it has not engaged me by then, it has lost me and is returned to the library or taken to a charity shop. With a short story, three or four pages are the maximum I allow (sometimes they are only five or six pages long in any case). A short story can entice us in without preamble or background information, and for that reason it has no excuse. It must not bore us even for a second.

If a short story has no excuse for being dull, it has even less reason to be bland. As I selected the stories for this anthology, I found myself reading stories that made me laugh out loud, gasp and often weep. If a story did not arouse a strong response in me, then I did not select it. Even if it is elegaic or whimsical, it must still stir something deep in the pit of the stomach or make the heart race.

Some stories had such a strong effect on me that I had to put a collection down and do something different with the rest of my day. I could read nothing else. I needed to ponder it, or possibly read it for a second time. Muriel Spark's 'The First Year of My Life' (*Loss*) dazzled me with its brilliance. That was a day when I didn't need to do anything other than reflect on her wisdom. For different reasons, Alice Munro's 'Miles City, Montana' (*Loss*) rendered me incapable of continuing to read. She moves seamlessly from a description of a drowned boy's funeral to an incident on a family outing where we believe that one of the children will drown. Even the relief I felt at the story's relatively happy conclusion was not enough to lift my mood.

Quite often an anthology is named after the author's favourite short story, and if that were the case I would read the eponymous story first. More often, there is no particular entry point into an anthology (unless you are happy to read them in the order they appear, something I usually resisted) and in that case, there was no better guide than simply whether the title intrigued me. Who, for example, would not go straight to a story entitled 'How I Finally Lost My Heart' (Doris Lessing, *Love*), 'A Weight Problem' (Elspeth Davie, *Life*), 'How Did I Get Away with Killing One of the Biggest Lawyers in the State? It Was Easy.' (Alice Walker, *Life*) or even the intriguingly named: 'The Life You Save May Be Your Own' (Flannery O'Connor, *Loss*)?

A short story can be more surreal than many readers might tolerate with a novel and, perhaps, less grounded in reality. Succinctness sometimes allows a writer to explore ideas that may not sustain over a greater length. An example of this is Nicola Barker's 'Inside Information' (*Loss*), a shiningly original story told through the voice of an unborn child who is considering the suitability of its soon-to-be mother. Personally, I love the slightly quirky in a short story, but I would probably not be so patient if I had to listen to the voice of a foetus over three hundred pages.

I think the short story can give a writer the opportunity to experiment and to try a style or a voice that they would not use in the novel form, so there is often an element of freshness and surprise for the reader – and perhaps for the writer too.

For me, the stories that make the greatest impact are those that are the most emotional. On a few occasions, when I was reading in the library, I noted curious glances from my neighbours. They gave me sympathetic looks, but tactfully chose to ignore my tears, the context probably reassuring them that I was weeping over the fate of a fictional character rather than some personal catastrophe. Perhaps a few hours later, I would be shaking with suppressed laughter. I think I must have been a very annoying person with whom to share a desk.

I have divided the stories into three categories – *Love*, *Loss* and *Life* – but these titles are loose. Love is, of course, a central preoccupation of literature, but a love story is so often a story of loss, or indeed a story of life. Many of these stories take an amusing and sardonic look at love, so the division, though slightly artificial, is designed to give a reader the chance to read according to her or his mood. Many of them could appear under more than one heading and, I will admit, some stories could probably fit happily into all three categories.

LOSS

Many of the stories in *Loss* are tragic, some are shocking. All of them are emotional.

From Katherine Mansfield's almost unbearably poignant 'The Canary', which is written with a feather-light touch, to Alice Munro's 'Gravel', which is blunt to the point of brutality, I think few of these stories will leave readers cold.

There are lost lives, lost loves, lost innocence, a lost mother (Colette Paul's 'Renaissance'), lost breasts (Ellen Gilchrist's 'Indignities'), loss of hearing (Helen Simpson's 'Sorry?') and even a lost leopard (Anna Kavan's extraordinary 'A Visit').

'The First Year of My Life' by Muriel Spark takes the idea that babies are born omniscient and gradually lose their power and their knowledge. In this story, a baby is born in 1913, 'in the very worst year that the world had ever seen so far', and watches, dismayed, unsmiling, sardonic: 'My teeth were coming through very nicely in my opinion, and well worth all the trouble I was put to in bringing them forth. I weighed twenty pounds. On all the world's fighting fronts the men killed in action or dead of wounds numbered 8,538,315 and the warriors wounded and maimed were 21,219,452. With these figures in mind I sat up in my high chair and banged my spoon on the table.'

It is a profound story – a curious companion piece to others in the anthology in which the story is also told by a wise, all-knowing baby: Nicola Barker's masterful 'Inside Information' and Ali Smith's 'The Child' (*Life*) are especially engaging and fresh.

Carol Shields' 'Fragility', with its hinterland story of a disabled child and a couple's lost happiness, shares much of the pathos of Yiyun Li's 'After a Life', in which a dying child lies incarcerated in a small apartment. Both stories are agonising to read. Lorrie Moore's 'Agnes of Iowa' is similarly tragic but even more open-ended, with a couple doomed to live in perpetuity with their woes.

Susan Hill's 'Father, Father', a story of two daughters 'losing' their father to a second wife, their step-mother, is insightful and real, a common situation faultlessly described.

LOVE

In the volume entitled *Love*, love appears in all its guises and disguises. As Yiyun Li describes in 'Love in the Marketplace': 'A romance is more than a love story with a man.'

Perhaps maternal love is the most visceral of all loves. At least it felt so the first time I read the phenomenal 'My Son the Hero' by Clare Boylan. 'Reach' by Rachel Seiffert and 'The Turtle' by Roshi Fernando also powerfully evoke the strength of a mother's love, and 'Even Pretty Eyes Commit Crimes' by M. J. Hyland touches beautifully on the love between father and son.

In this section there is the painful poignancy of romantic love in Margaret Drabble's 'Faithful Lovers', love that is more like madness in 'Master' by Angela Carter and love that is unrecognised until it is too late in 'The Man from Mars' by

Margaret Atwood. There is love that for some reason is not meant to be. Chimamanda Ngozi Adichie writes about this in 'The Thing Around your Neck'. There is love as infatuation, short-lived and potentially destructive, in Jennifer Egan's 'The Watch Trick', and the making of love, sometimes kinkily, as in Anne Enright's 'Revenge'.

Many readers will know the experience of being haunted by an ex, and Alison Lurie writes vividly about the effect of lost or past loves in her characters' lives ('In the Shadow' and also the even more extraordinary 'Ilse's House').

LIFE

Life provides infinite shades of light and dark and in this section there are many curious tales and unusual settings. There is a handful of stories that made me ask: What on earth gave her this idea? Where did this come from? One example is 'The Axe' by Penelope Fitzgerald. It is a chilling horror story that takes place in the deceptively banal environment of an office and describes what happens when a man finds his job has been 'axed'. The narrator leaves us, as she should in such a story, with our hairs standing on end.

There is plenty of humour in this section and this is often provided by an unexpected or rather marvellous twist. 'How Did I Get Away with Killing One of the Biggest Lawyers in the State? It Was Easy.' by Alice Walker is flawless. And Penelope Lively's 'Corruption' is too, with the most brilliant visual image perhaps of any story – where a judge, involved in a pornography trial, takes some of his 'research papers' on holiday. A gust of wind sends copies of the offending magazines flying around the beach to be gathered by innocent children and even a woman who, until this moment, has been flirting with the judge. It is brilliantly comic. I felt I was watching the action unfold scene by scene, just as if I was watching a film.

There is a mildly pornographic element too in A. M. Homes' darkly comic 'A Real Doll'. It's almost about love, but more to do with sex. A boy uses his sister's Barbie as a sex toy and all sorts of jealousies ensue (Ken has an opinion, naturally). It's funny, outrageous and totally original.

Alison Lurie's 'Fat People' is once again funny, dark and unique. One could say it is about dieting, but that would only be one per cent of it. But, for me, Nicola Barker is the wittiest and often the most original. I chose three of her stories for the anthology but had to restrain myself from selecting so many more. In 'G-String', her powers of description had me laughing out loud: 'It felt like her G-string was making headway from between her buttocks up into her throat... now she knew how a horse felt when offered a new bit and bridle for the first time.' Most women will know how accurate this is. Needless to say, this is a hilarious tale right to the very end, where the woman ends up 'knickerless... a truly modern female'.

Ali Smith's 'The Child' is also comic and surreal. A baby with the voice of an adult is placed in a woman's supermarket trolley. It's the reverse of a baby-snatching drama, and is both farcical and strangely daring. It was one of my favourites, and visits to the supermarket have not been the same since...

Elspeth Davie's 'Change of Face' about a street artist is haunting as is her story 'A Weight Problem'. The situations she describes seem to have been magicked from thin air.

Other stories are slightly more shocking: a death may take place, but the loss is not, in itself, a focal point. It is perhaps more to do with learning. Margaret Atwood's very clever story, 'Betty', is about this. Over a small number of pages, one gets a strong sense of the narrator's identity, her stages of growing up and how she reinterprets the past in the light of her age and experience. It is full of wisdom.

Helen Simpson's story 'Ahead of the Pack' is brief but brilliant. The central notion is that we should have a quota of carbon points each day (in the same way that people on diets allow themselves a certain number of calories). It is such a clever idea that I wondered if it should not become a reality. What better way to ensure that we do not get 'in terms of [our] planetary profile... an absolutely vast arse'.

I happily included the slightly self-referential 'A Society' by Virginia Woolf, where the character of Poll is left a fortune by her father on condition that she reads all the books in the London Library. She declares them 'for the most part unutterably bad!' Having done most of my research for this anthology there, I can confirm that Poll is wrong.

I have had interesting discussions about whether there is a female 'voice' and whether women write differently from men. I believe there are some quintessentially feminine writers – and some whose writing provides no clues as to their identity. Angela Carter's 'The Bloody Chamber' (*Love*), for example, is neither masculine nor feminine. It is simply one of the most powerful, imaginative and sensual pieces of writing that I have ever come across. If I did not have the knowledge, I would certainly not be able to identify that A. M. Homes' stories are from a woman's pen. Her male protagonists are totally convincing and their 'voices' provocative and disturbing.

Some stories are so vivid that it is hard to imagine them as anything other than autobiography – even when the writer is female and the narrator is male. 'Before He Left the Family' by Carrie Tiffany (*Loss*) is a very matter-of-fact, no-blame narration of parental separation, but in subtle ways leaves the reader with little doubt over the effect this had on the sons. It is masterful storytelling. The male voice is very real.

I believe that many of the writers in this volume have the

ability to leave their gender behind in their writing, whether through deliberately disguising themselves behind a male narrator, or adopting a masculine sensibility. Once again, this is something that would be more difficult to sustain over the duration of an entire novel.

Short stories seem ideally suited to how many of us are reading now. They are perfect to read on an iPad, even on a phone. They can last as long as a short bus or train journey. They are complete in themselves – though from time to time they leave us hanging in mid-air with some kind of twist or ambiguity, as if this story we have in our hands is merely a beginning.

This is a very personal selection of my favourite stories. There will definitely be omissions (some of them accidental, some of them deliberate). Many of these writers were suggested by friends and colleagues. It seems that everyone has a favourite writer of short stories – and whenever I mentioned to people what I was doing they all insisted that I must read one author or another. I always followed up on recommendations, but I did not always find that I shared their taste.

It's been a glorious adventure putting this book together. I hope readers will share some of my excitement and enthusiasm and use it as a starting point for their own explorations into this extraordinary genre.

Victoria Hislop
June 2014

Adapted from the introduction to *The Story: Love Loss and The Lives of Women* (Head of Zeus, 2013)

THE CANARY

Katherine Mansfield

Katherine Mansfield (1888–1923) was born in Wellington, New Zealand. After moving to England at nineteen, Mansfield secured her reputation as a writer with the story collection *Bliss*, published in 1920. She reached the height of her powers with her 1922 collection *The Garden Party*. Her last five years were shadowed by tuberculosis; she died from the disease at the age of thirty-four.

…You see that big nail to the right of the front door? I can scarcely look at it even now and yet I could not bear to take it out. I should like to think it was there always even after my time. I sometimes hear the next people saying, 'There must have been a cage hanging from there.' And it comforts me. I feel he is not quite forgotten.

… You cannot imagine how wonderfully he sang. It was not like the singing of other canaries. And that isn't just my fancy. Often, from the window I used to see people stop at the gate to listen, or they would lean over the fence by the mock-orange for quite a long time – carried away. I suppose it sounds absurd to you – it wouldn't if you had heard him – but it really seemed to me he sang whole songs, with a beginning and an end to them.

For instance, when I'd finished the house in the afternoon, and changed my blouse and brought my sewing on to the verandah here, he used to hop, hop, hop from one perch to the other, tap against the bars as if to attract my attention, sip a little water, just as a professional singer might, and then break into a song so exquisite that I had to put my needle down to listen to him. I can't describe it; I wish I could. But it was always the same, every afternoon, and I felt that I understood every note of it.

… I loved him. How I loved him! Perhaps it does not matter so very much what it is one loves in this world. But love something one must! Of course there was always my little house and the garden, but for some reason they were never enough. Flowers respond wonderfully, but they don't sympathise. Then I loved the evening star. Does that sound ridiculous? I used to go into the backyard, after sunset, and wait for it until it shone above the dark gum tree. I used to whisper, 'There you are, my darling.' And just in that first moment it seemed to be shining for me alone. It seemed to understand this ... something which is like longing, and yet it is not longing. Or regret – it is more like regret. And yet regret for what? I have much to be thankful for!

... But after he came into my life I forgot the evening star; I did not need it any more. But it was strange. When the Chinaman who came to the door with birds to sell held him up in his tiny cage, and instead of fluttering, fluttering, like the poor little goldfinches, he gave a faint, small chirp, I found myself saying, just as I had said to the star over the gum tree, 'There you are, my darling.' From that moment he was mine!

... It surprises even me now to remember how he and I shared each other's lives. The moment I came down in the morning and took the cloth off his cage he greeted me with a drowsy little note. I knew it meant 'Missus! Missus!' Then I hung him on the nail outside while I got my three young men their breakfasts, and I never brought him in, to do his cage, until we had the house to ourselves again. Then, when the washing-up was done, it was quite a little entertainment. I spread a newspaper over a corner of the table and when I put the cage on it he used to beat with his wings, despairingly, as if he didn't know what was coming. 'You're a regular little actor,' I used to scold him. I scraped the tray, dusted it with fresh sand, filled his seed and water tins, tucked a piece of chickweed and half a chili between the bars. And I am perfectly certain he understood and appreciated every item of this little performance. You see by nature he was exquisitely neat. There was never a speck on his perch. And you'd only to see him enjoy his bath to realise he had a real small passion for cleanliness. His bath was put in last. And the moment it was in he positively leapt into it. First he fluttered one wing, then the other, then he ducked his head and dabbled his breast feathers. Drops of water were scattered all over the kitchen, but still he would not get out. I used to say to him, 'Now that's quite enough. You're only showing off.' And at last out he hopped and standing on one leg he began to peck himself dry. Finally he gave a shake, a flick, a twitter and he lifted his throat – Oh, I can hardly bear to recall it. I was always cleaning the knives by then. And it almost seemed to me the knives sang too, as I rubbed them bright on the board.

... Company, you see, that was what he was. Perfect company. If you have lived alone you will realise how precious that is. Of course there were my three young men who came in to supper every evening, and sometimes they stayed in the dining-room afterwards reading the paper. But I could not expect them to be interested in the little things that made my day. Why should they be? I was nothing to them. In fact, I overheard them one evening talking about me on the stairs as 'the Scarecrow'. No matter. It doesn't matter. Not in the least. I quite understand. They are young. Why should I mind? But I remember feeling so especially thankful that I was not quite alone that evening. I told him, after they had gone. I said, 'Do you know what they call Missus?' And he put his head on one side and looked at me with his little bright eye until I could not help laughing. It seemed to amuse him.

... Have you kept birds? If you haven't, all this must sound, perhaps, exaggerated. People have the idea that birds are heartless, cold little creatures, not like dogs or cats. My washerwoman used to say every Monday when she wondered why I didn't keep 'a nice fox terrier', 'There's no comfort, Miss, in a canary.' Untrue! Dreadfully untrue! I remember one night. I had had a very awful dream – dreams can be terribly cruel – even after I had woken up I could not get over it. So I put on my dressing-gown and came down to the kitchen for a glass of water. It was a winter night and raining hard. I suppose I was half asleep still, but through the kitchen window, that hadn't a blind, it seemed to me the dark was staring in, spying. And suddenly I felt it was unbearable that I had no one to whom I could say 'I've had such a dreadful dream,' or – 'Hide me from the dark.' I even covered my face for a minute. And then there came a little 'Sweet! Sweet!' His cage was on the table, and the cloth had slipped so that a chink of light shone through. 'Sweet! Sweet!' said the darling little fellow again, softly, as much as to say, 'I'm here, Missus. I'm here!' That was so beautifully comforting that I nearly cried.

... And now he's gone. I shall never have another bird, another pet of any kind. How could I? When I found him, lying on his back, with his eye dim and his claws wrung, when I realised that never again should I hear my darling sing, something seemed to die in me. My breast felt hollow, as if it was his cage. I shall get over it. Of course. I must. One can get over anything in time. And people always say I have a cheerful disposition. They are quite right. I thank God I have.

... All the same, without being morbid, or giving way to – to memories and so on, I must confess that there does seem to me something sad in life. It is hard to say what it is. I don't mean the sorrow that we all know, like illness and poverty and death. No, it is something different. It is there, deep down, deep down, part of one, like one's breathing. However hard I work and tire myself I have only to stop to know it is there, waiting. I often wonder if everybody feels the same. One can never know. But isn't it extraordinary that under his sweet, joyful little singing it was just this – sadness? – Ah, what is it? – that I heard.

A WALK IN THE WOODS

Elizabeth Bowen

Elizabeth Bowen (1899–1973) was an Irish novelist and short story writer. She published her first book, a collection of short stories entitled *Encounters*, in 1923. During World War II Bowen wrote the novel, *The Heat of the Day* and a collection of stories, *The Demon Lover and Other Stories*, which won her universal praise for their depiction of wartime London. She was awarded a CBE in 1948. Her final novel, *Eva Trout, or Changing Scenes* won the James Tait Black Memorial Prize in 1969 and was shortlisted for the Man Booker Prize.

The mysterious thing was that the woods were full of people – though they showed a front of frondy depth and silence, inviolable and sifted through with sun. They looked like a whole element, like water, possible to behold but not to enter, in which only the native creature can exist. But this was a deception. Once inside them, it was only at a few moments that the solitary walker could feel himself alone, and lovers found it hard to snatch unregarded kisses. For those few moments when nobody was in sight, the glades of bronze bracken, the wet, green rides leading off still seemed to be the edge of another world. The brown distances, the deep hollows welled with magic, forlorn silence, as though they were untrodden. But what was likely to be the last fine Sunday of autumn had brought Londoners, or people from suburbs on this side of the city, in hundreds into these woods, which lay open, the People's property – criss-crossed by tarmac roads on which yellow leaves stuck. The people who came here were mostly well-to-do, for you needed a car to get here without effort. So saloon cars, run off the roads between the wide-apart birch-trees, were packed flank to flank, like shining square-rumped tin pigs, in the nearby glades. Inside a few of these cars people remained sitting with the wireless on – but mostly they had got out, yawned, stretched, and scattered in threes and fours.

Most of the Londoners lacked a sense of direction. Directly they were out of the sight of the road, an atavistic fear of the woods invaded them. Willing or unwilling they walked in circles, coming back again and again to make certain they had not lost their cars – in which had often been left a tea-basket, an overcoat of some value, or an old lady, an aunt or a grandmother. Not to be sure where one is induces panic – and yet the sensation of being lost was what they unconsciously looked for on this holiday – they had come to the woods. The sounds of bolder people whistling to dogs, of mackintoshes rustling against the bracken reassured them made them strike in deeper.

Walking between the pillars of the trees, the men squared their shoulders – as though they inherited savage dignity. The matronly women, heavy in fur coats – which, just taken out after the summer, shed a smell of camphor – protestingly rolled as they walked on their smart heels. They looked about them, dissatisfied, acquisitive, despising the woods because they belonged to everyone. Had they not profoundly dreaded to trespass, they would have preferred the property of some duke. Now and then, recalling a pottery vase at home, they would strip off their gloves and reach for a fanlike spray of gold beech leaves. Or, unwillingly stooping, they tugged at a frond of bracken – but that is hard to pick. Their faces stayed unrelaxed: there is no poetry for the middle-class woman in her middle years. Nature's disturbing music is silent for her; her short phase of instinctive life is over. She is raising, forcing upward the children she has, and driving her man on. Her features become bleak with narrow intention: she is riveted into society. Still, to touch the edge of Nature stands for an outing – you pack baskets and throng to the edge of forest or sea. The still, damp, glittering woods, the majestic death of the year were reflected in the opaque eyes of these women – hardly more human, very much less pathetic, than the glass eyes of the foxes some of them wore. In family parties the women and men parted; they did not speak to each other. The women walked more slowly to act as a brake. Where tracks narrowed between thickets or bracken the families went in files. The children escaped and kept chasing each other, cat-calling, round the trees. They were not allowed to run down the wet green rides.

Sometimes the thud of hooves was heard, and young people

on horseback crossed the end of a glade in coloured jerseys, with chins up, flaunting their bold happiness. The walkers, with a sort of animal envy, lowered their eyes and would not look after them. From couples of lovers clashing through the bracken, or standing suspended in love, fingers touching, in patches of sun, eyes were averted in a commenting way.

The riders thudding, across a glade were heard, not seen, by a couple in a thicket. These two, in a secret clearing at the foot of an oak, sat on a mackintosh eating sandwiches. They were very hungry. They had come to the edge of the woods in a Green Line bus, struck in and wandered for a long time now, looking for the place their fancy wanted. The woman, a city woman, refused to believe the woods had no undiscovered heart, if one could only come on it. Each time she had sighted the black of another tarmac road she had let out a persecuted sigh. The young man saw she was flagging, and he was hungry. He had found what she wanted by fighting through this thicket to the foot of the oak, then pulling her after him. In here they at least *saw* no one. They had spread the mackintosh, kissed, and opened the sandwiches.

'Listen,' she said. 'There go people riding.'

'Did you ever ride?'

'I did once.'

'On that farm?'

'Yes, that time,' she said, smiling quickly, touched that he should remember. She spoke often about her childhood, never about her girlhood – which was past, for she was ten years older than he. And her girlhood had been brief: she had married young. She watched him reach out for another sandwich, then gently and wilfully detained him by making her thumb and finger into a bracelet round his thin wrist. He pulled his wrist up to his lips and kissed the joint of her thumb. They enjoyed this play as seriously as lions. She shut her eyes, dropped her head back to let the sun through the branches fall on her forehead – then let his wrist go. He took the sandwich he wanted; she opened her eyes and saw him. 'You greedy boy.'

'Yes, I *am* greedy,' he said. '*You* know I'm greedy.'

She thrust both hands up to her cheeks and said: 'That's no good – *here.*'

'No, we've struck unlucky. I thought woods in winter—'

'It's still autumn. It's the fine Sunday.' Her face went narrow, as though she heard the crack of a whip: she opened a gap in their thicket by bending a branch back. With cautious, angry eyes they both looked through. A party of five people were filing through the bracken, about ten yards away. 'There they go,' she said. 'There go the neighbours. That's my life. Oh, God! Henry—'

'They can't hurt us.'

'You know they can. Look, eat that last sandwich, do.'

'What about you?'

'I don't want it: I cut them for you. Turkey and ham, that should be.'

'*I'm* a spoilt boy,' said Henry, taking the sandwich without any more fuss. She crumbled up the paper, drove it with the point of his stick into the soft earth at the foot of the oak and earthed it up alive. Then she brushed crumbs from the mackintosh with a downcast face, making a bed in which they dare not be. But Henry drew his long legs up, scrambled round like a dog and lay across the mackintosh with his head in Carlotta's lap. She stroked his stubborn dark hair back, leaned her bosom over his face and stroked his forehead with a terrible held-in tenderness. The whole weight of his body seemed to have gone into his head, which lay as heavy as a world on her thighs. His clerk's face was exposed to her touch and to the sky – generally so intent, over-expressive, nervous, the face was wiped into blank repose by her touch. He flung one hand across his chest and held a fold of her skirt. His spectacles, by reflecting the sky's light, hid his eyes from her, so she leaned over further and lifted them off gently. She looked into the blotted darkness of his pupils which, from being exposed like this, looked naked. Then he shut his eyes and put on the withdrawn smile of someone expecting sleep. 'You are so good,' he said.

'Sleep then ... go on, sleep ... '

'Will you?'

'Maybe. Sleep ... '

But she watched, with the bend of her spine against the tree, while he lay with his eyes shut. She saw that his will to sleep was a gentle way of leaving her for a little. She felt a tide of peace coming in – but then the tide turned: his forehead twitched. A bird trilled its unhopeful autumn song. He opened his eyes and said: 'It's awful, having no place.'

'But we make a place of our own.'

'But I get so tired – all this doesn't seem natural.'

'Oh, Henry – what's the good?'

'Well, *you've* often said that.'

'Then *you've* said, what's the good?'

'It was all very well at first,' he said, 'just knowing you. Just coming round to your place. Seeing you before Joe got back, or even: with Joe. I used to like you to have a place of your own – that was why I'd rather go with you than a girl.'

'That's what you want,' she said, 'just mothering. That's what Joe thinks; he doesn't think any harm. "Here comes your boy," he says; I think he's right, too: that's all you're really after.' She gently outlined his mouth with one of her fingertips.

But his mouth tightened. 'No, it's more than that now,' he said. '*You* know it's more than that.' He stared at the sky with his unfocused eyes – like a hare's eyes. 'I wanted what I've got; I wanted that all the time; I wanted that from the first – though it may once have been mixed up in the other dung. But ever *since* that, ever since we—'

'Do you wish we hadn't?'

'You don't know what you're saying. But I used to like your home; it was such a snug little place. I was happy there in a way: that's all gone now. I used to like Joe, too, one time. And now – it's awful ... *This* isn't what I imagined the first time I saw you. Hiding in woods like this – it isn't fit for you ... really.'

'It's my only life. You're my only life. My only way out. Before you came, I was walled in alive. I didn't know where to turn, I was burning myself out ... I don't mind where we go; so long as we get *away* from them ... And we do have these days when Joe's gone to his mother's.'

'But we've got no place ... When I was young I used to believe there was really some tremendous world and that one would get to it. A sort of a Shakespeare world. And I heard it in music, too. And I lived there for three days after I first met you. I once used to believe—'

'But you're young still.'

'Well, perhaps I do still.'

'I always have. That's our place.'

'But we ought to have some real place – I mean, I want you.'

'Oh, shut up,' she said. 'I—'

'Look, come on,' he said, getting up. 'Better walk on. This does no good. Let's walk on into the woods.'

'They're so full.'

'But they look empty.'

'Kiss once—'

They kissed. It was he who pulled apart. He gathered up her mackintosh on his arm and began to fight a way out for her through the thickets. As she stepped between the branches he held back, her lips shook and she looked quite blind. Her look attracted the notice of Muffet and Isabella, two schoolgirls who, walking arm-in-arm through the woods, had already started to stare and nudge each other on seeing the thicket of purple leaves shake. Any man and woman together made them giggle. They saw a haggard woman with dark red hair and a white face: something in her expression set them off giggling all the more. Henry disentangled the mackintosh from the last of the thicket; his consciousness of the girls staring and giggling made him look very young. His pride in Carlotta was wounded; his pity for her abased him. She was a married woman out with her neighbour's lodger. They both came from a newly developed suburb, and had met at the local debating society.

As he saw the girls' pink faces stuck open with laughter he saw why Carlotta hated her life. He saw why she towered like a statue out of place. She was like something wrecked and cast up on the wrong shore. When they met she had been one of these women going through life dutifully, and at the same time burning themselves up. Across the hall where they met, her forehead like no other woman's forehead, her impatient carriage, her deep eyes and held-in mouth, had been like a signal to him. He could not turn away. When they had talked, she excited, released, soothed him. Pride and a bitter feeling of misdirection had, up to that meeting, isolated them both. Passion broke down a wall in each of their lives. But her spirit was stronger than his, and so he was frightened of her ... Carlotta stumbled stepping out of the thicket, and put a hand on his elbow for support. Henry twitched his elbow away and strode ahead of her, lashing round at the bracken with his stick.

'Henry—'

'Look out, they're looking. Those girls behind. *Don't* look round—'

'All right,' she said. 'We can't be too careful, can we.' Henry did not know if she spoke in irony or sheer pain.

Muffet was spending the Sunday with Isabella, whose family lived not far from the Green Line bus stop. The girls were friends at the High School. They both wore dark-blue overcoats and walked bare-headed; their lively faces showed no particular character. They were allowed by their mothers to walk in the woods so long as they did not get talking to men: they had been told what happens to girls who do that – their minds were bulging with cautionary horrors. They had neither of them got boys yet: when they had got boys they would stop walking together. At present their walks were gay and enjoyable – on fine Sundays the woods were a great show for them: too soon this would be over, winter silence would fall.

This afternoon, in a fairly retired glade, they had come on a lonely car in which a couple embraced. They also inspected cars parked nearer the roadside, squinting in at grandmothers and the picnic baskets, running away in alarm from pairs of well-got-up women, upright in backs of cars like idols under glass cases, discontentedly waiting for their men to return. Or, intercepting a bar of wireless music, Isabella and Muffet would take a few dancing steps. They envied the thundering riders, the young lovers, the imperious owners of well-bred dogs ... Isabella and Muffet, anything but reluctant, hopped with impatience where brook and river meet. They were fifteen. They stared at everyone. At the same time they had a sense of propriety which was very easily offended.

They peered at the broken thicket, then turned to stare after the couple.

'My goodness,' said Isabella, '*she* looked silly!'

'Breaking trees, too,' said Muffet. 'That's against the law.'

'Besides being old enough to be his mother. She *was* old. Did you see her?'

'Perhaps she was his mother.'

'Mother my eye! But he gave her the push all right – did you see that? Did you see?'

'Going on at him like that.'

'Well, I call it a shame. It's a shame on him. He's a nice boy.'

'No, I call him sappy. I mean, at her age. Fancy him letting her.'

'Well, I tell you, I call it a shame.'

'Well, I tell you, it makes me laugh ... Look, let's go down there: I see people down there.' Isabella dug a bag of sweets out of her pocket and they sauntered on, both sucking, talking with cheeks blocked. 'Supposing you got offered a fur coat, what kind would you go for, nutria or kolinsky? ... If a boy that always went racing but that you were sweet on asked you to marry him, would you? ... Supposing you were going with a boy, then found out he was a trunk murderer ... '

'Oh, there's such a sweet dog, such a sweet fellow. Come, then!'

'My goodness,' said Isabella, 'it isn't half getting dark.'

'Well, what *do* you expect?'

'No, but the sun's gone in. And that's not mist, now; that's fog, that is.'

'They're starting two of those cars up.'

'Mother'll be starting to worry. Better be getting home.'

Yes, mist that had been the natural breath of the woods was thickening to fog, as though the not-distant city had sent out an infection. At dusk coming so suddenly and so early, the people felt a touch of animal fear – quickening their steps, they closed on each other in a disordered way, as though their instinct were to bolt underground. Wind or thunder, though more terrible in woods, do not hold this same threat of dissolution. The people packed back into their cars; the cars lurched on to the roads and started back to London in a solid stream. Down the rides, beginning to be deserted, the trees with their leaves still clinging looked despoiled and tattered. All day the woods had worn an heroic dying smile; now they were left alone to face death.

But this was still somebody's moment. There was still some daylight. The small lake, or big pool, clearly reflected in its black mirror the birches and reeds. A tall girl, with a not quite young porcelain face, folding her black fur collar round her throat with both hands, stood posing against a birch, having her photograph taken across the water by two young men at the other side of the lake. Bob, busy over the camera on a portable tripod, was an 'art' photographer: he could photograph Nature in the most difficult light. Therefore he could go far in search of her strange moods. He felt, thought, loved, even in terms of the Lens. He sold his work to papers, where it appeared with lines of poetry underneath. This girl over the water in the fog-smudged woods was to be called 'Autumn Evening'. Cecil, an old friend, behind Bob's shoulder, looked across at the girl.

Without breaking her pose, a born model's, she coughed, and shook under her fur coat. Cecil said cautiously: 'She's getting a bit cold, Bob.'

'*Tsssss!*' said Bob sharply. He had become his camera. His whole temperament crouched over his subject, like a lion over a bit of meat.

'Won't be long,' Cecil called across the lake.

'I'm all right,' said the girl, coughing again.

'Tell her not to grab her collar up,' Bob muttered. 'She's not supposed to look cold. She's got her coat all dragged up; it spoils the figure.'

'He says, not to grab your collar,' Cecil shouted.

'Right-o.' She let her collar fall open: Turning her head inside the fur corolla, she looked more obliquely across the lake. 'Is that better?'

'O.K ... *Ready!*' The slow exposure began.

People taking photographs in this half-light, this dream-light, made Carlotta and Henry stop to wonder. They stood back among the birches to be out of the way. Then the artistic tensity broke up; signals were exchanged across the water; the girl came round the lake to join the two young men. 'What's that floating?' she said. But they were busy packing up the camera. 'Should that be all right?' she said, but no one answered. Bob handed Cecil the tripod, shouldered his camera and they walked away from the lake with Bob's hand on his girl's shoulder.

'Do you think that photo will ever come out?' said Carlotta.

'I suppose he knows what he's doing ... I'd like to try with a camera ... '

'I'd sooner paint,' said Carlotta. They walked round the edge of the lake, looking across to where the girl had stood. 'She was pretty,' Carlotta said. She thought; 'She'll get her death. But I'd like to stand like that. I wish Henry *had* a camera. I wish I could give him one ... Against the photographer's shoulder-blade eternalized minutes were being carried away. Carlotta and Henry were both tired, what they saw seemed to belong in the past already. The light seemed to fade because of their own nerves. And still water in woods, in any part of the world, continues an everlasting terrible fairy tale, in which you are always lost, in which giants oppress. Now the people had gone, the lovers saw that this place was what they had been looking for all today. But they were so tired, each stood in an isolated dream.

'What *is* that floating?' she said.

Henry screwed up his eyes. 'A thermos.' He picked up a broken branch and, with an infinity of trouble, started to claw in, with the tip of the branch, the floating flask towards himself. Its cap was gone.

'But we don't want it, Henry.'

She might never have spoken – Henry's face was intent; he recklessly stood with one toe in the water. The ribbed aluminium cylinder, twirling under the touches of the branch, rode reluctantly in. Henry reached it eagerly out of the water, shook it. Its shattered inner glass coating rattled about inside – this, the light hollowness, the feel of the ribs in his grasp made Henry smile with almost crazy pleasure. 'Treasure!' he said, with a checked, excited laugh.

Carlotta smiled, but she felt her throat tighten. She saw Henry's life curve off from hers, like one railway line from another, curve off to an utterly different, and far-off destination. When she trusted herself to speak, she said as gently as possible: 'We'll have to be starting back soon. You know it's some way. The bus—'

'No, we won't miss that,' said Henry, rattling the flask and smiling.

SENTIMENT

Dorothy Parker

Dorothy Parker (1893–1967) was an American critic, satirical poet, and short story writer. Best known for her wit and eye for 20th-century foibles, Parker wrote book reviews, poetry and short fiction for the fledgling magazine the *New Yorker*. She wrote the screenplay for the Hitchcock film *Saboteur*, but her involvement with Communism led to her being blacklisted in Hollywood.

Oh, anywhere, *driver, anywhere – it doesn't matter. Just keep driving.*

It's better here in this taxi than it was walking. It's no good my trying to walk. There is always a glimpse through the crowd of someone who looks like him – someone with his swing of the shoulders, his slant of the hat. And I think it's he. I think he's come back. And my heart goes to scalding water and the buildings away and bend above me. No, it's better to be here. But I wish the driver would go fast, so fast that people walking by would be a long gray blur, and I could see no swinging shoulders, no slanted hat. It's bad stopping still in the traffic like this. People pass too slowly, too clearly, and always the next one might be – No, of course it couldn't be. I know that. Of course I know it. But it might be, it might.

And people can look in and see me, here. They can see if I cry. Oh, let them – it doesn't matter. Let them look and be damned to them.

Yes, you look at me. Look and look and look, you poor, queer tired woman. It's a pretty hat, isn't it? It's meant to be looked at. That's why it's so big and red and new, that's why it has these great soft poppies on it. Your poor hat is all weary and done with. It looks like a dead cat, a cat that was run over and pushed out of the way against the curbstone. Don't you wish you were I and could have a new hat whenever you pleased? You could walk fast, couldn't you, and hold your head high and raise your feet from the pavement if you were on your way to a new hat, a beautiful hat, a hat that cost more than ever you had? Only I hope you wouldn't choose one like mine. For red is mourning, you know. Scarlet red for a love that's dead. Didn't you know that?

She's gone now. The taxi is moving and she's left behind forever. I wonder what she thought when our eyes and our lives met. I wonder did she envy me, so sleek and safe and young. Or did she realize how quick I'd be to fling away all I have if I could bear in my breast the still, dead heart that she carries in hers. She doesn't feel. She doesn't even wish. She is done with hoping and burning, if ever she burned and she hoped. Oh, that's quite nice, it has a real lilt. She is done with hoping and burning, if ever she – Yes, it's pretty. Well – I wonder if she's gone her slow way a little happier, or, perhaps, a little sadder for knowing that there is one worse off than herself.

This is the sort of thing he hated so in me. I know what he would say. "Oh, for heaven's sake!" he would say. "Can't you stop that fool sentimentalizing? Why do you have to do it? Why do you *want* to do it? Just because you see an old charwoman on the street, there's no need to get sobbing about her. She's all right. She's fine. 'When your eyes and your lives met' – oh, come on now. Why, she never even saw you. And her 'still, dead heart,' nothing! She's probably on her way to get a bottle of bad gin and have a roaring time. You don't have to dramatize *everything*. You don't have to insist that *everybody's* sad. Why are you always so sentimental? Don't *do* it Rosalie." That's what he would say. I know.

But he won't say that or anything else to me, any more. Never anything else, sweet or bitter. He's gone away and he isn't coming back. "Oh, of course I'm coming back!" he said. "No, I don't know just when – I told you that. Ah, Rosalie, don't go making a national tragedy of it. It'll be a few months, maybe – and if ever two people needed a holiday from each other! It's nothing to cry about. I'll be back. I'm not going to stay away from New York forever."

But I knew. I knew. I knew because he had been far away from me long before he went. He's gone away and he won't come back. He's gone away and he won't come back, he's gone away and he'll never come back. Listen to the wheels saying it on and on and on. That's sentimental, I suppose. Wheels don't say anything Wheels can't speak. But I *hear* them.

I wonder why it's wrong to be sentimental. People are so contemptuous of feeling. "You wouldn't catch *me* sitting alone and mooning," they say. "Moon" is what they say when they mean remember, and they are so proud of not remembering. It's strange, how they pride themselves upon their lacks. "I never take anything seriously," they say. "I simply couldn't imagine," they say, "letting myself care so much that I could be hurt." They say. "No one person could be that important to *me*." And why, why do they think they're right?

Oh, who's right and who's wrong and who decides? Perhaps it was I who was right about that charwoman. Perhaps she *was* weary and still-hearted, and perhaps, for just that moment, she knew all about me. She needn't have been all right and fine and on her way for gin, just because he said so. Oh. Oh, I forgot. He didn't say so. He wasn't here; he isn't here. It was I, imagining what he would say. And I thought I heard him. He's always with me, he and all his beauty and his cruelty. But he mustn't be any more. I mustn't think of him. That's it, don't think of him. Yes. Don't breathe, either. Don't hear. Don't see. Stop the blood in your veins.

I can't go on like this. I can't, I can't. I cannot stand this frantic misery. If I knew it would be over in a day or a year or two months, I could endure it. Even if it grew duller sometimes and wilder sometimes, it could be borne. But it is always the same and there is no end.

> "*Sorrow like a ceaseless rain*
> *Beats upon my heart.*
> *People twist and scream in pain –*
> *Dawn will find them still again;*
> *This has neither wax nor wane.*
> *Neither stop nor start.*"

Oh, let's see – how does the next verse go? Something, something, something, something, something to rhyme with "wear." Anyway, it ends:

> *"All my thoughts are slow and brown:*
> *Standing up or sitting down*
> *Little matters, or what gown*
> *Or what shoes I wear."*

Yes, that's the way it goes. And it's right, it's so right. What is it to me what I wear? Go and buy yourself a big red hat with poppies on it – that ought to cheer you up. Yes – go buy it and loathe it. How am I to go on, sitting and staring and buying big red hats and hating them, and then sitting and staring again – day upon day upon day upon day? Tomorrow and tomorrow and tomorrow. How am I to drag through them like this?

But what else is there for me? "Go out and see your friends and have a good time," they say. "Don't sit alone and dramatize yourself." Dramatize yourself! If it be drama to feel a steady – no, a *ceaseless* rain beating upon my heart, then I do dramatize myself. The shallow people, the little people, how can they know what suffering is, how could their thick hearts be torn? Don't they know, the empty fools, that I could not see again the friends we saw together, could not go back to the places where he and I have been? For he's gone, and it's ended. It's ended, it's ended. And when it ends, only those places where you have known sorrow are kindly to you. If you revisit the scenes of your happiness, your heart must burst of its agony.

And that's sentimental, I suppose. It's sentimental to know that you cannot bear to see the places where once all was well with you, that you cannot bear reminders of a dead loveliness. Sorrow is tranquillity, remembered in emotion. It – oh, I think that's quite good. "Remembered in emotion" – that's a really nice reversal. I wish I could say it to him. But I won't say anything to him, ever again, ever, ever again. He's gone, and it's over, and I dare not think of the dead days. All my thoughts must be slow and brown, and I must—

Oh, no, no, no! Oh, the driver shouldn't go through this street! This was our street, this is the place of our love and our laughter. I can't do this, I can't, I can't. I will crouch down here, and hold my hands tight, tight over my eyes, so that I cannot look. I must keep my poor heart still, and I must be like the little, mean, dry-souled people who are proud not to remember.

But oh, I see it, I see it, even though my eyes are blinded. Though I had no eyes, my heart would tell me this street, out of all streets. I know it as I know my hands, as I know his face. Oh, why can't I be let to die as we pass through?

We must be at the florist's shop on the corner now. That's where he used to stop to buy me primroses, little yellow primroses massed tight together with a circle of their silver-backed leaves about them, clean and cool and gentle. He always said that orchids and camellias were none of my affair. So when there were no spring and no primroses, he would give me lilies-of-the-valley and little, gay rosebuds and mignonette and bright blue cornflowers. He said he couldn't stand the thought of me without flowers – it would be all wrong; I cannot bear flowers near me, now. And the little gray florist was so interested and so glad – and there was the day he called me "madam"! Ah, I can't, I can't.

And now we must be at the big apartment house with the big gold doorman. And the evening the doorman was holding the darling puppy on a big, long leash, and we stopped to talk to it, and he took it up in his arms and cuddled it, and that was the only time we ever saw the doorman smile! And next is the house with the baby, and he always would take off his hat and bow very solemnly to her, and sometimes she would give him her little starfish of a hand. And then is the tree with the rusty iron bars around it, where he would stop to turn and wave to me, as I leaned out the window to watch him. And people would look at him, because people always had to look at him, but he never noticed. It was our tree, he said; it wouldn't dream of belonging to anybody else. And very few city people had their own personal tree, he said. Did I realize that, he said.

And then there's the doctor's house, and the three thin gray houses and then – oh, God, we must be at our house now! Our house, though we had only the top floor. And I loved the long, dark stairs, because he climbed them every evening. And our little prim pink curtains at the windows, and the boxes of pink geraniums that always grew for me. And the little stiff entry and the funny mail-box, and his ring at the bell. And I waiting for him in the dusk, thinking he would never come; and yet the waiting was lovely, too. And then when I opened the door to him – Oh, no, no, no! Oh, no one could bear this. No one, no one.

Ah, why, why, why must I be driven through here? What torture could there be so terrible as this? It will be better if I uncover my eyes and look. I will see our tree and our house again, and then my heart will burst and I will be dead. I will look, I will look.

But where's the tree? Can they have cut down our tree – *our* tree? And where's the apartment house? And where's the florist's shop? And where – oh, where's our house, where's—

Driver, what street is this? Sixty-Fifth? Oh. No. Nothing, thank you. I – I thought it was Sixty-Third …

THE LOTTERY

Shirley Jackson

Shirley Jackson (1916–1965) was an American author best known for her story, 'The Lottery'. A prolific short story writer, Jackson also wrote six novels, one of which, *The Haunting of Hill House*, was nominated for the National Book Award in 1960. The Shirley Jackson Awards were established in 2007 to recognise outstanding achievement in the literature of psychological suspense, horror and the dark fantastic.

The morning of June 27th was clear and sunny, with the fresh warmth of a fun-summer day; the flowers were blossoming profusely and the grass was richly green. The people of the village began to gather in the square, between the post office and the bank, around ten o'clock; in some towns there were so many people that the lottery took two days and had to be started on June 26th, but in this village, where there were only about three hundred people, the whole lottery took less than two hours, so it could begin at ten o'clock in the morning and still be through in time to allow the villagers to get home for noon dinner.

The children assembled first, of course. School was recently over for the summer, and the feeling of liberty sat uneasily on most of them; they tended to gather together quietly for a while before they broke into boisterous play, and their talk was still of the classroom and the teacher; of books and reprimands. Bobby Martin had already stuffed his pockets full of stones, and the other boys soon followed his example, selecting the smoothest and roundest stones; Bobby and Harry Jones and Dickie Delacroix – the villagers pronounced this name "Deflacroy" – eventually made a great pile of stones in one corner of the square and guarded it against the raids of the other boys. The girls stood aside, talking among themselves, looking over their shoulders at the boys, and the very small children rolled in the dust or clung to the hands of their older brothers or sisters.

Soon the men began to gather, surveying their own children, speaking of planting and rain, tractors and taxes. They stood together, away from the pile of stones in the corner, and their jokes were quiet and they smiled rather than laughed. The women, wearing faded house dresses and sweaters, came shortly after their menfolk. They greeted one another and exchanged bits of gossip as they went to join their husbands. Soon the women, standing by their husbands, began to call to their children, and the children came reluctantly, having to be called four or five times. Bobby Martin ducked under his mother's grasping hand and ran, laughing, back to the pile of stones. His father spoke up sharply, and Bobby came quickly and took his place between his father and his oldest brother.

The lottery was conducted – as were the square dances, the teenage club, the Halloween program – by Mr. Summers, who had time and energy to devote to civic activities. He was a round-faced, jovial man and he ran the coal business, and people were sorry for him, because he had no children and his wife was a scold. When he arrived in the square, carrying the black wooden box, there was a murmur of conversation among the villagers, and he waved and called, "Little late today, folks." The postmaster, Mr. Graves, followed him, carrying a three-legged stool, and the stool was put in the center of the square and Mr. Summers set the black box down on it. The villagers kept their distance, leaving a space between themselves and the stool, and when Mr. Summers said, "Some of you fellows want to give me a hand?" there was a hesitation before two men, Mr. Martin and his oldest son, Baxter, came forward to hold the box steady on the stool while Mr. Summers stirred up the papers inside it.

The original paraphernalia for the lottery had been lost long ago, and the black box now resting on the stool had been put into use even before Old Man Warner, the oldest man in town, was born. Mr. Summers spoke frequently to the villagers about making a new box, but no one liked to upset even as much tradition as was represented by the black box. There was a story that the present box had been made with some pieces of the box that had preceded it, the one that had been constructed when the first people settled down to make a village here. Every year, after the lottery, Mr. Summers began talking again about a new box, but every year the subject was allowed to fade off without anything's being done. The black box grew shabbier each year, by now it was no longer completely black but splintered badly along one side to show the original wood color, and in some places faded or stained.

Mr. Martin and his oldest son, Baxter, held the black box securely on the stool until Mr. Summers had stirred the papers thoroughly with his hand. Because so much of the ritual had been forgotten or discarded, Mr. Summers had been successful in having slips of paper substituted for the chips of wood that had been used for generations. Chips of wood, Mr. Summers had argued, had been all very well when the village was tiny, but now that the population was more than three hundred and likely to keep on growing, it was necessary to use something that would fit more easily into the black box. The night before the lottery, Mr. Summers and Mr. Graves made up the slips of paper and put them in the box, and it was then taken to the safe of Mr. Summers' coal company and locked up until Mr. Summers was ready to take it to the square next morning. The rest of the year, the box was put away, sometimes one place, sometimes another; it had spent one year in Mr. Graves's barn and another year underfoot in the post office, and sometimes it was set on a shelf in the Martin grocery and left there.

There was a great deal of fussing to be done before Mr. Summers declared the lottery open. There were the lists to make up – of heads of families, heads of households in each family, members of each household in each family. There was the proper swearing-in of Mr. Summers by the postmaster, as the official of the lottery; at one time, some people remembered, there had been a recital of some sort, performed by the official of the lottery, a perfunctory, tuneless chant that had been rattled off duly each year; some people believed that the official of the lottery used to stand just so when he said or sang it, others believed that he was supposed to walk among the people, but years and years ago this part of the ritual had been allowed to lapse. There had been, also, a ritual salute, which the official of the lottery had had to use in addressing each person who came up to draw from the box, but this also had changed with time, until now it was felt necessary only for the official to speak to each person approaching. Mr. Summers was very good at all this; in his clean white shirt and blue jeans, with one hand resting carelessly on the black box, he seemed very proper and important as he talked interminably to Mr. Graves and the Martins.

Just as Mr. Summers finally left off talking and turned to the assembled villagers, Mrs. Hutchinson came hurriedly along the path to the square, her sweater thrown over her shoulders, and slid into place in the back of the crowd. "Clean forgot what day it was," she said to Mrs. Delacroix, who stood next to her, and they both laughed softly. "Thought my old man was out back slacking wood," Mrs. Hutchinson went on, "and then I looked out the window and the kids was gone, and then I remembered it was the twenty-seventh and came a-running." She dried her hands on her apron, and Mrs. Delacroix said, "You're in time, though. They're still talking away up there."

Mrs. Hutchinson craned her neck to see through the crowd and found her husband and children standing near the front. She tapped Mrs. Delacroix on the arm as a farewell and began to make her way through the crowd. The people separated good-humoredly to let her through; two or three people said, in voices just loud enough to be heard across the crowd, "Here comes your Missus Hutchinson," and "Bill, she made it after all." Mrs. Hutchinson reached her husband, and Mr. Summers, who had been waiting, said cheerfully, "Thought we were going to have to get on without you, Tessie." Mrs. Hutchinson said, grinning, "Wouldn't have me leave m'dishes in the sink, now, would you, Joe?" and soft laughter ran through the crowd as the people stirred back into position after Mrs. Hutchinson's arrival.

"Well, now," Mr. Summers said soberly, "guess we better get started, get this over with, so's we can go back to work. Anybody ain't here?"

"Dunbar," several people said. "Dunbar, Dunbar."

Mr. Summers consulted his list. "Clyde Dunbar," he said. "That's right. He's broke his leg, hasn't he? Who's drawing for him?"

"Me, I guess," a woman said, and Mr. Summers turned to look at her. "Wife draws for her husband," Mr. Summers said. "Don't you have a grown boy to do it for you, Janey?" Although Mr. Summers and everyone else in the village knew the answer perfectly well, it was the business of the official of the lottery to ask such questions formally. Mr. Summers waited with an expression of polite interest while Mrs. Dunbar answered.

"Horace's not but sixteen yet," Mrs. Dunbar said regretfully. "Guess I gotta fill in for the old man this year."

"Right," Mr. Summers said. He made a note on the list he was holding. Then he asked, "Watson boy drawing this year?"

A tall boy in the crowd raised his hand. "Here," he said. "I'm drawing for m'mother and me." He blinked his eyes nervously and ducked his head as several voices in the crowd said things like "Good fellow, Jack," and "Glad to see your mother's got a man to do it."

"Well," Mr. Summers said, "guess that's everyone. Old Man Warner make it?"

"Here," a voice said, and Mr. Summers nodded.

A sudden hush fell on the crowd as Mr. Summers cleared his throat and looked at the list. "All ready?" he called. "Now, I'll read the names – heads of families first – and the men come up and take a paper out of the box. Keep the paper folded in your hand without looking at it until everyone has had a turn. Everything clear?"

The people had done it so many times that they only half listened to the directions; most of them were quiet, wetting their lips, not looking around. Then Mr. Summers raised one hand high and said, "Adams." A man disengaged himself from the crowd and came forward. "Hi, Steve," Mr. Summers said, and Mr. Adams said, "Hi, Joe." They grinned at one another humorlessly and nervously. Then Mr. Adams reached into the black box and took out a folded paper. He held it firmly by one corner as he turned and went hastily back to his place in the crowd, where he stood a little apart from his family, not looking down at his hand.

"Allen," Mr. Summers said. "Anderson … Bentham."

"Seems like there's no time at all between lotteries any more," Mrs. Delacroix said to Mrs. Graves in the back row. "Seems like we got through with the last one only last week."

"Time sure goes fast," Mrs. Graves said.

"Clark … Delacroix."

"There goes my old man," Mrs. Delacroix said. She held her breath while her husband went forward.

"Dunbar," Mr. Summers said, and Mrs. Dunbar went steadily to the box while one of the women said, "Go on, Janey," and another said, "There she goes."

"We're next," Mrs. Graves said. She watched while Mr. Graves came around from the side of the box, greeted Mr. Summers gravely, and selected a slip of paper from the box. By now, all through the crowd there were men holding the small folded papers in their large hands, turning them over and over nervously. Mrs. Dunbar and her two sons stood together, Mrs. Dunbar holding the slip of paper.

"Harburt ... Hutchinson."

"Get up there, Bill," Mrs. Hutchinson said, and the people near her laughed.

"Jones."

"They do say," Mr. Adams said to Old Man Warner, who stood next to him, "that over in the north village they're talking of giving up the lottery."

Old Man Warner snorted. "Pack of crazy fools," he said. "Listening to the young folks, nothing's good enough for *them*. Next thing you know, they'll be wanting to go back to living in caves, nobody work any more, live *that* way for a while. Used to be a saying; about 'Lottery in June, corn be heavy soon.' First thing you know, we'd all be eating stewed chickweed and acorns. There's *always* been a lottery," he added petulantly. "Bad enough to see young Joe Summers up there joking with everybody."

"Some places have already quit lotteries," Mrs. Adams said.

"Nothing but trouble in *that*," Old Man Warner said stoutly. "Pack of young fools."

"Martin." And Bobby Martin watched his father go forward. "Overdyke ... Percy."

"I wish they'd hurry," Mrs. Dunbar said to her older son. "I wish they'd hurry."

"They're almost through," her son said.

"You get ready to run tell Dad," Mrs. Dunbar said.

Mr. Summers called his own name and then stepped forward precisely and selected a slip from the box. Then he called, "Warner."

"Seventy-seventh year I been in the lottery," Old Man Warner said as he went through the crowd. "Seventy-seventh time."

"Watson." The tall boy came awkwardly through the crowd. Someone said, "Don't be nervous, Jack," and Mr. Summers said, "Take your time, son."

"Zanini."

After that, there was a long pause, a breathless pause, until Mr. Summers, holding his slip of paper in the air, said, "All right, fellows." For a minute, no one moved, and then all the slips of paper were opened. Suddenly, all the women began to speak at once, saying, "Who is it?" "Who's got it?" "Is it the Dunbars?" "Is it the Watsons?" Then the voices began to say, "It's Hutchinson. It's Bill," "Bill Hutchinson's got it."

"Go tell your father," Mrs. Dunbar said to her older son.

People began to look around to see the Hutchinsons. Bill Hutchinson was standing quiet, staring down at the paper in his hand. Suddenly, Tessie Hutchinson shouted to Mr. Summers, "You didn't give him time enough to take any paper he wanted. I saw you. It wasn't fair!"

"Be a good sport, Tessie," Mrs. Delacroix called, and Mrs. Graves said, "All of us took the same chance."

"Shut up, Tessie," Bill Hutchinson said.

"Well, everyone," Mr. Summers said, "that was done pretty fast, and now we've got to be hurrying a little more to get done in time." He consulted his next list. "Bill," he said, "you draw for the Hutchinson family. You got any other households in the Hutchinsons?"

"There's Don and Eva," Mrs. Hutchinson yelled. "Make *them* take their chance!"

"Daughters draw with their husbands' families, Tessie," Mr. Summers said gently. "You know that as well as anyone else."

"It wasn't *fair*," Tessie said.

"I guess not, Joe," Bill Hutchinson said regretfully. "My daughter draws with her husband's family, that's only fair. And I've got no other family except the kids."

"Then, as far as drawing for families is concerned, it's you,"

Mr. Summers said in explanation, "and as far as drawing for households is concerned, that's you, too. Right?"

"Right," Bill Hutchinson said.

"How many lads, Bill?" Mr. Summers asked formally.

"Three," Bill Hutchinson said. "There's Bill, Jr., and Nancy, and little Dave. And Tessie and me."

"All right, then," Mr. Summers said. "Harry, you got their tickets back?"

Mr. Graves nodded and held up the slips of paper. "Put them in the box, then," Mr. Summers directed. "Take Bill's and put it in."

"I think we ought to start over," Mrs. Hutchinson said, as quietly as she could. "I tell you it wasn't *fair*. You didn't give him time enough to choose, everybody saw that."

Mr. Graves had selected the five slips and put them in the box, and he dropped all the papers but those onto the ground, where the breeze caught them and lifted them off.

"Listen, everybody," Mrs. Hutchinson was saying to the people around her.

"Ready, Bill?" Mr. Summers asked, and Bill Hutchinson, with one quick glance around at his wife and children, nodded.

"Remember," Mr. Summers said, "take the slips and keep them folded until each person has taken one. Harry, you help little Dave." Mr. Graves took the hand of the little boy, who came willingly with him up to the box. "Take a paper out of the box, Davy," Mr. Summers said. Davy put his hand into the box and laughed. "Take just one paper," Mr. Summers said. "Harry, you hold it for him." Mr. Graves took the child's hand and removed the folded paper from the tight fist and held it while little Dave stood next to him and looked up at him wonderingly.

"Nancy next," Mr. Summers said. Nancy was twelve, and her school friends breathed heavily as she went forward, switching her skirt, and took a slip daintily from the box. "Bill, Jr.," Mr. Summers said, and Billy, his face red and his feet over-large, nearly knocked the box over as he got a paper out. "Tessie," Mr. Summers said. She hesitated for a minute, looking around defiantly, and then set her lips and went up to the box. She snatched a paper out and held it behind her.

"Bill," Mr. Summers said, and Bill Hutchinson reached into the box and felt around, bringing his hand out at last with the slip of paper in it.

The crowd was quiet. A girl whispered, "I hope it's not Nancy," and the sound of the whisper reached the edges of the crowd.

"It's not the way it used to be," Old Man Warner said clearly. "People ain't the way they used to be."

"All right," Mr. Summers said. "Open the papers. Harry, you open little Dave's."

Mr. Graves opened the slip of paper and there was a general sigh through the crowd as he held it up and everyone could see that it was blank. Nancy and Bill, Jr., opened theirs at the same time, and both beamed and laughed, turning around to the crowd and holding their slips of paper above their heads.

"Tessie," Mr. Summers said. There was a pause, and then Mr. Summers looked at Bill Hutchinson, and Bill unfolded his paper and showed it. It was blank.

"It's Tessie," Mr. Summers said, and his voice was hushed. "Show us her paper, Bill."

Bill Hutchinson went over to his wife and forced the slip of paper out of her hand. It had a black spot on it, the black spot Mr. Summers had made the night before with the heavy pencil in the coal-company office. Bill Hutchinson held it up, and there was a stir in the crowd.

"All right, folks," Mr. Summers said. "Let's finish quickly."

Although the villagers had forgotten the ritual and lost the original black box, they still remembered to use stones. The pile of stones the boys had made earlier was ready; there were stones on the ground with the blowing scraps of paper that had come out of the box. Mrs. Delacroix selected a stone so large she had to pick it up with both hands and turned to Mrs. Dunbar. "Come on," she said. "Hurry up.'

Mrs. Dunbar had small stones in both hands, and she said, gasping for breath, "I can't run at all. You'll have to go ahead and I'll catch up with you."

The children had stones already, and someone gave little Davy Hutchinson a few pebbles.

Tessie Hutchinson was in the center of a cleared space by now, and she held her hands out desperately as the villagers moved in on her. "It isn't fair," she said. A stone hit her on the side of the head.

Old Man Warner was saying, "Come on, come on, everyone." Steve Adams was in the front of the crowd of villagers, with Mrs. Graves beside him.

"It isn't fair, it isn't right," Mrs. Hutchinson screamed, and then they were upon her.

THE LIFE YOU SAVE MAY BE YOUR OWN

Flannery O'Connor

Flannery O'Connor (1925–1964) was an American writer. An important voice in American literature, O'Connor published two novels and thirty-two short stories, as well as reviews and commentaries. Her *Complete Stories* won the US National Book Award for Fiction in 1972, and was voted Best of the National Book Awards in 2009.

The old woman and her daughter were sitting on their porch when Mr. Shiftlet came up their road for the first time. The old woman slid to the edge of her chair and leaned forward, shading her eyes from the piercing sunset with her hand. The daughter could not see far in front of her and continued to play with her fingers. Although the old woman lived in this desolate spot with only her daughter and she had never seen Mr. Shiftlet before, she could tell, even from a distance, that he was a tramp and no one to be afraid of. His left coat sleeve was folded up to show there was only half an arm in it and his gaunt figure listed slightly to the side as if the breeze were pushing him. He had on a black town suit and a brown felt hat that was turned up in the front and down in the back and he carried a tin tool box by a handle. He came on, at an amble, up her road, his face turned toward the sun which appeared to be balancing itself on the peak of a small mountain.

The old woman didn't change her position until he was almost into her yard; then she rose with one hand fisted on her hip. The daughter, a large girl in a short blue organdy dress, saw him all at once and jumped up and began to stamp and point and make excited speechless sounds.

Mr. Shiftlet stopped just inside the yard and set his box on the ground and tipped his hat at her as if she were not in the least afflicted; then he turned toward the old woman and swung the hat all the way off. He had long black slick hair that hung flat from a part in the middle to beyond the tips of his ears on either side. His face descended in forehead for more than half its length and ended suddenly with his features just balanced over a jutting steel-trap jaw. He seemed to be a young man but he had a look of composed dissatisfaction as if he understood life thoroughly.

"Good evening," the old woman said. She was about the size of a cedar fence post and she had a man's gray hat pulled down low over her head.

The tramp stood looking at her and didn't answer. He turned his back and faced the sunset. He swung both his whole and his short arm up slowly so that they indicated an expanse of sky and his figure formed a crooked cross. The old woman watched him with her arms folded across her chest as if she were the owner of the sun, and the daughter watched, her head thrust forward and her fat helpless hands hanging at the wrists. She had long pink-gold hair and eyes as blue as a peacock's neck.

He held the pose for almost fifty seconds and then he picked up his box and came on to the porch and dropped down on the bottom step. "Lady," he said in a firm nasal voice, "I'd give a fortune to live where I could see me a sun do that every evening."

"Does it every evening," the old woman said and sat back down. The daughter sat down too and watched him with a cautious sly look as if he were a bird that had come up very close. He leaned to one side, rooting in his pants pocket, and in a second he brought out a package of chewing gum and offered her a piece. She took it and unpeeled it and began to chew without taking her eyes off him. He offered the old woman a piece but she only raised her upper lip to indicate she had no teeth.

Mr. Shiftlet's pale sharp glance had already passed over everything in the yard – the pump near the corner of the house and the big fig tree that three or four chickens were preparing to roost in – and had moved to a shed where he saw the square rusted back of an automobile. "You ladies drive?" he asked.

"That car ain't run in fifteen year," the old woman said. "The day my husband died, it quit running."

"Nothing is like it used to be, lady," he said. "The world is almost rotten."

"That's right," the old woman said. "You from around here?"

"Name Tom T. Shiftlet," he murmured, looking at the tires.

"I'm pleased to meet you," the old woman said. "Name Lucynell Crater and daughter Lucynell Crater. What you doing around here, Mr. Shiftlet?"

He judged the car to be about a 1928 or '29 Ford. "Lady," he said, and turned and gave her his full attention, "lemme tell you something. There's one of these doctors in Atlanta that's taken a knife and cut the human heart – the human heart," he repeated, leaning forward; "out of a man's chest and held it in his hand," and he held his hand out, palm up, as if it were slightly weighted with the human heart, "and studied it like it was a day-old chicken, and lady," he said, allowing a long significant pause in which his head slid forward and his clay-colored eyes brightened, "he don't know no more about it than you or me."

"That's right," the old woman said.

"Why, if he was to take that knife and cut into every corner of it, he still wouldn't know no more than you or me. What you want to bet?"

"Nothing," the old woman said wisely. "Where you come from, Mr. Shiftlet?"

He didn't answer. He reached into his pocket and brought out a sack of tobacco and a package of cigarette papers and rolled himself a cigarette, expertly with one hand, and attached it in a hanging position to his upper lip. Then he took a box of wooden matches from his pocket and struck one on his shoe. He held the burning match as if he were studying the mystery of flame while it traveled dangerously toward his skin. The daughter began to make loud noises and to point to his hand and shake her finger at him, but when the flame was just before touching him, he leaned down with his hand cupped over it as if he were going to set fire to his nose and lit the cigarette.

He flipped away the dead match and blew a stream of gray into the evening. A sly look came over his face. "Lady," he said, "nowadays, people'll do anything anyways. I can tell you my name is Tom T. Shiftlet and I come from Tarwater, Tennessee, but you never have seen me before: how you know I ain't lying? How you know my name ain't Aaron Sparks, lady, and I come from

Singleberry, Georgia, or how you know it's not George Speeds and I come from Lucy, Alabama, or how you know I ain't Thompson Bright from Toolafalls, Mississippi?"

"I don't know nothing about you," the old woman muttered, irked.

"Lady," he said, "people don't care how they lie. Maybe the best I can tell you is, I'm a man; but listen lady," he said and paused and made his tone more ominous still, "what is a man?"

The old woman began to gum a seed. "What you carry in that tin box, Mr. Shiftlet?" she asked.

"Tools," he said, put back. "I'm a carpenter."

"Well, if you come out here to work, I'll be able to feed you and give you a place to sleep but I can't pay. I'll tell you that before you begin," she said.

There was no answer at once and no particular expression on his face. He leaned back against the two-by-four that helped support the porch roof. "Lady," he said slowly, "there's some men that some things mean more to them than money." The old woman rocked without comment and the daughter watched the trigger that moved up and down in his neck. He told the old woman then that all most people were interested in was money, but he asked what a man was made for. He asked her if a man was made for money, or what. He asked her what she thought she was made for but she didn't answer, she only sat rocking and wondered if a one-armed man could put a new roof on her garden house. He asked a lot of questions that she didn't answer. He told her that he was twenty-eight years old and had lived a varied life. He had been a gospel singer, a foreman on the railroad, an assistant in an undertaking parlor, and he had come over the radio for three months with Uncle Roy and his Red Creek Wranglers. He said he had fought and bled in the Arm Service of his country and visited every foreign land and that everywhere he had seen people that didn't care if they did a thing one way or another. He said he hadn't been raised thataway.

A fat yellow moon appeared in the branches of the fig tree as if it were going to roost there with the chickens. He said that a man had to escape to the country to see the world whole and that he wished he lived in a desolate place like this where he could see the sun go down every evening like God made it to do.

"Are you married or are you single?" the old woman asked.

There was a long silence. "Lady," he asked finally, "where would you find you an innocent woman today? I wouldn't have any of this trash I could just pick up."

The daughter was leaning very far down, hanging her head almost between her knees, watching him through a triangular door she had made in her overturned hair; and she suddenly fell in a heap on the floor and began to whimper. Mr. Shiftlet straightened her out and helped her get back in the chair.

"Is she your baby girl?" he asked.

"My only," the old woman said, "and she's the sweetest girl in the world. I wouldn't give her up for nothing on earth. She's smart too. She can sweep the floor, cook, wash, feed the chickens, and hoe. I wouldn't give her up for a casket of jewels."

"No," he said kindly, "don't ever let any man take her away from you."

"Any man come after her," the old woman said, "I'll have to stay around the place."

Mr. Shiftlet's eye in the darkness was focused on a part of the automobile bumper that glittered in the distance. "Lady," he said, jerking his short arm up as if he could point with it to her house and yard and pump, "there ain't a broken thing on this plantation that I couldn't fix for you, one-arm jackleg or not. I'm a man," he said with a sullen dignity, "even if I ain't a whole one. I got," he said, tapping his knuckles on the floor to emphasize the immensity of what he was going to say, "a moral intelligence!" and his face pierced out of the darkness into a shaft of doorlight and he stared at her as if he were astonished himself at this impossible truth.

The old woman was not impressed with the phrase. "I told you you could hang around and work for food," she said, "if you don't mind sleeping in that car yonder."

"Why listen, Lady," he said with a grin of delight, "the monks of old slept in their coffins!"

"They wasn't as advanced as we are," the old woman said.

The next morning he began on the roof of the garden house while Lucynell, the daughter, sat on a rock and watched him work. He had not been around a week before the change he had made in the place was apparent. He had patched the front and back steps, built a new hog pen, restored a fence, and taught Lucynell, who was completely deaf and had never said a word in her life, to say the word "bird." The big rosy-faced girl followed him everywhere, saying "Burrttddt ddbirrrttdt," and clapping her hands. The old woman watched from a distance, secretly pleased. She was ravenous for a son-in-law.

Mr. Shiftlet slept on the hard narrow back seat of the car with his feet out the side window. He had his razor and a can of water on a crate that served him as a bedside table and he put up a piece of mirror against the back glass and kept his coat neatly on a hanger that he hung over one of the windows.

In the evenings he sat on the steps and talked while the old woman and Lucynell rocked violently in their chairs on either side of him. The old woman's three mountains were black against the dark blue sky and were visited off and on by various planets and by the moon after it had left the chickens, Mr. Shiftlet pointed out that the reason he had improved this plantation was because he had taken a personal interest in it. He said he was even going to make the automobile run.

He had raised the hood and studied the mechanism and he said he could tell that the car had been built in the days when cars were really built. You take now, he said, one man puts in one bolt and another man puts in another bolt and another man puts in another bolt so that it's a man for a bolt. That's why you have to pay so much for a car: you're paying all those men. Now if you didn't have to pay but one man, you could get you a cheaper car and one that had had a personal interest taken in it, and it would be a better car. The old woman agreed with him that this was so.

Mr. Shiftlet said that the trouble with the world was that nobody cared, or stopped and took any trouble. He said he never would have been able to teach Lucynell to say a word if he hadn't cared and stopped long enough.

"Teach her to say something else," the old woman said.

"What you want her to say next?" Mr. Shiftlet asked.

The old woman's smile was broad and toothless and suggestive. "Teach her to say 'sugarpie,' " she said.

Mr. Shiftlet already knew what was on her mind.

The next day he began to tinker with the automobile and that evening he told her that if she would buy a fan belt, he would be able to make the car run.

The old woman said she would give him the money. "You see that girl yonder?" she asked, pointing to Lucynell who was sitting on the floor a foot away, watching him, her eyes blue even in the dark. "If it was ever a man wanted to take her away, I would say, 'No man on earth is going to take that sweet girl of mine away from me!' but if he was to say, 'Lady, I don't want to take her away, I want her right here,' I would say, 'Mister, I don't blame you none. I wouldn't pass up a chance to live in a permanent place and get the sweetest girl in the world myself. You ain't no fool,' I would say."

"How old is she?" Mr. Shiftlet asked casually.

"Fifteen, sixteen," the old woman said. The girl was nearly thirty but because of her innocence it was impossible to guess.

"It would be a good idea to paint it too," Mr. Shiftlet remarked. "You don't want it to rust out."

"We'll see about that later," the old woman said.

The next day he walked into town and returned with the parts he needed and a can of gasoline. Late in the afternoon, terrible noises issued from the shed and the old woman rushed out of the house, thinking Lucynell was somewhere having a fit. Lucynell was sitting on a chicken crate, stamping her feet and screaming, "Burrddttt! Bddurrddtttt!" but her fuss was drowned out by the car. With a volley of blasts it emerged from the shed, moving in a fierce and stately way. Mr. Shiftlet was in the driver's seat, sitting very erect. He had an expression of serious modesty on his face as if he had just raised the dead.

That night, rocking on the porch, the old woman began her business at once, "You want you an innocent woman, don't you?" she asked sympathetically. "You don't want none of this trash."

"No'm, I don't," Mr. Shiftlet said.

"One that can't talk," she continued, "can't sass you back or use foul language. That's the kind for you to have. Right there," and she pointed to Lucynell sitting cross-legged in her chair, holding both feet in her hands.

"That's right," he admitted. "She wouldn't give me any trouble."

"Saturday," the old woman said, "you and her and me can drive into town and get married."

Mr. Shiftlet eased his position on the steps.

"I can't get married right now," he said. "Everything you want to do takes money and I ain't got any."

"What you need with money?" she asked.

"It takes money," he said. "Some people'll do anything anyhow these days, but the way I think, I wouldn't marry no woman that I couldn't take on a trip like she was somebody. I mean take her to a hotel and treat her. I wouldn't marry the Duchesser Windsor," he said firmly, "unless I could take her to a hotel and give her something good to eat.

"I was raised thataway and there ain't a thing I can do about it. My old mother taught me how to do."

"Lucynell don't even know what a hotel is," the old woman muttered. "Listen here, Mr. Shiftlet," she said, sliding forward in her chair, "you'd be getting a permanent house and a deep well and the most innocent girl in the world. You don't need no money. Lemme tell you something: there ain't any place in the world for a poor disabled friendless drifting man."

The ugly words settled in Mr. Shiftlet's head like a group of buzzards in the top of a tree. He didn't answer at once. He rolled himself a cigarette and lit it and then he said in an even voice, "Lady, a man is divided into two parts, body and spirit."

The old woman clamped her gums together.

"A body and a spirit," he repeated. "The body, lady, is like a house: it don't go anywhere; but the spirit, lady, is like a automobile: always on the move, always ..."

"Listen, Mr. Shiftlet," she said, "my well never goes dry and my house is always warm in the winter and there's no mortgage on a thing about this place. You can go to the courthouse and see for yourself. And yonder under that shed is a fine automobile." She laid the bait carefully. "You can have it painted by Saturday. I'll pay for the paint."

In the darkness, Mr. Shiftlet's smile stretched like a weary snake waking up by a fire. After a second he recalled himself and said, "I'm only saying a man's spirit means more to him than anything else. I would have to take my wife off for the weekend without no regards at all for cost. I got to follow where my spirit says to go."

"I'll give you fifteen dollars for a weekend trip," the old woman said in a crabbed voice. "That's the best I can do."

"That wouldn't hardly pay for more than the gas and the hotel," he said. "It wouldn't feed her."

"Seventeen-fifty," the old woman said. "That's all I got so it isn't any use you trying to milk me. You can take a lunch."

Mr. Shiftlet was deeply hurt by the word "milk." He didn't doubt that she had more money sewed up in her mattress but he had already told her he was not interested in her money. "I'll make that do," he said and rose and walked off without treating with her further.

On Saturday the three of them drove into town in the car that the paint had barely dried on and Mr. Shiftlet and Lucynell were married in the Ordinary's office while the old woman witnessed. As they came out of the courthouse, Mr. Shiftlet began twisting his neck in his collar. He looked morose and bitter as if he had been insulted while someone held him. "That didn't satisfy me none," he said. "That was just something a woman in an office did, nothing but paper work and blood tests. What do they know about my blood? If they was to take my heart and cut it out," he said, "they wouldn't know a thing about me. It didn't satisfy me at all."

"It satisfied the law," the old woman said sharply.

"The law," Mr. Shiftlet said and spit. "It's the law that don't satisfy me."

He had painted the car dark green with a yellow band around it just under the windows. The three of them climbed in the front seat and the old woman said, "Don't Lucynell look pretty? Looks like a baby doll." Lucynell was dressed up in a white dress that her mother had uprooted from a trunk and there was a Panama hat on her head with a bunch of red wooden cherries on the brim. Every now and then her placid expression was changed by a sly isolated little thought like a shoot of green in the desert. "You got a prize!" the old woman said.

Mr. Shiftlet didn't even look at her.

They drove back to the house to let the old woman off and pick up the lunch. When they were ready to leave, she stood staring in the window of the car, with her fingers clenched around the glass. Tears began to seep sideways out of her eyes and run along the dirty creases in her face. "I ain't ever been parted with her for two days before," she said.

Mr. Shiftlet started the motor.

"And I wouldn't let no man have her but you because I seen you would do right. Good-by, Sugarbaby," she said, clutching at the sleeve of the white dress. Lucynell looked straight at her and didn't seem to see her there at all. Mr. Shiftlet eased the car forward so that she had to move her hands.

The early afternoon was clear and open and surrounded by pale blue sky. Although the car would go only thirty miles an hour, Mr. Shiftlet imagined a terrific climb and dip and swerve that went entirely to his head so that he forgot his morning bitterness. He had always wanted an automobile but he had never been able to afford one before. He drove very fast because he wanted to make Mobile by nightfall.

Occasionally he stopped his thoughts long enough to look at Lucynell in the seat beside him. She had eaten the lunch as soon as they were out of the yard and now she was pulling the cherries off the hat one by one and throwing them out the window. He became depressed in spite of the car. He had driven about a hundred miles when he decided that she must be hungry again and at the next small town they came to, he stopped in front of an aluminum-painted eating place called The Hot Spot and took her in and ordered her a plate of ham and grits. The ride had made her sleepy and as soon as she got up on the stool, she rested her head on the counter and shut her eyes. There was no one in The Hot Spot but Mr. Shiftlet and the boy behind the counter, a pale youth with a greasy rag hung over his shoulder. Before he could dish up the food, she was snoring gently.

"Give it to her when she wakes up," Mr. Shiftlet said. "I'll pay for it now."

The boy bent over her and stared at the long pink-gold hair and the half-shut sleeping eyes. Then he looked up and stared at Mr. Shiftlet. "She looks like an angel of Gawd," he murmured.

"Hitch-hiker," Mr. Shiftlet explained. "I can't wait. I got to make Tuscaloosa."

The boy bent over again and very carefully touched his finger to a strand of the golden hair and Mr. Shiftlet left.

He was more depressed than ever as he drove on by himself. The late afternoon had grown hot and sultry and the country had flattened out. Deep in the sky a storm was preparing very slowly and without thunder as if it meant to drain every drop of air from the earth before it broke. There were times when Mr. Shiftlet preferred not to be alone. He felt too that a man with a car had a responsibility to others and he kept his eye out for a hitchhiker. Occasionally he saw a sign that warned: "Drive carefully. The life you save may be your own."

The narrow road dropped off on either side into dry fields and here and there a shack or a filling station stood in a clearing. The sun began to set directly in front of the automobile. It was a reddening ball that through his windshield was slightly flat on the bottom and top. He saw a boy in overalls and a gray hat standing on the edge of the road and he slowed the car down and stopped in front of him. The boy didn't have his hand raised to thumb the ride, he was only standing there, but he had a small cardboard suitcase and his hat was set on his head in a way to indicate that he had left somewhere for good. "Son," Mr. Shiftlet said, "I see you want a ride."

The boy didn't say he did or he didn't but he opened the door of the car and got in, and Mr. Shiftlet started driving again. The child held the suitcase on his lap and folded his arms on top of it. He turned his head and looked out the window away from Mr. Shiftlet. Mr. Shiftlet felt oppressed. "Son," he said after a minute, "I got the best old mother in the world so I reckon you only got the second best."

The boy gave him a quick dark glance and then turned his face back out the window.

"It's nothing so sweet," Mr. Shiftlet continued, "as a boy's mother. She taught him his first prayers at her knee, she give him love when no other would, she told him what was right and what wasn't, and she seen that he done the right thing. Son," he said, "I never rued a day in my life like the one I rued when I left that old mother of mine."

The boy shifted in his seat but he didn't look at Mr. Shiftlet. He unfolded his arms and put one hand on the door handle.

"My mother was a angel of Gawd," Mr. Shiftlet said in a very strained voice. "He took her from heaven and giver to me and I left her." His eyes were instantly clouded over with a mist of tears. The car was barely moving.

The boy turned angrily in the seat. "You go to the devil!" he cried. "My old woman is a flea bag and yours is a stinking pole cat!" and with that he flung the door open and jumped out with his suitcase into the ditch.

Mr. Shiftlet was so shocked that for about a hundred feet he drove along slowly with the door still open. A cloud, the exact color of the boy's hat and shaped like a turnip, had descended over the sun, and another, worse looking, crouched behind the car. Mr. Shiftlet felt that the rottenness of the world was about to engulf him. He raised his arm and let it fall again to his breast, "Oh Lord!" he prayed. "Break forth and wash the slime from this earth!"

The turnip continued slowly to descend. After a few minutes there was a guffawing peal of thunder from behind and fantastic raindrops, like tin-can tops, crashed over the rear of Mr. Shiftlet's car. Very quickly he stepped on the gas and with his stump sticking out the window he raced the galloping shower into Mobile.

THE BLUSH

Elizabeth Taylor

Elizabeth Taylor (1912–1975) was a popular British novelist and short story writer. Her first novel, *At Mrs Lippincote's*, was published in 1945 and was followed by eleven more. Her short stories were published in various magazines and collected in four volumes. She also wrote a children's book.

They were the same age – Mrs Allen and the woman who came every day to do the housework. 'I shall never have children now,' Mrs Allen had begun to tell herself. Something had not come true; the essential part of her life. She had always imagined her children in fleeting scenes and intimations; that was how they had come to her, like snatches of a film. She had seen them plainly, their chins tilted up as she tied on their bibs at meal-times; their naked bodies had darted in and out of the water sprinkler on the lawn; and she had listened to their voices in the garden and in the mornings from their beds. She had even cried a little dreaming of the day when the eldest boy would go off to boarding-school; she pictured the train going out of the station; she raised her hand and her throat contracted and her lips trembled as she smiled. The years passing by had slowly filched from her the reality of these scenes – the gay sounds; the grave peace she had longed for; even the pride of grief.

She listened – as they worked together in the kitchen – to Mrs Lacey's troubles with her family, her grumblings about her grown-up son who would not get up till dinner-time on Sundays and then expected his mother to have cleaned his shoes for him; about the girl of eighteen who was a hairdresser and too full of dainty ways which she picked up from the women's magazines, and the adolescent girl who moped and glowered and answered back.

'My children wouldn't have turned out like that,' Mrs Allen thought, as she made her murmured replies. 'The more you do for some, the more you may,' said Mrs Lacey. But from gossip in the village which Mrs Allen heard she had done all too little. The children, one night after another, for years and years, had had to run out for parcels of fish and chips while their mother sat in the Horse and Jockey drinking brown ale. On summer evenings, when they were younger, they had hung about outside the pub: when they were bored they pressed their foreheads to the window and looked in at the dark little bar, hearing the jolly laughter, their mother's the loudest of all. Seeing their faces, she would swing at once from the violence of hilarity to that of extreme annoyance and, although ginger-beer and packets of potato crisps would be handed out through the window, her anger went out with them and threatened the children as they ate and drank.

'And she doesn't always care who she goes there *with*,' Mrs Allen's gardener told her.

'She works hard and deserves a little pleasure – she has her anxieties,' said Mrs Allen, who, alas, had none.

She had never been inside the Horse and Jockey, although it was nearer to her house than the Chequers at the other end of the village where she and her husband went sometimes for a glass of sherry on Sunday mornings. The Horse and Jockey attracted a different set of customers – for instance, people who sat down and drank, at tables all round the wall. At the Chequers no one ever sat down, but stood and sipped and chatted as at a cocktail party, and luncheons and dinners were served, which made it so much more respectable: no children hung about outside, because they were all at home with their nannies.

Sometimes in the evenings – so many of them – when her husband was kept late in London, Mrs Allen wished that she could go down to the Chequers and drink a glass of sherry and exchange a little conversation with someone; but she was too shy to open the door and go in alone: she imagined heads turning, a surprised welcome from her friends, who would all be safely in married pairs; and then, when she left, eyes meeting with unspoken messages and conjecture in the air.

Mrs Lacey left her at midday and then there was gardening to do and the dog to be taken for a walk. After six o'clock, she began to pace restlessly about the house, glancing at the clocks in one room after another, listening for her husband's car – the sound she knew so well because she had awaited it for such a large part of her married life. She would hear, at last, the tyres turning on the soft gravel, the door being slammed, then his footsteps hurrying towards the porch. She knew that it was a wasteful way of spending her years – and, looking back, she was unable to tell one of them from another – but she could not think what else she might do. Humphrey went on earning more and more money and there was no stopping him now. Her acquaintances, in wretched quandaries about where the next term's school-fees were to come from, would turn to her and say cruelly: 'Oh, *you're* all right, Ruth. You've no idea what you are spared.'

And Mrs Lacey would be glad when Maureen could leave school and 'get out earning'. '"I've got my geometry to do," she says, when it's time to wash up the tea-things. "I'll geometry you, my girl," I said. "When I was your age, I was out earning." '

Mrs Allen was fascinated by the life going on in that house and the children seemed real to her, although she had never seen them. Only Mr Lacey remained blurred and unimaginable. No one knew him. He worked in the town in the valley, six miles away, and he kept himself to himself; had never been known to show his face in the Horse and Jockey. 'I've got my own set,' Mrs Lacey said airily. 'After all, he's nearly twenty years older than me. I'll make sure neither of my girls follow my mistake. "I'd rather see you dead at my feet," I said to Vera.' Ron's young lady was lucky; having Ron, she added. Mrs Allen found this strange, for Ron had always been painted so black; was, she had been led to believe, oafish, ungrateful, greedy and slow to put his hands in his pockets if there was any paying out to do. There was also the matter of his shoe-cleaning, for no young woman would do what his mother did for him – or said she did. Always, Mrs Lacey would sigh and say: 'Goodness me, if only I was their age and knew what I know now.'

She was an envious woman: she envied Mrs Allen her pretty house and her clothes and she envied her own daughters their youth. 'If I had your figure,' she would say to Mrs Allen. Her own had gone: what else could be expected, she asked, when she had had three children? Mrs Allen thought, too, of all the brown ale she drank at the Horse and Jockey and of the reminiscences of meals past which came so much into her conversations. Whatever the cause was, her flesh, slackly corseted, shook as she trod heavily about the kitchen. In summer, with bare arms and legs she looked larger than ever. Although her skin was very white, the impression she gave was at once colourful – from her orange hair and bright lips and the floral patterns that she always wore. Her red-painted toe-nails poked through the straps of her fancy sandals; turquoise-blue beads were wound round her throat.

Humphrey Allen had never seen her; he had always left for the station before she arrived, and that was a good thing, his wife thought. When she spoke of Mrs Lacey, she wondered if he visualised a neat, homely woman in a clean white overall. She did not deliberately mislead him, but she took advantage of his indifference. Her relationship with Mrs Lacey and the intimacy of their conversations in the kitchen he would not have approved, and the sight of those calloused feet with their chipped nail-varnish and yellowing heels would have sickened him.

One Monday morning, Mrs Lacey was later than usual. She was never very punctual and had many excuses about flat bicycle-tyres or Maureen being poorly. Mrs Allen, waiting for her, sorted out all the washing. When she took another look at the clock, she decided that it was far too late for her to be expected at all. For some time lately Mrs Lacey had seemed ill and depressed; her eyelids, which were chronically rather inflamed, had been more angrily red than ever and, at the sink or ironing-board, she would fall into unusual silences, was absent-minded and full of sighs. She had always liked to talk about the 'change' and did so more than ever as if with a desperate hopefulness.

'I'm sorry, but I was ever so sick,' she told Mrs Allen, when she arrived the next morning. 'I still feel queerish. Such heartburn. I don't like the signs, I can tell you. All I crave is pickled walnuts, just the same as I did with Maureen. I don't like the signs one bit. I feel I'll throw myself into the river if I'm taken that way again.'

Mrs Allen felt stunned and antagonistic. 'Surely not at your age,' she said crossly.

'You can't be more astonished than me,' Mrs Lacey said, belching loudly. 'Oh, pardon. I'm afraid I can't help myself.'

Not being able to help herself, she continued to belch and

hiccough as she turned on taps and shook soap-powder into the washing-up bowl. It was because of this that Mrs Allen decided to take the dog for a walk. Feeling consciously fastidious and aloof she made her way across the fields, trying to disengage her thoughts from Mrs Lacey and her troubles; but unable to. 'Poor woman,' she thought again and again with bitter animosity.

She turned back when she noticed how the sky had darkened with racing, sharp-edged clouds. Before she could reach home, the rain began. Her hair, soaking wet, shrank into tight curls against her head; her woollen suit smelt like a damp animal. 'Oh, I am drenched,' she called out, as she threw open the kitchen door.

She knew at once that Mrs Lacey had gone, that she must have put on her coat and left almost as soon as Mrs Allen had started out on her walk, for nothing was done; the washing-up was hardly started and the floor was unswept. Among the stacked-up crockery a note was propped; she had come over funny, felt dizzy and, leaving her apologies and respects, had gone.

Angrily, but methodically, Mrs Allen set about making good the wasted morning. By afternoon, the grim look was fixed upon her face. 'How dare she?' she found herself whispering, without allowing herself to wonder what it was the woman had dared.

She had her own little ways of cosseting herself through the lonely hours, comforts which were growing more important to her as she grew older, so that the time would come when not to have her cup of tea at four-thirty would seem a prelude to disaster. This afternoon, disorganised as it already was, she fell out of her usual habit and instead of carrying the tray to the low table by the fire, she poured out her tea in the kitchen and drank it there, leaning tiredly against the dresser. Then she went upstairs to make herself tidy. She was trying to brush her frizzed hair smooth again when she heard the door bell ringing.

When she opened the door, she saw quite plainly a look of astonishment take the place of anxiety on the man's face. Something about herself surprised him, was not what he had expected. 'Mrs Allen?' he asked uncertainly and the astonishment remained when she had answered him.

'Well, I'm calling about the wife,' he said. 'Mrs Lacey that works here.'

'I was worried about her,' said Mrs Allen.

She knew that she must face the embarrassment of hearing about Mrs Lacey's condition and invited the man into her husband's study, where she thought he might look less out-of-place than in her brocade-smothered drawing-room. He looked about him resentfully and glared down at the floor which his wife had polished. With this thought in his mind, he said abruptly: 'It's all taken its toll.'

He sat down on a leather couch with his cap and his bicycle-clips beside him.

'I came home to my tea and found her in bed, crying,' he said. This was true. Mrs Lacey had succumbed to despair and gone to lie down. Feeling better at four o'clock, she went downstairs to find some food to comfort herself with; but the slice of dough-cake was ill-chosen and brought on more heartburn and floods of bitter tears.

'If she carries on here for a while, it's all got to be very different,' Mr Lacey said threateningly. He was nervous at saying what he must and could only bring out the words with the impetus of anger. 'You may or may not know that she's expecting.'

'Yes,' said Mrs Allen humbly. 'This morning she told me that she thought ...'

'There's no "thought" about it. It's as plain as a pikestaff.' Yet in his eyes she could see disbelief and bafflement and he frowned and looked down again at the polished floor.

Twenty years older than his wife – or so his wife had said – he really, to Mrs Allen, looked quite ageless, a crooked, bow-legged little man who might have been a jockey once. The expression about his blue eyes was like a child's: he was both stubborn and pathetic.

Mrs Allen's fat spaniel came into the room and went straight to the stranger's chair and began to sniff at his corduroy trousers.

'It's too much for her,' Mr Lacey said. 'It's too much to expect.'

To Mrs Allen's horror she saw the blue eyes filling with tears. Hoping to hide his emotion, he bent down and fondled the dog, making playful thrusts at it with his fist closed.

He was a man utterly, bewilderedly at sea. His married life had been too much for him, with so much in it that he could not understand.

'Now I know, I will do what I can,' Mrs Allen told him. 'I will try to get someone else in to do the rough.'

'It's the late nights that are the trouble,' he said. 'She comes in dog-tired. Night after night. It's not good enough. "Let them stay at home and mind their own children once in a while," I told her. "We don't need the money." '

'I can't understand,' Mrs Allen began. She was at sea herself now, but felt perilously near a barbarous, unknown shore and was afraid to make any movement towards it.

'I earn good money. For her to come out at all was only for extras. She likes new clothes. In the daytimes I never had any objection. Then all these cocktail parties begin. It beats me how people can drink like it night after night and pay out for someone else to mind their kids. Perhaps you're thinking that it's not my business, but I'm the one who has to sit at home alone till all hours and get my own supper and see next to nothing of my wife. I'm boiling over some nights. Once I nearly rushed out when I heard the car stop down the road. I wanted to tell your husband what I thought of you both.'

'My husband?' murmured Mrs Allen.

'What am I supposed to have, I would have asked him? Is she my wife or your sitter-in? Bringing her back at this time of night. And it's no use saying she could have refused. She never would.'

Mrs Allen's quietness at last defeated him and dispelled the anger he had tried to rouse in himself. The look of her, too, filled him with doubts, her grave, uncertain demeanour and the shock her age had been to him. He had imagined someone so much younger and – because of the cocktail parties – flighty. Instead, he recognised something of himself in her, a yearning disappointment. He picked up his cap and his bicycle-clips and sat looking down at them, turning them round in his hands. 'I had to come,' he said.

'Yes,' said Mrs Allen.

'So you won't ask her again?' he pleaded. 'It isn't right for her. Not now.'

'No, I won't,' Mrs Allen promised and she stood up as he did and walked over to the door. He stooped and gave the spaniel a final pat. 'You'll excuse my coming, I hope.'

'Of course.'

'It was no use saying any more to her. Whatever she's asked, she won't refuse. It's her way.'

Mrs Allen shut the front door after him and stood in the hall, listening to him wheeling his bicycle across the gravel. Then she felt herself beginning to blush. She was glad that she was alone, for she could feel her face, her throat, even the tops of her arms burning, and she went over to a looking-glass and studied with great interest this strange phenomenon.

THE SOUND
OF THE RIVER

Jean Rhys

Jean Rhys (1890–1979) was a novelist from Dominica, educated in the UK from the age of sixteen. Introduced in 1924 to the writer Ford Madox Ford, Rhys began to write short stories under his patronage. She is best known for her novel *Wide Sargasso Sea*, written as a 'prequel' to Charlotte Brontë's *Jane Eyre*.

The electric bulb hung on a short flex from the middle of the ceiling, and there was not enough light to read so they lay in bed and talked. The night air pushed out the curtains and came through the open window soft and moist.

'But what are you afraid of? How do you mean afraid?'

She said, 'I mean afraid like when you want to swallow and you can't.'

'All the time?'

'Nearly all the time.'

'My dear, really. You are an idiot.'

'Yes, I know.'

Not about this, she thought, not about this.

'It's only a mood,' she said. 'It'll go.'

'You're so inconsistent. You chose this place and wanted to come here, I thought you approved of it.'

'I do. I approve of the moor and the loneliness and the whole set-up, especially the loneliness. I just wish it would stop raining occasionally.'

'Loneliness is all very well,' he said, 'but it needs fine weather.'

'Perhaps it will be fine tomorrow.'

If I could put it into words it might go, she was thinking. Sometimes you can put it into words – almost – and so get rid of it – almost. Sometimes you can tell yourself I'll admit I was afraid today. I was afraid of the sleek smooth faces, the rat faces, the way they laughed in the cinema. I'm afraid of escalators and doll's eyes. But there aren't any words for this fear. The words haven't been invented.

She said, 'I'll like it again when the rain stops.'

'You weren't liking it just now, were you? Down by the river?'

'Well,' she said, 'no. Not much.'

'It was a bit ghostly down there tonight. What can you expect? Never pick a place in fine weather.' (Or anything else either he thought.) 'There are too many pines about,' he said. 'They shut you in.'

'Yes.'

But it wasn't the black pines, she thought, or the sky without stars, or the thin hunted moon, or the lowering, flat-topped hills, or the tor and the big stones. It was the river.

'The river is very silent,' she'd said. 'Is that because it's so full?'

'One gets used to the noise, I suppose. Let's go in and light the bedroom fire. I wish we had a drink. I'd give a lot for a drink, wouldn't you?'

'We can have some coffee.'

As they walked back he'd kept his head turned towards the water.

'Curiously metallic it looks by this light. Not like water at all.'

'It looks smooth as if it were frozen. And much wider.'

'Frozen – no. Very much alive in an uncanny way. Streaming hair,' he'd said as if he were talking to himself. So he'd felt it too. She lay remembering how the brown broken-surfaced, fast-running river had changed by moonlight. Things are more powerful than people. I've always believed that. (You're not my daughter if you're afraid of a horse. You're not my daughter if you're afraid of being seasick. You're not my daughter if you're afraid of the shape of a hill, or the moon when it is growing old. In fact you're not my daughter.)

'It isn't silent now is it?' she said. 'The river I mean.'

'No, it makes a row from up here.' He yawned. 'I'll put another log on the fire. It was very kind of Ransom to let us have that coal and wood. He didn't promise any luxuries of that sort when we took the cottage. He's not a bad chap, is he?'

'He's got a heart. And he must be wise to the climate after all.'

'Well I like it,' he said as he got back into bed, 'in spite of the rain. Let's be happy here.'

'Yes, let's.'

That's the second time. He said that before. He'd said it the first day they came. Then too she hadn't answered 'yes let's' at once because fear which had been waiting for her had come up to her and touched her, and it had been several seconds before she could speak.

'That must have been an otter we saw this evening,' he said, 'much too big for a water rat. I'll tell Ransom. He'll be very excited.'

'Why?'

'Oh, they're rather rare in these parts.'

'Poor devils, I bet they have an awful time if they're rare. What'll he do? Organize a hunt? Perhaps he won't, we've agreed that he's soft-hearted. This is a bird sanctuary, did you know? It's all sorts of things. I'll tell him about that yellow-breasted one. Maybe he'll know what it was.'

That morning she had watched it fluttering up and down the window pane – a flash of yellow in the rain. 'Oh what a pretty bird.' *Fear is yellow. You're yellow. She's got a broad streak of yellow. They're quite right, fear is yellow.* 'Isn't it pretty? And isn't it persistent? It's determined to get in …'

'I'm going to put this light out,' he said. 'It's no use. The fire's better.'

He struck a match to light another cigarette and when it flared she saw the deep hollows under his eyes, the skin stretched taut over his cheekbones, and the thin bridge of his nose. He was smiling as if he knew what she'd been thinking.

'Is there anything you're not afraid of in these moods of yours?'

'You,' she said. The match went out. *Whatever happened,* she thought. *Whatever you did. Whatever I did. Never you. D'you hear me?*

'Good.' He laughed. 'That's a relief.'

'Tomorrow will be fine, you'll see. We'll be lucky.'

'Don't depend on our luck. You ought to know better by this time,' he muttered. 'But you're the sort who never knows better. Unfortunately we're both the sort who never knows better.'

'Are you tired? You sound tired.'

'Yes,' He sighed and turned away, 'I am rather.' When she said, 'I must put the light on, I want some aspirin,' he didn't answer, and she stretched her arm over him and touched the switch of the dim electric bulb. He was sleeping. The lighted cigarette had fallen on to the sheet.

'Good thing I saw that,' she said aloud. She put the cigarette out and threw it through the window, found the aspirin, emptied the ashtray, postponing the moment when she must lie down stretched out straight, listening, when she'd shut her eyes only to feel them click open again.

'Don't go to sleep,' she thought lying there. 'Stay awake and comfort me. I'm frightened. There's something here to be frightened of, I tell you. Why can't you feel it? When you said, let's be happy, that first day, there was a tap dripping somewhere into a full basin, playing a gay and horrible tune. Didn't you hear it? I heard it. Don't turn away and sigh and sleep. Stay awake and comfort me.'

Nobody's going to comfort you, she told herself, you ought to know better. Pull yourself together. There was a time when you weren't afraid. Was there? When? When was that time? Of course there was. Go on. Pull yourself together, pull yourself to pieces. There was a time. There was a time. Besides I'll sleep soon. There's always sleeping, and it'll be fine tomorrow.

'I knew it would be fine today,' she thought when she saw the sunlight through the flimsy curtains. 'The first fine day we've had.'

'Are you awake,' she said. 'It's a fine day. I had such a funny dream,' she said, still staring at the sunlight. 'I dreamt I was walking in a wood and the trees were groaning and then I dreamt of the wind in telegraph wires, well a bit like that, only very loud. I can still hear it – really I swear I'm not making this up. It's still in my head and it isn't anything else except a bit like the wind in telegraph wires.'

'It's a lovely day,' she said and touched his hand.

'My dear, you are cold. I'll get a hot water bottle and some tea. I'll get it because I'm feeling very energetic this morning, you stay still for once!'

'Why don't you answer,' she said sitting up and peering at him. 'You're frightening me,' she said, her voice rising. 'You're frightening me. Wake up,' she said and shook him. As soon as she touched him her heart swelled till it reached her throat. It swelled and grew jagged claws and the claws clutched her driving in deep. 'Oh God,' she said and got up and drew the curtains and saw his face in the sun. 'Oh God,' she said staring at his face in the sun and knelt by the bed with his hand in her two hands not speaking not thinking any longer.

The doctor said, 'You didn't hear anything during the night?'

'I thought it was a dream.'

'Oh! You thought it was a dream. I see. What time did you wake up?'

'I don't know. We kept the clock in the other room because it had a loud tick. About half past eight or nine, I suppose.'

'You knew what had happened of course.'

'I wasn't sure. At first I wasn't sure.'

'But what did you do? It was past ten when you telephoned. What did you do?'

Not a word of comfort. Suspicion. He has small eyes and bushy eyebrows and he looks suspicious.

She said, 'I put on a coat and went to Mr Ransom's, where there's a telephone, I ran all the way but it seemed a long way.'

'But that oughtn't to have taken you more than ten minutes at the most.'

'No, but it seemed very long. I ran but I didn't seem to be moving. When I got there everybody was out and the room where the telephone is was locked. The front door is always open but he locks that room when he goes out. I went back into the road but there was no one there. Nobody in the house and nobody in the road and nobody on the slope of the hill. There were a lot of sheets and men's shirts hanging on a line waving. And the sun of course. It was our first day. The first fine day we've had.'

She looked at the doctor's face, stopped, and went on in a different voice.

'I walked up and down for a bit. I didn't know what to do. Then I thought I might be able to break the door in. So I tried and

I did. A board broke and I got in. But it seemed a long time before anybody answered.'

She thought, Yes, of course I knew. I was late because I had to stay here listening. I heard it then. It got louder and closer and it was in the room with me. I heard the sound of the river.

I heard the sound of the river.

A VISIT

Anna Kavan

Anna Kavan (1901–1968) was a British writer and painter. Having begun her career under her married name, Helen Ferguson, she suffered a nervous breakdown and became Anna Kavan, the protagonist of her 1930 novel *Let Me Alone*. Suffering from long-term drug addiction and bouts of mental illness, Kavan's life featured prominently in her work. She died of heart failure in 1968, soon after the publication of her most celebrated work, the novel *Ice*.

One hot night a leopard came into my room and lay down on the bed beside me. I was half asleep, and did not realize at first that it was a leopard. I seemed to be dreaming the sound of some large, soft-footed creature padding quietly through the house, the doors of which were wide open because of the intense heat. It was almost too dark to see the lithe, muscular shape coming into my room, treading softly on velvet paws, coming straight to the bed without hesitation, as if perfectly familiar with its position. A light spring, then warm breath on my arm, on my neck and shoulder, as the visitor sniffed me before lying down. It was not until later, when moonlight entering through the window revealed an abstract spotted design, that I recognized the form of an unusually large, handsome leopard stretched out beside me.

His breathing was deep though almost inaudible, he seemed to be sound asleep. I watched the regular contractions and expansions of the deep chest, admired the elegant relaxed body and supple limbs, and was confirmed in my conviction that the leopard is the most beautiful of all wild animals. In this particular specimen I noticed something singularly human about the formation of the skull, which was domed rather than flattened, as is generally the case with the big cats, suggesting the possibility of superior brain development inside. While I observed him, I was all the time breathing his natural odour, a wild primeval smell of sunshine, freedom, moon and crushed leaves, combined with the cool freshness of the spotted hide, still damp with the midnight moisture of jungle plants. I found this non-human scent, surrounding him like an aura of strangeness, peculiarly attractive and stimulating.

My bed, like the walls of the house, was made of palm-leaf matting stretched over stout bamboos, smooth and cool to the touch, even in the great heat. It was not so much a bed as a room within a room, an open staging about twelve feet square, so there was ample space for the leopard as well as myself. I slept better that night than I had since the hot weather started, and he too seemed to sleep peacefully at my side. The close proximity of this powerful body of another species gave me a pleasant sensation I am at a loss to name.

When I awoke in the faint light of dawn, with the parrots screeching outside, he had already got up and left the room. Looking out, I saw him standing, statuesque, in front of the house on the small strip of ground I keep cleared between it and the jungle. I thought he was contemplating departure, but I dressed and went out, and he was still there, inspecting the fringe of the dense vegetation, in which huge heavy hornbills were noisily flopping about.

I called him and fed him with some meat I had in the house. I hoped he would speak, tell me why he had come and what he wanted of me. But though he looked at me thoughtfully with his large, lustrous eyes, seeming to understand what I said, he did not answer, but remained silent all day. I must emphasize that there was no hint of obstinacy or hostility in his silence, and I did not resent it. On the contrary, I respected him for his reserve; and, as the silence continued unbroken, I gave up expecting to hear his voice. I was glad of the pretext for using mine and went on talking to him. He always appeared to listen and understand me.

The leopard was absent during much of the day. I assumed that he went hunting for his natural food; but he usually came back at intervals, and seldom seemed to be far away. It was difficult to see him among the trees, even when he was quite close, the pattern of his protective spots blended so perfectly with the pattern of sun-spots through savage branches. Only by staring with concentrated attention could I distinguish him from his background; he would be crouching there in a deep-shaded glade, or lying extended with extraordinary grace along a limb of one of the giant kowikawas, whose branch-structure supports less robust trees, as well as countless creepers and smaller growths. The odd thing was that, as soon as I'd seen him, he invariably turned his head as if conscious that I was watching. Once I saw him much further off, on the beach, which is only just visible from my house. He was standing darkly outlined against the water, gazing out to sea; but even at this distance, his head turned in my direction, though I couldn't possibly have been in his range of vision. Sometimes he would suddenly come indoors and silently go all through the house at a quick trot, unexpectedly entering one room after another, before he left again with the same mysterious abruptness. At other times he would lie just inside or outside, with his head resting on the threshold, motionless except for his watchful moving eyes, and the twitching of his sensitive nostrils in response to stimuli which my less acute senses could not perceive.

His movements were always silent, graceful, dignified, sure; and his large, dark eyes never failed to acknowledge me whenever we met in our daily comings and goings.

I was delighted with my visitor, whose silence did not conceal his awareness of me. If I walked through the jungle to visit someone, or to buy food from the neighbouring village, he would appear from nowhere and walk beside me, but always stopped before a house was in sight, never allowing himself to be seen. Every night, of course, he slept on the bed at my side. As the weeks passed he seemed to be spending more time with me during the day, sitting or lying near me while I was working, now and then coming close to gaze attentively at what I was doing.

Then, without warning, he suddenly left me. This was how it happened. The rainy season had come, bringing cooler weather; there was a chill in the early morning air, when he returned to my room as I finished dressing, and leaned against me for a moment. He had hardly ever touched me in daylight, certainly never in that deliberate fashion. I took it to mean that he wished me to do something for him, and asked what it was. Silently he led the way out of the house, pausing to look back every few steps to see whether I was coming, and into the jungle. The stormy sky was heavily clouded, it was almost dark under the trees, from which great drops of last night's rain splashed coldly on my neck and bare arms. As he evidently wanted me to accompany him further, I said I would go back for a coat.

However, he seemed to be too impatient to wait, lunging forward with long, loping strides, his shoulders thrusting like steel pistons under the velvet coat, while I reluctantly followed. Torrential rain began streaming down, in five minutes the ground was a bog, into which my feet sank at each step. By now I was shivering, soaked to the skin, so I stopped and told him I couldn't go on any further. He turned his head and for a long moment his limpid eyes looked at me fixedly, with an expression I could not read. Then the beautiful head turned away, the muscles slid and bunched beneath patterned fur, as he launched himself in a tremendous leap through the shining curtain of raindrops, and was instantly hidden from sight. I walked home as fast as I could, and changed into dry clothes. I did not expect to see him again before evening, but he did not come back at all.

Nothing of any interest took place after the leopard's visit. My life resumed its former routine of work and trivial happenings. The rains came to an end, winter merged imperceptibly into spring. I took pleasure in the sun and the natural world. I felt sure the leopard meant to return, and often looked out for him, but throughout this period he never appeared. When the sky hung pure and cloudless over the jungle, many-coloured orchids began to flower on the trees. I went to see one or two people I knew; a few people visited me in my house. The leopard was never mentioned in our conversations.

The heat increased day by day, each day dawned glassily clear. The atmosphere was pervaded by the aphrodisiac perfume of wild white jasmine, which the girls wove into wreaths for their necks and hair. I painted some large new murals on the walls of my house, and started to make a terrace from a mosaic of coloured shells. For months I'd been expecting to see the leopard, but as time kept passing without a sign of him, I was gradually losing hope.

The season of oppressive heat came round in due course, and the house was left open all night. More than at any other time, it was at night, just before falling asleep, that I thought of the leopard, and, though I no longer believed it would happen, pretended that

I'd wake to find him beside me again. The heat deprived me of energy, the progress of the mosaic was slow. I had never tried my hand at such work before, and being unable to calculate the total quantity of shells that would be required, I constantly ran out of supplies, and had to make tiring trips to the beach for more.

One day while I was on the shore, I saw, out to sea, a young man coming towards the land, standing upright on the crest of a huge breaker, his red cloak blowing out in the wind, and a string of pelicans solemnly flapping in line behind him. It was so odd to see this stranger, with his weird escort, approaching alone from the ocean on which no ships ever sailed, that my thoughts immediately connected him with the leopard: there must be some contact between them; perhaps he was bringing me news. As he got nearer, I shouted to him, called out greetings and questions, to which he replied. But because of the noise of the waves and the distance between us, I could not understand him. Instead of coming on to the beach to speak to me, he suddenly turned and was swept out to sea again, disappearing in clouds of spray. I was puzzled and disappointed. But I took the shells home, went on working as usual, and presently forgot the encounter.

Some time later, coming home at sunset, I was reminded of the young man of the sea by the sight of a pelican perched on the highest point of my roof. Its presence surprised me: pelicans did not leave the shore as a rule, I had never known one come as far inland as this. It suddenly struck me that the bird must be something to do with the leopard, perhaps bringing a message from him. To entice it closer, I found a small fish in the kitchen, which I put on the grass. The pelican swooped down at once, and with remarkable speed and neatness, considering its bulk, skewered the fish on its beak, and flew off with it. I called out, strained my eyes to follow its flight; but only caught a glimpse of the great wings flapping away from me over the jungle trees, before the sudden black curtain of tropical darkness came down with a rush.

Despite this inconclusive end to the episode, it revived my hope of seeing the leopard again. But there were no further developments of any description; nothing else in the least unusual occurred.

It was still the season when the earth sweltered under a simmering sky. In the afternoons the welcome trade wind blew through the rooms and cooled them, but as soon as it died down the house felt hotter than ever. Hitherto I had always derived a nostalgic pleasure from recalling my visitor; but now the memory aroused more sadness than joy, as I had finally lost all hope of his coming back.

At last the mosaic was finished and looked quite impressive, a noble animal with a fine spotted coat and a human head gazing proudly from the centre of the design. I decided it needed to be enclosed in a border of yellow shells, and made another expedition to the beach, where the sun's power was intensified by the glare off the bright green waves, sparkling as if they'd been sprinkled all over with diamonds. A hot wind whistled through my hair, blew the sand about, and lashed the sea into crashing breakers, above which flocks of sea birds flew screaming, in glistening clouds of spray. After searching for shells for a while I straightened up, feeling almost dizzy with the heat and the effort. It was at this moment, when I was dazzled by the violent colours and the terrific glare, that the young man I'd already seen reappeared like a mirage, the red of his flying cloak vibrating against the vivid emerald-green waves. This time, through a haze of shimmering brilliance, I saw that the leopard was with him, majestic and larger than life, moving as gracefully as if the waves were solid glass.

I called to him, and though he couldn't have heard me above the thundering of the surf, he turned his splendid head and gave me a long, strange, portentous look, just as he had that last time in the jungle, sparkling rainbows of spray now taking the place of rain. I hurried towards the edge of the water, then suddenly stopped, intimidated by the colossal size of the giant rollers towering over me. I'm not a strong swimmer, it seemed insane to challenge those enormous on-coming walls of water, which would certainly hurl me back contemptuously on to the shore with all my bones broken. Their exploding roar deafened me, I was half-blinded by the salt spray, the whole beach was a swirling, glittering dazzle, in which I lost sight of the two sea-borne shapes. And when my eyes brought them back into focus, they had changed direction, turned from the land, and were already a long way off, receding fast, diminishing every second, reduced to vanishing point by the hard, blinding brilliance of sun and waves.

Long after they'd disappeared, I stood there, staring out at that turbulent sea, on which I had never once seen any kind of boat, and which now looked emptier, lonelier, and more desolate than ever before. I was paralysed by depression and disappointment, and could hardly force myself to pick up the shells I'd collected and carry them home.

That was the last time I saw the leopard. I've heard nothing of him since that day, or of the young man. For a little while I used to question the villagers who lived by the sea, some of them said they vaguely remembered a man in a red cloak riding the water. But they always ended by becoming evasive, uncertain, and making contradictory statements, so that I knew I was wasting my time.

I've never said a word about the leopard to anyone. It would be difficult to describe him to these simple people, who can never have seen a creature even remotely like him, living here in the wilds as they do, far from zoos, circuses, cinemas and television. No carnivora, no large or ferocious beasts of any sort have ever inhabited this part of the world, which is why we can leave our houses open all night without fear.

The uneventful course of my life continues, nothing happens to break the monotony of the days. Sometime, I suppose, I may forget the leopard's visit. As it is I seldom think of him, except at night when I'm waiting for sleep to come. But, very occasionally he still enters my dreams, which disturbs me and makes me feel restless and sad. Although I never remember the dreams when I wake, for days afterwards they seem to weigh me down with the obscure bitterness of a loss which should have been prevented, and for which I am myself to blame.

OBSESSIONAL

Anna Kavan

Anna Kavan (1901–1968) was a British writer and painter. Having begun her career under her married name, Helen Ferguson, she suffered a nervous breakdown and became Anna Kavan, the protagonist of her 1930 novel *Let Me Alone*. Suffering from long-term drug addiction and bouts of mental illness, Kavan's life featured prominently in her work. She died of heart failure in 1968, soon after the publication of her most celebrated work, the novel *Ice*.

It happened between nine and ten in the evening, his usual time. The inner door of the lobby suddenly opened, just as if he'd let himself in with his key, and she turned her head.

The sheer, mad impossibility of his reappearing, now, all these months afterwards, did not check the instantaneous charge of purest joy that went through her like an electric shock. Many miracles had occurred in connection with him, and this could be one more, since cosmic rays and the mystery of mutation had committed them to each other – might they not come together without the body, and not only in dreams?

Already, before her reasoning brain killed the illusion, the words of welcome took shape, her muscles tensed for the suddenly youthful springing up that would take her to meet him, hands outstretched to bring him quickly into the room. 'Oh, I'm so glad you've come ...' Already, while in the act of turning, she'd seen his face crumpled in the hunted expression which always struck her as unbearably touching, though she could never decide if it was genuine or assumed, as he said with heart-tending humility – real or false, what did it matter? ... 'You must not be angry with me because I did not come to see you these last days. I wanted to come – but it has not been possible ...'

'Of course I'm not angry,' she would answer. 'All that matters that you're here now.' And everything would be perfect and understood, any need for explanation, any hint of criticism or sadness past would fade out with his troubled expression, his mouth widening in the warm, amused smile of his usual greeting, in confident anticipation of happiness.

Only of course he was not there this time. The door had opened, but nobody had come in. She got up to shut it, the flying fantasy leaving a black hiatus; in the midst of which she remembered that for once she was not alone, and, feeling the visitor's eyes following her with a question, turned back to him, her own eyes painful from straining to see what had never been visible.

'The wind must somehow have blown it open. Unless a ghost opened it.' She closed the door firmly, with unnecessary force, and returned to the friend; one of the very few who still – out of pity? Curiosity? Force of habit? – spent an occasional evening with her.

He nodded, smiling, with the amiable easy pretence of the unbeliever, tolerant enough to admit to ghosts of his own, before, rather obviously, changing the subject. Conversation continued, sounding unnaturally loud in her quiet room, which seemed to take on an air of pained surprise at the unaccustomed clatter of voices. But it was an effort for her to go on talking, and she soon fell silent, remaining absent, dispirited, more aware of the apparition that had failed to materialize than she was of the living guest, who left early, discouraged by her lack of interest in him, or in anything he could say, and was forgotten almost before he was out of the room.

It was always the same now, the ghost always coming between her and her life in the world, so much more important, since that lost being was still her only companion, and their now-obsolete relationship the one true human contact she would ever have.

The last time she had seen him in the flesh, all the vital force of his life stripped away, his sharpened face had confronted her with such a fearful fixed finality of sightless indifference that she had been frozen in mortal terror, engulfed by abysmal despair. After all the years of unfailing support, his huge, inhuman, deaf, blind inaccessibility was horrifying. He had not kept his promise. He had abandoned her, left her to suffer alone.

Since he'd gone, the world had become unnervingly strange. There was nothing she could do and nowhere she could go. She felt lost, lonely, dazed, deprived of everything, even of her identity, which was not strong enough to survive without his constant encouragement and reassurance. Isolation clamped down on her. For days she saw no one, spoke to no one. The telephone seldom rang. The strangers in the streets seemed frightening, as if they belonged to a different species, pushing, hard-faced, hurrying past her without a glance. Waiting to cross, standing in the middle of the road, traffic tearing in both directions, she had a sense of utter estrangement from the noisy, inconsequential chaos around her, as if she stood in a no-world, peering doubtfully at shadows, wondering if any of them were real.

Despite the frightful blow he'd inflicted on her by the act of ceasing to be, the man who had formerly filled her life was still her only reality. He had gone from the world. She would never see him again. And yet he was always with her, speaking to her, sharing her perceptions; he occupied her completely, leaving no room for life, excluding her from the world. Incapable of living without him, she had made him her ghostly reality. His ghost was better than nothing; it gave her no sense of the supernatural, in which she'd never believed, but at times seemed almost identical with the real man. Even more than while he had been alive, she was obsessed by him in a way that was not altogether pleasant, although, like an addiction, it was essential to her.

He waylaid her everywhere: in avenues with prancing equestrian statues, in tree-lined squares, tube stations, libraries, shops. She knew he was waiting for her in other countries: beside lakes and mountains, in hotels and clinics, at a certain café where all one evening he'd written verses and made drawings for her, under the doomed goggling eyes of the crowded trout in their tank. He naturally frequented the streets and parks where they'd walked so often. Forgotten conversations sprang up and struck her among the tables of restaurants where they'd been together. In the quiet streets of her own district, any half-glimpsed face of a passer-by was likely to startle her with the possibility of being his. She would wake in the morning with the conviction that he was coming to see her, and sit all day watching the door, afraid of missing him if she moved. Or she would suddenly feel him waiting impatiently for her somewhere, and in nightmare anxiety race from one of their old meeting places to another, hours later finding herself at home, exhausted, desolated, almost in tears, not sure whether she'd really been to all those places or only imagined she had.

A flimsy crumpled advertisement she took from the letterbox would, for a split second, become one of his scribbled notes, with an obscene cat drawn in the corner, the message scrawled in soft purple crayon illegible but for the words, 'The poor M was here …' She would rush to the telephone when it rang, expecting, for the first moment before the voice at the other end spoke in her ear, to hear his distraught voice utter her name. Almost daily, in her comings and goings about the town, a distant figure in a dark blue suit sliced her heart with an imagined resemblance. Hurrying out one day for a loaf of bread, suddenly she had a premonition. And, yes, there he was, walking in the same direction, among the people in front of her, bending forward slightly as if to thrust his way through them, hands and arms held a little away from him – there was no mistaking that characteristic prowling walk. But when she darted forward, eager and smiling, he became an elderly stranger with a heavy, morose face, and the ghostly illusion dissolved in the roar and diesel fumes of a passing bus. She did not wish to escape the consciousness of him, which nevertheless was a burden, like a dead body she carried about everywhere and couldn't bear to relinquish. Going into her workroom, she was half-surprised not to find him scrutinizing her latest paintings with a wry, enigmatic smile. Her disappointment darkened these paintings, already discoloured and splashed by the boredom and futility of her present existence. All her activities had become distasteful, dreary, a weariness to her. Everything she had ever done had been done for him. Why should she try to do anything now?

She wandered out restlessly into the darkening garden, feeling the cool dusk rising round her like water, filling the small space, already full of his inescapable aura. He had been in the habit of dropping in for a few minutes at about this time, roaming round the garden or sitting there till it got dark. Sometimes, if she'd been specially preoccupied with her work, she had wished he would not interrupt her, and this memory caused her a fresh pang. She never did any work these days, so he could come whenever he pleased – why wasn't he here now? As if the thought had invoked it, his hatless, hairless, dignified skull glimmered transparently for a second against the leaves at a spot where in other years he had planted beans. But directly afterwards there was only the deserted garden where nobody came any more, enclosed like a dark pool of twilight by trees and high walls, and containing nothing except her sadness and solitude and the silent watery chill of the rapidly deepening dusk. In the house, certain parts of the rooms, certain objects, always vividly evoked his image, and for these she could be prepared. It was the chance reminders, come upon unawares, that stabbed her most cruelly: a coat left on the settee, simulating his collapsed form sprawled on the green cushions, taking his pulse with two fingers, motionless with the fated calm of a man long familiar with the idea that any moment may be his last.

The haunted vacancy of these darkening ghostly rooms drove her out into the streets to calm herself by the effort of walking. But still the relentless seconds assailed her like arrows one after the other with piercing loneliness, loss. The lights came on, outlining the shapes of strangers, whose faces, limbs, voices, gestures, tormented her with momentary fragments of similarity, which flew away at a second glance. She even caught sight once, in a dark entry, of his spectral monocled countenance smiling inscrutably as it did from so many snapshots, leaving her with a famished longing so acute that it seemed physical, and hardly to be endured. If only, just once more, he would come in the reassuring solidity she had valued so lightly while it was accessible to her. She knew exactly how they would meet, his eyes finding hers with absolute certainty, but at once moving on, while his mouth undermined this pretence by breaking into the glad, intimate smile of greeting that always made her forget the other look of pretended indifference – distance – what? What was that element of elusiveness which had been there from the start, confirming itself in the end by his broken promise, like some ancient curse nobody believed in, which had finally come true after all?

The question remained unanswered. Deciding that she was tired enough to go home, she walked, dragging her feet wearily, through the emptying streets, not noticing anything, until arrested by the strong sense of his proximity, a few yards from the house where he'd lived all the time she had known him. Immediately she recalled the last painful occasion she'd been inside it, when his absence had been like a scream in the little rooms, where it was distressingly evident that no one now ever looked at the pictures, or took the books from the shelves. Certain small objects, special favourites he'd often stroked and held in his hands while he talked – a white jade fish, a painted Bengal tiger with a stiff string tail – had been incarcerated behind the glass doors of a cabinet, and glared out mournfully from their prison. She could not bear to see his beloved possessions uncared for, and, as soon as she was left alone for a minute, went out on to the stairs; where something impelled her to put her head round the door of his room, and she had instantly been struck down by most violent grief, as, in the act of reaching out to draw her towards the bed, his soft, strong hands disintegrated in thin air.

It seemed to her now that the door of the garage – the only place where there was room for his piano – was open and that he was playing inside; an illusion so powerful that she moved involuntarily to join him; then, collecting herself with an effort, walked on in the direction of her own street. Familiar music he'd often played followed her as she went, floating after her in the dark; muted, melancholy, incomplete passages that seemed to come from the middle of some long piece which never ended, the beginning of which she had never heard. The wistful, wandering notes affected her with an intolerable sadness. Nevertheless, at the corner she stopped to listen again; but now the faint sounds had faded out and she was alone in the silent and empty darkness.

Walking on, she wondered if it was safe to go to bed, if she would sleep now. Her legs ached with tiredness as she climbed the stairs and opened her door. The house looked dark and desolate inside. She went into the lobby, putting out one hand to switch off the outside light, and as she turned her head – never sure which switch controlled which bulb – to look down the staircase, a ghostly face glinted into her vision with an expression so heart-breakingly apologetic that she almost said aloud, 'Don't look like that. Nothing matters now that you're here.'

THE FIRST YEAR
OF MY LIFE

Muriel Spark

Muriel Spark (1918–2006) was a Scottish novelist best
known for her novel, *The Prime of Miss Jean Brodie*. In
2008 *The Times* named her in its list of the '50 Greatest
British Writers Since 1945'. Spark was twice shortlisted for
the Man Booker Prize and was awarded the Golden PEN
Award in 1998 by English PEN for her services to literature.
She became Dame Commander of the Order of the British
Empire in 1993.

I was born on the first day of the second month of the last year of
the First World War, a Friday. Testimony abounds that during the
first year of my life I never smiled. I was known as the baby whom
nothing and no one could make smile. Everyone who knew me
then has told me so. They tried very hard, singing and bouncing
me up and down, jumping around, pulling faces. Many times I was
told this later by my family and their friends; but, anyway, I knew
it at the time.

You will shortly be hearing of that new school of psychology,
or maybe you have heard of it already, which after long and far-
adventuring research and experiment has established that all of the
young of the human species are born omniscient. Babies, in their
waking hours, know everything that is going on everywhere in the
world, they can tune in to any conversation they choose, switch on
to any scene. We have all experienced this power. It is only after the
first year that it was brainwashed out of us, for it is demanded of
us by our immediate environment that we grow to be of use to it
in a practical way. Gradually, our know-all brain-cells are blacked
out although traces remain in some individuals in the form of ESP,
and in the adults of some primitive tribes.

It is not a new theory. Poets and philosophers, as usual, have been there first. But scientific proof is now ready and to hand. Perhaps the final touches are being put to the new manifesto in some cell at Harvard University. Any day now it will be given to the world, and the world will be convinced.

Let me therefore get my word in first, because I feel pretty sure, now, about the authenticity of my remembrance of things past. My autobiography, as I very well perceived at the time, started in the very worst year that the world had ever seen so far. Apart from being born bedridden and toothless, unable to raise myself on the pillow or utter anything but farmyard squawks or police-siren wails, my bladder and my bowels totally out of control, I was further depressed by the curious behaviour of the two-legged mammals around me. There were those black-dressed people, females of the species to which I appeared to belong, saying they had lost their sons. I slept a great deal. Let them go and find their sons. It was like the special pin for my nappies which my mother or some other hoverer dedicated to my care was always losing. These careless women in black lost their husbands and their brothers. Then they came to visit my mother and clucked and crowed over my cradle. I was not amused.

'Babies never really smile till they're three months old,' said my mother. 'They're not *supposed* to smile till they're three months old.'

My brother, aged six, marched up and down with a toy rifle over his shoulder.

> The grand old Duke of York
> He had ten thousand men;
> He marched them up to the top of the hill
> And he marched them down again.
>
> And when they were up, they were up
> And when they were down, they were down.
> And when they were neither down nor up
> They were neither up nor down.

'Just listen to him!'
'Look at him with his rifle!'

I was about ten days old when Russia stopped fighting. I tuned in to the Czar, a prisoner, with the rest of his family, since evidently the country had put him off his throne and there had been a revolution not long before I was born. Everyone was talking about it. I tuned in to the Czar. 'Nothing would ever induce me to sign the treaty of Brest-Litovsk,' he said to his wife. Anyway, nobody had asked him to.

At this point I was sleeping twenty hours a day to get my strength up. And from what I discerned in the other four hours of the day I knew I was going to need it. The Western Front on my frequency was sheer blood, mud, dismembered bodies, blistered crashes, hectic flashes of light in the night skies, explosions, total terror. Since it was plain I had been born into a bad moment in the history of the world, the future bothered me, unable as I was to raise my head from the pillow and as yet only twenty inches long. 'I truly wish I were a fox or a bird,' D. H. Lawrence was writing to somebody. Dreary old creeping Jesus. I fell asleep.

Red sheets of flame shot across the sky. It was 21st March, the fiftieth day of my life, and the German Spring Offensive had started before my morning feed. Infinite slaughter. I scowled at the scene, and made an effort to kick out. But the attempt was feeble. Furious and impatient for some strength, I wailed for my feed. After which I stopped wailing but continued to scowl.

> The grand old Duke of York
> He had ten thousand men ...

They rocked the cradle. I never heard a sillier song. Over in Berlin and Vienna the people were starving, freezing, striking, rioting and yelling in the streets. In London everyone was bustling to work and muttering that it was time the whole damn business was over.

The big people around me bared their teeth; that meant a smile, it meant they were pleased or amused. They spoke of ration cards for meat and sugar and butter.

Where will it all end?

I went to sleep. I woke and tuned in to Bernard Shaw who was telling someone to shut up. I switched over to Joseph Conrad who strangely enough, was saying precisely the same thing. I still didn't think it worth a smile, although it was expected of me any day now. I got on to Turkey. Women draped in black huddled and chattered in their harems; yak-yak-yak. This was boring, so I came back to home base.

In and out came and went the women in British black. My mother's brother, dressed in his uniform, came coughing. He had been poison-gassed in the trenches. *'Tout le monde à la bataille!'* declaimed Marshal Foch the old swine. He was now Commander-in-Chief of the Allied Forces. My uncle coughed from deep within his lungs, never to recover but destined to return to the Front. His brass buttons gleamed in the firelight. I weighed twelve pounds by now, I stretched and kicked for exercise seeing that I had a lifetime before me, coping with this crowd. I took six feeds a day and kept most of them down by the time the *Vindictive* was sunk in Ostend harbour, on which day I kicked with special vigour in my bath.

In France the conscripted soldiers leapfrogged over the dead on the advance and littered the fields with limbs and hands, or drowned in the mud. The strongest men on all fronts were dead before I was born. Now the sentries used bodies for barricades and the fighting men were unhealthy from the start. I checked my toes and fingers, knowing I was going to need them. *The Playboy of the Western World* was playing at the Court Theatre in London, but occasionally I beamed over to the House of Commons which made me drop off gently to sleep. Generally, I preferred the Western Front where one got the true state of affairs. It was essential to know the worst, blood and explosions and all, for one had to be prepared, as the boy scouts said. Virginia Woolf yawned and reached for her diary. Really, I preferred the Western Front.

In the fifth month of my life I could raise my head from my pillow and hold it up. I could grasp the objects that were held out to me. Some of these things rattled and squawked. I gnawed on them to get my teeth started. 'She hasn't smiled yet?' said the dreary old aunties. My mother, on the defensive, said I was probably one of those late smilers. On my wavelength Pablo Picasso was getting married and early in that month of July the Silver Wedding of King George V and Queen Mary was celebrated in joyous pomp at St Paul's Cathedral. They drove through the streets of London with their children. Twenty-five years of domestic happiness. A lot of fuss and ceremonial handing over of swords went on at the Guildhall where the King and Queen received a cheque for £53,000 to dispose of for charity as they thought fit. *Tout le monde à la bataille!* Income tax in England had reached six shillings in the pound. Everyone was talking about the Silver Wedding yak-yak-yak, and ten days later the Czar and his family, now in Siberia, were invited to descend to a little room in the basement. Crack, crack, went the guns; screams and blood all over the place, and that was the end of the Romanoffs. I flexed my muscles, 'A fine healthy baby,' said the doctor; which gave me much satisfaction.

Tout le monde à la bataille! That included my gassed uncle. My health had improved to the point where I was able to crawl in my playpen. Bertrand Russell was still cheerily in prison for writing something seditious about pacifism. Tuning in as usual to the Front Lines it looked as if the Germans were winning all the battles yet losing the war. And so it was. The upper-income people were upset about the income tax at six shillings to the pound. But all women over thirty got the vote. 'It seems a long time to wait,' said one of my drab old aunts, aged twenty-two. The speeches in the House of Commons always sent me to sleep which was why I missed, at the actual time, a certain oration by Mr Asquith following the armistice on 11th November. Mr Asquith was a greatly esteemed former prime minister later to be an Earl, and had been ousted by Mr Lloyd George. I clearly heard Asquith, in private, refer to Lloyd George as 'that damned Welsh goat'.

The armistice was signed and I was awake for that. I pulled myself on to my feet with the aid of the bars of my cot. My teeth were coming through very nicely in my opinion, and well worth all the trouble I was put to in bringing them forth. I weighed twenty pounds. On all the world's fighting fronts the men killed in action or dead of wounds numbered 8,538,315 and the warriors wounded and maimed were 21,219,452. With these figures in mind I sat up in my high chair and banged my spoon on the table. One of my mother's black-draped friends recited:

> I have a rendezvous with Death
> At some disputed barricade,

> When spring comes back with rustling shade
> And apple blossoms fill the air –
> I have a rendezvous with Death.

Most of the poets, they said, had been killed. The poetry made them dab their eyes with clean white handkerchiefs.

Next February on my first birthday, there was a birthday cake with one candle. Lots of children and their elders. The war had been over two months and twenty-one days. 'Why doesn't she smile?' My brother was to blow out the candle. The elders were talking about the war and the political situation. Lloyd George and Asquith, Asquith and Lloyd George. I remembered recently having switched on to Mr Asquith at a private party where he had been drinking a lot. He was playing cards and when he came to cut the cards he tried to cut a large box of matches by mistake. On another occasion I had seen him putting his arm around a lady's shoulder in a Daimler motor car, and generally behaving towards her in a very friendly fashion. Strangely enough she said, 'If you don't stop this nonsense immediately I'll order the chauffeur to stop and I'll get out.' Mr Asquith replied, 'And pray, what reason will you give?' Well anyway it was my feeding time.

The guests arrived for my birthday. It was so sad, said one of the black widows, so sad about Wilfred Owen who was killed so late in the war, and she quoted from a poem of his:

> What passing-bells for these who die as cattle?
> Only the monstrous anger of the guns.

The children were squealing and toddling around. One was sick and another wet the floor and stood with his legs apart gaping at the puddle. All was mopped up. I banged my spoon on the table of my high chair.

> But I've a rendezvous with Death
> At midnight in some flaming town;
> When spring trips north again this year,
> And I to my pledged word am true,
> I shall not fell that rendezvous.

More parents and children arrived. One stout man who was warming his behind at the fire, said, 'I always think those words of Asquith's after the armistice were so apt ... '

They brought the cake close to my high chair for me to see, with the candle shining and flickering above the pink icing. 'A pity she never smiles.'

'She'll smile in time,' my mother said, obviously upset.

'What Asquith told the House of Commons just after the war,' said that stout gentleman with his backside to the fire, '– so apt, what Asquith said. He said that the war has cleansed and purged the world, by God! recall his actual words: "All things have become new. In this great cleansing and purging it has been the privilege of our country to play her part ... "'

That did it, I broke into a decided smile and everyone noticed it, convinced that it was provoked by the fact that my brother had blown out the candle on the cake. 'She smiled!' my mother exclaimed. And everyone was clucking away about how I was smiling. For good measure I crowed like a demented raven. 'My baby's smiling!' said my mother.

'It was the candle on her cake,' they said.

The cake be damned. Since that time I have grown to smile quite naturally, like any other healthy and housetrained person, but when I really mean a smile, deeply felt from the core, then to all intents and purposes it comes in response to the words uttered in the House of Commons after the First World War by the distinguished, the immaculately dressed and the late Mr Asquith.

INDIGNITIES

Ellen Gilchrist

> Ellen Gilchrist (b. 1935) is an American author and poet who studied creative writing under Eudora Welty. Her 1981 collection of stories, *In the Land of Dreamy Dreams*, received immense critical acclaim and, in 1984, she won the National Book Award for her collection of stories, *Victory Over Japan*.

Last night my mother took off her clothes in front of twenty-six invited guests in the King's Room at Antoine's. She took off her Calvin Klein evening jacket and her beige silk wrap-around blouse and her custom-made brassiere and walked around the table letting everyone look at the place where her breasts used to be.

She had had them removed without saying a word to anyone. I'm surprised she told my father. I'm surprised she invited him to the party. He never would have noticed. He hasn't touched her in years except to hand her a check or a paper to sign.

After mother took off her blouse the party really warmed up. Everyone stayed until the restaurant closed. Teddy Lanier put the make on a waiter. Alice Lemle sang "A Foggy Day in London Town." A poet called Cherokee stood up on an antique chair, tore open her dress, and drew the sign for infinity on her chest with a borrowed Flair pen. Amalie DuBois sat down by the baked Alaska and began eating the meringue with her fingers.

Everyone followed us home. Someone opened the bar and Clarence Josephy sat down at the baby grand and began improvising. He always makes himself at home. There was a terrible period in my childhood when I thought he was going to be my father. I started going to mass with a little girl from Sacred Heart to pray he wouldn't move in and have breakfast with us every day. I even bought a crucifix. I had worked up to forty-six Hail Marys a day by the time my father came home from Australia and the crisis passed.

As soon as everyone was settled with a drink Mother went upstairs to change and I followed her. "Well, Mother," I said, "this takes the cake. You could have given me some warning. I thought I was coming home for a birthday party."

"I'm leaving it all to you, Melissa," she said. "Take my advice. Sell everything and fly to Paris."

I threw myself down on the bed with my hands over my ears, but she went tirelessly and relentlessly on. "This is your chance to rise above the categories," she said. "God knows I've done my best to teach you the relativity of it all." She sighed and shook her head, stepping into a long white dressing gown. I had always been a disappointment to her, that's for certain. No illicit drugs, no unwanted pregnancies, no lesbian affairs, no irate phone calls from teachers, never a moment's doubt that 1 was living up to my potential.

Melissa was born old, my mother always tells everyone, born with her fingers crossed.

"Why do you think you're dying, Mother?" I said. "Just tell me that, will you? Lots of women get breast cancer. It doesn't mean you're going to die."

"It means I'm going to die," she said. "And I'll tell you one thing. I am never setting foot inside that hospital again. I've never run across such a humorless unimaginative group in my life. And the food! Really, it's unforgivable."

"Mother," I said, trying to put my arms around her.

"Now, Melissa," she said, "let's save the melodrama for the bourgeoisie. I have a book for you to read." She always has a book for me to read. She has a book about everything. She reads the first chapter and the table of contents and the last three paragraphs and if she likes the theory she says APPROVED and goes on to the next book.

If she really likes the theory she writes the author and the publisher and buys twenty copies and gives them away to friends. She has ruined a lot of books for me that way. What real book could live up to one of mother's glowing and inaccurate descriptions?

It must be interesting to be her daughter, people say to me.

I don't know, I tell them. I've never tried it. I use her for a librarian.

The book she pressed upon me now was *Life after Life* by Raymond A. Moody, Jr., M.D. It was full of first-person accounts by men and women who were snatched from the jaws of death and came back to tell of their ecstatic experiences on the brink of nonbeing. The stories are remarkably similar. It seems the soul lifts off from the body like a sort of transparent angel and floats around the corpse. Then the person sees someone he is dying to talk to standing at the end of a tunnel swinging a lantern and waiting for him.

"But who are you in such a hurry to see, Mother," I said, "all of your friends are downstairs and you never liked your own parents."

"Perhaps Leonardo will be there. Perhaps Blake is waiting for me. Or Margaret Mead or Virginia Woolf."

"How old will you be in heaven, Mother?" I ask, being drawn into the fantasy.

"Oh, thirty-four I think. Attractive, yet intelligent enough to be interesting. What color was my hair at that age? The only thing I regret about all this is that I never had time to grow out my gray hair. I kept putting it off. Vanity, vanity."

"Mother, let's stop this."

"Right. Not another word." She sprayed herself with Shalimar and giving me a pat on the cheek went downstairs to her guests, leaving me alone in her room.

Her room is half of the second floor of a Queen Anne house designed by Thomas Sully in 1890.

There is a round bed on a dais with dozens of small soft pillows piled against a marble headboard. There is a quilt made by her great-grandmother's slaves and linen sheets the colors of the sky at evening.

Everything else in the room is white, white velvet, white satin, white silk, white marble, white painted wood.

There is a dressing table six feet long covered with every product ever manufactured by Charles of the Ritz.

There is a huge desk littered with papers and books, her unpublished poems, her short stories, her journals, her unfinished novels.

"Mother," I called, following her into the hall, "what about the novels. Who will finish the novels?"

"We'll give them to somebody who needs them," she called back. "Some poor person who doesn't have any."

I went downstairs to find her reclining on a love seat with her admirers sitting at her feet drinking brandy and helping plan the funeral.

I was surprised at how traditional her plans have become. Gone was the flag-shaped tombstone saying IT SEEMED LIKE A GOOD IDEA AT THE TIME. Gone the videotape machine in the mausoleum.

"Some readings from García Márquez," she was saying. "Lionel can do them in Spanish. Spanish always sounds so *religious*, don't you agree?"

"How long do you think it will be," Bartlett said.

"Not more than six months surely," Mother said. "February."

"I like a winter funeral myself," Eric said. "Especially in this climate."

The weather was perfect for the funeral. "Don't you know she *arranged* this," everyone kept saying. As we were entering the chapel a storm blew up quite suddenly. Rain beat on the walls and lightning flashed through the stained-glass windows.

Then, just as we were carrying the coffin outside, the sun broke from the clouds. "That was going too far," everyone agreed.

Later, a wind blew up from the east and continued to blow while we shoveled dirt on the coffin. "Really!" everyone muttered.

"Melissa," she had said to me, "swear you will never let strangers lower my box." So, while the gravediggers sat politely nearby wondering if we belonged to some new kind of cult, we cranked the coffin down and picked up the shovels.

Clarence turned on the tape player and we shoveled to Mahler for a while, then to Clementi, then Bach.

"I remember the night she chartered a plane and flew to California for the earthquake," Lionel said, pulling a feather out of his hat and dropping it in the hole. He was wearing a velvet suit and an enormous green hat with feathers. He looked like a prehistoric bird.

"Remember the year she learned to scuba dive," Selma said,

weeping all over her white tuxedo and dropping an onyx ring on top of the feather. "She didn't even know how to *swim*."

"I remember the week she played with me," I said. "I was four years old. She called and had a piano crate delivered and we turned it into a house and painted murals all over the walls. The title of our mural was Welsh Fertility Rites with Sheepdogs Rampant."

The wind kept on blowing and I kept on shoveling, staring down at all that was left of my childhood, now busily growing out yards and yards of two-toned hair.

THE PILL-BOX

Penelope Lively

Penelope Lively (b. 1933) is a critically acclaimed British author of fiction for both children and adults. She won the Carnegie Medal for children's fiction in 1973, for *The Ghost of Thomas Kempe*, and also the Man Booker Prize for her 1987 novel, *Moon Tiger*. Lively was made Dame Commander of the Order of the British Empire in the 2012 New Year Honours list.

The writer of a story has an infinity of choices. An infinity of narratives; an infinity of endings. The process of choosing, of picking this set of events rather than that, of ending up here rather than there – well, call it what you like: craft, art, accident, intuition.

Call it what you like, it's a curious process.

I teach Eng. Lit. Consequently I try to point this sort of thing out to the young. Life and literature – all that. Parallels; illuminations. I'm no mystic, but there's one thing that never ceases to astonish me: the fixity of things. That we live with it, accept it as we do. That we do not question that the course of events is thus, and never could be other. When you think of how nearly, at every moment, it is not.

Think of it. Stare it in the face and think of it.

I come out of my front gate, I bump into old Sanders next door, we have a chat ... Shift the point at which I emerge by ever so little, and I do not meet Sanders, we do not have a word about the cricket club dinner, he does not offer to drop over later with his Black & Decker and fix that shelf for me.

I cross the street, looking first to right and left, a lorry passes, I alight upon the pavement opposite.

I cross the street, not looking, first to right and left; the lorry driver's concentration lapses for a second, I am so much meat under his wheels.

Some bloke is gunned down in Sarajevo. In another country, evil is bred. And then and then and then ... A tired voice comes from a crackling wireless: there is war. "May God bless you all," he says.

A trigger jams. Elsewhere, a mad house-painter dies young of polio. And then, and then, and then ... 3rd September 1939 is a fine day, sunshine with a hint of showers.

Oh well *of course* you say, any fool can play those games. Intriguing but unproductive. We inhabit, after all, a definite world; facts are facts. The sequence of my life, of your life, of the public life.

Listen, then. I went up to the pill-box this evening – the wartime pill-box on the top.

The pill-box is on the brow of the hill and faces square down the lane. I take my time getting up there; it's a steep pull up and the outlook's half the point of the walk. I have a rest at the first gate, and then at the end by the oak, and again at the gate to Clapper's field. You get the view from there: the village down below you and the fields reaching away to the coast and the sea hanging at the edge of the green, a long grey smear with maybe a ship or two and on clear days the white glimmer of the steelworks over on the Welsh coast.

It was sited to cover anything coming up and heading on over the hill. Heading for the main road – that would have been the idea, I suppose. It would have had the village covered, too, and a good part of the valley. Very small it looks now, stuck there at the edge of the field: barely room for a couple of blokes inside. I never know why it's not been taken away – much longer and it'll be a historical monument I daresay and they'll slap a protection order on it. The field is rough grazing and always has been so I suppose no one's felt any great call to get rid of it. Dalton's field, it is; from time to time you find he's stashed some cattle feed away in the pill-box, or a few bags of lime. It comes in handy for the village lads, too, always has done: get your girl up there, nice bit of shelter ... I've made use of it that way myself in my time. Back in – oh, forty-seven or thereabouts. Yes, forty-seven, that spring it rained cats and dogs and there was flooding right left and centre. Rosie Parks, black curly hair and an answer to everything. Lying in there with the rain coming down in spears outside; "You lay off, Keith Harrison, I'm telling you ...", "Ah, come on, Rosie ..." Giggle giggle.

The rain started this evening when I was at the oak, just a sprinkle, and by the time I got to the top it was coming down hard and looked set in for a while so I ducked down into the pill-box to sit it out.

I was thinking about the past, in a vague kind of way – the war, being young. Looking out from inside the pill-box you see the countryside as a bright green rectangle, very clear, lots of detail, like a photo. And I've got good eyesight anyway, even at fifty-seven, just about a hundred per cent vision. I could see the new houses they've put up on the edge of the village and I was thinking that the place has changed a lot since I was a boy, and yet in other ways it hasn't. The new estate, the shop, cars at every door, telly aerials, main drainage; but the same names, by and large, same families, same taste to the beer, same stink from Clapper's silage in hot weather.

I can see the house where I was born, from the pill-box. And the one I live in now. The churchyard, where my parents are, God bless 'em. The recreation ground beside the church hall where we used to drill in 1941; those of us left behind, too old like Jim Blockley at sixty-odd, too young like me at seventeen-and-a-half, too wonky like the postmaster with his bronchitis, too valuable like the farmers and the doctor.

I can see the road, too – the road that takes me daily to work. Ten miles to Scarhead to try to drum a bit of sense and a bit of knowledge into forty fifteen-year-old heads. Full cycle. Back then, mine was the empty head, the bloke at the blackboard was ... was old Jenkins, Jenks. It's not been a mistake, coming back. I'd always thought I'd like to. The day I saw the advert, in the *Times Ed. Supp.*, I knew at once I'd apply. Yes, I thought, that's it, that's for me, end up back at home, why not? I've always thought of it as home, down here, wherever I've been – Nottingham, up in the north-east, London. Not that it's local boy made good, exactly. Teaching's a tidy enough occupation, they reckon down here, but not high-flying. Farmers do a sight better. I don't drive a Jag, like Tim Matlock who was in my class at the grammar and farms up on the county border now. Not that I care tuppence.

I lit a pipe to keep the midges off; the rain was coming down harder than ever. It looked as though I might have to pack in the rest of my walk. I opened the newspaper: usual stuff, miners reject pay offer, Middle East talks, rail fares up.

When I heard the first voice I thought there was someone outside in the field – some trick of the acoustics, making it sound as though it were in the pill-box.

"They're bloody coming!" he said.

And then another bloke, a young one, a boy, gave a sort of grunt. You knew, somehow, he was on edge. His voice had that crack to it, that pitch of someone who's keyed up, holding himself in. Shit-scared.

"Can I have a look, Mr Barnes? Oh God – I see them. Heading straight up."

How can I put it? Describe how it was. The words that come to mind are banal, clichés: eery, unearthly, uncanny.

They were there, but they were not. They were in the head, but yet were outside it. There were two men, an old and a younger, who spoke from some other dimension; who were there with me in the pill-box and yet also were not, could not be, had never been.

Listen again.

"Give me them field-glasses ... They've set Clapper's barn on fire. There's more tanks on the Scarhead road – six, seven ... They'll be at the corner in a few minutes now, son."

And the young chap speaks again. "O.K.," he says. "O.K., I'm ready."

The voices, you understand, are overlaid by other noises, ordinary noises: the rain on the roof of the pill-box, sheep, a tractor in the lane. The tractor goes past but the voices don't take a blind bit of notice. The old bloke tells the other one to pass him another clip of ammo. "You all right, son?" he says, the boy answers that he is all right. There is that high sharp note in his voice, in both their voices.

There is a silence.

And then they come back.

"I can see him now. Armoured car. Two."

"O.K. Yes. I've got them."

"Hold it. Hold it, son ..."

"Yes. Right ..."

"Hold it. Steady. When they get to the oak."

"O.K., Mr Barnes."

And everything is quiet again. A quiet you could cut with a knife. The inside of the pill-box is tight-strung, waiting; it is both a moment in time and a time that is going on for ever, will go on for ever. I drop my tobacco tin and it clatters on the concrete floor but the sound does not break that other quiet, which, I now realise, is somewhere else, is something else.

The old bloke says, "Fire!"

And then they are both talking together. There is no other sound, nothing, just their voices. And the rain.

The boy says, "I got him, my God. I got him!" and the other one says, "Steady. Re-load now. Steady. Wait till the second one's moving again. Right. Fire!"

"We hit him!"

"He's coming on ..."

"Christ there's another behind!"

"Bastards! Jerry bastards!"

And the boy cries, "That's for my dad! And that's for my mum! Come on then, bloody come on then ..."

"Steady, son. Hold it a minute, there's a ..."

"What's he doing, Christ he's ..."

"He's got a grenade. Keep on firing, for God's sake. Keep him covered."

And suddenly they go quiet. Quite quiet. Except that just once the old bloke says something. He says, "Don't move, Keith, keep still, I'm coming over, I ..."

He says, "Keith?"

And there is nothing more.

I went on sitting there. The quietness left the inside of the pill-box, that other quietness. The tractor came back down the lane again. The rain stopped. A blackbird started up on the roof of the pill-box. Down in the valley there was a patch of sunlight slap on the village; the church very bright, a car windscreen flashing, pale green of the chestnuts in the pub car park.

I knew, now, that from the first moment there'd been something about that young chap's voice. The boy.

Mr Barnes. Joe Barnes worked the manor farm in the war. He

left here some time ago, retired to Ilfracombe; he died a year or two back.

I was in his platoon, in 1941. I've not thought of him in years. Couldn't put a face to him, now. He died of cancer in a nursing-home in Ilfracombe. Didn't he?

Or.

Or he died in a pill-box up on the hill above the village, long ago. Him and a boy called Keith. In which case the pill-box is no longer there nor I take it the village nor the whole bloody place at least not in any way you or I could know it.

No young fellow called Keith ever put his hand up the skirt of Rosie Parks in that pill-box, nor did another bloke, a fifty-seven year old teacher of English, walk up that way of an evening for a smoke and a look at the view.

I came out, filled my pipe, looked down at the village. All right, yes, I thought to myself – interesting, the imaginative process. The mind churning away, putting pictures to a line of thought. I dozed off in there.

Later I knew I did not imagine it. I heard it. Heard them. So what do you make of that? Eh? What can anyone make of it? How, having glimpsed the possibility of the impossible, can the world remain as steady as you had supposed?

Suppose that the writer of a story were haunted, in the mind, for ever, by all those discarded alternatives, by the voices of all those assorted characters. Forced to preserve them always as the price of creative choice.

Then suppose, by the same token, that just once in a while it is given to any one of us to experience the inconceivable. To push through the barrier of what we know into the heady breathtaking unbearable ozone of what we cannot contemplate. Did that happen to me? In the pill-box on the hill on a summer Monday evening, with the world steady under my feet and the newspaper in my hand, telling me what's what, how the world is, where we are?

MILES CITY, MONTANA

Alice Munro

Alice Munro (b. 1931) is a Canadian short story writer and winner of the 2009 Man Booker International Prize, which honours her complete body of work. She has been awarded Canada's Governor General's Award for Fiction three times, the Giller Prize twice and is a perennial contender for the Nobel Prize for Fiction. She was awarded the National Book Critics Circle Award in 1998 for her collection *The Love of a Good Woman*.

My father came across the field carrying the body of the boy who had been drowned. There were several men together, returning from the search, but he was the one carrying the body. The men were muddy and exhausted, and walked with their heads down, as if they were ashamed. Even the dogs were dispirited, dripping from the cold river. When they all set out, hours before, the dogs were nervy and yelping, the men tense and determined, and there was a constrained, unspeakable excitement about the whole scene. It was understood that they might find something horrible.

The boy's name was Steve Gauley. He was eight years old. His hair and clothes were mud-colored now and carried some bits of dead leaves, twigs, and grass. He was like a heap of refuse that had been left out all winter. His face was turned in to my father's chest, but I could see a nostril, an ear, plugged up with greenish mud.

I don't think so. I don't think I really saw all this. Perhaps I saw my father carrying him, and the other men following along, and the dogs, but I would not have been allowed to get close enough to see something like mud in his nostril. I must have heard someone talking about that and imagined that I saw it. I see his face unaltered except for the mud – Steve Gauley's familiar, sharp-honed, sneaky-looking face – and it wouldn't have been like that; it would have been bloated and changed and perhaps muddied all over after so many hours in the water.

To have to bring back such news, such evidence, to a waiting family, particularly a mother, would have made searchers move heavily, but what was happening here was worse. It seemed a worse shame (to hear people talk) that there was no mother, no woman at all – no grandmother or aunt, or even a sister – to receive Steve Gauley and give him his due of grief. His father was a hired man, a drinker but not a drunk, an erratic man without being entertaining, not friendly but not exactly a troublemaker. His fatherhood seemed accidental, and the fact that the child had been left with him when the mother went away, and that they continued living together, seemed accidental. They lived in a steep-roofed, gray-shingled hillbilly sort of house that was just a bit better than a shack – the father fixed the roof and put supports under the porch, just enough and just in time – and their life was held together in a similar manner; that is, just well enough to keep the Children's Aid at bay. They didn't eat meals together or cook for each other, but there was food. Sometimes the father would give Steve money to buy food at the store, and Steve was seen to buy quite sensible things, such as pancake mix and macaroni dinner.

I had known Steve Gauley fairly well. I had not liked him more often than I had liked him. He was two years older than I was. He would hang around our place on Saturdays, scornful of whatever I was doing but unable to leave me alone. I couldn't be on the swing without him wanting to try it, and if I wouldn't give it up he came and pushed me so that I went crooked. He teased the dog. He got me into trouble – deliberately and maliciously, it seemed to me afterward – by daring me to do things I wouldn't have thought of on my own: digging up the potatoes to see how big they were when they were still only the size of marbles, and pushing over the stacked firewood to make a pile we could jump off. At school, we never spoke to each other. He was solitary, though not tormented. But on Saturday mornings, when I saw his thin, self-possessed figure sliding through the cedar hedge, I knew I was in for something and he would decide what. Sometimes it was all right. We pretended we were cowboys who had to tame wild horses. We played in the pasture by the river, not far from the place where Steve drowned. We were horses and riders both, screaming and neighing and bucking and waving whips of tree branches beside a little nameless river that flows into the Saugeen in southern Ontario.

The funeral was held in our house. There was not enough room at Steve's father's place for the large crowd that was expected because of the circumstances. I have a memory of the crowded room but no picture of Steve in his coffin, or of the minister, or of wreaths of flowers. I remember that I was holding one flower, a white narcissus, which must have come from a pot somebody forced indoors, because it was too early for even the forsythia bush or the trilliums and marsh marigolds in the woods. I stood in a row of children, each of us holding a narcissus. We sang a children's hymn, which somebody played on our piano: "When He Cometh, When He Cometh, to Make Up His Jewels." I was wearing white ribbed stockings, which were disgustingly itchy, and wrinkled at the knees and ankles. The feeling of these stockings on my legs is mixed up with another feeling in my memory. It is hard to describe. It had to do with my parents. Adults in general but my parents in particular. My father, who had carried Steve's body from the river, and my mother, who must have done most of the arranging of this funeral. My father in his dark-blue suit and my mother in her brown velvet dress with the creamy satin collar. They stood side by side opening and closing their mouths for the hymn, and I stood removed from them, in the row of children, watching. I felt a furious and sickening disgust. Children sometimes have an access of disgust concerning adults. The size, the lumpy shapes, the bloated power. The breath, the coarseness, the hairiness, the horrid secretions. But this was more. And the accompanying anger had nothing sharp and self-respecting about it. There was no release, as when I would finally bend and pick up a stone and throw it at Steve Gauley. It could not be understood or expressed, though it died down after a while into a heaviness, then just a taste, an occasional taste – a thin, familiar misgiving.

Twenty years or so later, in 1961, my husband, Andrew, and I got a brand-new car, our first – that is, our first brand-new. It was a Morris Oxford, oyster-colored (the dealer had some fancier name for the color) – a big small car, with plenty of room for us and our two children. Cynthia was six and Meg three and a half.

Andrew took a picture of me standing beside the car. I was wearing white pants, a black turtleneck, and sunglasses. I lounged against the car door, canting my hips to make myself look slim.

"Wonderful," Andrew said. "Great. You look like Jackie Kennedy." All over this continent probably, dark-haired, reasonably slender young women were told, when they were stylishly dressed or getting their pictures taken, that they looked like Jackie Kennedy.

Andrew took a lot of pictures of me, and of the children, our house, our garden, our excursions and possessions. He got copies made, labelled them carefully, and sent them back to his mother and his aunt and uncle in Ontario. He got copies for me to send to my father, who also lived in Ontario, and I did so, but less regularly than he sent his. When he saw pictures he thought I had already sent lying around the house, Andrew was perplexed and annoyed. He liked to have this record go forth.

That summer, we were presenting ourselves, not pictures. We were driving back from Vancouver, where we lived, to Ontario, which we still called "home," in our new car. Five days to get there, ten days there, five days back. For the first time, Andrew had three weeks' holiday. He worked in the legal department at B. C. Hydro.

On a Saturday morning, we loaded suitcases, two thermos bottles – one filled with coffee and one with lemonade – some fruit and sandwiches, picture books and coloring books, crayons, drawing pads, insect repellent, sweaters (in case it got cold in the mountains), and our two children into the car. Andrew locked the house, and Cynthia said ceremoniously, "Goodbye, house."

Meg said, "Goodbye, house." Then she said, "Where will we live now?"

"It's not goodbye forever," said Cynthia. "We're coming back. Mother! Meg thought we weren't ever coming back!"

"I did not," said Meg, kicking the back of my seat.

Andrew and I put on our sunglasses, and we drove away, over the Lions Gate Bridge and through the main part of Vancouver. We shed our house, the neighborhod, the city, and – at the crossing point between Washington and British Columbia – our country. We were driving east across the United States, taking the most northerly route, and would cross into Canada again at Sarnia, Ontario. I don't know if we chose this route because the

Trans-Canada Highway was not completely finished at the time or if we just wanted the feeling of driving through a foreign, a very slightly foreign, country – that extra bit of interest and adventure.

We were both in high spirits. Andrew congratulated the car several times. He said he felt so much better driving it than our old car, a 1951 Austin that slowed down dismally on the hills and had a fussy-old-lady image. So Andrew said now.

"What kind of image does this one have?" said Cynthia. She listened to us carefully and liked to try out new words such as "image." Usually she got them right.

"Lively," I said. "Slightly sporty. It's not show-off."

"It's sensible, but it has class," Andrew said. "Like my image."

Cynthia thought that over and said with a cautious pride, "That means like you think you want to be, Daddy?"

As for me, I was happy because of the shedding. I loved taking off. In my own house, I seemed to be often looking for a place to hide – sometimes from the children but more often from the jobs to be done and the phone ringing and the sociability of the neighborhood. I wanted to hide so that I could get busy at my real work, which was a sort of wooing of distant parts of myself. I lived in a state of siege, always losing just what I wanted to hold on to. But on trips there was no difficulty. I could be talking to Andrew, talking to the children and looking at whatever they wanted me to look at – a pig on a sign, a pony in a field, a Volkswagen on a revolving stand – and pouring lemonade into plastic cups, and all the time those bits and pieces would be flying together inside me. The essential composition would be achieved. This made me hopeful and lighthearted. It was being a watcher that did it. A watcher, not a keeper.

We turned east at Everett and climbed into the Cascades. I showed Cynthia our route on the map. First I showed her the map of the whole United States, which showed also the bottom part of Canada. Then I turned to the separate maps of each of the states we were going to pass through. Washington, Idaho, Montana, North Dakota, Minnesota, Wisconsin. I showed her the dotted line across Lake Michigan, which was the route of the ferry we would take. Then we would drive across Michigan to the bridge that linked the United States and Canada at Sarnia, Ontario. Home.

Meg wanted to see, too.

"You won't understand," said Cynthia. But she took the road atlas into the back seat.

"Sit back," she said to Meg. "Sit still. I'll show you."

I could hear her tracing the route for Meg, very accurately, just as I had done it for her. She looked up all the states' maps, knowing how to find them in alphabetical order.

"You know what that line is?" she said. "It's the road. That line is the road we're driving on. We're going right along this line."

Meg did not say anything.

"Mother, show me where we are right this minute," said Cynthia.

I took the atlas and pointed out the road through the mountains, and she took it back and showed it to Meg. "See where the road is all wiggly?" she said. "It's wiggly because there are so many turns in it. The wiggles are the turns." She flipped some pages and waited a moment. "Now," she said, "show me where we are." Then she called to me, "Mother, she understands! She pointed to it! Meg understands maps!"

It seems to me now that we invented characters for our children. We had them firmly set to play their parts. Cynthia was bright and diligent, sensitive, courteous, watchful. Sometimes we teased her for being too conscientious, too eager to be what we in fact depended on her to be. Any reproach or failure, any rebuff, went terribly deep with her. She was fair-haired, fair-skinned, easily showing the effects of the sun, raw winds, pride, or humiliation. Meg was more solidly built, more reticent – not rebellious but stubborn sometimes, mysterious. Her silences seemed to us to show her strength of character, and her negatives were taken as signs of an imperturbable independence. Her hair was brown, and we cut it in straight bangs. Her eyes were a light hazel, clear and dazzling.

We were entirely pleased with these characters, enjoying the contradictions as well as the confirmations of them. We disliked the heavy, the uninventive, approach to being parents. I had a dread of turning into a certain kind of mother – the kind whose body sagged, who moved in a woolly-smelling, milky-smelling fog, solemn with trivial burdens. I believed that all the attention these mothers paid, their need to be burdened, was the cause of colic, bed-wetting, asthma. I favored another approach – the mock desperation, the inflated irony of the professional mothers who wrote for magazines. In those magazine pieces, the children were splendidly self-willed, hard-edged, perverse, indomitable. So were the mothers, through their wit, indomitable. The real-life mothers I warmed to were the sort who would phone up and say, "Is my embryo Hitler by any chance over at your house?" They cackled clear above the milky fog.

We saw a dead deer strapped across the front of a pickup truck.

"Somebody shot it," Cynthia said. "Hunters shoot the deer."

"It's not hunting season yet," Andrew said. "They may have hit it on the road. See the sign for deer crossing?"

"I would cry if we hit one," Cynthia said sternly.

I had made peanut-butter-and-marmalade sandwiches for the children and salmon-and-mayonnaise for us. But I had not put any lettuce in, and Andrew was disappointed.

"I didn't have any," I said.

"Couldn't you have got some?"

"I'd have had to buy a whole head of lettuce just to get enough for sandwiches, and I decided it wasn't worth it."

This was a lie. I had forgotten.

"They're a lot better with lettuce."

"I didn't think it made that much difference." After a silence, I said, "Don't be mad."

"I'm not mad. I like lettuce on sandwiches."

"I just didn't think it mattered that much."

"How would it be if I didn't bother to fill up the gas tank?"

"That's not the same thing."

"Sing a song," said Cynthia. She started to sing:

> "*Five little ducks went out one day,*
> *Over the hills and far away.*
> *One little duck went*
> *'Quack-quack-quack.'*
> *Four little ducks came swimming*
> *back.*"

Andrew squeezed my hand and said, "Let's not fight."

"You're right. I should have got lettuce."

"It doesn't matter that much."

I wished that I could get my feelings about Andrew to come together into a serviceable and dependable feeling. I had even tried writing two lists, one of things I liked about him, one of things I disliked – in the cauldron of intimate life, things I loved and things I hated – as if I hoped by this to prove something, to come to a conclusion one way or the other. But I gave it up when I saw that all it proved was what I already knew – that I had violent contradictions. Sometimes the very sound of his footsteps seemed to me tyrannical, the set of his mouth smug and mean, his hard, straight body a barrier interposed – quite consciously, even dutifully, and with a nasty pleasure in its masculine authority – between me and whatever joy or lightness I could get in life. Then, with not much warning, he became my good friend and most essential companion. I felt the sweetness of his light bones and serious ideas, the vulnerability of his love, which I imagined to be much purer and more straightforward than my own. I could be greatly moved by an inflexibility, a harsh propriety, that at other times I scorned. I would think how humble he was, really, taking on such a ready-made role of husband, father, breadwinner, and how I myself in comparison was really a secret monster of egotism. Not so secret, either – not from him.

At the bottom of our fights, we served up what we thought were the ugliest truths. "I know there is something basically selfish and basically untrustworthy about you," Andrew once said. "I've always known it. I also know that that is why I fell in love with you."

"Yes," I said, feeling sorrowful but complacent.

"I know that I'd be better off without you."

"Yes. You would."

"You'd be happier without me."

"Yes."

And finally – finally – racked and purged, we clasped hands and laughed, laughed at those two benighted people, ourselves. Their grudges, their grievances, their self-justification. We leapfrogged over them. We declared them liars. We would have wine with dinner, or decide to give a party.

I haven't seen Andrew for years, don't know if he is still thin, has gone completely gray, insists on lettuce, tells the truth, or is hearty and disappointed.

We stayed the night in Wenatchee, Washington, where it hadn't rained for weeks. We ate dinner in a restaurant built about a tree – not a sapling in a tub but a tall, sturdy cottonwood. In the early-morning light, we climbed out of the irrigated valley, up dry, rocky, very steep hillsides that would seem to lead to more hills, and there on the top was a wide plateau, cut by the great Spokane and Columbia rivers. Grainland and grassland, mile after mile. There were straight roads here, and little farming towns with grain elevators. In fact, there was a sign announcing that this county we were going through, Douglas County, had the second-highest wheat yield of any county in the United States. The towns had planted shade trees. At least, I thought they had been planted, because there were no such big trees in the countryside.

All this was marvellously welcome to me. "Why do I love it so much?" I said to Andrew. "Is it because it isn't scenery?"

"It reminds you of home," said Andrew. "A bout of severe nostalgia." But he said this kindly.

When we said "home" and meant Ontario, we had very different places in mind. My home was a turkey farm, where my father lived as a widower, and though it was the same house my mother had lived in, had papered, painted, cleaned, furnished, it showed the effects now of neglect and of some wild sociability. A life went on in it that my mother could not have predicted or condoned. There were parties for the turkey crew, the gutters and pluckers, and sometimes one or two of the young men would be living there temporarily, inviting their own friends and having their own impromptu parties. This life, I thought, was better for my father than being lonely, and I did not disapprove, had certainly no right to disapprove. Andrew did not like to go there, naturally enough, because he was not the sort who could sit around the kitchen table with the turkey crew, telling jokes. They were intimidated by him and contemptuous of him, and it seemed to me that my father, when they were around, had to be on their side. And it wasn't only Andrew who had trouble. I could manage those jokes, but it was an effort.

I wished for the days when I was little, before we had the turkeys. We had cows, and sold the milk to the cheese factory. A turkey farm is nothing like as pretty as a dairy farm or a sheep farm. You can see that the turkeys are on a straight path to becoming frozen carcasses and table meat. They don't have the pretense of a life of their own, a browsing idyll, that cattle have, or pigs in the dappled orchard. Turkey barns are long, efficient buildings – tin sheds. No beams or hay or warm stables. Even the smell of guano seems thinner and more offensive than the usual smell of stable manure. No hints there of hay coils and rail fences and songbirds and the flowering hawthorn. The turkeys were all let out into one long field, which they picked clean. They didn't look like great birds there but like fluttering laundry.

Once, shortly after my mother died, and after I was married – in fact, I was packing to join Andrew in Vancouver – I was at home alone for a couple of days with my father. There was a freakishly heavy rain all night. In the early light, we saw that the turkey field was flooded. At least, the low-lying parts of it were flooded – it was like a lake with many islands. The turkeys were huddled on these islands. Turkeys are very stupid. (My father would say, "You know a chicken? You know how stupid a chicken is? Well, a chicken is an Einstein compared with a turkey.") But they had managed to crowd to higher ground and avoid drowning. Now they might push each other off, suffocate each other, get cold and die. We couldn't wait for the water to go down. We went out in an old rowboat we had. I rowed and my father pulled the heavy, wet turkeys into the boat and we took them to the barn. It was still raining a little. The job was difficult and absurd and very uncomfortable. We were laughing. I was happy to be working with my father. I felt close to all hard, repetitive, appalling work, in which the body is finally worn out, the mind sunk (though sometimes the spirit can stay marvellously light), and I was homesick in advance for this life and this place. I thought that if Andrew could see me there in the rain, red-handed, muddy, trying to hold on to turkey legs and row the boat at the same time, he would only want to get me out of there and make me forget about it. This raw life angered him. My attachment to it angered him. I thought that I shouldn't have married him. But who else? One of the turkey crew?

And I didn't want to stay there. I might feel bad about leaving, but I would feel worse if somebody made me stay.

Andrew's mother lived in Toronto, in an apartment building looking out on Muir Park. When Andrew and his sister were both at home, his mother slept in the living room. Her husband, a doctor, had died when the children were still too young to go to school. She took a secretarial course and sold her house at Depression prices, moved to this apartment, managed to raise her children, with some help from relatives – her sister Caroline, her brother-in-law Roger. Andrew and his sister went to private schools and to camp in the summer.

"I suppose that was courtesy of the Fresh Air fund?" I said once, scornful of his claim that he had been poor. To my mind, Andrew's urban life had been sheltered and fussy. His mother came home with a headache from working all day in the noise, the harsh light of a department-store office, but it did not occur to me that hers was a hard or admirable life. I don't think she herself believed that she was admirable – only unlucky. She worried about her work in the office, her clothes, her cooking, her children. She worried most of all about what Roger and Caroline would think.

Caroline and Roger lived on the east side of the park, in a handsome stone house. Roger was a tall man with a bald, freckled head, a fat, firm stomach. Some operation on his throat had deprived him of his voice – he spoke in a rough whisper. But everybody paid attention. At dinner once in the stone house – where all the dining-room furniture was enormous, darkly glowing, palatial – I asked him a question. I think it had to do with Whittaker Chambers, whose story was then appearing in the *Saturday Evening Post*. The question was mild in tone, but he guessed its subversive intent and took to calling me Mrs. Gromyko, referring to what he alleged to be my "sympathies." Perhaps he really craved an adversary, and could not find one. At that dinner, I saw Andrew's hand tremble as he lit his mother's cigarette. His Uncle Roger had paid for Andrew's education, and was on the board of directors of several companies.

"He is just an opinionated old man," Andrew said to me later. "What is the point of arguing with him?"

Before we left Vancouver, Andrew's mother had written,

"Roger seems quite intrigued by the idea of your buying a small car!" Her exclamation mark showed apprehension. At that time, particularly in Ontario, the choice of a small European car over a large American car could be seen as some sort of declaration – a declaration of tendencies Roger had been sniffing after all along.

"It isn't that small a car," said Andrew huffily.

"That's not the point," I said. "The point is, it isn't any of his business!"

We spent the second night in Missoula. We had been told in Spokane, at a gas station, that there was a lot of repair work going on along Highway 2, and that we were in for a very hot, dusty drive, with long waits, so we turned onto the interstate and drove through Coeur d'Alene and Kellogg into Montana. After Missoula, we turned south toward Butte, but detoured to see Helena, the state capital. In the car, we played Who Am I?

Cynthia was somebody dead, and an American, and a girl. Possibly a lady. She was not in a story. She had not been seen on television. Cynthia had not read about her in a book. She was not anybody who had come to the kindergarten, or a relative of any of Cynthia's friends.

"Is she human?" said Andrew, with a sudden shrewdness.

"No! That's what you forgot to ask!"

"An animal," I said reflectively.

"Is that a question? Sixteen questions!"

"No, it is not a question. I'm thinking. A dead animal."

"It's the deer," said Meg, who hadn't been playing.

"That's not fair!" said Cynthia. "She's not playing!"

"What deer?" said Andrew.

I said, "Yesterday."

"The day before," said Cynthia. "Meg wasn't playing. Nobody got it."

"The deer on the truck," said Andrew.

"It was a lady deer, because it didn't have antlers, and it was an American and it was dead," Cynthia said.

Andrew said, "I think it's kind of morbid, being a dead deer."

"I got it," said Meg.

Cynthia said, "I think I know what morbid is. It's depressing."

Helena, an old silver-mining town, looked forlorn to us even in the morning sunlight. Then Bozeman and Billings, not forlorn in the slightest – energetic, strung-out towns, with miles of blinding tinsel fluttering over used-car lots. We got too tired and hot even to play Who Am I? These busy, prosaic cities reminded me of similar places in Ontario, and I thought about what was really waiting there – the great tombstone furniture of Roger and Caroline's dining room, the dinners for which I must iron the children's dresses and warn them about forks, and then the other table a hundred miles away, the jokes of my father's crew. The pleasures I had been thinking of – looking at the countryside or drinking a Coke in an old-fashioned drugstore with fans and a high, pressed-tin ceiling – would have to be snatched in between.

"Meg's asleep," Cynthia said. "She's so hot. She makes me hot in the same seat with her."

"I hope she isn't feverish," I said, not turning around.

What are we doing this for, I thought, and the answer came – to show off. To give Andrew's mother and my father the pleasure of seeing their grandchildren. That was our duty. But beyond that we wanted to show them something. What strenuous children we were, Andrew and I, what relentless seekers of approbation. It was as if at some point we had received an unforgettable, indigestible message – that we were far from satisfactory, and that the most commonplace success in life was probably beyond us. Roger dealt out such messages, of course – that was his style – but Andrew's mother, my own mother and father couldn't have meant to do so. All they meant to tell us was "Watch out. Get along." My father, when I was in high school, teased me that I was getting to think I was so smart I would never find a boyfriend. He would have forgotten that in a week. I never forgot it. Andrew and I didn't forget things. We took umbrage.

"I wish there was a beach," said Cynthia.

"There probably is one," Andrew said. "Right around the next curve."

"There isn't any curve," she said, sounding insulted.

"That's what I mean."

"I wish there was some more lemonade."

"I will just wave my magic wand and produce some," I said.

"Okay, Cynthia? Would you rather have grape juice? Will I do a beach while I'm at it?"

She was silent, and soon I felt repentant. "Maybe in the next town there might be a pool," I said. I looked at the map. "In Miles City. Anyway, there'll be something cool to drink."

"How far is it?" Andrew said.

"Not so far," I said. "Thirty miles, about."

"In Miles City," said Cynthia, in the tones of an incantation, "there is a beautiful blue swimming pool for children, and a park with lovely trees."

Andrew said to me, "You could have started something."

But there was a pool. There was a park, too, though not quite the oasis of Cynthia's fantasy. Prairie trees with thin leaves – cottonwoods and poplars – worn grass, and a high wire fence around the pool. Within this fence, a wall, not yet completed, of cement blocks. There were no shouts or splashes; over the entrance I saw a sign that said the pool was closed every day from noon until two o'clock. It was then twenty-five after twelve.

Nevertheless I called out, "Is anybody there?" I thought somebody must be around, because there was a small truck parked near the entrance. On the side of the truck were these words: "We have Brains, to fix your Drains. (We have Roto-Rooter too.)"

A girl came out, wearing a red lifeguard's shirt over her bathing suit. "Sorry, we're closed."

"We were just driving through," I said.

"We close every day from twelve until two. It's on the sign." She was eating a sandwich.

"I saw the sign," I said. "But this is the first water we've seen for so long, and the children are awfully hot, and I wondered if they could just dip in and out – just five minutes. We'd watch them."

A boy came into sight, behind her. He was wearing jeans and a T-shirt with the words "Roto-Rooter" on it.

I was going to say that we were driving from British Columbia to Ontario, but I remembered that Canadian place names usually meant nothing to Americans. "We're driving right across the country," I said. "We haven't time to wait for the pool to open. We were just hoping the children could get cooled off."

Cynthia came running up barefoot behind me. "Mother. Mother, where is my bathing suit?" Then she stopped, sensing the serious adult negotiations. Meg was climbing out of the car – just wakened, with her top pulled up and her shorts pulled down, showing her pink stomach.

"Is it just those two?" the girl said.

"Just the two. We'll watch them."

"I can't let any adults in. If it's just the two, I guess I could watch them. I'm having my lunch." She said to Cynthia, "Do you want to come in the pool?"

"Yes, please," said Cynthia firmly.

Meg looked at the ground.

"Just a short time, because the pool is really closed," I said. "We appreciate this very much," I said to the girl.

"Well, I can eat my lunch out there, if it's just the two of them." She looked toward the car as if she thought I might try to spring some more children on her.

When I found Cynthia's bathing suit, she took it into the changing room. She would not permit anybody, even Meg, to see her naked. I changed Meg, who stood on the front seat of the car. She had a pink cotton bathing suit with straps that crossed and buttoned. There were ruffles across the bottom.

"She *is* hot," I said. "But I don't think she's feverish."

I loved helping Meg to dress or undress, because her body still had the solid unself-consciousness, the sweet indifference, something of the milky smell, of a baby's body. Cynthia's body had long ago been pared down, shaped and altered, into Cynthia. We all liked to hug Meg, press and nuzzle her. Sometimes she would scowl and beat us off, and this forthright independence, this ferocious bashfulness, simply made her more appealing, more apt to be tormented and tickled in the way of family love.

Andrew and I sat in the car with the windows open. I could hear a radio playing, and thought it must belong to the girl or her boyfriend. I was thirsty, and got out of the car to look for a concession stand, or perhaps a soft-drink machine, somewhere in the park. I was wearing shorts, and the backs of my legs were slick with sweat. I saw a drinking fountain at the other side of the park and was walking toward it in a roundabout way, keeping to the shade of the trees. No place became real till you got out of the car. Dazed with the heat, with the sun on the blistered houses, the pavement, the burned grass, I walked slowly. I paid attention to a squashed leaf, ground a Popsicle stick under the heel of my sandal, squinted at a trash can strapped to a tree. This is the way you look at the poorest details of the world resurfaced, after you've been driving for a long time – you feel their singleness and precise location and the forlorn coincidence of your being there to see them.

Where are the children?

I turned around and moved quickly, not quite running, to a part of the fence beyond which the cement wall was not completed. I could see some of the pool. I saw Cynthia, standing about waist-deep in the water, fluttering her hands on the surface and discreetly watching something at the end of the pool, which I could not see. I thought by her pose, her discretion, the look on her face, that she must be watching some byplay between the lifeguard and her boyfriend. I couldn't see Meg. But I thought she must be playing in the shallow water – both the shallow and deep ends of the pool were out of my sight.

"Cynthia!" I had to call twice before she knew where my voice was coming from. "Cynthia! Where's Meg?"

It always seems to me, when I recall this scene, that Cynthia turns very gracefully toward me, then turns all around in the water – making me think of a ballerina on point – and spreads her arms in a gesture of the stage. "Dis-ap-peared!"

Cynthia was naturally graceful, and she did take dancing lessons, so these movements may have been as I have described. She did say "Disappeared" after looking all around the pool, but the strangely artificial style of speech and gesture, the lack of urgency, is more likely my invention. The fear I felt instantly when I couldn't see Meg – even while I was telling myself she must be in the shallower water – must have made Cynthia's movements seem unbearably slow and inappropriate to me, and the tone in which she could say "Disappeared" before the implications struck her (or was she covering, at once, some ever-ready guilt?) was heard by me as quite exquisitely, monstrously self-possessed.

I cried out for Andrew, and the lifeguard came into view. She was pointing toward the deep end of the pool, saying, "What's that?"

There, just within my view, a cluster of pink ruffles appeared, a bouquet, beneath the surface of the water. Why would a lifeguard stop and point, why would she ask what that was, why didn't she just dive into the water and swim to it? She didn't swim; she ran all the way around the edge of the pool. But by that time Andrew was over the fence. So many things seemed not quite plausible – Cynthia's behavior, then the lifeguard's – and now I had the impression that Andrew jumped with one bound over this fence, which seemed about seven feet high. He must have climbed it very quickly, getting a grip on the wire.

I could not jump or climb it, so I ran to the entrance, where there was a sort of lattice gate, locked. It was not very high, and I did pull myself over it. I ran through the cement corridors, through the disinfectant pool for your feet, and came out on the edge of the pool.

The drama was over.

Andrew had got to Meg first, and had pulled her out of the water. He just had to reach over and grab her, because she was swimming somehow, with her head underwater – she was moving toward the edge of the pool. He was carrying her now, and the lifeguard was trotting along behind. Cynthia had climbed out of the water and was running to meet them. The only person aloof from the situation was the boyfriend, who had stayed on the bench at the shallow end, drinking a milkshake. He smiled at me, and I thought that unfeeling of him, even though the danger was past. He may have meant it kindly. I noticed that he had not turned the radio off, just down.

Meg had not swallowed any water. She hadn't even scared herself. Her hair was plastered to her head and her eyes were wide open, golden with amazement.

"I was getting the comb," she said. "I didn't know it was deep."

Andrew said, "She was swimming! She was swimming by herself. I saw her bathing suit in the water and then I saw her swimming."

"She nearly drowned," Cynthia said. "Didn't she? Meg nearly drowned."

"I don't know how it could have happened," said the lifeguard. "One moment she was there, and the next she wasn't."

What had happened was that Meg had climbed out of the water at the shallow end and run along the edge of the pool toward the deep end. She saw a comb that somebody had dropped lying on the bottom. She crouched down and reached in to pick it up, quite deceived about the depth of the water. She went over the edge and slipped into the pool, making such a light splash that nobody heard – not the lifeguard, who was kissing her boyfriend, or Cynthia, who was watching them. That must have been the moment under the trees when I thought, Where are the children? It must have been the same moment. At that moment, Meg was slipping, surprised, into the treacherously clear blue water.

"It's okay," I said to the lifeguard, who was nearly crying. "She can move pretty fast." (Though that wasn't what we usually said about Meg at all. We said she thought everything over and took her time.)

"You swam, Meg," said Cynthia, in a congratulatory way. (She told us about the kissing later.)

"I didn't know it was deep," Meg said. "I didn't drown."

We had lunch at a take-out place, eating hamburgers and fries at a picnic table not far from the highway. In my excitement, I forgot to get Meg a plain hamburger, and had to scrape off the relish and mustard with plastic spoons, then wipe the meat with a paper napkin, before she would eat it. I took advantage of the trash can there to clean out the car. Then we resumed driving east, with the car windows open in front. Cynthia and Meg fell asleep in the back seat.

Andrew and I talked quietly about what had happened. Suppose I hadn't had the impulse just at that moment to check on the children? Suppose we had gone uptown to get drinks, as we had thought of doing? How had Andrew got over the fence? Did he jump or climb? (He couldn't remember.) How had he reached Meg so quickly? And think of the lifeguard not watching. And Cynthia, taken up with the kissing. Not seeing anything else. Not seeing Meg drop over the edge.

Disappeared.

But she swam. She held her breath and came up swimming.

What a chain of lucky links.

That was all we spoke about – luck. But I was compelled to picture the opposite. At this moment, we could have been filling out forms. Meg removed from us, Meg's body being prepared for shipment. To Vancouver – where we had never noticed such a thing as a graveyard – or to Ontario? The scribbled drawings she had made this morning would still be in the back seat of the car. How could this be borne all at once, how did people bear it? The plump, sweet shoulders and hands and feet, the fine brown hair, the rather satisfied, secretive expression – all exactly the same as when she had been alive. The most ordinary tragedy. A child drowned in a swimming pool at noon on a sunny day. Things tidied up quickly. The pool opens as usual at two o'clock. The lifeguard is a bit shaken up and gets the afternoon off. She drives away with her boyfriend in the Roto-Rooter truck. The body sealed away in some kind of shipping coffin. Sedatives, phone calls, arrangements. Such a sudden vacancy, a blind sinking and shifting. Waking up groggy from the pills, thinking for a moment it wasn't true. Thinking if only we hadn't stopped, if only we hadn't taken this route, if only they hadn't let us use the pool. Probably no one would ever have known about the comb.

There's something trashy about this kind of imagining, isn't there? Something shameful. Laying your finger on the wire to get the safe shock, feeling a bit of what it's like, then pulling back. I believed that Andrew was more scrupulous than I about such things, and that at this moment he was really trying to think about something else.

When I stood apart from my parents at Steve Gauley's funeral and watched them, and had this new, unpleasant feeling about them, I thought that I was understanding something about them for the first time. It was a deadly serious thing. I was understanding that they were implicated. Their big, stiff, dressed-up bodies did not stand between me and sudden death, or any kind of death. They gave consent. So it seemed. They gave consent to the death of children and to my death not by anything they said or thought but by the very fact that they had made children – they had made me. They had made me, and for that reason my death – however grieved they were, however they carried on – would seem to them anything but impossible or unnatural. This was a fact, and even then I knew they were not to blame.

But I did blame them. I charged them with effrontery, hypocrisy. On Steve Gauley's behalf, and on behalf of all children, who knew that by rights they should have sprung up free, to live a new, superior kind of life, not to be caught in the snares of vanquished grown-ups, with their sex and funerals.

Steve Gauley drowned, people said, because he was next thing to an orphan and was let run free. If he had been warned enough and given chores to do and kept in check, he wouldn't have fallen from an untrustworthy tree branch into a spring pond, a full gravel pit near the river – he wouldn't have drowned. He was neglected, he was free, so he drowned. And his father took it as an accident, such as might happen to a dog. He didn't have a good suit for the funeral, and he didn't bow his head for the prayers. But he was the only grownup that I let off the hook. He was the only one I didn't see giving consent. He couldn't prevent anything, but he wasn't implicated in anything, either – not like the others, saying the Lord's Prayer in their unnaturally weighted voices, oozing religion and dishonor.

At Glendive, not far from the North Dakota border, we had a choice – either to continue on the interstate or head northeast, toward Williston, taking Route 16, then some secondary roads that would get us back to Highway 2.

We agreed that the interstate would be faster, and that it was important for us not to spend too much time – that is, money – on the road. Nevertheless we decided to cut back to Highway 2.

"I just like the idea of it better," I said.

Andrew said, "That's because it's what we planned to do in the beginning."

"We missed seeing Kalispell and Havre. And Wolf Point. I like the name."

"We'll see them on the way back."

Andrew's saying "on the way back" was a surprising pleasure to me. Of course, I had believed that we would be coming back, with our car and our lives and our family intact, having covered all that distance, having dealt somehow with those loyalties and problems, held ourselves up for inspection in such a foolhardy way. But it was a relief to hear him say it.

"What I can't get over," said Andrew, "is how you got the signal. It's got to be some kind of extra sense that mothers have."

Partly I wanted to believe that, to bask in my extra sense. Partly I wanted to warn him – to warn everybody – never to count on it.

"What I can't understand," I said, "is how you got over the fence."

"Neither can I."

So we went on, with the two in the back seat trusting us, because of no choice, and we ourselves trusting to be forgiven, in time, for everything that had first to be seen and condemned by those children: whatever was flippant, arbitrary, careless, callous – all our natural, and particular, mistakes.

FRAGILITY

Carol Shields

Carol Shields (1935–2003) was an American-born Canadian writer. She is best known for her 1993 novel *The Stone Diaries*, which won the Pulitzer Prize as well as the Governor General's Award in Canada. Shields published ten novels, three collections of poetry and five collections of short stories.

We are flying over the Rockies on our way to Vancouver, and there sits Ivy with her paperback. I ask myself Should I interrupt and draw her attention to the grandeur beneath us?

In a purely selfish sense, watching Ivy read is as interesting as peering down at those snowy mountains. She turns the pages of a book in the same way she handles every object, with a peculiar respectful gentleness, as though the air around it were more tender than ordinary air. I've watched her lift a cup of tea with this same abstracted grace, cradling a thick mug in a way that transforms it into something precious and fragile. It's a gift some people have.

I decide not to disturb her; utterly absorbed in what she's reading, she's seen the Rockies before.

In the seat ahead of us is a young man wearing a bright blue jacket – I remember that once I had a similar jacket in a similar hue. Unlike us, he's clearly flying over the Rockies for the first time. He's in a half-standing position at the window, snapping away with his camera, pausing only to change the film. From where I'm sitting I can see his intense, eager trigger hand, his steadying elbow, his dropped lower lip. In a week he'll be passing his slides around the office, holding them delicately at their edges up to the light. He might set up a projector and screen them one evening in his living room; he might invite a few friends over, and his wife – who will resemble the Ivy of fifteen years ago – will serve coffee and wedges of cheese cake; these are the Rockies, he'll say – magnificent, stirring, one of the wonders of the continent.

I tell myself that I would give a great deal to be in that young man's shoes, but this is only a half-truth, the kind of lie Ivy and I sometimes spin for our own amusement. We really don't want to go back in time. What we envy in the young is that fine nervous edge of perception, the ability to take in reality afresh. I suppose, as we grow older, that's what we forfeit, acquiring in its place a measure of healthy resignation.

Ivy puts down her book suddenly and reaches for my hand. A cool, light, lazy touch. She's smiling.

"Good book?"

"Hmmm," she says, and stretches.

Now, as a kind of duty, I point out the Rockies.

"Beautiful," she exclaims, leaning toward the window.

And it is beautiful. But unfortunately the plane is flying at a height that extracts all sense of dimension from the view. Instead of snow-capped splendor, we see a kind of Jackson Pollock dribbling of white on green. It's a vast abstract design, a linking of incised patterns, quite interesting in its way, but without any real suggestion of height, or majesty.

"It looks a little like a Jackson Pollock," Ivy says in that rhythmic voice of hers.

"Did you really say that?"

"I think so." Her eyebrows go up, her mouth crimps at the edges. "At least, if I didn't, someone did."

I lift her hand – I can't help myself – and kiss her fingertips.

"And what's that for?" she asks, still smiling.

"An attack of poignancy."

"A serious new dietary disease, I suppose," Ivy says, and at that moment the steward arrives with our lunch trays.

Ivy and I have been to Vancouver fairly often on business trips or for holidays. This time it's different; in three months we'll be moving permanently to Vancouver, and now the two of us are engaged in that common-enough errand, a house-hunting expedition.

Common, I say, but not for us.

We know the statistics: that about half of all North Americans move every five years, that we're a rootless, restless, portable society. But for some reason, some failing on our part or perhaps simple good fortune, Ivy and I seem to have evaded the statistical pattern. The small stone-fronted, bow-windowed house we bought when Christopher was born is the house in which we continue to live after twenty years.

If there had been another baby, we would have considered a move, but we stayed in the same house in the middle of Toronto. It was close to both our offices and close too to the clinic Christopher needed. Curiously enough, most of our neighbors also stayed there year after year. In our neighborhood we know everyone. When the news of my transfer came, the first thing Ivy said was, "What about the Mattisons and the Levensons? What about Robin and Sara?"

"We can't very well take everyone on the street along with us."

"Oh Lordy," Ivy said, and bit her lip. "Of course not. It's only—"

"I know," I said.

"Maybe we can talk Robin and Sara into taking their holidays on the coast next year. Sara always said—"

"And we'll be back fairly often. At least twice a year."

"If only—"

"If only what?"

"Those stupid bulbs." (I love the way Ivy pronounces the word *stupid: stewpid*, giving it a patrician lift.)

"Bulbs?"

"Remember last fall, all those bulbs I put in?"

"Oh," I said, remembering.

She looked at me squarely: "You don't mind as much as I do, do you?"

"Of course I do. You know I do."

"Tell me the truth."

What could I say? I've always been impressed by the accuracy of Ivy's observations. "The truth is—"

"The truth is—?" she helped me along.

"I guess I'm ready."

"Ready for what?" Her eyes filled with tears. This was a difficult time for us. Christopher had died in January. He was a tough kid and lived a good five years longer than any of us ever thought he would. His death was not unexpected, but still, Ivy and I were feeling exceptionally fragile.

"Ready for what?" she asked again.

"For something," I admitted. "For anything, I guess."

The first house we look at seems perfect. The settled neighborhood is dense with trees and shrubbery, and reminds us both of our part of Toronto. There are small repairs that need doing but nothing major. Best of all, from the dining room there can be seen a startling lop of blue water meeting blue sky.

I point this out to Ivy; a view was one of the things we had put on our list. There is also a fireplace, another must, and a capacious kitchen with greenhouse windows overlooking a garden.

"And look at the bulbs," I point out. "Tulips halfway up. Daffodils."

"Lilies," Ivy says.

"I think we've struck it lucky," I tell the real-estate woman who's showing us around, a Mrs. Marjorie Little. ("Call me Marge," she'd said to us with west-coast breeziness.)

Afterward, in the car, Ivy is so quiet I have to prompt her. "Well?"

Marge Little, sitting at the wheel, peers at me, then at Ivy.

"It's just," Ivy begins, "it's just so depressing."

Depressing? I can't believe she's saying this. A view, central location, a fireplace. Plus bulbs.

"Well," Ivy says slowly, "it's a divorce house. You must have noticed?"

I hadn't. "A divorce house? How do you know?"

"I looked in the closets. Her clothes were there but *his* weren't."

"Oh."

"And half the pictures had been taken off the wall. Surely you noticed that."

I shake my head.

"I know it sounds silly, but wouldn't you rather move into a house with some good" – she pauses – "some good vibrations?"

"Vibrations?"

"Did you notice the broken light in the bathroom? I'll bet someone threw something at it. In a rage."

"We could always fix the light. And the other things. And with our own furniture—"

Ivy is an accountant. Once I heard a young man in her firm

describe her as a *crack* accountant. For a number of years now she's been a senior partner. When this same young man heard she was leaving because of my transfer, he couldn't help ragging her a little, saying he thought women didn't move around at the whim of their husbands anymore, and that, out of principle, she ought to refuse to go to Vancouver or else arrange some kind of compromise life – separate apartments, for instance, with weekend rendezvous in Winnipeg.

Ivy had howled at this. She's a positive, good-natured woman and, as it turned out, she had no trouble finding an opening in a good Vancouver firm, at senior level. As I say, she's positive. Which is why her apprehension over good or bad vibrations is puzzling. Can it be she sees bad times ahead for the two of us? Or is it only that she wants solid footing after these long years with Christopher? Neither of us is quite glued back together again. Not that we ever will be.

"I can't help it," Ivy is saying. "It just doesn't feel like a lucky house. There's something about—"

Marge Little interrupts with a broad smile. "I've got all kinds of interesting houses to show you. Maybe you'll like the next one better."

"Does it have good vibes?" Ivy asks, laughing a little to show she's only half-serious.

"I don't know," Marge Little says. "They don't put that kind of info on the fact sheet."

The next house is perched on the side of the canyon. No, that's not quite true. It is, in fact, falling into the canyon. I notice, but don't mention, the fact that the outside foundation walls are cracked and patched. Inside, the house is alarmingly empty; the cool settled air seems proof that it's been vacant for some time.

Marge consults her fact sheet. Yes, the house has been on the market about six months. The price has been reduced twice. But – she glances at us – perhaps we noticed the foundation …

"Yes," I say. "Hopeless."

"Damn," Ivy says.

We look at two more houses; both have spectacular views and architectural distinction. But one is a bankruptcy sale and the other is a divorce house. By now I'm starting to pick up the scent:

it's a compound of petty carelessness and strenuous neglect, as though the owners had decamped in a hurry, angry at the rooms themselves.

To cheer ourselves up, the three of us have lunch in a sunny Broadway restaurant. It seems extraordinary that we can sit here and see mountains that are miles away; the thought that we will soon be able to live within sight of these mountains fills us with optimism. We order a little wine and linger in the sunlight. Vancouver is going to be an adventure. We're going to be happy here. Marge Little, feeling expansive, tells us about her three children and about the problem she has keeping her weight down. "Marge Large they'll be calling me soon," she says. It's an old joke, we sense, and the telling of it makes us feel we're old friends. She got into the business, she says, because she loves houses. And she has an instinct for matching houses with people. "So don't be discouraged," she tells us. "We'll find the perfect place this afternoon."

We drive through narrow city streets to a house where a famous movie idol grew up. His mother still lives in the house, a spry, slightly senile lady in her eighties. The tiny house – we quickly see it is far too small for us – is crowded with photographs of the famous son. He beams at us from the hallway, from the dining room, from the bedroom bureau.

"Oh, he's a good boy. Comes home every two or three years," his mother tells us, her large teeth shining in a diminished face. "And once I went down there, all the way down to Hollywood, on an airplane. He paid my way, sent me a ticket, I saw his swimming pool. They all have swimming pools. He has a cook, a man who does all the meals, so I didn't have to lift a finger for a whole week. What an experience, like a queen. I have some pictures someplace I could show you—"

"That would be wonderful," Marge Little says, "but" – she glances at her watch – "I'm afraid we have another appointment."

"—I saw those pictures just the other day. Now where—? I think they're in this drawer somewhere. Here, I knew it. Take a look at this. Isn't that something? That's his swimming pool. Kidney-shaped. He's got another one now, even bigger."

"Beautiful," Ivy says.

"And here he is when he was little. See this? He'd be about nine there. We took a trip east. That's him and his dad standing by Niagara Falls. Here's another—"

"We really have to—"

"A good boy. I'll say that for him. Didn't give any trouble. Sometimes I see his movies on the TV and I can't believe the things he does; with women and so on. I have to pinch myself and say it's only pretend—"

"I think—"

"I'm going into this senior-citizen place. They've got a nice TV lounge, big screen, bigger than this little, bitty one, color too. I always—"

"Sad," Ivy says, when we escape at last and get into the car.

"The house or the mother?" I ask her.

"Both."

"At least it's not a D.H." (This has become our shorthand expression for divorce house.)

"Wait'll you see the next place," Marge Little says, swinging into traffic. "The next place is fabulous."

Fabulous, yes. But far too big. After that, in a fit of desperation, we look at a condo. "I'm not quite ready for this," I have to admit.

"No garden," Ivy says in a numb voice. She looks weary, and we decide to call it a day.

The ad in the newspaper reads: WELL-LOVED FAMILY HOME. And Ivy and Marge Little and I are there, knocking on the door, at nine-thirty in the morning.

"Come in, come in," calls a young woman in faded jeans. She has a young child on one hip and another – they must be twins – by the hand. Sunlight pours in the front window and there is freshly baked bread cooling on the kitchen counter.

But the house is a disaster, a rabbit warren of narrow hallways and dark corners. The kitchen window is only feet away from a low brick building where bodywork is being done on imported sports cars. The stairs are uneven. The bedroom floors slope, and the paint is peeling off the bathroom ceiling.

"It just kills us to leave this place," the young woman says. She's following us through the rooms, pointing with unmistakable sorrow at the wall where they were planning to put up shelving, at the hardwood floors they were thinking of sanding. Out of the blue, they got news of a transfer.

Ironically, they're going to Toronto, and in a week's time they'll be there doing what we're doing, looking for a house they can love. "But we just know we'll never find a place like this," she tells us with a sad shake of her head. "Not in a million zillion years."

After that we lose track of the number of houses. The day bends and blurs, square footage, zoning regulations, mortgage schedules, double-car garages, cedar siding only two years old – was that the place near that little park? No, that was the one on that little crescent off Arbutus. Remember? The one without the basement.

Darkness is falling as Marge Little drives us back to our hotel. We are passing hundreds – it seems like thousands – of houses, and we see lamps being turned on, curtains being closed. Friendly smoke rises from substantial chimneys. Here and there, where the curtains are left open, we can see people sitting down to dinner. Passing one house, I see a woman in a window, leaning over with a match in her hand, lighting a pair of candles. Ivy sees it too, and I'm sure she's feeling as I am, a little resentful that everyone but us seems to have a roof overhead.

"Tomorrow for sure," Marge calls cheerily. (Tomorrow is our last day. Both of us have to be home on Monday.)

"I suppose we could always rent for a year." Ivy says this with low enthusiasm.

"Or," I say, "we could make another trip in a month or so. Maybe there'll be more on the market."

"Isn't it funny? The first house we saw, remember? In a way, it was the most promising place we've seen."

"The one with the view from the dining room? With the broken light in the bathroom?"

"It might not look bad with a new fixture. Or even a skylight."

"Wasn't that a divorce house?" I ask Ivy.

"Yes," she shrugs, "but maybe that's just what we'll have to settle for."

"It *was* listed at a good price."

"I live in a divorce house," Marge Little says, pulling in front of our hotel. "It's been a divorce house for a whole year now."

"Oh, Marge," Ivy says. "I didn't mean—" she stops. "Forgive me."

"And it's not so bad. Sometimes it's darned cheerful."

"I just—" Ivy takes a breath. "I just wanted a lucky house. Maybe there's no such thing—"

"Are you interested in taking another look at the first house? I might be able to get you an appointment this evening. That is, if you think you can stand one more appointment today."

"Absolutely," we say together.

This time we inspect the house inch by inch. Ivy makes a list of the necessary repairs, and I measure the window for curtains. We hadn't realized that there was a cedar closet off one of the bedrooms. The lights of the city are glowing through the dining-room window. A spotlight at the back of the house picks out the flowers just coming into bloom. There'll be room for our hi-fi across from the fireplace. The basement is dry and very clean. The wallpaper in the downstairs den is fairly attractive and in good condition. The stairway is well proportioned and the banister is a beauty. (I'm a sucker for banisters.) There's an alcove where the pine buffet will fit nicely. Trees on both sides of the house should give us greenery and privacy. The lawn, as far as we can tell, seems to be in good shape. There's a lazy Susan in the kitchen, also a built-in dishwasher, a later model than ours. Plenty of room for a small table and a couple of chairs. The woodwork in the living room has been left natural, a wonder since so many people, a few years back, were painting over their oak trim.

Ivy says something that makes us laugh. "Over here," she says, "over here is where we'll put the Christmas tree." She touches the edge of one of the casement windows, brushes it with the side of her hand and says, "It's hard to believe that people could live in such a beautiful house and be unhappy."

For a moment there's silence, and then Marge says, "We could put in an offer tonight. I don't think it's too late. What do you think?"

And now, suddenly it's the next evening, and Ivy and I are flying back to Toronto. Here we are over the Rockies again, crossing them this time in darkness. Ivy sits with her head back, eyes closed, her shoulders so sharply her own; she's not quite asleep, but not quite awake either.

Our plane seems a fragile vessel, a piece of jewelry up here between the stars and the mountains. Flying through dark air like this makes me think that life itself is fragile. The miniature accidents of chromosomes can spread unstoppable circles of grief. A dozen words carelessly uttered can dismantle a marriage. A few gulps of oxygen are all that stand between us and death.

I wonder if Ivy is thinking, as I am, of the three months ahead, of how tumultuous they'll be. There are many things to think of when you move. For one, we'll have to put our own house up for sale. The thought startles me, though I've no idea why.

I try to imagine prospective buyers arriving for appointments, stepping through our front door with polite murmurs and a sharp eye for imperfections.

They'll work their way through the downstairs, the kitchen (renewed only four years ago), the living room (yes, a real fireplace, a good draft), the dining room (small, but you can seat ten in a pinch). Then they'll make their way upstairs (carpet a little worn, but with lots of wear left). The main bedroom is fair size (with good reading lamps built in, also bookshelves).

And then there's Christopher's bedroom.

Will the vibrations announce that here lived a child with little muscular control, almost no sight or hearing and no real consciousness as that word is normally perceived? He had, though – and perhaps the vibrations will acknowledge the fact – his own kind of valor and perhaps his own way of seeing the world. At least Ivy and I always rewallpapered his room every three years or so out of a conviction that he took some pleasure in the sight of ducks swimming on a yellow sea. Later, it was sail boats; then tigers and monkeys dodging jungle growth, then a wild op-art checkerboard; and then, the final incarnation, a marvelous green cave of leafiness with amazing flowers and impossible birds sitting in branches.

I can't help wondering if these prospective buyers, these people looking for God only knows what, if they'll enter this room and feel something of his fragile presence alive in a fragile world.

Well, we shall see. We shall soon see.

THE MERRY WIDOW

Margaret Drabble

Margaret Drabble (b. 1939) is a British novelist, biographer and critic. Awarded a CBE in 1980, Drabble was promoted to Dame Commander of the Order of the British Empire in the 2008 Birthday Honours. In 2011, she was awarded the Golden PEN Award by English PEN for a lifetime's distinguished service to literature.

When Philip died, his friends and colleagues assumed that Elsa would cancel the holiday. Elsa knew that this would be their assumption. But she had no intention of cancelling. She was determined upon the holiday. During Philip's unexpectedly sudden last hours, and in the succeeding weeks of funeral and condolence and letters from banks and solicitors, it began to take an increasingly powerful hold upon her imagination. If she were honest with herself, which she tried to be, she had not been looking forward to the holiday while Philip was alive: it would have been yet another dutifully endured, frustrating, saddening attempt at reviving past pleasures, overshadowed by Philip's increasing ill health and ill temper. But without Philip, the prospect brightened. Elsa knew that she would have to conceal her growing anticipation, for it was surely not seemly for so recent a widow to look forward so eagerly to something as mundane as a summer holiday – although it was not, she reasoned with herself, as though she were contemplating an extravagant escapade. Their plans had been modest enough – no Swans tour of the Greek isles, no luxury hotel, not even a little family pension with check tablecloths and local wine in the Dordogne, but a fortnight in a rented cottage in Dorset. A quiet fortnight in late June. An unambitious arrangement, appropriate for such a couple as Philip and Elsa, Elsa and Philip.

Perhaps, she thought, as she threw away old socks and parcelled suits for Oxfam and the Salvation Army, as she cancelled subscriptions to scholarly periodicals, perhaps she should try to imply to these well-meaning acquaintances that she felt a spiritual *need* to go to Dorset, a need for solitude, for privacy, a need to recover in tranquillity and new surroundings from the shock (however expected a shock) of Philip's death? And indeed, such an implication would not be so far from the truth, except for the fact that the emotion she expected to experience in Dorset was not grief, but joy. She needed to be alone, to conceal from prying eyes her relief, her delight in her new freedom and, yes, her joy.

This was unseemly, but it was so. She had been absolutely fed up to the back teeth with Philip, she said to herself, gritting those teeth tightly as she wrote to increase the standing order for oil delivery, as she rang the plumber to arrange to have a shower attachment fitted to the bathroom tap. Why on earth shouldn't she have a shower attachment, at her age, with her pension and savings? Her jaw ached with retrospective anger. How mean he had become, how querulous, how determined to thwart every pleasure, to interfere with every friendship. Thanks to Philip, she had no friends left, and that was why she was looking forward with a voluptuous, sensuous, almost feverish longing to the delights of solitude. To get away, away from all these ruined relationships, these false smiles, these old tweed suits and pigeonholes full of papers – to be alone, not to have to pretend, to sleep and wake alone, unobserved.

It had not been Philip's fault, she told others, that he had become 'difficult'. It had been the fault of the illness. It had been bad luck, to be struck down like that when not yet sixty, bad luck to have such constant nagging pain, bad luck to be denied one's usual physical exercise and pleasures, one's usual diet. But of course in her heart she thought it *was* Philip's fault. Illness had merely accentuated his selfishness, his discreet malice, his fondness for putting other people in their place. Illness gave him excuses for behaving badly – but he had *always* behaved badly. He had seized upon illness as a gift, had embraced it as his natural state. When younger, he had made efforts to control his tongue, his witticisms at the expense of others, his desire to prove the rest of the world ignorant, foolish, ill-mannered. Illness had removed the controls, had given him licence. He had seemed to enjoy humiliating her in public, complaining about her behind her back, undermining her when they sat alone together watching television. It had reached the stage where she could not express the slightest interest in any television programme without his launching an attack on her taste, her interests, her habits of mind. If she watched the news, she was news-obsessed, media-obsessed, brain-washed into submission by the news-madness of the programme planners; if she watched tennis or athletics or show-jumping, he would lecture her on the evils of competitive sport; if she watched wildlife documentaries, he would mock her for taking an interest in badgers and butterflies when she ought to be attending to the problems of the inner cities; if she watched a comedy series, he would call her escapist, and the comedy would be attacked as cosy middle-class fantasy or as a glorification of working-class subculture. Whatever she watched was wrong, and if she watched nothing – why, she was a television snob, unable to share the simple pleasures of Everyman. Night after night, at an oblique angle, through the small screen, he had abused her. It was not television he hated, it was her.

There was no television in Dorset. Apologetically, the owners of the little Mill House had explained that the valley was too deep for good reception, the picture quality too poor to make it worth providing a set. Good, Philip had said, but he had not meant it. If he had lived, if he had been alive to go on this Dorset holiday, he would undoubtedly have found some devious way to complain about its absence. Her lack of conversation, perhaps, would have been trundled out: better a mindless television programme, he would have declared, than your small talk, your silences.

Dead he was, now, and there would be no complaints. No television, and no complaints. There would be silence.

The evening before her departure, Elsa Palmer sat alone in the drawing-room with a tray of bread and cheese and pickle, and tomato salad, and milk chocolate digestive biscuits, and a pile of road maps, and her bird book, and her butterfly book, and her flower book, and her Pevsner. The television was on, but she was not watching it. She ate a bit of cheese, and wrote down road numbers in an orderly way. A10, A30, A354. There didn't seem to be any very obvious way of getting to Dorset from Cambridge, but that made the exercise of plotting a route all the more entertaining. She would pass through towns she did not know, get stuck in high streets she had never seen, drive past hedgerows banked with unfamiliar flowers. Alone, with her car radio. If she took a wrong turning, nobody would reprimand her. If she chose to listen to Radio 2, nobody would know. She could stop for a cup of coffee, she could eat a sandwich from her knee and drop crumbs on her skirt. And, at the end of the journey, there would be the Mill House, where nothing would remind her of Philip. She would lose herself in the deep Dorset countryside, so different from these appalling, over-farmed, open East Anglian wastes. There would be a whole fortnight of walkings and wanderings, of scrambling up coastal paths and rambling through woods, of collecting specimens and identifying them from her books in the long, light, solitary evenings. Unobserved, uncriticized.

Philip, of late, had taken increasingly strongly against her passion for identifications. 'What's in a name?' he would say, when she tried to remember a variety of sweet pea, or to spot a distant little brown bird at the end of the garden. As he always beat her down in argument by sheer persistence (and anyway, was it fair to argue with an ill man?) she had never been able to defend her own pleasure in looking things up in reference books. It had seemed a harmless pleasure, until Philip attacked it. Harmless, innocent, and proper for the wife of a university lecturer. An interest in flowers and butterflies. What could be wrong with that? By some sleight of reasoning he had made it seem sinister, joyless, life-denying. He had made her feel it to be a weakness, a symptom of a character defect. She would never work out quite how he had managed it.

The Lulworth Skipper. A local little butterfly that haunts Lulworth Cove. She looked at its portrait and smiled approvingly. Yes, she would walk along the Dorset Coast Path, with the Ordnance Survey map in her pocket, and go to Lulworth, and search for the Lulworth Skipper. And if she did not find it, nobody would know she had been defeated. Her pleasure would be her own, her disappointment her own.

Marriage has warped me, thought Elsa Palmer the next day, as she dawdled through Biggleswade. Marriage is unnatural, thought Elsa Palmer, as she stopped at the red light of some roadworks ini Aylesbury.

Marriage and maternity. She thought of her children, her

grandchildren. They had all attended the funeral, dutifully. She had found herself bored by them, irritated with them. After years and years of cravenly soliciting their favours, of begging them to telephone more often, of blackmailing them into coming for Christmas (or, lately, into inviting herself and Philip for Christmas), she now, suddenly, had found herself bored, had admitted herself to be bored. Stuart was a slob, Harriet was a pedantic chip off the old block (and always ill, my God, what stories of migraines and backaches, and she was only twenty-nine) and even young Ben had been incredibly tedious about his new car. And the grandchildren – whining, sniffing, poking their noses, kicking the furniture, squabbling, with their awful London accents and their incessant demands for sweets. Spoiled brats, the lot of them. Elsa smiled, comfortably, to herself, as she sailed through the landscape, divinely, enchantingly, rapturously alone. The weather responded to her mood; the sun shone, huge white clouds drifted high, vast shadows fell on the broad trees and the green-gold trees. An Indian summer, in June.

She had cautioned herself against disappointment at her journey's end; could the mill really be as charming as it appeared in its photographs? Was there some undisclosed flaw, some blot in the immediate landscape, some pylon or pig farm on its doorstep? Maybe, maybe: but some charm it must surely have, and the description of the little river flowing through the house and the garden, dividing the front garden from the little paddock at the back, could not be wholly fictitious. There were trout in the stream, she was assured. She pictured herself reclining in a deckchair, lying on a rug on the grass, reading a book, sipping a drink, looking up every now and then to gaze at the trout in the shallows, the waving weed. Inexpressibly soothing, she found this image of herself.

And the mill, when finally she arrived in the late afternoon, was no disappointment. It was smaller than it looked in the photographs, but houses always are, and it was right on the road, but the road was a small road, a country road, a delightful road, and she liked the way the garden gate opened onto a flinty courtyard where she parked her car. Rustic, unpretentious. A little lawn, with a wooden table; creepers growing up the house; a nesting blackbird watching anxiously, boldly, curiously; and beyond the lawn, the little river, the River Cerne itself, which flowed right through what was to be, for a whole fortnight, her own little property. The border was paved, and next to the idle mill wheel was a low stone wall, warm from the day's sun. She sat on it, and saw the promised trout flicker. It was all that she had hoped. There was a little bridge over the river, leading to the tree-shaded, thickly hedged paddock, part also of her property. You can sit there, the owners had assured her, quite out of sight of the road. If you don't like to sit down on the lawn at the front, they had said, it's quite private, through the back.

Quite private. She savoured the concept of privacy. She would save her exploration of it until she had collected the key and been shown round, until she had unpacked and made herself at home.

The interior of the house, as displayed to her by Mrs Miller from the village, was perhaps a little too rustic-smart: she was introduced to a shining wooden kitchen table and benches with diamond-shaped holes carved in them, a lot of glossy bright brown woodwork, an open light wooden staircase up to an upper floor and a semi-galleried sitting-room, a brass horseshoe and a brass kettle, and a disconcerting fox's mask grinning down from a wall. It was all newly decorated, spick and span. But the millstone was still there, and the ancient machinery of the mill could still be seen in the back rooms of the house, and through the heart of the house flowed the noisy, companionable sound of water. Elsa liked it all very much. She even liked the varnished wood and the fox's mask. Philip would have hated them, would have been full of witticisms about them, but she liked them very much. They were not to her taste, but she felt instantly at home with them. 'It's lovely,' she said, brightly, to Mrs Miller, hoping Mrs Miller would take herself off as soon as she had explained the intricacies of the electricity meter and revealed the contents of the kitchen cupboards. 'Oh, I'm sure I'll find everything I need,' she said, noting that milk, bread and butter had been provided. She was touched by the thoughtfulness of her absent landlords.

Mrs Miller vanished, promptly, tactfully. Elsa Palmer was alone. She wandered from room to room, examining the objects that make themselves at home in holiday cottages – an earthenware jug of dried flowers, a songbook open on the piano, a Visitors' Book, an umbrella-stand, a children's tricycle under the stairs, a stone hot-water bottle, a clock in a glass case, a print of a hunting scene. They made her feel amazingly irresponsible. She felt that for the first time for years she had no housekeeping cares in the world. She could live on Kit Kat or KiteKat and no one would comment. She could starve, and no one would care. Contemplating this freedom, she unpacked her clothes and laid them neatly in empty, paper-lined, mothballed, impersonal drawers, and made up the double bed in the low-ceilinged bedroom, and went downstairs. It was early evening. She could hear the sound of the mill stream. She unpacked her groceries: eggs, cheese, long-life milk, tins of tuna fish, onions, potatoes, a little fruit. A bottle of gin, a bottle of white wine, a few bottles of tonic.

With a sense of bravado, she poured herself a gin and tonic. Philip had always poured the drinks; in his lifetime she would no more have thought of pouring one for herself than she would have expected Philip to make an Irish stew. The thought of Philip struggling with an Irish stew struck her as irresistibly comic; she smliled to herself. Now Philip was dead, she could laugh at him at last. She adorned her gin and tonic with ice cubes and a slice of lemon. A merry widow.

The evening sun was mellow. It was one of the longest days of the year. She wandered out into the flinty courtyard and over to the little lawn. She sat on the low stone wall and sipped her drink. She watched a flock of long-tailed finches fluttering in a small tree. Tomorrow, if they returned, she would sit here and identify them. She thought they would return.

The weeds swayed and poured in the stream. Water crowfoot blossomed above the surface, its roots trailing. Trout rippled, stationary yet supple and subtle, motionless yet full of movement.

She sat and gazed as water and time flowed by. Then she rose and wandered over the little hidden wooden bridge to inspect the unseen paddock on the far side. As she crossed the bridge, a startled moorhen dislodged itself with great noise and splashing and she saw some chicks scrambling clumsily upstream. And there was the paddock – a long, triangular plot of land, planted with fruit trees, bordered on one side by a fence, on another by the stream and on the third by a high, irregular, ancient row of mixed tree and hedge, at the bottom of which ran another little tributary. The paddock, she discovered, was a sort of island. The music of the water was soft and reassuring. The grass was deep, knee-high. The stream was fringed with all sorts of wild flowers, growing in rich profusion and disorder – forget-me-not, valerian, comfrey, buttercup and many other species that she could not at once distinguish. A wild garden, overgrown, secret, mysterious. Nobody could overlook her here.

She sipped her gin and tonic and wandered through the long grasses in the cool of the evening. A deep, healing peace possessed her. She stood on the little triangular point of her island, where the two streams met, and stood on a tree root at the end of her promontory, gazing at a view that could not have altered much in a thousand years. A field of wheat glowed golden to her left, rising steeply to a dark purple wood. Long shadows fell. A small, steep view. The small scale of her little kingdom was peculiarly comforting. A few hundred yards of modest wilderness. She would sit here, perhaps, in the afternoons. Perhaps she would sleep a little, on a rug, under a fruit tree, in the sun, listening to the sound of water. Pleasant plans formed themselves in her imagination as she wandered slowly back and over the little bridge, plucking as she went a spray of blue forget-me-not. She would look it up, after her supper, in the flower book. How impatient Philip would have been with such a plan! It's *obviously* a forget-me-not, *anyone* can see it's a forget-me-not, Philip would have said, and anyway, who cares what it is? But he would have put it more wittily than that, more hurtfully than that, in words that, thank God, she did not have to invent for him. For he was not here, would never be there again.

Later, reading her flower book, examining the plant more closely, she discovered that it wasn't a forget-me-not at all. Its leaves were all wrong, and it was too tall. It was probably a borage, hairy borage – and after a while, she settled for green alkanet. *Anchusa sempervirens.* 'Small clusters of flat white-eyed bright blue flowers, rather like a forget-me-not or speedwell ...' Yes, that was it. *Rather like*. Rather like, but not identical. Similar, but not the same. This distinction delighted her. She would forget it, she knew, but for the moment it delighted her. She was not very good at flowers, and forgot most of the names she so painstakingly established. At her age she found it difficult to retain new information, almost impossible to enlarge her store of certainties from the hundred

names she had learned, half a century ago, as a brownie in the
Yorkshire Dales. But the inability did not diminish her pleasure,
it increased it. Philip had never been able to understand this.
The safety, the comfort of the familiar wellthumbed pages; the
safety, the comfort of the familiar process of doubt, comparison,
temporary certainty. Yes, there it was. Green alkanet.

Her dreams that night were violent and free. Horses raced
through dark fields, waterfalls plunged over crags, clouds heaped
ominously in a black sky. But when she woke, the morning was
serene and blue and filled with birdsong. She made herself a mug of
coffee and sat outside, watching the odd car pass, the village bus,
an old woman walking a dog. She planned her day. She would walk
the mile and a half into the village, do a little shopping, visit the
church, buy a newspaper, wander back, read her novel, eat a little
lunch, then go and lie on a rug on the long grass in the paddock.
The next day, she would be more ambitious perhaps, she would go
for a real walk, a mapped walk. But today, she would be quiet. The
luxury of knowing that nothing and no one could interfere with her
prospect made her feel momentarily a little tearful. Had she really
been so unhappy for so long? She saw the little long-tailed finches
fluttering in the tree. They had returned to charm her.

Philip, she reflected, as she sat on the wall reading, would not
have approved her choice of novel. She was reading a Margery
Allingham omnibus, nostalgically, pointlessly. Philip had despised
detective stories. He had mocked her pleasure in them. And indeed
they *were* a bit silly, but that was the point of them. Yes, that
was the point. After lunch, she took Margery Allingham into the
paddock, with a rug and her sunhat, and lay under an apple tree.
Impossible to explain, to the young, the satisfaction of sleeping
in the afternoon. How can you *enjoy* being asleep, her children
used to ask her. Now they too, parents themselves, were glad of
a siesta, of an afternoon nap. Elsa lay very still. She could hear
the moorhen with its chicks. She lifted her eyes from the page and
saw a little brown water rat swimming upstream. A fringe of tall
plants and weeds shimmered and blurred before her eyes. Sedges,
reeds, cresses ... yes, later she would look them all up. She nodded,
drooped. She fell asleep.

After an hour she woke, from dreams of grass and gardens, to find her dream continuing. She was possessed by a great peace. She lay there, gazing at the sky. She could feel her afflictions, her irritations, her impatiences leaving her. They loosened their little hooks and drifted off. She would be redeemed, restored, forgiven.

The day passed smoothly into the evening, and gin and tonic, and the identification of long-tailed finches, and a reading of Pevsner. She marked churches she might or might not visit, and smiled at Pevsner's use of the phrase 'life-size angels'. Who was to know the life size of an angel? Had it not once been thought that millions of them might dance on the point of a pin? Might not an angel be as tall as an oak tree, as vast and powerful as a leviathan?

She slept like an angel, and woke to another blue uninterrupted day of laziness. She decided not to make a long excursion. She would spend another whole day in the delights of her new terrain. She repeated her walk to the village of the previous morning, she returned to a little lunch, she took herself off again to the paddock with her rug and her Margery Allingham. Already she had established the charm of routine, of familiarity. She felt as though she had been here forever. She read, nodded, dozed, and fell asleep.

When she woke, half an hour later, she knew at once that she was no longer alone. She sat up hastily, guiltily, rearranging her hat, straightening her cotton skirt over her bare knees, reaching for her glasses, trying to look as though she had never dozed off in an afternoon in her life. Where was the intruder? Who had aroused her? Discreetly, but with mounting panic, she surveyed her triangle of paddock – and yes, there, at the far end, she could see another human being. An old man, with a scythe. She relaxed, slightly; a rustic old character, a gardener of some sort, annoying and embarrassing to have been caught asleep by him, but harmless enough, surely? Yes, quite harmless. What was he up to? She shaded her eyes against the afternoon sun.

He appeared to be cutting the long grass. The long grass of her own paddock.

Oh dear, thought Elsa Palmer to herself. What a shame. She wanted him to stop, to go away at once. But what right had she to stop him? He must belong to the Mill House, he was clearly fulfilling his horticultural obligations to his absentee employers.

Slowly, as she sat and watched him, the full extent of the disaster began to sink in. Not only was her solitude invaded, not only had she been observed asleep by a total stranger, but this total stranger was even now in the act of cutting back the very foliage, the very grasses that had so pleased her. She watched him at work. He scythed and sawed. He raked and bundled. Could he see her watching him? It made her feel uncomfortable, to watch this old man at work, in the afternoon, on a hot day, as she sat idling with Margery Allingham on a rug. She would have to get up and go. Her paddock was ruined, at least for this afternoon. Furtively she assembled her possessions and began to creep away back to the house. But he spotted her. From the corner of the triangle, a hundred yards and more away, he spotted her. He saluted her with an axe and called to her. 'Nice day,' he called. 'Not disturbing you, am I?'

'No, no, of course not,' she called back, faintly, edging away, edging back towards the little wooden bridge. Stealthily she retreated. He had managed to hack only a few square yards; it was heavy going, it would take him days, weeks to finish off the whole plot ...

Days, weeks. That evening, trapped in her front garden, on her forecourt, she saw him cross her bridge, within yards of her, several times, with his implements, with his wheelbarrows full of rubbish. She had not dared to pour herself a gin and tonic; it did not seem right. Appalled, she watched him, resisting her impulse to hide inside her own house. On his final journey, he paused with his barrow. 'Hot work,' he said, mopping his brow. He was a terrible old man, gnarled, brown, toothless, with wild white hair. 'Yes, hot work,' she faintly agreed. What was she meant to do? Offer him a drink? Ask him in? Make him a pot of tea? He stood, resting on his barrow, staring at her.

'Not in your way, am I?' he asked.

She shook her head.

'On your own, are you?' he asked. She nodded, then shook her head. 'A peaceful spot,' he said.

'Yes,' she said.

'I'll be back in the morning,' he said. But, for the moment, did not move. Elsa stood, transfixed. They stared at one another. Then he sighed, bent down to tweak out a weed from the gravel, and moved slowly, menacingly on.

Elsa was shattered. She retired into her house and poured herself a drink, more for medicine than pleasure. Could she trust him to have gone? What if he had forgotten something? She lurked indoors for twenty minutes, miserably. Then, timidly, ventured out. She crept back across the bridge to inspect the damage he had done at the far end of the paddock. Well, he was a good workman. He had made an impression on nature; he had hacked and tidied to much effect. Cut wood glared white, severed roots in the river bank bled, great swathes of grass and flowers and sedge lay piled in a heap. He had made a devastation. And at this rate, it would take him a week, a fortnight, to work his way round. To level the lot. If that was his intention, which it must be. I'll be back in the morning, he had said. Distractedly plucking at sedges, she tried to comfort herself. She could go for walks, she could amuse herself, further afield, she could lie firmly in her deckchair on the little front lawn. She had a right. She had paid. It was her holiday.

Pond sedge. *Carex acutiformis*. Or great pond sedge, *Carex riparia*? She gazed at the flower book, as night fell. It did not seem to matter much what kind of sedge it was. Carnation sedge, pale sedge, drooping sedge. As Philip would have said, who cared? Elsa drooped. She drooped with disappointment.

Over the next week the disappointment intensified. Her worst fears were fulfilled. Day by day, the terrible old man returned with his implements, to hack and spoil and chop. She had to take herself out, in order not to see the ruination of her little kingdom. She went for long walks, along white chalky ridges, through orchid-spotted shadows, through scrubby little woods, past fields of pigs, up Roman camps, along the banks of other rivers, as her own river was steadily and relentlessly stripped and denuded. Every evening she crept out to inspect the damage. The growing green diminished, retreated, shrank. She dreaded the sight of the old man with the scythe. She dreaded the intensity of her own dread. Her peace of mind was utterly destroyed. She cried, in the evenings, and wished she had a television set to keep her company. At night she dreamed of Philip. In her dreams he was always angry, he shouted at her and mocked her, he was annoyed beyond the grave.

*

I am going mad, she told herself, as the second week began, as she watched the old man once more cross the little bridge, after the respite of Sunday. I must have been mad already, to let so small a thing unbalance me. And I thought I was recovering. I thought I could soon be free. But I shall never be free, when so small a thing can destroy me.

She felt cut to the root. The sap bled out. She would be left a dry low stalk.

I might as well die, she said to herself, as she tried to make herself look again at her flower book, at her Pevsner, at her old companions. No others would she ever have, and these had now failed her.

Worst of all were the old man's attempts at conversation. He liked to engage her, despite her obvious reluctance, and she, as though mesmerized, could not bring herself to avoid him. It was the banality of these conversational gambits that delayed her recognition of his identity, his identification. They misled her. For he was an old bore, ready to comment on the weather, the lateness of the bus, the cricket. Elsa Palmer had no interest in cricket, did not wish to waste time conversing with an old man about cricket, but found herself doing so nevertheless. For ten minutes at a time she would listen to him as he rambled on about names that meant nothing to her, about matches of yesteryear. Why was she so servile, so subdued? What was this extremity of fear that gripped her as she listened?

He was hacking away her own life, this man with a scythe. Bundling it up, drying it out for the everlasting bonfire. But she did not let herself think this. Not yet.

It was on the last evening of his hacking and mowing that Elsa Palmer defeated the old man. She had been anticipating his departure with mixed feelings, for when he had finished the paddock would be flat and he would be victorious. He would have triumphed over Nature, he would depart triumphant, this old man of the river bank.

She saw him collect his implements for the last time, saw him pause with his wheelbarrow for the last time. Finished, now, for the year, he said. A good job done. Feebly, she complimented him, thinking of the poor shaven discoloured pale grass, the amputated stumps of the hedgerow. For the last time they discussed the weather and the cricket. He bade her goodbye, wished her a pleasant holiday. She watched him trundle his barrow through the gate, and across the road, and on, up the hillside, to the farm. He receded. He had gone.

And I, thought Elsa, am still alive.

She leaned on the gate and breathed deeply. She gathered her courage. She summoned all her strength.

I am still alive, thought Elsa Palmer. Philip is dead, but I, I have survived the Grim Reaper.

And it came to her as she stood there in the early evening fight that the old man was not Death, as she had feared, but Time. Old Father Time. *He* is the one with the scythe. She had feared that the old man was Death calling for her, as he had called for Philip, but no, he was only Time, Time friendly, Time continuing, Time healing. What had he said, of the paddock? 'Finished for the year,' he had said. But already, even now at this instant, it was beginning to grow again, and next June it would be as dense, as tangled, as profuse as ever, awaiting his timely, friendly scythe. Not Death, but Time. Similar, but not identical. She had named him, she had identified him, she had recognized him, and he had gone harmlessly away, leaving her in possession of herself, of her place, of her life. She breathed deeply. The sap began to flow. She felt it flow in her veins. The frozen water began to flow again under the bridge. The trout darted upstream. Yes, Old Father Time, *he* is the one with the scythe. Death is that other one. Death is the skeleton. Already, the grass was beginning to grow, the forget-me-nots and green alkanets were recovering.

Rejoicing, she went indoors, to her flower book. It glowed in the lamplight, it lived again. She settled down, began to turn the pages. Yes, there they were, forget-me-not, green alkanet – and what about brooklime? Was it a borage or a speedwell? She gazed at the colour plates, reprieved, entranced. Widespread and common in wet places. She turned the pages of her book, naming names. Time had spared her, Time had trundled his scythe away. Philip had been quite wrong, wrong all along. Elsa smiled to herself in satisfaction. Philip was dead because he had failed to recognize his adversary.

Death had taken him by surprise, death unnamed, unrecognized, unlabelled. Lack of recognition had killed Philip. Whereas I, said Elsa, I have conversed with and been spared by the Grim Reaper.

She turned the pages, lovingly. *Carex acutiformis, Carex riparia.* Tomorrow she would get to grips with the sedges. There were still plenty left, at the far end of the paddock, in the difficult corner by the overhanging alder. Tomorrow she would go and pick some specimens. And maybe, when she went back to Cambridge, she would enrol for that autumn course on Italian Renaissance Art and Architecture. She didn't really know much about iconography, but she could see that it had its interest. Well, so did everything, of course. Everything was interesting.

She began to wish she had not been so mean, so unfriendly. She really ought to have offered that old man a cup of tea.

THE I OF IT

A. M. Homes

A. M. Homes (b. 1961) is an American writer known for her controversial novels and unusual stories. She released her first collection of short stories, *The Safety of Objects*, in 1990. In 2013 she won the Women's Prize for Fiction with her novel *May We Be Forgiven*.

I am sitting naked on a kitchen chair, staring at it. My jeans and underwear are bunched up at my ankles. I walked from the bathroom to here, shuffling one foot in front of the other as though in shackles.

This has been a terrible week. I have been to the doctor. It is evening and I am sitting at my table staring down. I half wish that it had done what was threatened most in cases of severe abuse and fallen off. If I had found it lying loose under the sheets or pushed down to the bottom of the bed, rubbing up against my ankle, I could have picked it up lovingly, longingly. I could have brought it to eye level and given it the kind of inspection it truly deserved; I would have admired it from every angle, and then kept it in my dresser drawer.

I have an early memory of discovering this part of myself, discovering it as something neither my mother or sisters had. I played with it, knowing mine was the only one in the house, admiring its strength, enjoying how its presence seemed to mean so much to everyone. They were always in one way or another commenting on its existence from the manner in which they avoided it when they dried me from the tub to the way they looked out the car window when we stopped on long road trips and I stood by the highway releasing a thin yellow stream that danced in the wind.

This stab of maleness was what set me apart in a house of women; it was what comforted me most in that same house, knowing that I would never be like them.

From the time I first noticed that it filled me with warmth as I twirled my fingers over its top, I felt I had a friend. I walked to and from school and noisily up and down the stairs in our house, carrying it with me, slightly ahead of me, sharing its confidence.

I was a beautiful boy, or so they said. If I stood in my school clothes in front of the mirror I did not see anything special. My haircut was awful, my ears stuck out like telephone receivers, my eyes, while blue, seemed to disappear entirely when I smiled. And yet when I stood in front of the same mirror naked, I danced at the sight of myself, incredibly and inexcusably male.

I had no desire to be beautiful or good. Somehow, I suspect because it did not come naturally, I longed to be bad. I wanted to misbehave, to prove to myself that I could stand the sudden loss of my family's affection. I wanted to do terrible, horrible things and then be excused simply because I was a boy and that's what boys do, especially boys without fathers. I had the secret desire to frighten others. But I was forever a pink-skinned child, with straight blond hair, new khaki pants, white socks, and brown shoes.

My only true fear was of men. Having grown up without fathers, brothers, or uncles, men were completely unfamiliar to me, their naked selves only accidentally seen in bathhouses or public restrooms. They lived behind extra long zippers, hidden, like something in a freak show you'd pay to see once and only once. Their ungraceful parts hung deeply down, buried in a weave of hair that wound itself denser as it got closer as if to protect the world from the sight of such a monster. As I grew older, I taught myself to enjoy what was frightening.

I never wore underwear. Inside my jeans, it lay naked, rubbing the blue denim white. I went out in the evenings to roam among men, to display myself, to parade, to hunt. I was what everyone wanted, white, clean, forever a boy. They wanted to ruin me as a kind of revenge. It was part of my image to look unavailable but the truth was anyone could have me. I liked ugly men. Grab your partner and do-si-do. Change partners. I kissed a million of them. I opened myself to them and them to me. I walked down the street nearly naked with it in the lead. It was pure love in the sense of loving oneself and loving the sensation.

I was alive, incredibly, joyously. Even in the grocery store or the laundromat, every time someone's eyes passed over me, holding me for a second, I felt a boost that sent me forward and made me capable of doing anything. Every hour held a sensuous moment, a romantic possibility. Each person who looked at me and smiled, cared for me. To be treasured by those who weren't related, to whom I meant nothing, was the highest form of a compliment.

Men, whose faces I didn't recognize, bent down to kiss me as I sat eating lunch in sidewalk cafes. I kissed them back and whispered, It was good seeing you. And when my lunch dates asked who that was, I simply smiled.

I felt celebrated. Every dream was a possibility. It was as though I would never be afraid again. I remember being happy.

I look down on it and begin to weep. I do not understand what has happened or why. I am sickened by myself, and yet cannot stand the sensation of being so revolted. It is me, I tell myself. It is me, as though familiarity should be a comfort.

I remember when the men I met were truly strangers; our private parts went off in search of each other like dogs on a leash sniffing each other while the owners look away. I remember still, after that, meeting a man, and looking at him, looking at him days and months in a row and each time loving him.

I feel like I should wear rubber gloves for fear of touching myself or someone else. I have never felt so dangerous. I am weeping and it frightens me.

A friend told me about a group of men who make each other feel better, more hopeful, good about their bodies.

I picture a room full of men, sitting on folding chairs. They begin as any sort of meeting that welcomes strangers; they go around the room, first names only. They talk a little bit, and then finally, as though the talking is the obligatory introductory prayer, the warning of what is to follow, the cue to begin the incantation, they slowly take off their clothing, sweaters and shoes first. They silently stand up, and drop their pants to the floor. The sight of a circle of naked men and folding chairs is exciting. Those who can, rise to the occasion and fire their poison jets into the air. It is wonderful. A great relief. They are saying something. They are angry. Men shuffle around in a circle doing it until they collapse. I imagine that one time someone died at a meeting. He came and he died. When he fell, the group used it as inspiration. They did it again, over him, and it was all so much better then.

I can no longer love. I cannot possess myself as I did before. I can never again possess it, as it possessed me.

I am in my apartment screaming at nothing. This is the most horrible thing that ever happened, I am furious. I deserve better than this. I am a good boy. Truly I am. I am sorry. I am so sorry.

I look down on it and it seems to look up at me. I want it to apologize for wanting the world, literally. I have the strongest desire to punish it, to whack it until it screams, beat it until it is bloody and runs off to hide, shaking in a corner, but I can't. I cannot turn my back so quickly, and besides it is already lying there pale and weak, as if it is dead.

I see sick men, friends that have shriveled into strangers, unwelcome in hospitals and at home. They can't think or breathe, and still as they go rattling towards death, it never loses an ounce, it lies fattened, untouched in the darkness between their legs. It is strikingly an ornament, a reminder of the past.

Should I ask for a divorce? A separation from myself on the grounds that this part of me that is more male than I alone could ever be has betrayed me. We no longer have anything in common except profound depression and disbelief. I have lost my best friend, my playmate from childhood, myself. I have lost what I loved most deeply. I wish to be compensated.

I let a napkin from the table fall across it, and then quickly whisk it away, *Voilà*, like I am doing a magic trick. I look down upon my lap as if expecting to see a bunch of flowers or a white rabbit in its place.

I remember the first man who unzipped my pants while I stood motionless, eyes turned down. I allowed myself to peek, to see it in his hand.

"It is a beautiful thing," he said, lifting it like a treasure and touching it gently.

I kick off my jeans and run from room to room. I look out onto the city that once seemed so big and has now shrunken so that it is no more than a garden surrounding my apartment. I stand naked in the window, my hands flat against the glass. My reflection is clear.

There is no escaping myself. My lips press against the window. I am a beautiful boy. I feel the familiar warmth that rises when I am being taken in. In the apartment directly across from mine I see a man watching me, his hand upon himself. He seems wonderful through the glass, someone I could be with forever. He smiles. I slide the window open and lean towards the air. I am no longer safe, I step up onto the sill and spring forward into the night.

THE FIRST TIME

Marina Warner

Marina Warner (b. 1946) is a British writer of fiction, criticism and history. Her works include novels and short stories as well as studies of art, myths, symbols and fairytales. Her 1988 novel, *The Lost Father*, was shortlisted for the Man Booker Prize and she won the 2012 National Book Critics Circle Award for her non-fiction work, *Stranger Magic*. Warner was elected a Fellow of the Royal Society of Literature in 1984 and she was awarded a CBE in 2008.

The serpent had decided to diversify; the market economy demanded ir. Jeans, soft drinks, bicycles and sunglasses had learned to present themselves in subtly different guises; so could he.

He took a training course in nutrition. In his first job (for he showed talent), he was issued with an instantly printed label identifying him as 'Lola – Trainee Customer Service Assistant', and he wangled himself a pitch on the Tropical Fruit stand in the Tropical Fruit promotion that was taking place in order to add a little cheer to the London winter.

To attract the customers' attention, the serpent now known as Lola was togged up in tropical splendour and he put on his deepest and brownest syrupy voice to match. There were OAPS with plastic shopping bags on wheels and hair in their noses; they tasted the little cubes of fragrant juicy this and that which Lola had cut up and flagged with their proper name and country of origin, but one said he would think about it, dear, and another made a face and said the stringy bits were too stringy. Lola wasn't sure the game was worth the candle in their case. She was after brighter prizes. The serpent in her liked fresh material; he hoped for a challenge. (Though pity, it would turn out after all, wasn't unknown to him.)

Then Lola spotted a candidate: a likely lass, a young one made just as she fancied, quite ready for pleasure, pleasure of every sort, a hard green bright slip of a girl, barely planted but taking root, and so she held out in her direction a nifty transparent plastic cup like a nurse's for measuring out dosages in hospital, with one of the tasty morsels toothpicked and labelled inside it, and urged her to eat. (She was speaking aloud in the new soft brown demerara voice, but under her breath she was cooing and hissing in another voice altogether which she hoped her young shopper would listen to, secretly. This was a trick the serpent had perfected over centuries of practice.)

'Come here, my little girly, I have just the thing for a cold day, bring some sunshine back into your life.

(I know what it's like, it's written all over you. He fucked you to death three days ago – oh, is it a whole week? – and you haven't heard from him since. Your face is pale, your brow is wan and you can't understand what you did wrong. Well, you can tell me all about it)

'There's nothing Lola your Trainee Customer Service Assistant can't provide. It's Tropical Fruit week – just move over this way – we have passion fruit and pawpaw (that's papaya by another name) and prickly pear and pitahaya and guava and tamarillo and phylaris and grenadilla. Not to mention passion fruit. Each one has been flown here from the lands of milk and honey where they grow naturally, as in the original garden of paradise, and they're full of just that milk and honey, I'm telling you, you can hear the palm trees bending in the breeze on the beach and the surf breaking in creamy froth on the sand and they reach the parts other things don't reach

(the tingly bits, the melting bits and rushes-to-the head and the rushes to places elsewhere than the head – well I shan't go on, but your troubles are at an end if you just come a little bit closer, so I can pick up the signals in your dear little fluttering heart, my sweet, and whisper in your ear)

'As I say, it's Tropical Fruit week and this is the Tropical Fruit stand! With a dozen different varieties of fruit from all over the world, many new, exciting and delicious flavours for you to sample, and

> (let me add this under my breath so only you can hear –
> they all have different powers they can work wonders in
> all kinds of different ways – they're guaranteed to fix up
> your little problems before you can snap your fingers and
> say What the hell, and what the hell, I know all about that,
> I know the hell you're in, believe me.
>
> And I also know – I do – how to stop it hurting, my
> dear little one)

'I should know, because I'm fresh from the Healthy Eating consultancy course in our company headquarters in Stanton St James, Gloucestershire. We were given an intensive fortnight of nutritional experience, and so there's nothing I can't tell you now about fruit–'

And the serpent, to his great joy, saw that the young girl was getting interested and coming closer, with her shopping list crumpled under one hand on the bar of the supermarket trolley and the other twiddling a strand of her hair near her chin, as she drew near to look at Lola's spread of little plastic cups with pieces of fruit in each one, so close that Lola could hear her thinking,

i was all clenched up cos i was scared it's not everyday i do it you know in fact i don't do it very often though looking at me you might think so and i like to make out i'm a one cos otherwise you look a bit of a wimp don't you i mean everyone else is doing it, aren't they? and my mother said keep smiling the men don't like scenes they don't like glooms if you want to drive a man away just keep that down at the mouth look on your face and the wind'll change men don't like a woman all down in the dumps who'd want to spend a minute with you it'd be like passing the time of day with a ghoul

And Lola took charge of the situation, it was her job to bring a little sunshine back into winter; pleasure was her speciality. So she began,

'Take mango for instance, now the instructions say, "Make sure the rind is rosy-yellow and slightly yielding to the touch – green mangoes are inedible." Just like it says there, on the label, a mango, when it's properly ripe and ready, is full and juicy and its sweetness runs all over your hands and gives off this deep rich scent –'

(I don't have to go on, do I? A good man is going to know that and if he don't know it, he's no good and you can drop him, my sweet, and find another one who understands these things. The first point you must get into your little head, sweetheart, is that if you were clenched up like you said it wasn't anybody's fault but his –)

i tried to be lighthearted and cheerful while it was going on but it kept getting to me all the same and making me sad, sex does that to you it lifts you up but it doesn't last it drops you down again from a great height and now i can't concentrate on anything cos i keep seeing him doing things to me and me doing them back i was trying to keep a brave face on it but i know i was disappointing not passionate like he knows it from other girls it wasn't new to him like it was to me he knows that i could sense it but i don't like the neighbours to hear anything cos when they're at it and i hear and mum is out and i'm alone it makes me feel funny

Lola carries on, talking over the girl's thoughts, which are coming across to her loud and clear. 'Take this guava for instance,' she tells her. 'It's in perfect condition. Sometimes when you pierce one of these fruits, they're not quite ripe yet. You have to wait for the ones that aren't ready, you can't rush them. But the ones that are overripe, gone soft and spongy, you have to throw those away ...'

(don't you worry any more, my little girly, you'll be fine. You're just lacking confidence, that's all it is, and you wanted to please him, when really you should just think how much pleasure there's in it for you. Never forget that, it's the first rule. My sweet little girly, you're a perfect little girly and he's a fool if I know men – and I do – forget him and find another one who'll appreciate you)

it's a bit shocking, really, i didn't expect such a mess, both of us leaking this and that, i did melt at first, stickiness afterwards he seemed to like it, he held on to me tight, he asked me if i cared for him and i said i did; and his heart was thumping and it seemed like a promise it was a promise, it must have been some kind of a promise ... but then nothing not another sight of him not a word what did I do wrong what can i do now

> (when he comes back and he will you know he'll be round with his tongue hanging out you must be ready so come closer still – you are a sweet and tender pretty little girl, aren't you, yum yum, no wonder he liked you he's probably just frightened of coming back because your hold on him's too strong believe me, I know. You're at just that dangerous age, and your hair smells good, vanilla and grass and peach and a trace of sweat, that's good, very good –)

The young girl's head was very near Lola now, as she bent over the little measuring cups with their pink and yellow and crimson offerings, sniffing at this one and that one, daring, daring to taste one.

'Peaches don't count as Tropical but they have restorative powers too, I'm telling you, and now we can grow them all the year round, that's the wonder of modern agronomy – agronomy – the science of growing foods

> (anyhow, darling, just any one of these Tropical Fruits will give him what he wants from you and then you'll have him in the palm of your hand. Try slipping him a fat cactus fruit, with the spines cut off, mind – or if you're ambitious, try pawpaw – papaya by another name as I was saying and it's no accident that this is papa-fare, ha ha. It's a fruit for daddy's girls, firm and slippery, yes!)

'and its juice makes an excellent meat tenderiser if you want to add it to a marinade or you can just open it and eat it all, yes, seeds and all – Or there's tamarillo here, it's full of rich pulp under the tight shiny skin and the flavour's sweet and sour when it's ripe, and has many culinary uses, in desserts as well as savoury dishes

... Eat it when the skin's turned a deep red, and the fruit's firm but yielding to gentle pressure ...'

> (that's right, you start giggling, you'll be fine even if it's all over with him there'll soon be another one – I'm telling you, live for passion there's nothing better and that's the second rule and all men and women are fools who don't grasp it)

it began like that he said, Trust me, and then you open up first your mouth and his mouth and then, well ... sometimes i envy men, they know what other women are like, i wonder if i'm like the other ones, he must have had lots he felt like he knew what he was doing, i was a bit scared, he's older than me just two years but it makes a difference and he's got a reputation at school that's what made me interested in the first place so i bit down on my fears, other girls do it all the time i must get on with mum's shopping it might give that assistant ideas, my hanging around here maybe i should try one of her fruits she looks silly standing there in that tropical outfit with the headcloth and the fruit earrings dangling and the bangles over her surgical gloves she's using a little sharp knife with these funny knobbly and lumpy fruits she's egging on to Customers, the OAPs with their shopping bags on wheels and their nose hair sprouting, so now it's my turn and i point to one of the little plastic cups with the fruit inside on a toothpick and she's saying to me,

'Go on try, you're under no obligation to purchase – I don't even have the fruits here on my stand, you have to go to the fruit and veg. section and choose your own. We're here to educate the public, to raise the standards of nutrition and health in the households of this country, especially where there are children and young people, growing up

> (like you, my dear, so silky and soft and lovely with just that whiff of unwashed ...)

'There's pitahaya for you too – firm as a pear and slightly perfumed, like rose petals – it's refreshing! Here, you can eat it like a dessert fruit, you peel it like this, lengthways, the rind comes off smoothly, it's related to the prickly pear but this one hasn't got any prickles. Or you can slice it into salads – add a dash of colour to your salad bowl, keep the winter at bay with Tropical Fruit from the parts of the world where frost can't reach and the sun always shines, scoop out the pink flesh and taste the sunshine!'

we didn't use anything it seemed mean to ask him to as if i thought he was diseased or something so now i don't know i could be pregnant – are you happy to be pregnant? the ads ask – i could be i suppose – i can feel something inside me it's like a letter y it's either a sperm wriggling or it's one of those cells they go on about on the telly reproducing itself all wrong and giving me aids

(now that was silly very silly you can't have the pleasure that's due to you, my girl, if you're careless, that's the third rule. But if you bend your ear I'll let you in on the way to have fun – never do that again, this time you'll be all right, I can tell, I can see and hear things other people can't and)

'There's nothing like fresh fruit to build up your immune system, clean out your insides, keep you healthy and lean and full of energy ...

(as I say, you're in luck this time but don't try anything like that again)

'... in these days of pollution and other problems – I mean we've all wised up to the devastation of the rain forests and their connection to ... well, I shan't talk about meat-eating because we still have a butcher's counter here – all free range, of course – but anyway what with acid rain and the hole in the ozone layer and the thinning of the oxygen supply and the little creepy-crawly things out of the tap in your water – you need Fruit! Fresh fruit, goes straight to the immune system and kick-starts it into a new life ...'

Eventually, the serpent was successful: his fresh, young, sad target dropped her mother's shopping list somewhere on the floor of the supermarket and forgot everything that was on it and came home instead with

> 1 mango
> 1 pitahaya
> 2 pawpaws
> 4 guavas
> 2 tamarillos
> 6 passion fruit
> and 13p change

Her mother said, 'Where's the shopping I asked you to get?' And so her daughter told her about Lola, about the Tropical Fruit stand and Tropical Fruit week. She kept quiet, however, about some of the other matters that had passed between her and the sales assistant.

Her mother scolded, her mother railed: 'In my day, an apple a day kept the doctor away – now you have to have –' she picked up the guavas and the soft but firm mango and the tubular and prickle-free pitahaya and smooth and slippery pawpaw – 'What do you do with this stuff anyway?'

'I've brought the leaflet – look!'

'Apples were good enough for us, and they should be good enough for you. And when I write down a pound of apples on the shopping list I mean a pound of apples, I don't mean any of this fancy rubbish. Your generation doesn't understand the meaning of no – you just believe in self, self, self, you want mote, more, more. You think only of your own pleasure. You'll be the ruin of me. I don't know, I try to bring you up right ...'

'Plump and rounded or long and thin, it has a distinctive firmness of texture and delicacy of aroma ...' her daughter began, reading from the recipe leaflet provided, and she thought she heard her mother stifle a snort as she kept on with the Tropical Fruit week promotion package.

if he doesn't come back that lady was right i'll just find another one what she said made sense he thought he was something but was he anything to write home about anyhow i feel better about it already I'll go back to school and i'll just make out it meant nothing to me nothing and i don't care about him she was wicked she was strong i liked her

Lola was still at the stand, back in the shop, doing her patter, to other customers passing by:

'Guava, passion fruit, tamarillo! Let me just tell you exactly how you can put each one to good use –'

And meanwhile she was thinking,

(my little girly, you're young, you're inexperienced, but you'll soon know so much. You'll look back on this and you'll laugh or you won't even remember that you ever felt so pale and wan. In fact you might even look back and wish that you could feel something as sweet and real and true as this first-time pain you were feeling till I taught you the three principles of pleasure and set you on my famous primrose path)

The mother took the leaflet out of her daughter's hand and scanned it impatiently; and read:

For a happy and healthy life!
Take fresh fruit in season.
Squeeze.

INSIDE INFORMATION

Nicola Barker

Nicola Barker (b. 1966) is a British novelist and short story writer. Her novel, *Wide Open*, won the IMPAC Dublin Literary Award in 2000, and another, *Darkmans*, was shortlisted for the Man Booker Prize in 2007.

Martha's social worker was under the impression that by getting herself pregnant, Martha was looking for an out from a life of crime.

She couldn't have been more wrong.

'First thing I ever nicked,' Martha bragged, when her social worker was initially assigned to her, 'very first thing I ever stole was a packet of Lil-lets. I told the store detective I took them as a kind of protest. You pay 17½ per cent VAT on every single box. Men don't pay it on razors, you know, which is absolutely bloody typical.'

'But you stole other things, too, on that occasion, Martha.'

'Fags and a bottle of Scotch. So what?' she grinned. 'Pay VAT on those too, don't you?'

Martha's embryo was unhappy about its assignment to Martha. Early on, just after conception, it appealed to the higher body responsible for its selection and placement. This caused something of a scandal in the After-Life. The World-Soul was consulted – a democratic body of pinpricks of light, an enormous institution – which came, unusually enough, to a rapid decision.

'Tell the embryo,' they said, 'hard cheese.'

The embryo's social worker relayed this information through a system of vibrations – a language which embryos alone in the Living World can produce and receive. Martha felt these conversations only as tiny spasms and contractions.

Being pregnant was good, Martha decided, because store detectives were much more sympathetic when she got caught. Increasingly, they let her off with a caution after she blamed her bad behaviour on dodgy hormones.

The embryo's social worker reasoned with the embryo that all memories of the After-Life and feelings of uncertainty about placement were customarily eradicated during the trauma of birth. This was a useful expedient. 'Naturally,' he added, 'the nine-month wait is always difficult, especially if you've drawn the short straw in allocation terms, but at least by the time you've battled your way through the cervix, you won't remember a thing.'

The embryo replied, snappily, that it had never believed in the maxim that Ignorance is Bliss. But the social worker (a corgi in its previous incarnation) restated that the World-Soul's decision was final.

As a consequence, the embryo decided to take things into its own hands. It would communicate with Martha while it still had the chance and offer her, if not an incentive, at the very least a moral imperative.

Martha grew larger during a short stint in Wormwood Scrubs. She was seven months gone on her day of release. The embryo was now a well-formed foetus, and, if its penis was any indication, it was a boy. He calculated that he had, all things being well, eight weeks to change the course of Martha's life.

You see, the foetus was special. He had an advantage over other, similarly situated, disadvantaged foetuses. This foetus had Inside Information.

In the After-Life, after his sixth or seventh incarnation, the foetus had worked for a short spate as a troubleshooter for a large pharmaceutical company. During the course of his work and research, he had stumbled across something so enormous, something so terrible about the World-Soul, that he'd been compelled to keep this information to himself, for fear of retribution.

The rapidity of his assignment as Martha's future baby was, in part, he was convinced, an indication that the World-Soul was aware of his discoveries. His soul had been snatched and implanted in Martha's belly before he'd even had a chance to discuss the matter rationally. In the womb, however, the foetus had plenty of time to analyse his predicament. *It was a cover-up!* He was being gagged, brainwashed and railroaded into another life sentence on earth.

*

In prison, Martha had been put on a sensible diet and was unable to partake of the fags and the sherry and the Jaffa cakes which were her normal dietary staples. The foetus took this opportunity to consume as many vital calories and nutrients as possible. He grew at a considerable rate, exercised his knees, his feet, his elbows, ballooned out Martha's belly with nudges and pokes.

In his seventh month, on their return home, the foetus put his plan into action. He angled himself in Martha's womb, at just the right angle, and with his foot, gave the area behind Martha's belly button a hefty kick. On the outside, Martha's belly was already a considerable size. Her stomach was about as round as it could be, and her navel, which usually stuck inwards, had popped outwards, like a nipple.

By kicking the inside of her navel at just the correct angle, the foetus – using his Inside Information – had successfully popped open the lid of Martha's belly button like it was an old-fashioned pill-box.

Martha noticed that her belly button was ajar while she was taking a shower. She opened its lid and peered inside. She couldn't have been more surprised. Under her belly button was a small, neat zipper, constructed out of delicate bones. She turned off the shower, grabbed hold of the zipper and pulled it. It unzipped vertically, from the middle of her belly to the top. Inside she saw her foetus, floating in brine. 'Hello,' the foetus said. 'Could I have a quick word with you, please?'

'This is incredible!' Martha exclaimed, closing the zipper and opening it again. The foetus put out a restraining hand. 'If you'd just hang on a minute I could tell you how this was possible ...'

'It's so weird!' Martha said, closing the zipper and getting dressed.

Martha went to Tesco's. She picked up the first three items that came to hand, unzipped her stomach and popped them inside. On her way out, she set off the alarms – the bar-codes activated them, even from deep inside her – but when she was searched and scrutinized and interrogated, no evidence could be found of her hidden booty. Martha told the security staff that she'd consider legal action if they continued to harass her in this way.

When she got home, Martha unpacked her womb. The foetus,

squashed into a corner, squeezed up against a tin of Spam and a packet of sponge fingers, was intensely irritated by what he took to be Martha's unreasonable behaviour.

'You're not the only one who has a zip, you know,' he said. 'All pregnant women have them; it's only a question of finding out how to use them, from the outside, gaining the knowledge. But the World-Soul has kept this information hidden since the days of Genesis, when it took Adam's rib and reworked it into a zip with a pen-knife.'

'Shut it,' Martha said. 'I don't want to hear another peep from you until you're born.'

'But I'm trusting you,' the foetus yelled, 'with this information. It's my salvation!'

She zipped up.

Martha went shopping again. She shopped sloppily at first, indiscriminately, in newsagents, clothes shops, hardware stores, chemists. She picked up what she could and concealed it in her belly.

The foetus grew disillusioned. He re-opened negotiations with his social worker. 'Look,' he said, 'I know something about the World-Soul which I'm willing to divulge to my earth-parent Martha if you don't abort me straight away.'

'You're too big now,' the social worker said, fingering his letter of acceptance to the Rotary Club which preambled World-Soul membership. 'And anyway, it strikes me that Martha isn't much interested in what you have to say.'

'Do you honestly believe,' the foetus asked, 'that any woman on earth in her right mind would consider a natural birth if she knew that she could simply unzip?'

The social worker replied coldly: 'Women are not kangaroos, you cheeky little foetus. If the World-Soul has chosen to keep the zipper quiet then it will have had the best of reasons for doing so.'

'But if babies were unzipped and taken out when they're ready,' the foetus continued, 'then there would be no trauma, no memory loss. Fear of death would be a thing of the past. We could eradicate the misconception of a Vengeful God.'

'And all the world would go to hell,' the social worker said.

'How can you say that?'

The foetus waited for a reply, but none came.

Martha eventually sorted out her priorities. She shopped in Harrods and Selfridges and Liberty's. She became adept at slotting things of all conceivable shapes and sizes into her belly. Unfortunately, the foetus himself was growing quite large. After being unable to fit in a spice rack, Martha unzipped and addressed him directly. 'Is there any possibility,' she asked, 'that I might be able to take you out prematurely so that there'd be more room in there?'

The foetus stared back smugly. 'I'll come out,' he said firmly, 'when I'm good and ready.'

Before she could zip up, he added, 'And when I do come out, I'm going to give you the longest and most painful labour in Real-Life history. I'm going to come out sideways, doing the can-can.'

Martha's hand paused, momentarily, above the zipper. 'Promise to come out very quickly,' she said, 'and I'll nick you some baby clothes.'

The foetus snorted in a derisory fashion. 'Revolutionaries,' he said, 'don't wear baby clothes. Steal me a gun, though, and I'll fire it through your spleen.'

Martha zipped up quickly, shocked at this vindictive little bundle of vituperation she was unfortunate enough to be carrying. She smoked an entire packet of Marlboro in one sitting, and smirked, when she unzipped, just slightly, at the coughing which emerged.

The foetus decided that he had no option but to rely on his own natural wit and guile to foil both his mother and the forces of the After-Life. He began to secrete various items that Martha stole in private little nooks and crannies about her anatomy.

On the last night of his thirty-sixth week, he put his plan into action. In his arsenal: an indelible pen, a potato, a large piece of cotton from the hem of a dress, a thin piece of wire from the supports of a bra, all craftily reassembled. In the dead of night, while Martha was snoring, he gradually worked the zip open from the inside, and did what he had to do.

The following morning, blissfully unaware of the previous night's activities, Martha went out shopping to Marks and Spencer's. She picked up some Belgian chocolates and a bottle of port, took hold of her zipper and tried to open her belly. It wouldn't open. The zipper seemed smaller and more difficult to hold.

'That bastard,' she muttered, 'must be jamming it up from the inside.' She put down her booty and headed for the exit. On her way out of the shop, she set off the alarms.

'For Chrissakes!' she told the detective, 'I've got nothing on me!' And for once, she meant it.

Back home, Martha attacked her belly with a pair of nail scissors. But the zip wasn't merely jammed, it was meshing and merging and disappearing, fading like the tail end of a bruise. She was frazzled. She looked around for her cigarettes. She found her packet and opened it. The last couple had gone, and instead, inside, was a note.

> *Martha,* [the note said] *I have made good my escape, fully intact. I sewed a pillow into your belly. On the wall of your womb I've etched and inked an indelible bar-code. Thanks for the fags.*
>   *Love, Baby.*

'But you can't do that!' Martha yelled. 'You don't have the technology!' She thought she heard a chuckle, behind her. She span around. On the floor, under the table, she saw a small lump of afterbirth, tied up into a neat parcel by an umbilical cord. She could smell a whiff of cigarette smoke. She thought she heard laughter, outside the door, down the hall. She listened intently, but heard nothing more.

DESIDERATUS

Penelope Fitzgerald

Penelope Fitzgerald (1916–2000) was a Man Booker Prize-winning British novelist, poet, essayist and biographer. In 2008, *The Times* included her in a list of the '50 Greatest British Writers Since 1945' and, in 2012, the *Observer* named her final novel, *The Blue Flower*, as one of 'The 10 Best Historical Novels'. A collection of Fitzgerald's short stories, *The Means of Escape*, and a volume of her non-fiction writings, *A House of Air*, were published posthumously.

Jack Digby's mother never gave him anything. Perhaps, as a poor woman, she had nothing to give, or perhaps she was not sure how to divide anything between the nine children. His godmother, Mrs Piercy, the poulterer's wife, did give him something, a keepsake, in the form of a gilt medal. The date on it was September the 12th, 1663, which happened to be Jack's birthday, although by the time she gave it him he was eleven years old. On the back there was the figure of an angel and a motto, *Desideratus*, which, perhaps didn't fit the case too well, since Mrs Digby could have done with fewer, rather than more, children. However, it had taken the godmother's fancy.

Jack thanked her, and she advised him to stow it away safely, out of reach of the other children. Jack was amazed that she should think anywhere was out of the reach of his little sisters. 'You should have had it earlier, when you were born,' said Mrs Piercy, 'but those were hard times.' Jack told her that he was very glad to have something of which he could say, This is my own, and she answered, though not with much conviction, that he mustn't set too much importance on earthly possessions.

He kept the medal with him always, only transferring it, as the year went by, from his summer to his winter breeches. But anything you carry about with you in your pocket you are bound to lose sooner or later. Jack had an errand to do in Hending, but there was nothing on the road that day, neither horse nor cart, no hope of cadging a lift, so after waiting for an hour or so he began to walk over by the hill path.

After about a mile the hill slopes away sharply towards Watching, which is not a village and never was, only a single great house standing among its outbuildings almost at the bottom of the valley. Jack stopped there for a while to look down at the smoke from the chimneys and to calculate, as anyone might have done, the number of dinners that were being cooked there that day.

If he dropped or lost his keepsake he did not know it at the time, for as is commonly the case he didn't miss it until he got home again. Then he went through his pockets, but the shining medal was gone and he could only repeat, 'I had it when I started out.' His brothers and sisters were of no help at all. They had seen nothing. What brother or sister likes being asked such questions?

The winter frosts began and at Michaelmas Jack had the day off school and thought, I had better try going that way again. He halted, as before, at the highest point, to look down at the great house and its chimneys, and then at the ice under his feet, for all the brooks, ponds, and runnels were frozen on every side of him, all hard as bone. In a little hole or depression just to the left hand of the path, something no bigger than a small puddle, but deep, and by now set thick with greenish ice as clear as glass, he saw, through the transparency of the ice, at the depth of perhaps twelve inches, the keepsake that Mrs Piercy had given him.

He had nothing in his hand to break the ice. Well then, Jack Digby, jump on it, but that got him nowhere, seeing that his wretched pair of boots was soaked right through. 'I'll wait until the ice has gone,' he thought. 'The season is turning, we'll get a thaw in a day or two.'

On the next Sunday, by which time the thaw had set in, he was up there again, and made straight for the little hole or declivity, and found nothing. It was empty, after that short time, of ice and even of water. And because the idea of recovering the keepsake had occupied his whole mind that day, the disappointment made him feel lost, like a stranger to the country. Then he noticed that there was an earthenware pipe laid straight down the side of the hill, by way of a drain, and that this must very likely have carried off the water from his hole, and everything in it. No mystery as to where it led, it joined another pipe with a wider bore, and so down, I suppose, to the stable-yards, thought Jack. His Desideratus had been washed down there, he was as sure of that now as if he'd seen it go.

Jack had never been anywhere near the house before, and did not care to knock at the great kitchen doors for fear of being taken for a beggar. The yards were empty. Either the horses had been taken out to work now that the ground was softer or else – which was hard to believe – there were no horses at Watching. He went back to the kitchen wing and tried knocking at a smallish side entrance. A man came out dressed in a black gown, and stood there peering and trembling.

'Why don't you take off your cap to me?' he asked.

Jack took it off, and held it behind his back, as though it belonged to someone else.

'That is better. Who do you think I am?'

'No offence, sir,' Jack replied, 'but you look like an old schoolmaster.'

'I am a schoolmaster, that is, I am tutor to this great house. If you have a question to ask, you may ask it of me.'

With one foot still on the step, Jack related the story of his godmother's keepsake.

'Very good,' said the tutor, 'you have told me enough. Now I am going to test your memory. You will agree that this is not only necessary, but just.'

'I can't see that it has anything to do with my matter,' said Jack.

'Oh, but you tell me that you dropped this-or-that in such-and-such a place, and in that way lost what had been given to you. How can I tell that you have truthfully remembered all this? You know that when I came to the door you did not remember to take your cap off.'

'But that—'

'You mean that was only lack of decent manners, and shows that you come from a family without self-respect. Now, let us test your memory. Do you know the Scriptures?'

Jack said that he did, and the tutor asked him what happened, in the fourth chapter of the Book of Job, to Eliphaz the Temanite, when a vision came to him in the depth of the night.

'A spirit passed before his face, sir, and the hair of his flesh stood up.'

'The hair of his flesh stood up,' the tutor repeated. 'And now, have they taught you any Latin?' Jack said that he knew the word that had been on his medal, and that it was *Desideratus*, meaning long wished-for.

'That is not an exact translation,' said the tutor. Jack thought, he talks for talking's sake.

'Have you many to teach, sir, in this house?' he asked, but the tutor half closed his eyes and said, 'None, none at all. God has not blessed Mr Jonas or either of his late wives with children. Mr Jonas has not multiplied.'

If that is so, Jack thought, this schoolmaster can't have much work to do. But now at last here was somebody with more sense, a house-keeperish-looking woman, come to see why the side-door was open and letting cold air into the passages. 'What does the boy want?' she asked.

'He says he is in search of something that belongs to him.'

'You might have told him to come in, then, and given him a glass of wine in the kitchen,' she said, less out of kindness than to put the tutor in his place. 'He would have been glad of that, I daresay.'

Jack told her at once that at home they never touched wine. 'That's a pity,' said the housekeeper. 'Children who are too strictly prohibited generally turn out drunkards.' There's no pleasing these people, Jack thought.

His whole story had to be gone through again, and then again when they got among the servants in one of the pantries. Yet really there was almost nothing to tell, the only remarkable point being that he should have seen the keepsake clearly through almost a foot of ice. Still nothing was said as to its being found in any of the yards or ponds.

Among all the to-ing and fro-ing another servant came in, the man who attended on the master, Mr Jonas, himself. His arrival caused a kind of disquiet, as though he were a foreigner. The master, he said, had got word that there was a farm-boy, or a schoolboy, in the kitchens, come for something that he thought was his property.

'But all this is not for Mr Jonas's notice,' cried the tutor. 'It's a story of child's stuff, a child's mischance, not at all fitting for him to look into.'

The man repeated that the master wanted to see the boy.

The other part of the house, the greater part, where Mr Jonas lived, was much quieter, the abode of gentry. In the main hall Mr Jonas himself stood with his back to the fire. Jack had never before been alone or dreamed of being alone with such a person. What a pickle, he thought, my godmother, Mrs Piercy, has brought me into.

'I daresay you would rather have a sum of money,' said Mr Jonas, not loudly, 'than whatever it is that you have lost.'

Jack was seized by a painful doubt. To be honest, if it was to be a large sum of money, he would rather have that than anything. But Mr Jonas went on, 'However, you had better understand me more precisely. Come with me.' And he led the way, without even looking round to see that he was followed.

At the foot of the wide staircase Jack called out from behind, 'I think, sir, I won't go any further. What I lost can't be here.'

'It's poor-spirited to say "I won't go any further",' said Mr Jonas.

Was it possible that on these dark upper floors no one else was living, no one was sleeping? They were like a sepulchre, or a barn at the end of winter. Through the tall passages, over uneven floors, Mr Jonas, walking ahead, carried a candle in its candlestick in each hand, the flames pointing straight upwards. I am very far from home, thought Jack. Then, padding along behind the master of the house, and still twisting his cap in one hand, he saw in dismay that the candle flames were blown over to the left, and a door was open to the right.

'Am I to go in there with you, sir?'

'Are you afraid to go into a room?'

Inside it was dark and in fact the room probably never got much light, the window was so high up. There was a glazed jug and basin, which reflected the candles, and a large bed which had no curtains, or perhaps, in spite of the cold, they had been drawn back. There seemed to be neither quilts nor bedding, but a boy was lying there in a linen gown, with his back towards Jack, who saw that he had red or reddish hair, much the same colour as his own.

'You may go near him, and see him more clearly,' Mr Jonas said. 'His arm is hanging down, what do you make of that?'

'I think it hangs oddly, sir.'

He remembered what the tutor had told him, that Mr Jonas had not multiplied his kind, and asked, 'What is his name, sir?' To this he got no answer.

Mr Jonas gestured to him to move nearer, and said, 'You may take his hand.'

'No, sir, I can't do that.'

'Why not? You must touch other children very often. Wherever you live, you must sleep the Lord knows how many in a bed.'

'Only three in a bed at ours,' Jack muttered.

'Then touch, touch.'

'No, sir, no, I can't touch the skin of him!'

Mr Jonas set down his candles, went to the bed, took the boy's wrist and turned it, so that the fingers opened. From the open fingers he took Jack's medal, and gave it back to him.

'Was it warm or cold?' they asked him later. Jack told them that it was cold. Cold as ice? Perhaps not quite as cold as that.

'You have what you came for,' said Mr Jonas. 'You have taken back what was yours. Note that I don't deny it was yours.'

He did not move again, but stood looking down at the whiteish heap on the bed. Jack was more afraid of staying than going, although he had no idea how to find his way through the house, and was lucky to come upon a back staircase which ended not where he had come in but among the sculleries, where he managed to draw back the double bolts and get out into the fresh air.

'Did the boy move,' they asked him, 'when the medal was taken away from him?' But by this time Jack was making up the answers as he went along. He preferred, on the whole, not to think much about Watching. It struck him, though, that he had been through a good deal to get back his godmother's present, and he quite often wondered how much money Mr Jonas would in fact have offered him, if he had had the sense to accept it. Anyone who has ever been poor – even if not as poor as Jack Digby – will sympathize with him in this matter.

AGNES OF IOWA

Lorrie Moore

Lorrie Moore (b. 1957) is an American writer, known for her humorous and poignant short stories. Moore has published three collections: *Self-Help*, *Like Life*, and *Birds of America*, which was a *New York Times* bestseller. She has contributed to the *Paris Review* and the *New Yorker* and published three novels, one of which, *A Gate at the Stairs*, was shortlisted for the 2010 Orange Prize.

Her mother had given her the name Agnes, believing that a good-looking woman was even more striking when her name was a homely one. Her mother was named Cyrena, and was beautiful to match, but had always imagined her life would have been more interesting, that she herself would have had a more dramatic, arresting effect on the world and not ended up in Cassell, Iowa, if she had been named Enid or Hagar or Maude. And so she named her first daughter Agnes, and when Agnes turned out not to be attractive at all, but puffy and prone to a rash between her eyebrows, her hair a flat and bilious hue, her mother backpedaled and named her second daughter Linnea Elise (who turned out to be a lovely, sleepy child with excellent bones, a sweet, full mouth, and a rubbery mole above her lip that later in life could be removed without difficulty, everyone was sure).

Agnes herself had always been a bit at odds with her name. There was a brief period in her life, in her mid-twenties, when she had tried to pass it off as French – she had put in the accent grave and encouraged people to call her "On-yez." This was when she was living in New York City, and often getting together with her cousin, a painter who took her to parties in TriBeCa lofts or at beach houses or at mansions on lakes upstate. She would meet a lot of not very bright rich people who found the pronunciation of her name intriguing. It was the rest of her they were unclear on. "On-yez, where are you from, dear?" asked a black-slacked, frosted-haired woman whose skin was papery and melanomic with suntan. "Originally." She eyed Agnes's outfit as if it might be what in fact it was: a couple of blue things purchased in a department store in Cedar Rapids.

"Where am I from?" Agnes said it softly. "Iowa." She had a tendency not to speak up.

"*Where?*" The woman scowled, bewildered.

"Iowa," Agnes repeated loudly.

The woman in black touched Agnes's wrist and leaned in confidentially. She moved her mouth in a concerned and exaggerated way, like a facial exercise. "No, dear," she said. "*Here* we say *O-hi-o*."

That had been in Agnes's mishmash decade, after college. She had lived improvisationally then, getting this job or that, in restaurants or offices, taking a class or two, not thinking too far ahead, negotiating the precariousness and subway flus and scrimping for an occasional manicure or a play. Such a life required much exaggerated self-esteem. It engaged gross quantities of hope and despair and set them wildly side by side, like a Third World country of the heart. Her days grew messy with contradictions. When she went for walks, for her health, cinders would spot her cheeks and soot would settle in the furled leaf of each ear. Her shoes became unspeakable. Her blouses darkened in a breeze, and a blast of bus exhaust might linger in her hair for hours. Finally, her old asthma returned and, with a hacking, incessant cough, she gave up. "I feel like I've got five years to live," she told people, "so I'm moving back to Iowa so that it'll feel like fifty."

When she packed up to leave, she knew she was saying good-bye to something important, which was not that bad, in a way, because it meant that at least you had said hello to it to begin with, which most people in Cassell, Iowa, she felt, could not claim to have done.

A year and a half later, she married a boyish man twelve years her senior, a Cassell realtor named Joe, and together they bought a house on a little street called Birch Court. She taught a night class at the Arts Hall and did volunteer work on the Transportation Commission in town. It was life like a glass of water: half-empty, half-full. Half-full. Half-full. Oops: half-empty. Over the years, she and Joe tried to have a baby, but one night at dinner, looking at each other in a lonely way over the meat loaf, they realized with shock that they probably never would. Nonetheless, after six years, they still tried, vandalizing what romance was left in their marriage.

"Honey," she would whisper at night when he was reading under the reading lamp and she had already put her book away and curled toward him, wanting to place the red scarf over the lamp shade but knowing it would annoy him and so not doing it. "Do you want to make love? It would be a good time of month."

And Joe would groan. Or he would yawn. Or he would already be asleep. Once, after a long, hard day, he said, "I'm sorry, Agnes. I guess I'm just not in the mood."

She grew exasperated. "You think *I'm* in the mood?" she said. "I don't want to do this any more than you do," and he looked at her in a disgusted way, and it was two weeks after that that they had the sad dawning over the meat loaf.

At the Arts Hall, formerly the Grange Hall, Agnes taught the Great Books class, but taught it loosely, with cookies. She let her students turn in poems and plays and stories that they themselves had written; she let them use the class as their own little time to be creative. Someone once even brought in a sculpture: an electric one with blinking lights.

After class, she sometimes met with students individually. She recommended things for them to write about or read or consider in their next project. She smiled and asked if things were going well in their lives. She took an interest.

"You should be stricter," said Willard Stauffbacher, the head of the Instruction Department; he was a short, balding musician who liked to tape on his door pictures of famous people he thought he looked like. Every third Monday, he conducted the monthly departmental meeting – aptly named, Agnes liked to joke, since she did indeed depart mental. "Just because it's a night course doesn't mean you shouldn't impart standards," Stauffbacher said in a scolding way. "If it's piffle, use the word *piffle*. If it's meaningless, write *meaningless* across the top of every page." He had once taught at an elementary school and once at a prison. "I feel like I do all the real work around here," he added. He had posted near his office a sign that read RULES FOR THE MUSIC ROOM:

I will stay in my seat unless [sic] permission to move.
I will sit up straight.
I will listen to directions.
I will not bother my neighbor.
I will not talk when Mr. Stauffbacher is talking.
I will be polite to others.
I will sing as well as I can.

Agnes stayed after one night with Christa, the only black student in her class. She liked Christa a lot – Christa was smart and funny, and Agnes sometimes liked to stay after with her to chat. Tonight, Agnes had decided to talk Christa out of writing about vampires all the time.

"Why don't you write about that thing you told me about that time?" Agnes suggested.

Christa looked at her skeptically. "What thing?"

"The time in your childhood, during the Chicago riots, walking with your mother through the police barricades."

"Man, I lived that. Why should I want to write about it?"

Agnes sighed. Maybe Christa had a point. "It's just that I'm no help to you with this vampire stuff," Agnes said. "It's formulaic, genre fiction."

"You would be of more help to me with *my childhood*?"

"Well, with more serious stories, yes."

Christa stood up, perturbed. She grabbed her vampire story back. "You with all your Alice Walker and Zora Hurston. I'm just not interested in that anymore. I've done that already. I read those books years ago."

"Christa, please don't be annoyed." *Please do not talk when Mr. Stauffbacher is talking.*

"You've got this agenda for me."

"Really, I don't at all," said Agnes. "It's just that – you know what it is? It's that I'm just sick of these vampires. They're so roaming and repeating."

"If you were black, what you're saying might have a different spin. But the fact is, you're not," Christa said, and picked up her coat and strode out – though ten seconds later, she gamely stuck her head back in and said, "See you next week."

"We need a visiting writer who's black," Agnes said in the next depart mental meeting. "We've never had one." They were looking at their budget, and the readings this year were pitted against Dance Instruction, a program headed up by a redhead named Evergreen.

"The Joffrey is just so much central casting," said Evergreen, apropos of nothing. As a vacuum cleaner can start to pull up the actual thread of a carpet, her brains had been sucked dry by too much yoga. No one paid much attention to her.

"Perhaps we can get Harold Raferson in Chicago," Agnes suggested.

"We've already got somebody for the visiting writer slot," said Stauffbacher coyly. "An Afrikaner from Johannesburg."

"What?" said Agnes. Was he serious? Even Evergreen barked out a laugh.

"W. S. Beyerbach. The university's bringing him in. We pay our five hundred dollars and we get him out here for a day and a half."

"Who?" asked Evergreen.

"This has already been decided?" asked Agnes.

"Yup." Stauffbacher looked accusingly at Agnes. "I've done a lot of work to arrange for this. *I've* done all the work!"

"Do less," said Evergreen.

When Agnes first met Joe, they'd fallen madly upon each other. They'd kissed in restaurants; they'd groped, under coats, at the movies. At his little house, they'd made love on the porch, or the landing of the staircase, against the wall in the hall by the door to the attic, filled with too much desire to make their way to a real room.

Now they struggled self-consciously for atmosphere, something they'd never needed before. She prepared the bedroom carefully. She played quiet music and concentrated. She lit candles – as if she were in church, praying for the deceased. She donned a filmy gown. She took hot baths and entered the bedroom in nothing but a towel, a wild fishlike creature of moist, perfumed heat. In the nightstand drawer she still kept the charts a doctor once told her to keep, still placed an X on any date she and Joe actually had sex. But she could never show these to her doctor; not now. It pained Agnes to see them. She and Joe looked like worse than bad shots. She and Joe looked like idiots. She and Joe looked dead.

Frantic candlelight flickered on the ceiling like a puppet show. While she waited for Joe to come out of the bathroom, Agnes lay back on the bed and thought about her week, the bloody politics of it, how she was not very good at politics. Once, before he was elected, she had gone to a rally for Bill Clinton, but when he was late and had kept the crowd waiting for over an hour, and when the sun got hot and bees began landing on people's heads, when everyone's feet hurt and tiny children began to cry and a state assemblyman stepped forward to announce that Clinton had stopped at a Dairy Queen in Des Moines and that was why he was late – Dairy Queen! – she had grown angry and resentful and apolitical in her own sweet-starved thirst and she'd joined in with some other people who had started to chant, "Do us a favor, tell us the flavor."

Through college she had been a feminist – basically: she shaved her legs, *but just not often enough*, she liked to say. She signed day-care petitions, and petitions for Planned Parenthood. And although she had never been very aggressive with men, she felt strongly that she knew the difference between feminism and Sadie Hawkins Day – which some people, she believed, did not.

"Agnes, are we out of toothpaste or is this it – oh, okay, I see."

And once, in New York, she had quixotically organized the ladies' room line at the Brooks Atkinson Theatre. Because the play was going to start any minute and the line was still twenty women long, she had gotten six women to walk across the lobby with her to the men's room. "Everybody out of there?" she'd called in timidly, allowing the men to finish up first, which took a while, especially with other men coming up impatiently and cutting ahead in line. Later, at intermission, she saw how it should have been done. Two elderly black women, with greater expertise in civil rights, stepped very confidently into the men's room and called out, "Don't mind us, boys. We're coming on in. Don't mind us."

"Are you okay?" asked Joe, smiling. He was already beside her. He smelled sweet, of soap and minty teeth, like a child.

"I think so," she said, and turned toward him in the bordello light of their room. He had never acquired the look of maturity anchored in sorrow that burnished so many men's faces. His own sadness in life – a childhood of beatings, a dying mother – was like quicksand, and he had to stay away from it entirely. He permitted no unhappy memories spoken aloud. He stuck with the same mild cheerfulness he'd honed successfully as a boy, and it made him seem fatuous – even, she knew, to himself. Probably it hurt his business a little.

"Your mind's wandering," he said, letting his own eyes close.

"I know." She yawned, moved her legs onto his for warmth, and in this way, with the candles burning into their tins, she and Joe fell asleep.

The spring arrived cool and humid. Bulbs cracked and sprouted, shot up their green periscopes, and on April first, the Arts Hall offered a joke lecture by T. S. Eliot, visiting scholar. "The Cruelest Month," it was called. "You don't find that funny?" asked Stauffbacher.

April fourth was the reception for W. S. Beyerbach. There was to be a dinner afterward, and then Beyerbach was to visit Agnes's Great Books class. She had assigned his second collection of sonnets, spare and elegant things with sighing and diaphanous politics. The next afternoon there was to be a reading.

Agnes had not been invited to the dinner, and when she asked about this, in a mildly forlorn way, Stauffbacher shrugged, as if it were totally out of his hands. I'm a *published poet*, Agnes wanted to say. She *had* published a poem once – in *The Gizzard Review*, but still!

"It was Edie Canterton's list," Stauffbacher said. "I had nothing to do with it."

She went to the reception anyway, annoyed, and when she planted herself like a splayed and storm-torn tree near the cheese, she could actually feel the crackers she was eating forming a bad paste in her mouth and she became afraid to smile. When she finally introduced herself to W. S. Beyerbach, she stumbled on her own name and actually pronounced it "On-yez."

"On-yez," repeated Beyerbach in a quiet Englishy voice.

Condescending, she thought. His hair was blond and white, like a palomino, and his eyes were blue and scornful as mints. She could see he was a withheld man; although some might say *shy*, she decided it was *withheld*: a lack of generosity. Passive-aggressive. It was causing the people around him to squirm and blurt things nervously. He would simply nod, the smile on his face faint and vaguely pharmaceutical. Everything about him was tight and coiled as a door spring. From living in *that country*, thought Agnes. How could he live in that country?

Stauffbacher was trying to talk heartily about the mayor. Something about his old progressive ideas, and the forthcoming convention center. Agnes thought of her own meetings on the Transportation Commission, of the mayor's leash law for cats, of his new squadron of meter maids and bicycle police, of a councilman the mayor once slugged in a bar. "Now, of course, the mayor's become a fascist," said Agnes in a voice that sounded strangely loud, bright with anger.

Silence fell all around. Edie Canterton stopped stirring the punch. Agnes looked about her. "Oh," she said. "Are we not supposed to use *that word* in this room?" Beyerbach's expression went blank. Agnes's face burned in confusion.

Stauffbacher appeared pained, then stricken. "More cheese, anyone?" he asked, holding up the silver tray.

After everyone left for dinner, she went by herself to the Dunk 'N Dine across the street. She ordered the California BLT and a cup of coffee, and looked over Beyerbach's work again: dozens of images of broken, rotten bodies, of the body's mutinies and betrayals, of the body's strange housekeeping and illicit pets. At the front of the book was a dedication – *To DFB (1970–1989)*. Who could that be? A political activist, maybe. Perhaps it was the young woman referred to often in his poems, "a woman who had thrown aside the unseasonal dress of hope," only to look for it again "in the blood-blooming shrubs." Perhaps if Agnes got a chance, she would ask him. Why not? A book was a public thing, and its dedication was part of it. If it was too personal a question for him, *tough*. She would find the right time, she decided. She paid the check, put on her jacket, and crossed the street to the Arts Hall, to meet

Beyerbach by the front door. She would wait for the moment, then seize it.

He was already at the front door when she arrived. He greeted her with a stiff smile and a soft "Hello, Onyez," an accent that made her own voice ring coarse and country-western.

She smiled and then blurted, "I have a question to ask you." To her own ears, she sounded like Johnny Cash.

Beyerbach said nothing, only held the door open for her and then followed her into the building.

She continued as they stepped slowly up the stairs. "May I ask to whom your book is dedicated?"

At the top of the stairs, they turned left down the long corridor. She could feel his steely reserve, his lip-biting, his shyness no doubt garbed and rationalized with snobbery, but so much snobbery to handle all that shyness, he could not possibly be a meaningful critic of his country. She was angry with him. *How can you live in that country?* she again wanted to say, although she remembered when someone had once said that to her – a Danish man on Agnes's senior trip abroad to Copenhagen. It had been during the Vietnam War and the man had stared meanly, righteously. "The United States – how can you live in that country?" the man had asked. Agnes had shrugged. "A lot of my stuff is there," she'd said, and it was then that she first felt all the dark love and shame that came from the pure accident of home, the deep and arbitrary place that happened to be yours.

"It's dedicated to my son," Beyerbach said finally.

He would not look at her, but stared straight ahead along the corridor floor. Now Agnes's shoes sounded very loud.

"You lost a son," she said.

"Yes," he said. He looked away, at the passing wall, past Stauffbacher's bulletin board, past the men's room, the women's room, some sternness in him broken, and when he turned back, she could see his eyes filling with water, his face a plethora, reddened with unbearable pressure.

"I'm so sorry," Agnes said.

Side by side now, their footsteps echoed down the corridor toward her classroom; all the anxieties she felt with this mournfully quiet man now mimicked the anxieties of love. What should she say? It must be the most unendurable thing to lose a child. Shouldn't he say something of this? It was his turn to say something.

But he would not. And when they finally reached her classroom, she turned to him in the doorway and, taking a package from her purse, said simply, in a reassuring way, "We always have cookies in class."

Now he beamed at her with such relief that she knew she had for once said the right thing. It filled her with affection for him. Perhaps, she thought, that was where affection began: in an unlikely phrase, in a moment of someone's having unexpectedly but at last said the right thing. *We always have cookies in class.*

She introduced him with a bit of flourish and biography. Positions held, universities attended. The students raised their hands and asked him about apartheid, about shantytowns and homelands, and he answered succinctly, after long sniffs and pauses, only once referring to a question as "unanswerably fey," causing the student to squirm and fish around in her purse for something, nothing, Kleenex perhaps. Beyerbach did not seem to notice. He went on, spoke of censorship, how a person must work hard not to internalize a government's program of censorship, since that is what a government would like best, for *you* to do it *yourself*, and how he was not sure he had not succumbed. Afterward, a few students stayed and shook his hand, formally, awkwardly, then left. Christa was the last. She, too, shook his hand and then started chatting amiably. They knew someone in common – Harold Raferson in Chicago! – and as Agnes quickly wiped the seminar table to clear it of cookie crumbs, she tried to listen, but couldn't really hear. She made a small pile of crumbs and swept them into one hand.

"Good night," sang out Christa when she left.

"Good night, Christa," said Agnes, brushing the crumbs into the wastebasket.

Now she stood with Beyerbach in the empty classroom. "Thank you so much," she said in a hushed way. "I'm sure they all got quite a lot out of that. I'm very sure they did."

He said nothing, but smiled at her gently.

She shifted her weight from one leg to the other. "Would you like to go somewhere and get a drink?" she asked. She was standing close to him, looking up into his face. He was tall, she saw now.

His shoulders weren't broad, but he had a youthful straightness to his carriage. She briefly touched his sleeve. His suitcoat was corduroy and bore the faint odor of clove. This was the first time in her life that she had ever asked a man out for a drink.

He made no move to step away from her, but actually seemed to lean toward her a bit. She could feel his dry breath, see up close the variously hued spokes of his irises, the grays and yellows in the blue. There was a sprinkling of small freckles near his hairline. He smiled, then looked at the clock on the wall. "I would love to, really, but I have to get back to the hotel to make a phone call at ten-fifteen." He looked a little disappointed – not a lot, thought Agnes, but certainly a little.

"Oh, well," she said. She flicked off the lights and in the dark he carefully helped her on with her jacket. They stepped out of the room and walked together in silence, back down the corridor to the front entrance of the hall. Outside on the steps, the night was balmy and scented with rain. "Will you be all right walking back to your hotel?" she asked. "Or—"

"Oh, yes, thank you. It's just around the corner."

"Right. That's right. Well, my car's parked way over there. So I guess I'll see you tomorrow afternoon at your reading."

"Yes," he said, "I shall look forward to that."

"Yes," she said. "So shall I."

The reading was in the large meeting room at the Arts Hall and was from the sonnet book she had already read, but it was nice to hear the poems again, in his hushed, pained tenor. She sat in the back row, her green raincoat sprawled beneath her on the seat like a leaf. She leaned forward, onto the seat ahead of her, her back an angled stem, her chin on double fists, and she listened like that for some time. At one point, she closed her eyes, but the image of him before her, standing straight as a compass needle, remained caught there beneath her lids, like a burn or a speck or a message from the mind.

Afterward, moving away from the lectern, Beyerbach spotted her and waved, but Stauffbacher, like a tugboat with a task, took his arm and steered him elsewhere, over toward the side table with the little plastic cups of warm Pepsi. We are both men, the gesture seemed to say. We both have *back* in our names. Agnes put on her green coat. She went over toward the Pepsi table and stood. She drank a warm Pepsi, then placed the empty cup back on the table. Beyerbach finally turned toward her and smiled familiarly. She thrust out her hand. "It was a wonderful reading," she said. "I'm very glad I got the chance to meet you." She gripped his long, slender palm and locked thumbs. She could feel the bones in him.

"Thank you," he said. He looked at her coat in a worried way. "You're leaving?"

She looked down at her coat. "I'm afraid I have to get going home." She wasn't sure whether she really had to or not. But she'd put on the coat, and it now seemed an awkward thing to take off.

"Oh," he murmured, gazing at her intently. "Well, all best wishes to you, Onyez."

"Excuse me?" There was some clattering near the lectern.

"All best to you," he said, something retreating in his expression.

Stauffbacher suddenly appeared at her side, scowling at her green coat, as if it were incomprehensible.

"Yes," said Agnes, stepping backward, then forward again to shake Beyerbach's hand once more; it was a beautiful hand, like an old and expensive piece of wood. "Same to you," she said. Then she turned and fled.

For several nights, she did not sleep well. She placed her face directly into her pillow, then turned it some for air, then flipped over to her back and opened her eyes, staring at the far end of the room through the stark angle of the door frame toward the tiny light from the bathroom which illumined the hallway, faintly, as if someone had just been there.

For several days, she thought perhaps he might have left her a note with the secretary, or that he might send her one from an airport somewhere. She thought that the inadequacy of their good-bye would haunt him, too, and that he might send her a postcard as elaboration.

But he did not. Briefly, she thought about writing him a letter, on Arts Hall stationery, which for money reasons was no longer the stationery, but photocopies of the stationery. She knew he had flown to the West Coast, then off to Tokyo, then Sydney, then back to Johannesburg, and if she posted it now, perhaps he would receive it when he arrived. She could tell him once more how interesting it had been to meet him. She could enclose her poem from *The Gizzard Review*. She had read in the newspaper an article about bereavement – and if she were her own mother, she could send him that, too.

Thank God, thank God, she was not her mother.

Spring settled firmly in Cassell with a spate of thundershowers. The perennials – the myrtle and grape hyacinths – blossomed around town in a kind of civic blue, and the warming air brought forth an occasional mosquito or fly. The Transportation Commission meetings were dreary and long, too often held over the dinner hour, and when Agnes got home, she would replay them for Joe, sometimes bursting into tears over the parts about the photoradar or the widening interstate.

When her mother called, Agnes got off the phone fast. When her sister called about her mother, Agnes got off the phone even faster. Joe rubbed her shoulders and spoke to her of carports, of curb appeal, of asbestos-wrapped pipes.

At the Arts Hall, she taught and fretted and continued to receive the usual memos from the secretary, written on the usual scrap paper – except that the scrap paper this time, for a while, consisted of the extra posters for the Beyerbach reading. She would get a long disquisition on policies and procedures concerning summer registration, and she would turn it over and there would be his face – sad and pompous in the photograph. She would get a simple phone message – "Your husband called. Please phone him at the office" – and on the back would be the ripped center of Beyerbach's nose, one minty eye, an elbowish chin. Eventually, there were no more, and the scrap paper moved on to old contest announcements, grant deadlines, Easter concert notices.

At night, she and Joe did yoga to a yoga show on TV. It was part of their effort not to become their parents, though marriage, they knew, held that hazard. The functional disenchantment, the sweet habit of each other had begun to put lines around her mouth, lines that looked like quotation marks – as if everything she said had already been said before. Sometimes their old cat, Madeline, a fat and pampered calico reaping the benefits of life with a childless couple during their childbearing years, came and plopped herself down with them, between them. She was accustomed to much nestling and appreciation and drips from the faucet, though sometimes she would vanish outside, and they would not see her for days, only to spy her later, in the yard, dirty and matted, chomping a vole or eating old snow.

For Memorial Day weekend, Agnes flew with Joe to New York, to show him the city for the first time. "A place," she said, "where if you're not white and not born there, you're not automatically a story." She had grown annoyed with Iowa, the pathetic thirdhand manner in which the large issues and conversations of the world were encountered, the oblique and tired way history situated itself there – if ever. She longed to be a citizen of the globe!

They roller-skated in Central Park. They looked in the Lord & Taylor windows. They went to the Jofffey. They went to a hair salon on Fifty-seventh Street and there she had her hair dyed red. They sat in the window booths of coffee shops and got coffee refills and ate pie.

"So much seems the same," she said to Joe. "When I lived here, everyone was hustling for money. The rich were. The poor were. But everyone tried hard to be funny. Everywhere you went – a store, a manicure place – someone was telling a joke. A *good* one." She remembered it had made any given day seem bearable, that impulse toward a joke. It had been a determined sort of humor, an intensity mirroring the intensity of the city, and it seemed to embrace and alleviate the hard sadness of people having used one another and marred the earth the way they had. "It was like brains having sex. It was like every brain was a sex maniac." She looked down at her pie. "People really worked at it, the laughing," she said. "People need to laugh."

"They do," said Joe. He took a swig of coffee, his lips out over the cup in a fleshy flower. He was afraid she might cry – she was getting that look again – and if she did, he would feel guilty and lost and sorry for her that her life was not here anymore, but in a far and boring place now with him. He set the cup down and tried to smile. "They sure do," he said. And he looked out the window at the rickety taxis, the oystery garbage and tubercular air, seven pounds of chicken giblets dumped on the curb in front of the restaurant where they were. He turned back to her and made the face of a clown.

"What are you doing?" she asked.

"It's a clown face."

"What do you mean, 'a clown face?'" Someone behind her was singing "I Love New York," and for the first time she noticed the strange irresolution of the tune.

"A regular clown face is what I mean."

"It didn't look like that."

"No? What did it look like?"

"You want me to do the face?"

"Yeah, do the face."

She looked at Joe. Every arrangement in life carried with it the sadness, the sentimental shadow, of its not being something else, but only itself: she attempted the face – a look of such monstrous emptiness and stupidity that Joe burst out in a howling sort of laughter, like a dog, and then so did she, air exploding through her nose in a snort, her head thrown forward, then back, then forward again, setting loose a fit of coughing.

"Are you okay?" asked Joe, and she nodded. Out of politeness, he looked away, outside, where it had suddenly started to rain. Across the street, two people had planted themselves under the window ledge of a Gap store, trying to stay dry, waiting out the downpour, their figures dark and scarecrowish against the lit window display. When he turned back to his wife – his sad young wife – to point this out to her, to show her what was funny to a man firmly in the grip of middle age, she was still bent sideways in her seat, so that her face fell below the line of the table, and he could only see the curve of her heaving back, the fuzzy penumbra of her thin spring sweater, and the garish top of her bright, new, and terrible hair.

CURVED IS THE LINE
OF BEAUTY

Hilary Mantel

Hilary Mantel (b. 1952) is a British writer who has twice been awarded the Man Booker Prize for the 2009 novel, *Wolf Hall*, and, in 2012, for *Bring Up the Bodies*, making her the first woman to receive the award twice. She has published twelve novels and one collection of short stories, *Learning to Talk*.

When I was in my middle childhood my contemporaries started to disappear. They vanished from the mill-town conurbations and the Manchester back-streets, and their bodies – some of them, anyway – were found buried on the moors. I was born on the edge of this burial ground, and had been instructed in its ways. Moorland punished those who were in the wrong place at the wrong time. It killed those who were stupid and those who were unprepared. Ramblers from the city, feckless boys with bobble hats, would walk for days in circles, till they died of exposure. The rescue parties would be baffled by dank fogs, which crept over the landscape like sheets drawn over corpses. Moorland was featureless except for its own swell and eddy, its slow waves of landscape rising and falling, its knolls, streams and bridle paths which ran between nowhere and nowhere; its wetness underfoot, its scaly patches of late snow, and the tossing inland squall that was its typical climate. Even in mild weather its air was wandering, miasmic, like memories that no one owns. When raw drizzle and fog invaded the streets of the peripheral settlements, it was easy to feel that if you stepped out of your family house, your street, your village, you were making a risky move; one mistake, and you would be lost.

The other way of being lost, when I was a child, was by being damned. Damned to hell that is, for all eternity. This could happen very easily if you were a Catholic child in the 1950s. If the speeding driver caught you at the wrong moment – let us say, at the midpoint between monthly confessions – then your dried-up soul could snap from your body like a dead twig. Our school was situated handily, so as to increase the risk, between two bends in the road. Last-moment repentance is possible, and stress was placed on it. You might be saved, if, in your final welter of mashed bones and gore, you remembered the correct formula. So it was really all a matter of timing. I didn't think it might be a matter of mercy. Mercy was a theory that I had not seen in operation. I had only seen how those who wielded power extracted maximum advantage from every situation. The politics of the playground and classroom are as instructive as those of the parade ground and the Senate. I understood that, as Thucydides would later tell me, 'the strong exact what they can, and the weak yield what they must'.

Accordingly, if the strong said, 'We are going to Birmingham,' to Birmingham you must go. We were going to make a visit, my mother said. To whom, I asked; because we had never done this before. To a family we had not met, she said, a family we did not yet know. In the days after the announcement I said the word 'family' many times to myself, its crumbly soft sound like a rusk in milk, and I carried its scent with me, the human warmth of chequered blankets and the yeast smell of babies' heads.

In the week before the visit, I went over in my mind the circumstances that surrounded it. I challenged myself with a few contradictions and puzzles which these circumstances threw up. I analysed who *we* might be, we who were going to make the visit: because that was not a constant or a simple matter.

The night before the visit I was sent to bed at eight – even though it was the holidays and Saturday next day. I opened the sash window and leaned out into the dusk, waiting till a lonely string of street lights blossomed, far over the fields, under the upland shadow. There was a sweet grassy fragrance, a haze in the twilight; *Dr Kildare's* Friday-night theme tune floated out from a hundred TV sets, from a hundred open windows, up the hill, across the reservoir, over the moors; and as I fell asleep I saw the medics in their frozen poses, fixed, solemn and glazed, like heroes on the curve of an antique jar.

I once read of a jar on which this verse was engraved:

Straight is the line of duty;
Curved is the line of beauty.
Follow the straight line; thou shalt see
The curved line ever follow thee.

At five o'clock, a shout roused me from my dreams. I went downstairs in my blue spotted pyjamas to wash in hot water from the kettle, and I saw the outline of my face, puffy, in the light like grey linen tacked to the summer window. I had never been so far from home; even my mother had never, she said, been so far. I was excited and excitement made me sneeze. My mother stood in the kitchen in the first uncertain shaft of sun, making sandwiches with cold bacon and wrapping them silently, sacramentally, in greaseproof paper.

We were going in Jack's car, which stood the whole night, these last few months, at the kerb outside our house. It was a small grey car, like a jelly mould, out of which a giant might turn a foul jelly of profanity and grease. The car's character was idle, vicious and sneaky. If it had been a pony you would have shot it. Its engine spat and steamed, its underparts rattled; it wanted brake shoes and new exhausts. It jibbed at hills and sputtered to a halt on bends. It ate oil, and when it wanted a new tyre there were rows about having no money, and there was slamming the door so hard that the glass of the kitchen cupboard rattled in its grooves.

The car brought out the worst in everybody who saw it. It was one of the first cars on the street, and the neighbours, in their mistaken way, envied it. Already sneerers and ill-wishers of ours, they were driven to further spite when they saw us trooping out to the kerb carrying all the rugs and kettles and camping stoves and raincoats and wellington boots that we took with us for a day at the seaside or the zoo.

There were five of *us*, now. Me and my mother; two biting, snarling, pinching little boys; Jack. My father did not go on our trips. Though he still slept in the house – the room down the corridor, the one with the ghost – he kept to his own timetables and routines, his Friday jazz club, and his solitary sessions of syncopation, picking at the piano, late weekend afternoons, with a remote gaze. This had not always been his way of life. He had once taken me to the library. He had taken me out with my fishing net. He had taught me card games and how to read a racecard; it might not have been a suitable accomplishment for an eight-year-old, but any skill at all was a grace in our dumb old world.

But those days were now lost to me. Jack had come to stay with us. At first he was just a visitor and then without transition he seemed to be always there. He never carried in a bag, or unpacked clothes; he just came complete as he was. After his day's work he would drive up in the evil car, and when he came up the steps and through the front door, my father would melt away to his shadowy evening pursuits. Jack had a brown skin and muscles beneath his shirt. He was your definition of a man, if a man was what caused alarm and shattered the peace.

To amuse me, while my mother combed the tangles out of my hair, he told me the story of David and Goliath. It was not a success. He tried his hardest – as I tried also – to batten down my shrieks. As he spoke his voice slid in and out of the London intonations with which he had been born; his brown eyes flickered, caramel and small, the whites jaundiced. He made the voice of Goliath, but – to my mind – he was lacking in the David department.

After a long half-hour, the combing was over. My vast weight of hair studded to my skull with steel clips, I pitched exhausted from the kitchen chair. Jack stood up, equally exhausted, I suppose; he would not have known how often this needed to happen. He liked children, or imagined he did. But (owing to recent events and my cast of mind) I was not exactly a child, and he himself was a very young man, too inexperienced to navigate through the situation in which he had placed himself, and he was always on the edge, under pressure, chippy and excitable and quick to take offence. I was afraid of his flaring temper and his irrationality: he argued with brute objects, kicked out at iron and wood, cursed the fire when it wouldn't light. I flinched at the sound of his voice, but I tried to keep the flinch inwards.

When I look back now I find in myself – in so far as I can name what I find – a faint stir of fellow feeling that is on the way to pity.

It was Jack's quickness of temper, and his passion for the underdog, that was the cause of our trip to Birmingham. We were going to see a friend of his, who was from Africa. You will remember that we have barely reached the year 1962, and I had never seen anyone from Africa, except in photographs, but the prospect in itself was less amazing to me than the knowledge that Jack had a friend. I thought friends were for children. My mother seemed to think that you grew out of them. Adults did not have friends. They had relatives. Only relatives came to your house. Neighbours might come, of course. But not to our house. My mother was now the subject of scandal and did not go out. We were all the subject of scandal, but some of us had to. I had to go to school, for instance. It was the law.

It was six in the morning when we bundled into the car, the two little boys dropped sleep-stunned beside me on to the red leather of the back seat. In those days it took a very long time to get anywhere. There were no motorways to speak of. Fingerposts were still employed, and we did not seem to have the use of a map. Because my mother did not know left from right, she would cry 'That way, that way!' whenever she saw a sign and happened to read it. The car would swerve off in any old direction and Jack would start cursing and she would shout back. Our journeys usually found us bogged in the sand at Southport, or broken down by the drystone wall of some Derbyshire beauty spot, the lid of the vile spitting engine propped open, my mother giving advice from the wound-down window: fearful advice, which went on till Jack danced with rage on the roadway or on the uncertain sand, his voice piping in imitation of a female shriek; and she, heaving up the last rags of self-control, heaving them into her arms like some dying diva's bouquet, would drop her voice an octave and claim, 'I don't talk like that.'

But on this particular day, when we were going to Birmingham, we didn't get lost at all. It seemed a miracle. At the blossoming hour of ten o'clock, the weather still fine, we ate our sandwiches, and I remember that first sustaining bite of salted fat, sealing itself in a plug to the hard palate: the sip of Nescafé to wash it down, poured steaming from the flask. In some town we stopped for petrol. That too passed without incident.

I rehearsed, in my mind, the reason behind the visit. The man from Africa, the friend, was not now but had once been a workmate of Jack. And they had spoken. And his name was Jacob. My mother had told me, don't say 'Jacob is black', say 'Jacob is coloured'.

What, coloured? I said. What, striped? Like the towel which, at that very moment, was hanging to dry before the fire? I stared at it; the stripes had run together to a patchy violet-grey. I felt it; the fibres were stiff as dried grass. Black, my mother said, is not the term polite people use. And stop mauling that towel!

So now, the friend, Jacob. He had been, at one time, living in Manchester, working with Jack. He had married a white girl. They had gone to get lodgings. At every door they had been turned away. No room at the inn. Though Eva was expecting. Especially because she was expecting. Even the stable door was bolted, it was barred against them, NO COLOUREDS, the signs said.

Oh, merrie England! At least people could spell in those days. They didn't write NO COLOURED'S or 'NO' COLOUREDS. That's about all you can say for it.

So: Jacob unfolded to Jack this predicament of his: no house, the insulting notices, the pregnant Eva. Jack, quickly taking fire, wrote a letter to a tabloid newspaper. The newspaper, quick to spot a cause, took fire also. There was naming and shaming; there was a campaign. Letters were written and questions were asked. The next thing you knew, Jacob had moved to Birmingham, to a new job. There was a house now, and a baby, indeed two. Better days were here. But Jacob would never forget how Jack had taken up the cudgels. That, my mother said, was the phrase he had used.

David and Goliath, I thought. My scalp prickled, and I felt steel pins cold against it. Last night had been too busy for the combing. My hair fell smoothly down my back, but hidden above the nape of my neck there was a secret pad of fuzziness which, if slept on for a second night, would require a howling hour to unknot.

The house of Jacob was built of brick in a quiet colour of brown, with a white-painted gate and a tree in a tub outside. One huge window stared out at a grass verge, with a sapling; and the road curved away, lined with similar houses, each in their own square of garden. We stepped out of the heat of the car and stood jelly-legged on the verge. Behind the plate glass was a stir of movement, and Jacob opened the front door to us, his face breaking into a smile. He was a tall slender man, and I liked the contrast of his white shirt with the soft sheen of his skin. I tried hard not to say, even to think, the term that is not the one polite people use. Jacob, I said to myself, is quite a dark lavender, verging on purple on an overcast day.

Eva came out from behind him. She had a compensatory pallor, and when she reached out, vaguely patting at my little brothers, she did it with fingers like rolled dough. Well, well, the adults said. And, this is all very nice. Lovely, Eva. And fitted carpets. Yes, said Eva. And would you like to go and spend a penny? I didn't know this phrase. Wash your hands, my mother said. Eva said, run upstairs, poppet.

At the top of the stairs there was a bathroom, not an arrangement I had reason to take for granted. Eva ushered me into it, smiling, and clicked the door behind her. Standing at the basin and watching myself in the mirror, I washed my hands carefully with Camay soap. Maybe I was dehydrated from the journey, for I didn't seem to need to do anything else. I hummed to myself, 'You'll look a little lovelier ... each day ... with fabulous *Camay*.' I didn't look around much. Already I could hear them on the stairs, shouting that it was their turn. I dried carefully between my fingers with the towel behind the door. There was a bolt on this door and I thought for a moment of bolting myself in. But a familiar pounding began, a head-butting, a thudding and a giggling, and I opened the door so that my brothers fell in at it and I went downstairs to do the rest of the day.

Everything had been fine, till the last hour of the journey. 'Not long to go,' my mother had said, and suddenly swivelled in her seat. She watched us, silent, her neck craning. Then she said, 'When we are visiting Jacob, don't say "Jack". It's not suitable. I want you to say,' and here she began to struggle with words, '"Daddy ... Daddy Jack".'

Her head, once more, faced front. Studying the line of her cheek, I thought she looked sick. It had been a most unconvincing performance. I was almost embarrassed for her. 'Is this just for today?' I asked. My voice came out cold. She didn't answer.

When I got back into the downstairs room they were parading Eva's children, a toddler and a baby, and remarking that it was funny how it came out, so you had one butter-coloured and one bluish, and Jacob was saying, too, that it was funny how it came out and you couldn't ever tell, really, it was probably beyond the scope of science as we know it today. The sound of a pan rocking on the gas jet came from the kitchen, and there was a burst of wet steam, and some clanking; Eva said, carrots, can't take your eye off them. Wiping her hands on her apron, she made for the door and melted into the steam. My eyes followed her. Jacob smiled and said, so how is the man who took up the cudgels?

We children ate in the kitchen – my family, that is, because the two babies sat in their own high chairs by Eva and sucked gloop from a spoon. There was a little red table with a hinged flap, and Eva propped the back door open so that the sunlight from the garden came in. We had vast pale slices of roast pork, and gravy that was beige and so thick it kept the shape of the knife. Probably if I am honest about what I remember, I think it is the fudge texture of this gravy that stays in my mind, better even than the afternoon's choking panic, the tears and prayers that were now only an hour or so away.

After our dinner Tabby came. She was not a cat but a girl, and the niece of Jacob. Enquiries were made of me: did I like to draw? Tabby had brought a large bag with her, and from it she withdrew sheets of rough coloured paper and a whole set of coloured pencils, double-ended. She gave me a quick, modest smile, and a flicker of her eyes. We settled down in a corner, and began to make each other's portrait.

Out in the garden the little boys grubbed up worms, shrieked, rolled the lawn with each other and laid about with their fists. I thought that the two coloured babies, now snorting in milky sleep, would be doing the same thing before long. When one of the boys fetched the other a harder clout than usual, the victim would howl, 'Jack! Jack!'

My mother stood looking over the garden. 'That's a lovely shrub, Eva,' she said. I could see her through the angle made by the open door of the kitchen; her high-heeled sandals planted squarely on the lino. She was smaller than I had thought, when I saw her beside the floury bulk of Eva, and her eyes were resting on something further than the shrub: on the day when she would leave the moorland village behind her, and have a shrub of her own. I bent my head over the paper and attempted the blurred line of Tabby's cheek, the angle of neck to chin. The curve of flesh, its soft bloom, eluded me; I lolled my pencil point softly against the paper, feeling I wanted to roll it in cream, or in something vegetable-soft but tensile, like the fallen petal of a rose. I had already noticed, with interest, that Tabby's crayons were sharpened down in a similar pattern to the ones I had at home. She had little use for gravy colour and still less for bl***k. Almost as unpopular was the double-ended crayon in morbid mauve/dark pink. Most popular with her was gold/green: as with me. On those days when I was tired of crayoning, and started to play that the crayons were soldiers, I had to imagine that gold/green was a drummer boy, so short was he.

On the rough paper, my pencil snagged; at once, my reverie was interrupted. I took in a breath. I bit my lip. I felt my heart begin to beat: an obscure insult, trailing like the smell of old vegetable water, seemed to hang in the air. This paper is for kids, I thought; it's for babies who don't know how to draw. My fingers gripped the crayon. I held it like a dagger. My hand clenched around it. At my toppest speed, I began to execute cartoon men, with straight jointless limbs, and brown 'O's for heads, with wide grinning mouths, jug ears; petty Goliaths with slatted mouths, with five fingerbones splaying from their wrists.

Tabby looked up. Shh, shh … she said; as if soothing me.

I drew children rolling in the grass, children made of two circles with a third 'O' for their bawling mouths.

Jacob came in, laughing, talking to Jack over his shoulder, '… so I tell him, if you want a trained draughtsman for £6 a week, man, you can whistle for him!'

I thought, I won't call Jack anything, I won't give him a name. I'll nod my head in his direction so they'll know who I mean. I'll even point to him, though polite people don't point. Daddy Jack! *Daddy Jack!* They can whistle for him!

Jacob stood over us, smiling softly. The crisp turn of his collar, the top button released, disclosed his velvet, quite dark-coloured throat. 'Two nice girls,' he said. 'What have we here?' He picked up my paper. 'Talent!' he said. 'Did you do this, honey, by yourself?'

He was looking at the cartoon men, not my portrait of Tabby, those tentative strokes in the corner of the page; not at the tilt of her jaw, like a note in music. 'Hey, Jack,' he said, 'now this is good, I can't believe it at her young age.' I whispered, 'I am nine,' as if I wanted to alert him to the true state of affairs. Jacob waved the paper around, delighted. 'I could well say this is a prodigy,' he said. I turned my face away. It seemed indecent to look at him. In that one moment it seemed to me that the world was blighted, and that every adult throat bubbled, like a garbage pail in August, with the syrup of rotting lies.

I see them, now, from the car window, children any day, on any road; children going somewhere, disconnected from the routes of adult intent. You see them in twos or threes, in unlikely combinations, sometimes a pair with a little one tagging along, sometimes a boy with two girls. They carry, it might be, a plastic bag with something secret inside, or a stick or box, but no obvious plaything; sometimes a ratty dog processes behind them. Their faces are intent and their missions hidden from adult eyes; they have a geography of their own, urban or rural, that has nothing to do with the milestones and markers that adults use. The country through which they move is older, more intimate than ours. They have their private knowledge of it. You do not expect this knowledge to fail.

There was no need to ask if we were best friends, me and Tabby, as we walked the narrow muddy path by the water. Perhaps it was a canal, but a canal was not a thing I'd seen, and it seemed to me more like a placid inland stream, silver-grey in colour, tideless though not motionless, fringed by sedge and tall grasses. My fingers were safely held in the pad of Tabby's palm, and there was a curve of light on the narrow, coffee-coloured back of her hand. She was a head taller than me, willowy, cool to the touch, even at the hot end of this hot afternoon. She was ten and a quarter years old, she said; lightly, almost as if it were something to shrug away. In her free hand she held a paper bag, and in this bag – which she had taken from her satchel, her eyes modestly downcast – were ripe plums. They were – in their perfect dumpling under my fingertips, in their cold purple blush – so fleshy that to notch your teeth against

their skin seemed like becoming a teatime cannibal, a vampire
for a day. I carried my plum in my palm, caressing it, rolling it
like a dispossessed eye, and feeling it grow warm from the heat of
my skin. We strolled, so, abstinent; till Tabby pulled at my hand,
stopped me, and turned me towards her, as if she wanted a witness.
She clenched her hand. She rolled the dark fruit in her fist, her
eyes on mine. She raised her fist to her sepia mouth. Her small
teeth plunged into ripe flesh. Juice ran down her chin. Casually,
she wiped it. She turned her face full to mine, and for the first time
I saw her frank smile, her lips parted, the gap between her front
teeth. She flipped my wrist lightly, with the back of her fingers; I
felt the sting of her nails. 'Let's go on the wrecks,' she said.

It meant we must scramble through a fence. Through a gap
there. I knew it was illicit. I knew no would be said: but then what,
this afternoon, did I care for no? Under the wire, through the snag
of it, the gap already widened by the hands of forerunners, some
of whom must have worn double-thickness woollen double-knit
mittens to muffle the scratch against their flesh. Once through the
wire, Tabby went, 'Whoop!'

Then soon she was bouncing, dancing in the realm of the dead
cars. They were above our head to the height of three. Her hands
reached out to slap at their rusting door-sills and wings. If there
had been glass in their windows, it was strewn now at our feet.
Scrapes of car paint showed, fawn, banana, a degraded scarlet. I
was giddy, and punched my fingers at metals: it crumbled, I was
through it. For that moment only I may have laughed; but I do not
think so.

She led me on the paths to the heart of the wrecks. We play
here, she said, and towed me on. We stopped for a plum each. We
laughed. 'Are you too young to write a letter?' she asked. I did not
answer. 'Have you heard of penfriends? I have one already.'

All around us, the scrapyard showed its bones. The wrecks
stood clear now, stack on stack, against a declining yellow light.
When I looked up they seemed to foreshorten, these carcasses, and
bear down on me; gaping windows where faces once looked out,
engine cavities where the air was blue, treadless tyres, wheel arches
gaping, boots unsprung and empty of bags, unravelling springs
where seats had been; and some wrecks were warped, reduced as if

by fire, bl***kened. We walked, sombre, cheeks bulging, down the
paths between. When we had penetrated many rows in, by blind
corners, by the swerves enforced on us by the squishy corrosion of
the sliding piles, I wanted to ask, why do you play here and who
do you mean by *we*, can I be one of your friends or will you forget
me, and also can we go now please?

Tabby ducked out of sight, around some rotting heap. I heard
her giggle. 'Got you!' I said. 'Yes!' She ducked, shying away, but my
plum stone hit her square on the temple, and as it touched her flesh
I tasted the seducing poison which, if you crack a plum stone, your
tongue can feel. Then Tabby broke into a trot, and I chased her:
when she skidded to a halt, her flat brown sandals making brakes
for her, I stopped too, and glanced up, and saw we had come to a
place where I could hardly see the sky. Have a plum, she said She
held the bag out. I am lost, she said. We are, we are, lost. I'm afraid
to say.

What came next I cannot, you understand, describe in clock-
time. I have never been lost since, not utterly lost, without the
sanctuary of sense; without the reasonable hope that I will and
can and deserve to be saved. But for that next buried hour, which
seemed like a day, and a day with fading light, we ran like rabbits:
pile to pile, scrap to scrap, the wrecks towering, as we went deeper,
for twenty feet above our heads. I could not blame her. I did not.
But I did not see how I could help us either.

If it had been the moors, some ancestral virtue would have
propelled me, I felt, towards the metalled road, towards a stream
bed or cloud that would have conveyed me, soaked and beaten,
towards the A57, towards the sanctuary of some stranger's car;
and the wet inner breath of that vehicle would have felt to me,
whoever owned it, like the wet protective breathing of the belly of
the whale. But here, there was nothing alive. There was nothing I
could do, for there was nothing natural. The metal stretched, friable,
bl***k, against evening light. We shall have to live on plums for
ever, I thought. For I had the sense to realise that the only incursion
here would be from the wreckers' ball. No flesh would be salvaged
here; there would be no rescue team. When Tabby reached for my
hand, her fingertips were cold as ball-bearings. Once, she heard
people calling. Men's voices. She said she did. I heard only distant,

formless shouts. They are calling our names, she said. Uncle Jacob, Daddy Jack. They are calling for us.

She began to move, for the first time, in a purposive direction. 'Uncle Jacob!' she called. In her eyes was that shifty light of unconviction that I had seen on my mother's face – could it be only this morning? 'Uncle Jacob!' She paused in her calling, respectful, so I could call in my turn. But I did not call. I would not, or I could not? A scalding pair of tears popped into my eyes. To know that I lived, I touched the knotted mass of hair, the secret above my nape: my fingers rubbed and rubbed it, round and round. If I survived, it would have to be combed out, with torture. This seemed to militate against life; and then I felt, for the first time and not the last, that death at least is straightforward. Tabby called, 'Uncle Jacob!' She stopped, her breath tight and short, and held out to me the last plum stone, the kernel, sucked clear of flesh.

I took it without disgust from her hand. Tabby's troubled eyes looked at it. It sat in my palm, a shrivelled brain from some small animal. Tabby leaned forward. She was still breathing hard. The edge of her littlest nail picked at the convolutions. She put her hand against her ribs. She said, 'It is like the map of the world.'

There was an interval of praying. I will not disguise it. It was she who raised the prospect. 'I know a prayer,' she said. I waited. 'Little Jesus, meek and mild ...'

I said, 'What's the good of praying to a baby?'

She threw her head back. Her nostrils flared. Prayers began to run out of her.

'Now I lay me down, to sleep,
 – I pray the Lord my soul to keep'
Stop, I said.
'If I should die before I wake—'

My fist, before I even knew it, clipped her across the mouth.

After a time, she raised her hand there. A fingertip trembled against the corner of her lip, the crushed flesh like velvet. She crept her lip downwards, so that for a moment the inner membrane showed, dark and bruised. There was no blood.

I said, 'Aren't you going to cry?'

She said, 'Are you?'

I couldn't say, I never cry. It was not true. She knew it. She said softly, it is all right if you want to cry. You're a Catholic, aren't you? Don't you know a Catholic prayer?

Hail Mary, I said. She said, teach it me. And I could see why: because night was falling: because the sun lay in angry streaks across farther peaks of the junkyard. 'Don't you have a watch?' she whispered. 'I have one it is Timex, but it is at home, in my bedroom.' I said, I have a watch it is Westclox, but I am not allowed to wind it, it is only to be wound by Jack. I wanted to say, and often he is tired, it is late, my watch is winding down, it is stopping but I dare not ask, and when next day it's stopped there's bellowing, only I can do a bleeding thing in this bleeding house. (Door slam.)

There is a certain prayer which never fails. It is to St Bernard; or by him, I was never quite clear. Remember oh most loving Virgin Mary, that it is a thing *unheard of* that anyone *ever* beseeched thy aid, craved thy intercession or implored thy help and was left forsaken. I thought that I had it, close enough – they might not be the exact words but could a few errors matter, when you were kicking at the very gate of the Immaculate herself? I was ready to implore, ready to crave: and this prayer, I knew, was the best and most powerful prayer ever invented. It was a clear declaration that heaven must help you, or go to hell! It was a taunt, a challenge, to Holy Mary, Mother of God. Get it fixed! Do it now! It is a thing *unheard* of! But just as I was about to begin, I realised I must not say it after all. Because if it didn't work …

The strength seemed to drain away then, from my arms and legs. I sat down, in the deep shadows of the wrecks, when all the indications were that we should keep climbing. I wasn't about to take a bet on St Bernard's prayer, and live my whole life knowing it was useless. My life might be long, it might be very long. I must have thought there were worse circumstances, in which I'd need to deal this final card from my sleeve.

'Climb!' said Tabby. I climbed. I knew – did she? – that the rust might crumble beneath us and drop us into the heart of the wrecks. Climb, she said, and I did: each step tested, so that I learned the resistance of rotting metal, the play and the give beneath my feet, the pathetic cough and wheeze of it, its abandonment and mineral despair. Tabby climbed. Her feet scurried, light, skipping, the soles of her sandals skittering and scratching like rats. And then, like

stout Cortez, she stopped, pointed, and stared. 'The woodpiles!'
I gazed upwards into her face. She swayed and teetered, six feet
above me. Evening breeze whipped her skirt around her stick legs.
'The woodpiles!' Her face opened like a flower.

What she said meant nothing to me, but I understood the
message. We are out! she cried. Her arm beckoned me. Come on,
come on! She was shouting down to me, but I was crying too hard
to hear. I worked myself up beside her: crab arms, crab legs, two
steps sideways for every step forward. She reached down and
scooped at my arm, catching at my clothes, pulling, hauling me up
beside her. I shook myself free. I pulled out the stretched sleeve of
my cardigan, eased the shape into the wool, and slid it back past
my wrist. I saw the light on the still body of water, and the small
muddy path that had brought us there.

'Well, you girls,' Jacob said, 'don't you know we came calling?
Didn't you hear us?'

Well, suppose I did, I thought, Suppose she was right. I can just
hear myself, can't you, bawling, here, Daddy Jack, here I am! Come
and save me, Daddy Jack!

It was seven o'clock. They had been composing sandwiches and
Jacob had been for ice cream and wafers. Though missed, we had
never been a crisis. The main point was that we should be there for
the right food at the right time.

The little boys slept on the way home, and I suppose so did I.
The next day, next week, next months are lost to me. It startles me
now that I can't imagine how I said goodbye to Tabby, and that I
can't even remember at what point in the evening she melted away,
her crayons in her satchel and her memories in her head. Somehow,
with good fortune on our side for once, my family must have rolled
home; and it would be another few years before we ventured so
far again.

The fear of being lost comes low these days on the scale of fears
I have to live with. I try not to think about my soul, lost or not
(though it must be thirty years since my last confession), and I
don't generally have to resort to that covert shuffle whereby some
women turn the map upside down to count off the road junctions.

They say that females can't read maps and never know where they are, but in the year 2000 the Ordnance Survey appointed its first woman director, so I suppose that particular slander loses its force. I married a man who casts a professional eye on the lie of the land, and would prefer me to direct with reference to tumuli, stream beds and ancient monuments. But a finger tracing the major routes is enough for me, and I just say nervously, 'We are about two miles from our turn-off or maybe, of course, we are not.' Because they are always tearing up the contour lines, ploughing under the map, playing hell with the cartography that last year you were sold as *le dernier cri*.

As for the moorland landscape, I know now that I have left it far behind. Even those pinching little boys in the back seat share my appreciation of wild-flower verges and lush arable acres. It is possible, I imagine, to build a home on firm ground, a home with long views. I don't know what became of Jacob and his family: did I hear they went home to Africa? Of Tabby, I never heard again. But in recent years, since Jack has been wandering in the country of the dead, I see again his brown skin, his roving caramel eyes, his fretting rage against power and its abuses: and I think perhaps that he was lost all his life, and looking for a house of justice, a place of safety to take him in.

In the short term, though, we continued to live in one of those houses where there was never any money, and doors were slammed hard. One day the glass did spring out of the kitchen cupboard, at the mere touch of my fingertips. At once I threw up my hands, to protect my eyes. Between my fingers, for some years, you could see the delicate scars, like the ghosts of lace gloves, that the cuts left behind.

FATHER, FATHER

Susan Hill

> Susan Hill (b. 1942) is a British author, best known for her
> novel *The Woman in Black*, which was adapted into a
> long-running stage show in London's West End. She won
> the Somerset Maugham Award in 1971 for *I'm the King of
> the Castle*, and was awarded a CBE in 2012.

'I never realised,' Nita said, standing beside the washbasin rinsing
out a tooth glass. Kay was turning a face flannel over and over
between her hands, quite pointlessly.

'Dying. Do you mean about dying?'

'That. Yes.'

They were silent, contemplating it, the truth sinking in at last
with the speaking of the word. In the room across the landing their
mother was dying.

'I really meant Father.'

Naturally they had always seemed happy. Theirs had been the
closest of families for thirty-seven years, Raymond and Elinor, Nita
and Kay the two little girls. People used to point them out: 'The
happy family.'

So they had taken it for granted that he loved her, as they loved
her, fiercely and full of pride in her charm and her warmth and her
skill, loved her more than they loved him, if they had ever had to
choose. Not that they did not love their father. But he was a man,
and that itself set him outside their magic ring. They simply did not
know him. Not as they knew one another, and knew her.

'But not this.'

Not this desperate, choking, terrified devotion, this anguish by
her bed, this distraught clinging. This was a love they could not
recognise and did not know how to deal with – and even, in a
way, resented. And so they fussed over him, his refusal to eat, his
red eyes, the flesh withering on his frame; they took him endless
cups of tea, coffee, hot water with lemon, but otherwise could not

face his anguished, embarrassing love, and the fear on his face, his openness to grief.

The end was agony, though perhaps it was more so for them, for their mother seemed unaware of it all now. She had slipped down out of reach.

It lasted for hours. There was a false alarm. The doctor came. Next she rallied, and even seemed about to wake briefly, before drowning again.

They had both gone to sleep, Nita on the sewing-room sofa under a quilt, Kay in the kitchen rocking chair, slumped awkwardly across her arm. But some change woke them and they both went into the hall, looking at one another in terror, scarcely believing, icy calm. They went up the stairs without speaking.

Afterwards, and for the rest of their lives, the picture was branded on their minds and the branding marks became deeper and darker and more ineradicable with everything that happened. So that what might have been a tender, fading memory became a bitter scar. Their father was kneeling beside the bed. He had her hand between both of his and clutched to his breast, and his tears were splashing down onto it and running over it. Every few minutes a groan came from him, a harsh, raw sound which appalled them.

The lamp was on, tipped away from her face and the golden-yellow curtains she had chosen for their cheerful brightness during the day were now dull topaz. The bedside table was a litter of bottles and pots of medicines.

Her breathing was hoarse, as if her chest was a gravel bed through which water was trying to strain. Now and then it heaved up and collapsed down again. But the rest of her body was almost flat to the bed, almost a part of it. She was so thin, the bedclothes were scarcely lifted.

Nita felt for Kay's hand and pressed until it hurt, though neither of them was aware of it. Their father was still bent over the figure on the bed, still holding, holding on.

And then, shocking them, everything stopped. There was a rasping breath, and after it, nothing, simply nothing at all, and the world stopped turning and waited, though what was being waited for they could not have told.

That split second fell like a drop of balm in the tumult of her dying and their distress, so that long afterwards each of them would try to recall it for comfort. But almost at once it was driven out by the cataract of grief and rage that poured from their father. The bellow of pain that horrified them so that in the end they fled down to the sitting room, and held each other and wept, but quietly, and with a restraint and dignity that was shared and unspoken.

There was to be a funeral tea, though not many would come. She had outlived most of her relatives and had needed few friends, their family unit had been so tight, yielding her all she had wanted.

But those who did come must be properly entertained.

Nita and Kay arrived back before the rest to prepare, though the work had been done by Mrs Willis and her daughter.

The hall was cool. Nita, standing in front of the mirror to take off her hat and tidy her hair, caught her sister's eye. They were exhausted. The whole day, like the whole week, seemed unreal, something they had floated through. Their father had wept uncontrollably in the church, and at the graveside bent forward so far, as the coffin was lowered, that they had half-feared he was about to pitch himself in after it.

Behind Nita, Kay's face was pinched, the eye sockets bruise-coloured. There was everything to say. There was nothing to say. The clock ticked.

She will never hear it tick again, Nita thought.

For a second, then, the truth found an entrance and a response, but there was no time, the cars had returned, there were footsteps on the path, voices. The truth retreated again.

They turned, faces composed. Nita opened the door.

Every day for the next six months they thought that he would die too. If he did not, it was not any will to live that prevented it. He scarcely ate. He saw no one. He scarcely spoke. He had always been interested in money, money was his work, his hobby, his passion. Now, the newspapers lay unopened, bank letters and packets of company reports gathered dust. For much of the time he sat in the drawing room opposite his wife's chair. Often he wept. Whenever he could persuade Nita or Kay to sit with him he talked about their mother. Within the half-year she had achieved sainthood and become perfect in the memory, every detail about her sacred, every aspect of their marriage without flaw.

'I miss her,' Kay said, one evening in October. They were in the kitchen, tidying round, putting away, laying the table for breakfast.

Nita sat down abruptly. The kitchen went silent. It had been said. Somehow, until now, they had not dared.

'Yes.'

'I miss laughing with her over the old photographs, I miss watching her embroider. Her hands.'

'People don't now, do they? There used to be all those little shops for silks and threads and transfers.'

They thought of her sewing box, in the drawing room by the French windows, and the last, intricate piece, unfinished on the round wood frame.

'Things will never be the same, Kay.'

'But they will get better. Surely they'll get better.'

'I suppose so.'

'Perhaps – we ought at least to start looking at some of the things.'

The sewing box, her desk, the drawers and wardrobe in her bedroom. Clothes, earrings, hair-brushes, letters, embroidery silks were spread out for inspection in their minds.

'You read about people quarrelling with their mothers.'

'We never quarrelled.'

'You couldn't.'

'You read about it being the natural way of things.'

'Quarrelling is not obligatory.'

They caught one another's eye and Nita laughed. The laughter grew, and took them gradually over; they laughed until they cried, and sat back exhausted, muscles aching, and the laughter broke something, some seal that had been put on life to keep it down.

Outside Nita's room, they held one another, knowing that the laughter had marked a change. In the study, hearing their laughter coming faintly from the distant kitchen, their father let misery and loneliness and self-pity wash over him, and sank back, submerging himself under the wave.

What would life be like? They did not know. Each morning they went out of the house together, at the same time, and parted at the end of the next street. Nita walked on, to her hospital reception desk. Kay caught her bus to the department store where she was Ladies' Fitter.

At six they met again, and walked home. And so, life was the same, it went on in the old way – yet it did not. Even the shape of the trees in the avenue seemed changed. When they neared the house something came over them, some miasma of sorrow and fear and uncertainty, and a sort of dread.

Each knew that the other felt it, but neither spoke of it; they spoke, as before, of the ordinary details of the day, the weather, the news of the town.

And in each of their minds was always the question – will today be different? Will this be the day when he wakes from the terrible paralysis of misery?

But when the door opened into the cool, silent hall and the light caught the bevel of the mirror, they knew at once that after all, this was not the day, and went in to hang their coats and empty this or that bag, to wash and tidy before going in to him.

The medicines had been thrown away and a few bills and receipts and shopping lists, otherwise he would allow nothing to be sorted or moved or cleared.

Everything must remain as she had left it.

Once, a few days after the funeral, Kay had crept into her mother's bedroom and sat on the bed, which the nurse had stripped and re-made with fresh linen, as if, somehow, her mother might come back and it must be ready for her. And she had been everywhere in the room. Kay had touched the dressing gown behind the door, and the touch had disturbed the faint fine smell of the violet talcum powder and soap her mother had used, and brought her back even more vividly.

Six months later, nothing had been moved, but going into the room again, in search of her mother's old address book, she had sensed the difference at once. There was a hollow, she was no longer there. The bedroom was quite empty of her.

Kay had found, as she stood for a few moments at the window looking out over the garden, that she could not conjure her mother up in any way, could not picture her, could not remember the sound of her voice. When she touched the dressing gown, the smell had gone.

'Father ought to go in there now,' she said, going in to Nita. 'Surely it might ...'

Her sister shook her head.

'Perhaps Dr Boyle—'

'But he isn't ill.'

'I suppose not.'

'Perhaps you are right though, about the room.'

'What should we say?'

They imagined what words might conceivably serve, where they might possibly begin.

'It would be best to be straightforward,' Nita said at last.

'Could you?'

'I – I think I must.'

But two days later, it was Kay who spoke, coming into the drawing room and finding it in darkness, so that she startled him by clicking on the light.

There had been some petty irritations during the day and she was suffering from a cold; if it had not been for those things she might never have confronted him, would never have had the courage.

'Whatever are you doing sitting here in the dark again, Father? Whatever good is this going to do any of us?'

She saw that she had shocked him and his shock gave her nerve.

'It is six months since Mother died, half a year. What good are you doing? We have to go out, carry on a life. That's how it should be, how it has to be. Do you think we haven't felt it and missed her as much as you? Do you suppose she would think well of you, hiding away, wringing your hands? You've interest in nothing, concern for nothing. You're in the half-dark. Have you wondered how it is for us, coming back to it at the end of every day?'

She heard herself as she might hear someone in a play. She was not startled or made afraid by her own voice, or the passion with which she had spoken. She simply heard herself, with interest but without emotion and when she stopped speaking she heard the silence.

Her father was staring at her, his face brick-red, his mouth working.

She began to shake.

It was Nita who saved them, coming without any warning into the room.

'Kay?'

She looked at her sister, at her father, at the two shocked faces and though she had heard nothing of what had been said, the force of it seemed to press down upon the silence that filled the room and Nita understood the enormity of what had happened.

'Kay?'

But Kay was frozen, she could neither speak nor move, could scarcely even breathe.

And then he got up and without looking at either of them, blundered out of the room, and through the hall towards the stairs.

When they returned home the following evening he was not in the house. He had left before ten, Mrs Willis said, in a taxi which was taking him in to the city.

By the time he returned they had gone to bed, though both were lying awake, turning the events over in their minds. Both heard his key in the lock, his footsteps, the closing of his bedroom door. Both thought of creeping along the corridor to the other. Neither did.

The next day, the pattern was the same, and so, until the end of that week, on the Saturday, he ate lunch and supper with them. But something in his look forbade them to refer to any of it. Kay was terrified of catching his eye.

'He is my father, why should I be afraid of him?'

The news was on the television, the one programme they always watched, as they had watched it every night with their mother. Somehow, speaking over the voices on it seemed to Kay like not quite speaking at all.

The news ended. Nita got up.

'He should be grateful to us,' she said and her voice rose. 'Grateful!'

Her sister's face had flushed and Kay saw that there were tears in her eyes.

'It had to stop and I didn't have the courage to say it.'

She went quickly out of the room. Kay stared at the blank screen, and quite suddenly, her mother's face came to mind; she saw her as she had been, long before the illness, saw her grey, neatly parted hair and the soft cheeks, saw her smiling, pleased, patient expression. She had gone and now she had come back.

The television screen remained opaque and grey.

'Yes,' Kay said to herself. 'Yes.'

As she left the sewing room where they kept the television set her father came out of his study and instinctively Kay stepped back, acutely conscious of what had been said earlier.

'Kay.'

She found herself reaching out, and then held by him, her face against his sleeve, pressed into the cloth, smelling his soap and the faint smell of his city day which brought her childhood back to envelop her and hold her as he held her himself.

Nothing else was said after the one word 'Kay' and in a second or two he disengaged himself gently and went down the passage towards the side door that led to the garden. Every night, until the last weeks of her mother's life, he had gone there at the end of the evening to smoke a single small cigar. Kay went up to her bedroom and opened the window and after a moment the smell of the smoke came to her from the garden below.

She felt a rush of the most exhilarating happiness, as the anxiety and gloom of the past weeks fell away. The house had been sunk into the dreary aftermath of their mother's death for so long that she had forgotten even the small, pleasant details of everyday life until now, when one of them had been given back. They were all weary, their flesh felt dead, their skins grey, their movements were slow; there had been no lightness in anything, the subdued atmosphere had become usual, their father's isolated uncommunicated grief suffocating everything that might have been enjoyed or anticipated.

She leaned further out of the window, intent on catching as much as possible of the smell of his cigar smoke.

We have come through it, she thought. We have come through.

She was not rash enough to expect life to be everything that it had been. Their mother was dead. Nothing could alter that, nothing lessened the pain though the death had been 'a blessing'.

But something had changed at last. They had all moved on and surely for good.

She waited at the open window until the last trace of smoke had faded from the air and the only smell was of night, and grass and the earth. Then she got into bed, and slept like something new born.

And indeed, slowly, gradually the mood in the house lightened. Their father spoke to them, went out, returned with the evening paper, opened letters, worked at his desk. There was no laughter yet, and no social life. Friends and neighbours were not invited. But they had all of them lost the habit of that and did not feel any particular need yet to re-acquire it.

'In the summer,' Nita said.

'Perhaps we could have one of the old summer garden parties.'

'I wonder – do you think Father has given any thought to a holiday?'

Such small exchanges lightened their days. There was no sense of urgency or anxiety, no need to push forward too fast. But when they spoke of their mother now it was with smiling reminiscence, only tinged at the edges with sorrow.

On a Wednesday evening, almost eight months after the death, they walked down the avenue together as usual, and into the house.

'Hello?'

Sometimes they returned first, sometimes he did, and so one or other always called out.

'Hello?'

It was late spring but exceptionally warm. The drawing-room door was open. Nita went through.

The French windows were also open. From the garden came voices speaking quietly together.

'Kay.'

'What's wrong?'

'There is – there's someone in the garden with Father.'

They looked at one another, recognising the next step taken, the next stage reached.

'Good,' Kay said. 'Isn't that good?'

Though they had to wait and absorb it, take in the feeling of strangeness. No one else had been in the house since the day of the funeral. Now someone was here, some old friend of his, some neighbour, and although if asked they would each have said that they welcomed it, nevertheless it felt like a violation of something that had grown to become sacred.

The clock ticked in the hall behind them.

'Oh goodness,' Kay said, half-laughing with impatience at their own hesitation, and walked boldly out through the open windows onto the terrace.

The scene, and the next moments that passed, took their place in the series of ineradicable pictures etched into their minds, joining their mother's deathbed, the funeral, the sight of their father leaning over the grave.

Two garden chairs were drawn up on either side of the small table. Two cups and saucers, the teapot, milk jug and sugar bowl stood on the table. That fact alone they had difficulty in absorbing, and wondered wildly how the tea had come to be made and found its way out there.

Hearing them, their father turned, but did not get up.

Kay and Nita hesitated like children uncertain of what to say or do next, needing permission to come forward. They were on the outside of a charmed circle.

'Here you are!' he said.

After another moment, and as one, they began to cross the grass.

'This is a friend of mine – Leila. Leila Crocker.' He gestured expansively. 'My daughters. Nita. Kay.'

They knew, Nita said afterwards. They knew absolutely and at once and their stomachs plunged like lifts down a deep shaft, leaving only nausea.

The garden froze, the colours were blanched out of everything, the leaves stiffened, the trees went dead. Unbelievably, instinctively, impossibly, they knew.

She stood. Said, 'How very nice.'

Under their feet, deep below the grass and turf, the earth seemed to shift and heave treacherously, shaking their confidence, throwing them off balance. The sky tipped and ended up on its side, like a house after a bomb had fallen.

At the moment of death, it is said, a person's past rushes towards them, but it was the whole of the future that they saw, in the instant between taking in the presence of the woman with their father, and her words; and in composing themselves to greet her, they saw what was to come in every aspect and detail, it seemed.

'But that cannot have been so,' Nita said, years later. Yet it had. They knew that absolutely.

But all they saw was a woman, of perhaps forty-five, perhaps a few years less or a few years more, who wore a cherry-red suit and had hair formed in an extraordinary bolster above her brow, and who was called Leila Crocker.

'Leila,' she said quickly; 'please call me that.'

They would not. At once they retreated into themselves like snails touched on the tenderest tips of their horns. They could not possibly call her Leila, and so they called her nothing at all.

'I'm afraid the tea will have gone cold.' And she touched the china pot with the blue ribbon pattern. Nita and Kay flinched, though giving no outward sign. The last woman to have touched the blue ribbon teapot had been their mother.

'Not that we've left much of it I'm afraid.'

Their father's voice sounded quite different to them. Lighter, younger, the tone oddly jovial. Everything about him was lighter and younger. He sat back smiling, leaning back in the garden chair, looking at the blue ribbon teapot, and at the woman.

'No please.' Nita made a strange little gesture, like a half-bow. 'Don't worry. We always make tea freshly.'

No one moved then. No one else spoke.

We make a tableau, Kay thought, or one of those old pictures. 'Tea in the Garden' – no, 'A Visitor to Tea'.

Their father might have spoken then, might have told them to take their freshly made tea into the garden to join them. The woman might have said, observing their evening routine, that she must go. But he did not, she did not; they sat, as if waiting to resume an interrupted conversation, so that in the end it was Nita who broke the tableau, by turning and going quickly back across the lawn and through the open French window into the house. Kay gave a half-smile, as if in some kind of hopeless explanation or apology – though meaning neither – before following her sister.

Just at the window, she glanced quickly back, expecting them to be watching, feeling their eyes on her. But her father and the woman were turned towards one another, both leaning forwards slightly, their eager conversation eagerly resumed.

We might not have been here, Kay thought.

In the kitchen, Nita dropped the lid of the kettle and the sound went on reverberating on the tiled floor, even after she had bent impatiently to pick it up.

Rain poured off the roofs of the houses they walked past and the early blossom lay in sad, sodden little heaps in the gutter. Spring had retreated behind banked, swollen clouds and a cold wind.

'Perhaps it is time for us to leave home,' Kay said into the umbrella with which she was trying to shield her head and face. Nita stopped dead and lifted her own umbrella to stare at her sister and the rain flowed off it down her neck.

'Even without ... well, there will surely be changes. Perhaps we should institute our own.'

'Why must there be changes?'

'Aren't we rather too old to be living at home still?'

Kay was thirty-five, Nita about thirty-seven. They looked older. Felt older.

'But wherever would we go to? Where would you want to go?'

'A flat?'

'Do you like flats?'

'Not particularly.'

'We are perfectly happy and comfortable as we are.'

'Yes.'

They turned the corner. Each had had a private inner glimpse into the rooms of a small flat, and looked quickly away.

'Besides.'

The rest was unspoken, and perfectly understood. Besides, Nita would have continued, now that she has come to the house there is all the more reason than ever for us to stay.

Every afternoon since that first day when they had stepped into the garden and seen their father sitting with Leila Crocker over the blue ribbon teapot, they had dreaded coming home and finding her there again. Twice already they had done so. Once, the two of them had been seated in exactly the same place in the garden, the table and the tea things between them so that they might never have moved at all.

The next time, Leila Crocker had been coming along the passage from the downstairs cloakroom as they opened the front door. None of them had known what to say.

Now, Kay turned her key in the lock, pushed the door slowly and waited. They both waited, listening. But the house was empty, they could feel at once. It felt and sounded and smelled empty. The clock ticked. Nita took both umbrellas out to the scullery.

At the end of the television news, when Kay had switched off the set, their father had not come home.

'He has never said anything.'

'Perhaps he has nothing to say.'

'He has told us nothing about her. Wouldn't it be usual – to tell something?'

'What is "usual"? I don't think I know.'

'No.'

It was not that he had behaved secretively, or evasively, or avoided them. Things had gone on exactly as before. Except that in some vital, deep-rooted way, they had not. Because always, no matter how he behaved, the woman was between the three of them.

The taxi came for him each morning. He went out, returned, sometimes very late, opened his letters, read the newspaper, worked at his desk, smoked his single late cigar. When they were all together, he ate with them. When he was not at home, they had no idea of where he was and could not ask.

The house seemed suddenly imbued with meaning, redolent of their past and precious to them. Every door handle and window-pane and cupboard. Every book and curtain and step on the stairs. The mirror in the hall and the clock and the blue ribbon teapot, all seemed to hold the life of their family within every atom, to be infinitely more than household objects made of wood and glass and metal and china and paint. Every touch and footstep, the echo of every word spoken, was part of the fabric and substance of the house. At night they lay and wrapped it round themselves and held it to them.

They were possessive, passionate and jealous of it and everything it contained. The feeling they had for it was as strong and vital as their love for their father and the memory of their mother. They were shocked by the power of it.

They could not say that they liked Leila Crocker. They could not say that they disliked her.

'Her hair is very tightly permed,' Kay said.

'But her shoes are good.'

At the department store during one lunch hour Kay had suddenly told the other fitter about it. Anne McKay's hirsute face had lit up.

'Oh, Kay, that is so very nice! Isn't that nice for him? I think that's lovely.'

What is 'lovely'? Kay thought, panicking. I have told her that he brought a woman to tea. Her face betrayed her terror. Anne McKay reached out and touched her arm. They were seated in the old broken-down basket chairs in the dusty little staffroom.

'I meant how lovely for him to have some companionship. I know you miss your mother, of course you do, but life has to move on.'

Does it? Why does it? Why can it not stay as it is? Kay took a bite from her sandwich but could not swallow it.

'You won't be at home for ever, will you? Either of you.'

Won't we? Why not? Why should we ever leave? Who could make us?

Kay jumped up, and went to the cloakroom and there spat the piece of sandwich violently into the lavatory basin.

'I suppose,' Nita said, hearing about it later, 'that companionship is important.'

'He has us. He isn't alone.'

'We should try to be fair.'

'What is "unfair"?'

'We are – well, isn't it quite different?'

'From what?'

'I mean, it is just a different kind of companionship – friendship. Of course it is, Kay.'

But what the nature of the friendship or companionship was they could not have said.

*

It had been raining for almost a week, but now, as they walked the last hundred yards down the avenue, the sun came out and shone in their faces and reflected watery gold on the wet pavement and the house roof.

'We must try to be fair,' Nita said again.

They quickened their steps.

But the house was empty, as it was empty every evening for the next week, and after that, it seemed, was never empty again. It was the speed of it all that horrified them, the speed which was, Kay said, unnecessary and unseemly.

'And rather hurtful.'

But their father was now oblivious to everything except the woman he was to marry. For he would marry Leila Crocker, he said, telling them, with neither warning nor ceremony, the next time he spent an evening at home with them.

'I should like you to know,' he had said, laying down his soup spoon, 'that I have asked Leila to be my wife.'

The room went deathly silent and, it seemed to Kay and Nita, deathly cold. A chill mist seemed to creep in under the door and the window frame, curling itself round them so that they actually shivered. They could not look at him or at one another. They could do nothing.

'I have found a very dear companion, a very fine person with whom to share the rest of my life. Your mother – her illness and her death – were – very difficult. I had not imagined – of course you hardly know Leila, but you will come to know her, and to love and admire her, I am quite certain of it. Quite certain.'

He beamed innocently from one to the other.

'This is going to be a very happy home once more.'

It was like their bereavement all over again but in a way worse, because death was the final certainty, and this was uncertain, this would go on and on. Their whole lives would change but they did not know how. Their future would be entirely different but they could not picture it.

That first night, after he had told them, the silence had been so terrible, his eager, beaming face so open and expectant, that Nita had prayed to die, then, there, rather than have to face any of it and

Kay had wished her tongue cut out, for any words she might feel able to utter would be wrong and false and surely choke her.

In the end, after what might have been a minute or a lifetime, their father said, 'I hope very much that you are pleased.'

Kay swallowed.

'Of course, your mother—'

Nita leaped up, pushing her chair back with such force that it toppled and crashed over behind her. 'She – Mother has nothing to do with this – please do not talk about Mother.'

'Perhaps—' Kay heard her own voice, strangled and peculiar. 'Perhaps you may be able to understand what a shock this is.'

'But you *are* happy for me? You do share this happiness with me?'

His face was that of a child anxious for approval, and their feelings as they looked at him were impossible, confused, painful.

'She has given me a new life.'

They fled.

The next morning Nita woke Kay up before seven o'clock.

'I am going to the service. Will you come?'

Kay turned onto her back. They had not been to church since the Sunday after the funeral.

'What will you pray for?'

'Guidance.'

'For him?'

'For ourselves.'

'For it to end – for this – this thing to be over.'

Nita sat down on her sister's bed. 'I think,' she said carefully, 'that it will not.'

'No.'

'And I find I cannot cope with – I have never felt like this in my life.'

'What do you feel?'

'I think it is hatred. And anger. Great anger.'

'Betrayal.'

'Is it?'

'But not us – it is not us he is betraying.'

'No.'

'It is indecent. He is an old man.'

'Perhaps if it had been in a few years' time.'

'That is the worst, isn't it? Think of all those tears. All that – and how to think it was all lies and falseness.'

'Oh I don't think it was. He did—'

'Love Mother?'

'Yes.'

'Then how could he?'

'If I don't deal with this terrible hatred it will become destructive of everything. I hardly slept.'

'Burrowing.'

'Yes. It's like that. A canker. Will you come?'

'No.'

'We have to try. We must try.'

'For her sake?'

'No, for him. Of course for him.'

'Do you like her?'

'We barely know her. I only say we should try.'

'You are too good.'

Kay turned over and pressed her face hard into her pillow. Her mother seemed to be somewhere in the depths of it, as she was everywhere now, smiling, patient. Betrayed. 'You will have to go by yourself,' Kay said, tears pouring down her face.

The city restaurant had been full at ten minutes past one and so they had been obliged to share a table. That was how they had met.

'I suppose she had been on the lookout for just such a man, eating alone.'

'Kay—'

'Unfair?'

'Yes.'

'It is all unfair.'

'She is very nice to us.'

'Why should she not be?'

'We have not been altogether nice to her – we have perhaps been rather unwelcoming.'

'Of course we have. She is unwelcome.'

Though so far Leila Crocker had behaved impeccably. She had been reserved, friendly hut never effusive. Pleasant and careful.

'It really is difficult to dislike her,' Nita said.

'I don't care for her clothes.'

'Well they are perfectly good clothes.'

'Oh yes. *Good* clothes.'

Leila Crocker wore smart suits in plain colours, alternating them week by week, cherry-red, ice-blue, camel, mauve. She was, she said, personal assistant to a managing director. The second rime she came to the house, she told them that she was forty-four.

'Why did she suppose her age was of any interest to us? It is no business of ours.'

Their father was almost thirty years older. They could not talk to him.

'I hope that things will go on as they always have,' he said.

'How can they? How can anything ever be as it was?'

Kay ran her finger over and over the closed lid of the piano.

'He is destroying all of it.'

'Do stop doing that.'

'Do you suppose he ever thinks – thinks of Mother?'

'Surely he must.'

'What? What can he think?'

'You will take off the veneer.'

'There is no one else left to defend her memory.'

'Is that what we are for?'

'What else?'

'It is almost as though thirty-seven years had somehow—'

'Well they have not.' Kay spoke in a raw, furious whisper.

'Do stop doing that. I think I shall go mad,' Nita shouted, then went quite silent. They stared at one another fearfully.

'Look,' Kay said after a moment. 'Look what is happening, what it is making us do. Everything is cracking and splintering and being destroyed. Even us.'

A month after Leila Crocker had first come to the house, Nita found her in the kitchen one evening.

'I am cooking for us all.'

'Oh, there is no need. I was going to make omelettes with a salad.'

'I'm sure you would prefer roast chicken.'

'And then,' Nita said, going in, trembling, to her sister's room, 'I noticed it.'

'Noticed what?'

'How can he think of doing such a thing? How can he?'

The light had caught the ring on Leila Crocker's hand as she had reached out to one of the kitchen taps.

Kay laid down her pen. Her diary was open on the desk in front of her.

'The diamond hoop with the small sapphires?'

'Yes.'

Though their mother had rarely worn it, saying it was too special, too dressy, it was to be kept for very special occasions, and those had rarely come, in such quiet, self-contained lives.

'Are you sure?'

The words came out of Kay's mouth as heavy and cold and separate as marbles.

'Go down and see for yourself. If he has to give her a ring – well, people naturally do—'

'Not the ring that belonged to their wife of thirty-seven years who has been dead for under a year. I think not.'

At two o'clock in the morning, Kay went into her sister's room and, after hesitating a moment, her bed.

'Ninny?' She had not used the name for twenty years.

'I'm not asleep.'

'I don't think I can bear it.'

'I know.'

'I feel as if I were a child.'

'What would other people do? Different kinds of people?'

Kay thought of Anne McKay, and Mrs Willis. 'Do you – do you believe she can know?'

They lay, picturing their mother, floating somewhere nearby, smiling, patient.

Is it for her? Nita thought, feeling her sister's warmth to the side of her. As children they had often crept into one another's beds. Is it really for Mother's sake that I mind what is happening more than I have ever minded anything apart from her dying?

But in the end she turned on her side and took her sister's hand and, after a few moments, slept, exhausted by the impossible, unanswerable questions.

'We cannot possibly go to the wedding,' Kay had said. But of course they did, and somehow got through the service, at which there were three hymns and two readings and Leila Crocker wore cream lace. The church and the hotel room afterwards were full of strangers. Their father's face was flushed with excitement and open devotion.

Somehow, they got through all of it. Somehow, they stayed until the car had left the hotel courtyard, waved at by the strangers.

In the avenue, Kay stopped, took off her jacket and shook it out until the few paper rose petals drifted into the gutter.

The two weeks that followed were extraordinarily happy. They felt an unreal sense of freedom and contentment, in the house by themselves, answerable to no one. The sun shone; they set the table up on the terrace and ate supper there, and, at the weekend, breakfast and lunch as well.

They put a shield around themselves. Neither referred to their father or to the marriage. When postcards arrived, first from Rome, and then from Florence, they read and then discarded them without a word.

But on the morning they were due to return Nita cut fresh branches of philadelphus and put them in jugs about the house.

'We have to try. We have a duty to try. Things may go perfectly well.'

From the very beginning they did not, though whose fault it was none of them could have told.

It was difficult to share their home with another, difficult to accept her as having precedence over them, difficult that she and their father slept in the same room, the old room in which their mother had slept in the years before her last illness, difficult to get used to changes of daily routine and the presence of their stepmother's possessions hanging in wardrobes, filling drawers, displacing the old order of things. Difficult to find someone else in the house every evening when they returned home, at supper, at breakfast and for the whole of every weekend.

'Difficult, difficult, difficult,' Kay said, walking faster than usual up the avenue.

But difficult might have become less so. They might perhaps have adapted themselves to the new arrangement, in the end. Difficult was not painful or hurtful and it was pain and hurt which came very quickly.

'What is happening?' Nita said as they rounded the corner, and saw the removal van outside the house. 'What is happening?'

They almost ran.

It was nearly over. The work had been going on for most of the day. All the old furniture from their mother's sewing room and the small sitting room, as well as from the bedroom in which she had died, had gone. In the sitting room were a new, bright-blue sofa and chair, and a glass-fronted cabinet. The sewing room and bedroom were empty.

Their father met them in the hall, saw their faces, but could not manage to meet their eyes.

After that everything disintegrated, everything was swept away, or so it felt. Their mother's clothes were cleared, and her papers. The photographs of her about the drawing room and their father's study disappeared, though her pearls and her two pairs of good earrings did not go, their stepmother wore them.

'How dare she?' Kay said, banging into her father's study. 'How dare she take Mother's things, her personal things, how could you let her?'

'Please lower your voice. I remember that when your mother passed away –'

'Died. She died.'

'—you – and Nita – you said you would prefer not to have those things. As I understood.'

'That did not give – your wife – the right to appropriate them.'

He stood up. 'I gave them to her. I wanted her to have them. Leila took nothing.'

'How could you give them – you?'

'I think, I believe, that it is what—'

'If you say it is what Mother would have wanted, I think I shall kill you.'

'Kay—'

'You let her throw out our mother's furniture – clear her things.'

'We did it together. It was time.'

'For who?'

'For me.'

'You are a blind, cruel, besotted, foolish old man.'

At the top of the stairs, she almost collided heavily with Nita.

'Whatever is happening? Why were you screaming?'

In her own room, Kay sobbed tears of bitter pain and rage.

Nita had closed the door. 'It is very hard,' she said. 'I hate this. I mind it as much as you do. I mind it for Mother's sake and for us, but screaming at Father is not right – he loves her, he is besotted with her. He cannot see that she is doing anything wrong.'

'He is being treacherous, utterly treacherous. He was married to Mother for almost forty years. He loved her, he saw her die and almost went mad with grief. We had to watch all that, bear all that. He has utterly, utterly betrayed her, bringing that woman here, marrying her in such haste, such a few months after – and making that – that vulgar display, that wedding – giving her Mother's jewellery, helping her throw Mother's things away – taking down the photographs.

'She has no idea, none. She is completely insensitive and I do not care for her, I wish she had never come here – but I don't blame her and I do not hate her. I blame him. I hate him. I can't forgive him – I cannot –'

The tears this time were not of anger, but of misery and grief at everything lost, and after a moment Nita cried with her for the same loss, of their mother and of everything that had been hers, and for the loss of him, the loss of all love, for it seemed that their father had taken everything from them, and given it to his wife, taken his love for them and for their mother and theirs for him, taken his loyalty and sense of what was right. Taken their home and their place in it.

They sat holding one another on Kay's bed as the light faded,

and the empty room below and the empty room next door were
like hollow caves carved out of their own hearts.

They lived in the house for another five months, and in that time
everything changed, piece by piece. Everything that was old and
familiar and belonged to their past went and was replaced by
the new, the strange, until only their father's study and their own
rooms remained unaltered. They scarcely spoke to him, avoided
him altogether if they could. To their stepmother they were polite,
with all the careful, wary courtesy of strangers, but they saw, in her
face, in her eyes, that she was indifferent to them.

'They neither need nor want us,' Nita said, 'that much is clear
without anything being said.'

They felt invisible, quite supplanted, quite irrelevant. One
evening they drew a circle on the street map, and began to look
within it. They could not have borne to change their routine, the
walk to the same bus stop, the return together. It was all that was
left to them, apart from their jobs, and their own shared life.

When they found a flat which would do, Kay told their
father, who said nothing. 'You have your own lives to lead,' their
stepmother said brightly; 'naturally you do.'

The flat was really quite pleasant. The sitting room had wide
windows overlooking the chestnut trees that lined the quiet street.
The rooms were freshly painted. They grew used to not having a
garden, particularly as it was winter when they moved in.

They wondered from time to time whether they had judged Leila
Crocker, as they still thought of her, correctly, whether she had
cornered their father into a meeting, marriage, the clearing away
of his past, or whether she had in fact been blameless and the fault
was his, but it came to matter less and less just as, to their surprise,
they were able to remember their mother more clearly in the flat
than they had in the old house. She had come with them, she was
there every evening on their return, in her photograph, which was
everywhere, and with her invisible yet smiling, patient presence.

They thought as little as possible about their father and their
old home, though it was the memories of home which gave them
the greatest pain, striking without warning, because of the way the
sun shone suddenly through a window, or the banging of a gate. At

these moments, the past would wash over them and drown them in itself. Their years of childhood and young womanhood were fresher and more vivid than the previous day so that it seemed they might simply have opened the door and walked back into them.

Their habits firmed, hardened, their natures set. Routine became all-important. They came to dread any disturbance, any hint of the unfamiliar.

Their father's new marriage had nothing to do with them.

'It is far better,' Kay said; 'it is the only way.' And all the while believed it.

But very occasionally, Nita got up before her and went to the early service. Kay could never be persuaded. It was the only rift between them, and slight enough, apart from the day Nita let the blue ribbon teapot slip out of her hands onto the floor of the kitchenette, where it smashed into far too many pieces for there to be the slightest hope of repair. Walking into the room a moment later, Kay found her sister standing, staring down at the shards of china and, recognising them, she began to scream, furiously, uncontrollably, her voice rising and rising, until Nita's face took on a look of pain, and panic, and, as Kay's scream intensified, of fear.

RENAISSANCE

Colette Paul

> Colette Paul is a Scottish author. She has published one
> book of short stories, *Whoever You Choose to Love*, which
> was shortlisted for the Glenfiddich Spirit of Scotland
> Writer's Award. She won the Royal Society of Authors
> Tom-Gallon Trust Award in 2005.

My mum was generally a cheerful person. It was her misfortune
that she had borne a child who was neither cheerful, nor endowed
with finer feelings, as she was. She was always telling me that
when I was a baby I used to lie completely quiet and still for hours
and people would say to her, 'Are you sure that baby's alive?'
and sometimes she herself wondered. She couldn't understand it
because she came from a family of lookers-on-the-bright-side. It
was in the genes.

'Our family motto,' she said, 'was if you break a leg, just be
thankful you didn't break two legs.'

We only went up to Granny Philips's twice a year, and I never
found her and Grandpa very cheery. There was plastic covering the
sofa and tables, and the only time they smiled was when their dog,
Gertrude, came into the room. The conversation revolved around
Gertrude – they loved her more than they loved each other – and
Sam, Mum's brother, who had depression, and still lived at home.

'You *think* you've got depression,' Mum would say to him, 'but
answer me this. Do people in Africa have depression? Do they
have time to get depressed when they've got to walk to the well
and work in the fields? Can they just stay in bed all day, watching
cartoons and thinking how miserable they are?'

'I suppose not,' Sam would say, slumped in his seat, looking
more and more depressed.

Mum's one beef was that she never went to university. This was
the only subject that was immune to her abrasive brand of looking
on the bright side. If she had gone, she said, she would have studied

English. She had won a prize at school for an essay entitled 'Why We Read'. She could remember whole poems, and could recite them off by heart to prove it. One of them was 'The Donkey' by Chesterton. For this one she adopted a low, sad voice, and stood rooted to the spot as if she were possessed by the spirit of the donkey. When it came to *Fools! For I also had my hour* she would fairly belt the line out. I disliked these performances. I found them sentimental, and never knew what to say when she had finished and was looking at me with such sad triumph. Once I asked her what happened to the donkey afterwards, and she got annoyed and said he just went back to being an ugly donkey, but that that wasn't the point.

Mum cited my dad as the reason she didn't go to university. She said she would have thrived in such an atmosphere, but that he didn't want her thriving. He wanted a good little doctor's wife. Dad said the real reason was that Mum didn't have the qualifications to get into university, and that having a good head for poetry didn't mean she was brainy anyway. It just meant she had a good memory. This was the one thing he could say that truly enraged Mum. Usually she ignored his drunken rants, the rants where he would call everyone he knew rotten bastards and elaborate endlessly on the ways they had wronged him. But she couldn't let a slur on her intelligence pass by without comment.

'I'm not the one who had to re-sit their exams three times,' she'd say.

Other times she'd mention her IQ, or the fact that Dad had been scared to try a tomato until he was twenty-one, or that he'd only ever read one book in his life. She never mentioned the most obvious thing, that he was killing off what was left of his brain with alcohol. She ignored what she didn't want to face, and made it seem somehow bad-mannered to mention the obvious. So I never mentioned it either.

I spent most of my time with Mum, and didn't see Dad very much. He worked late, and often wouldn't be home until I'd gone to bed. My response to him was complicated by the fact that he was so changeable. When he was sober he was gentle and easy to be with. We would play draughts or chess together, or take a walk to the beach and skim pebbles. He didn't talk very much and was more comfortable showing me how to do things. By the time I was nine I could put someone in the recovery position, wire a plug, and tie knots to shame the Boy Scouts. Dad never talked about his life, but I felt he was sad, and when he was sober I felt sorry for him. He had a doleful, refugee look about him, as if he didn't belong with the people around him and was ready to apologize at any moment for his presence. I never thought about him being a doctor, and I was always surprised at Christmas time when he would bring home presents his patients had given him. (Unfortunately it was mostly bottles of whisky, which meant a lot of Xmas cheer for Dad, and not much for Mum and me.) For a little while his black bag with his medical equipment inside – his props, Dad called them – fascinated me. The props looked so alien and authoritative, yet Dad could wield them and interpret their signals. When I asked him about them he explained what they were used for, and said they were easy to handle once you knew how.

'Anyone can do it,' he said, and I believed him and stopped being impressed.

By the time I was twelve he was drunk or hung over more often than he was sober. One afternoon, just before the summer holidays, Mum came into my room and told me we were moving.

'Your father's lost his job,' she said. 'He's in disgrace.'

'What'd he do?' I said.

Mum walked over to the window and stared outside. Then she came over and put her hands on my shoulders.

'Don't hunch,' she said, 'it makes you look like an old woman.'

'I'm not hunching,' I said.

She said it would be good for us to live somewhere new, but she didn't sound as if she believed it.

'You'll miss your friends,' she said, 'but you'll make new ones. And so will I. It'll be exciting.'

'I don't have any friends,' I said, which was true.

'Well, that's even better then,' she said, 'you won't miss anyone. I'll tell you what I'll miss. I'll miss Lucy, and I'll miss the book group –'

I interrupted to remind her that she didn't even like the book group, and when she denied it I cited the week before when she told me they weren't a very bright bunch, and all they wanted to do was gossip and read Joanna Trollope novels.

'I did not say that,' said Mum, 'and even if I did, it doesn't mean I won't miss them. When I think of them discussing *Pride and Prejudice* without me ... I have a lot to say about that book,' she added ominously.

I said I was sure they'd miss her too, and Mum surprised me by smiling hesitantly and saying, 'Do you think they will?'

It was on the tip of my tongue to say, *No, they'll crack open the party poppers*, but I looked at her face and said, 'Of course they'll miss you. You're the life and soul of that book group.'

'I'm sure that's not true,' she said, in a way that made me believe she thought it was very true indeed, 'but it's very nice of you to say so.'

She went on for another ten minutes about what she'd miss – the beach, the house, the weather – until she stopped and said there must be *something* I'd miss.

'I don't know yet,' I said. 'I won't know until we're gone.'

I saw her looking at me, willing me to mention something we could share together.

'I might miss the tree,' I said, 'in the front garden.'

'Oh, the tree!' she said in sudden delight. 'I love that tree. When you were little, you and I used to sit under that tree for hours in the summertime. You used to stare up at the leaves and there wouldn't be a peep out of you. I used to wonder what you were thinking, you looked so serious for a baby.'

'I was probably thinking I wish Mum wouldn't stick me under this stupid tree for hours,' I said, and Mum laughed.

'And there was me,' she said, 'thinking you were deep.'

It was an eternal disappointment to her that I wasn't deep, as she had hoped, but just quiet. Mum's criteria for deepness were pretty arbitrary anyway – they involved liking poetry and crying at sad films, as she did. I scuppered my chances of ever being deep by laughing during the graveyard scene in *Who Will Love My Children*.

'Anyway,' she said, 'we'll be together, you and me. That's what matters.'

'And Dad,' I said, but Mum kissed the back of my head and didn't say anything to that.

We arrived in Glasgow one rainy Friday night, two days into my summer holidays. Mum said Glasgow meant dear green place, but it didn't look very green. We passed groups of dark high-rise flats, shabby rows of shops, huge billboard stands. A fat girl behind the counter of a fish-and-chip shop stuck her two fingers up at me as we waited at the traffic lights.

'Would you look at that,' said Mum, 'she must be very unhappy.'

But the girl didn't look unhappy at all. She looked like she wanted to bash someone, preferably me. When I said this to Mum, she replied that my outlook on life was superficial.

'Any psychologist worth his salt will tell you,' she said, 'that behind every bully is a very scared, very sad person.'

I rolled my eyes and looked out of the window. It had begun to strike me, in the past year, that Mum could be a bit dim. It wouldn't matter, I thought, if she wasn't so pleased with herself.

'I agree with Cara,' Dad said suddenly. It startled me to hear his voice because I'd forgotten he was there. What can you say to someone who agrees with you? I said nothing and we rolled into Waver Street in silence.

The delivery van arrived the next morning, and we spent the next few days unpacking. The house was too small for all our things, and we had to start piling stuff into cupboards. The first things to go were Mum's pictures, which looked wrong on the murky, floral walls. Then old photo albums, vases, toiletry sets, my old christening gown, her old christening gown. Hoarding was the one indulgence Mum allowed herself. She never threw anything away without a wrench of her heart. She got nostalgic about an old clay bear she'd made at school, and angry and disappointed reading my old school reports, which, apart from maths which Mum didn't rate anyway, were roundly bad. One entry particularly incensed her for its inelegance and atrocious spelling:

Cara may be a good student if she paid atention in class. As it is, she pays no attention, and is not a good student.

'She certainly didn't beat around the bush,' Mum said. We were sitting on the living-room floor, the papers scattered around us.

'They all say the same,' she said. 'Why do you think that is?' She gave me a concentrated look, as if my answer was the most important thing in the whole world. I hated that look.

'I don't know,' I said and shrugged. 'Because I don't pay attention?'

From upstairs came the sound of Dad laughing. I'd taken his lunch up to their room earlier and he'd been watching a Jerry Springer show about people who wanted to marry their pets. He'd pointed to the telly with his vodka bottle and said it just wasn't right to get engaged to your horse.

'Well,' said Mum sharply, 'you'll need to start paying attention. You're going into second year after the summer, that's when the wheat's separated from the chaff. I want to see you in the wheat pile.'

I said what if I liked it in the chaff pile, and Mum said to stop being facetious. 'Stupidness doesn't suit anyone,' she said.

This brought on a reverie about her own thwarted ambition, what she could have excelled in (anything she wanted!) if she'd been given the chances and opportunities I had.

'I just soaked up knowledge,' she said. 'I was thankful for it. How many other people,' she said, 'can recite the whole of "Hail to thee blithe spirit! Bird that never wert" off by heart?'

That same day, Mum decided we should introduce ourselves to the neighbours. Only one woman answered our knock, and we had to call out our business before she would open the door.

'I thought you were those Jehovah Witnesses,' she said.

'Oh no,' said Mum. 'Though hopefully we bring good news,' she added in an excruciatingly jolly voice.

Shelia was round and solid as a Christmas pudding. Her t-shirt said FCUK OFF although her expression alone conveyed this message. I was intimidated by her, but also impressed by the short thrift she gave Mum.

'Well then, I'm busy,' she said after a few minutes, practically shutting the door in our faces. I'd never seen Mum dismissed before: she was used to regimenting people's emotional responses to match her own.

'Not a congenial person at all,' Mum said when we got home.

'Behind every bully is a very scared, very sad person,' I said, pleased with myself.

We saw Shelia again a few nights later. She came to the door late on Saturday night to tell Mum that Dad was passed out at the bottom of the street. At first Mum tried to pretend she didn't know what Shelia was talking about. This was pretty futile, as Dad had been sitting in the garden for the past two days saluting everyone who went past.

'Well, he must have a twin,' said Shelia, 'and it's conked out down the road.'

'Okay, well thank you for letting us know,' said Mum brightly.

We went down the road to get him. He had a cut down one side of his face, and was muttering something about shitheads. Mum gave him a hanky for his face, but he groggily swiped it away.

'You! What do you care?' he said, slurring his words.

'We both care,' I said, desperate to get him off the street.

'She doesn't. She wouldn't spit on me if I was on fire.'

'Don't be ridiculous,' said Mum. 'Grab his other arm, Cara.'

'You'd probably laugh your head off,' he said, a note of girlish hysteria creeping into his voice. 'You'd have a ball!'

I tried to lift his arm to pull him up, but it was no use. He was too heavy and making no attempt to help us. He stumbled up himself, calling us a couple of fuckers before he lurched away.

Things got back to normal pretty quickly. Dad got a job, I don't know how he managed it, working in a doctor's surgery in Bearsden. His drinking eased up, and became confined to frantic, demented bouts of one or two days. We hardly noticed him except when he was drunk. It was like realizing you had a ghost only when you heard its manacles rattle. Sometimes he would come into my room. He always used a pretext: he wanted to seal my window, bleed the radiator. He would hang around afterwards and maybe say something like: 'That was five flus today. There's something going around.'

'Mmm,' I'd say.

'Have you been feeling okay? No temperature, no aches and pains?'

'Nope.'

'Good.' He would muse on this quietly for a few minutes. Then he would get up and say, 'Well, tell me if you feel anything coming on.'

A month after we moved in he came in to show me a big card everyone had signed for his birthday. He pointed out all the names and told me what job each of them did at the surgery. Everyone had written a message, which he read out in embarrassed pleasure.

'They all call you Teddy,' I said. 'Not William?'

'I know,' said Dad. 'That's their nickname for me.'

He told me that the last time he'd had a nickname was at school. The boys in his class called him walnut face, because of his acne. But, as Dad pointed out, that wasn't really a nickname.

'That was just people being cruel,' he said.

Later that night I asked Mum if she'd seen the card. We were side by side at the sink, Mum washing, me drying. She was humming a tune and broke off, smiling at me as if she'd just realized I was there.

'The card,' I said, 'did you see it?'

'Of course I saw it,' she said. 'It was very nice.'

'He seems quite popular,' I said, handing her back a plate with a tomato sauce stain. It was one of her principles to be sloppy about housework.

'Yes, people always take to your father. He has a very modest way about him, people like that.'

'Is that why you liked him?' I asked, and Mum said she supposed it must have been.

'It's so long ago now,' she said. 'I was just turned eighteen when we got married. You don't know your own mind at that age. All I wanted was to be grown-up, have a house, a husband, a big wedding. Idiotic,' she said, 'that was just the word for me at that age.'

She smiled fondly at the thought of her younger, idiotic self, and went back to humming her tune.

If anything, Mum was happier after we moved to Glasgow. She joined a hill-walking club and went on jaunts with them every Saturday. She came back late in the evening, full of the joys. Scotland had the most beautiful scenery – she described it rapturously – and the people in the group were the most interesting and well-informed people you could hope to meet.

'It's so invigorating,' she said after the first meeting, 'to meet people who understand you. People you can talk to.'

'Are they all loonies too, then?' I said, but Mum was in a good mood and just laughed.

I got to know everyone in the hill-walking group on a first-name basis. Velma, a retired schoolteacher, wonderful for her age, but you didn't want to get stuck as her partner because her arthritis slowed her down considerably. Gina and Tom, the couple who got on well, and Clair and Philip, who didn't. Betty the librarian, who didn't seem interested when Mum tried to engage her on the subject of literature. The person she talked most about, though, was a divorcee called Brian. He taught a communication course in a college in Hamilton, and his life had been a life compounded of misfortune. His parents died in a car crash, his sister was a recovering drug-addict, his ex-wife a jealous psychotic.

'But he doesn't let life get him down,' said Mum, admiration shining through her voice. 'He just refuses.'

He revealed his life to her on these walks, supposedly because she was a good listener, and empathetic to boot. He said these were rare qualities.

We finished the dishes, and Mum dried her hands and said she'd better get ready. She was meeting the hill-walking group in the pub at seven.

'That's the second time this week you're going out,' I said. 'Not including Saturday.'

Mum said she was in the house all day with me, wasn't she allowed to see her friends at night? 'Humans are social animals,' she said, 'they need other people to spark off.'

'For hearty outdoor types, you spend a lot of time in the pub,' I said.

'I don't know why you're being like this. You've got Barbara now. I don't stop you seeing her.'

In fact, I wished Mum would stop me seeing Barbara. She was someone I was scared *not* to be friends with. She was thirteen, a year older than me, and none of the other girls in the street would hang around with her. Barbara said it was because they were snobs, but the real reason was that she hit them. I didn't know if she hit them because they didn't like her, or if they didn't like her because she hit them. The thing was that Barbara insisted on being involved in everything they were doing. There were four girls, all about our ages, that lived in Waver Street. When it was hot as it had been for weeks, they spread blankets on the street and lounged around on them. They read magazines, painted each other's nails, plaited their hair with beads. Barbara was bony, with a greyish, old-china tinge to her skin. She had heavy, greasy black hair, thick eyebrows, and a huge nose that she often stroked self-consciously. She didn't look like the kind of girl who could get away with thinking she was pretty, or worth decorating.

The first time I met her was one of those hot days. I was sitting with the girls, whose names I'd instantly forgotten, trying to decide how I could escape home without seeming rude. I was going through what Mum called a beefy stage, and I towered above them in height and girth. They were asking each other questions from a 'How Good A Friend Are You?' quiz in a magazine. Barbara came along and stood beside the blanket.

'Ask me,' she said fiercely, halfway between a threat and a plea. One of the girls, a bossy, vicious blonde, said, 'Why, Barbara? You don't have any friends.'

'I do so,' said Barbara. 'and they're better than any of you.'

'Unless you count her nits,' another girl said, and they all tittered.

'I don't have nits,' Barbara said flatly. 'You have nits.'

'Very clever,' said the blonde one. 'How long did it take you to think that one up, Barbara?'

They all ignored her after that, but Barbara kept standing there. And then suddenly she swooped down and walloped one of them on the face. The girls jumped apart, shouting, but not before Barbara had managed to rain a few more blows on them. It all lasted only a few minutes. Barbara stopped abruptly and walked away, giving me a half-hearted push on her way past.

A few days later I was down at the disused railway line at the back of Waver Street. I was walking up and down the tracks, bored, when Barbara appeared.

'Hey, you,' she said, 'what's your name?'

'Cara,' I said.

'What kind of name's that?' she said, and I shrugged. She sat at the edge of the platform and swung her legs over the edge.

'Everyone says your dad's an alkie,' she said.

'He's not. He's a doctor.'

'Doesn't matter anyway. They say things about me, too, that aren't true. They make me so mad.'

'I'd better go,' I said after a few minutes of silence.

She was picking a scab on her knee and didn't look up. 'See you around,' she said as I walked away.

Barbara was very definite about what she wanted to do, and more and more she wanted me to accompany her while she did it. Even though I didn't like her, it never occurred to me to say no to her. At first we just walked around the streets. Then Barbara started to invite me to her house. The curtains were never open, but the sun shone through them and showed up dust everywhere. There were ashtrays, and old newspapers, and dirty plates and cups lying around; a smell of old cat-food permeated the house. Barbara's room was the worst. There were clothes all over the floor, mixed up with plates and bowls crusted with dried-on food. A box of cereal with cornflakes spilling out of it lay in the corner of her room for weeks. The only things that Barbara took care of were her old, beat-up trumpet, and her cassette player. She had two tapes – Simply Red and Louis Armstrong – and she made us listen to them right through, in total silence. The other thing she liked to do was rifle through her mum's bedroom. She would pull all her clothes out of the wardrobe, onto the bed, and run her hands tenderly through them, as if she were touching skin.

'Has your mum got this many clothes?' she asked me once.

I didn't know what to say: her mum's clothes were cheap and pretty ordinary looking. I couldn't understand their appeal.

'I don't know,' I said. 'I suppose so.'

'One day I'm going to have even more than this.'

She held up a red, silky blouse, smelt it, and then passed it to me.

'That's the perfume she wears,' she said. 'It costs thirty-two pounds, and that's just for a tiny bottle.'

It was in her mum's bedroom that she showed me the photographs. She got them out of a drawer where they'd been hidden under piles of underwear. They were of normal size, bad quality. A woman bending over and spreading her bum cheeks; lying on her back with her legs splayed; on all fours like a dog. On and on. Barbara looked at each of them carefully, seriously, before passing them to me. Someone was playing a radio outside, and apart from that it was deadly quiet.

'Why's your mum got these?' I said at last.

"They're of her, stupid.'

'They're disgusting,' I said, and Barbara said, 'I know,' and gathered them up and hid them away again.

A few days later I met her mum for the first time. I was sitting in Barbara's room, listening to her practise her trumpet. She couldn't play a note on it; she just blew into it as hard as she could and wiggled her fingers about. She told me that the best musicians in the world were self-taught. We heard the front door open, and then someone's feet coming up the stairs. Barbara stopped and shouted, 'Mum?'

'You don't need to holler like that, Barbara,' said her mum. She stood in the doorway, a dumpy, baggy woman wearing jeans and a denim jacket. Her brown hair was tied in a ponytail, and she had a weary, fleshy face that looked like it couldn't be bothered to decide on an expression. She looked round the room blankly; she didn't say hello, or ask me my name, as all the mums I'd ever met did.

'Do you want to hear my trumpet Mum?' said Barbara in a plaintive voice I'd never heard her use before.

'Not just now,' she sighed. 'I've got to go out again.'

I felt myself staring at her, and turned away. Trying to connect her with the woman in the photographs was like trying to imagine what ice-cream sprinkled with salt would taste like. Except more disturbing.

'Where're you going?' said Barbara.

'Phil's taking me out.'

She left and we heard her bedroom door close.

'You need to go now,' said Barbara, pushing me towards the door. 'I want to see my mum.'

I got home, relieved at how normal and orderly everything looked. The gate, the curtains pulled efficiently at either side of the window.

They made Barbara's house seem a Gothic extravagance of my imagination, and my involvement in her life slipped away: I forgot her.

The kitchen door was open. I could hear Mum's voice. And then a man's voice. They were at the kitchen table drinking tea.

'I ask you,' Mum was saying, 'whoever heard of Lady Macbeth urinating in the middle of the stage? And then the three witches wearing sunglasses! I nearly fell off my seat.'

'It's just shock value these days,' the man said. 'They want to grind your face in the shit, as Pinter said.'

'Oh,' said Mum, and paused. I could tell she didn't know who Pinter was. 'Just lamentable,' she said after a few seconds, 'that's what it was.'

'What was?' I said suddenly, walking into the kitchen. They hadn't noticed me and Mum was surprised.

'Well hello to you too,' she said. 'Cara, this is Brian from the group, Brian this is Cara.'

'Hello there,' he said.

'Hi.'

I walked over to the cupboard and got out a packet of crisps. 'Put those back,' Mum shouted over. 'It'll be lunch soon, I don't want you stuffing your face with rubbish.'

'I'm *starving*.'

'You don't look starving. Quite the opposite.'

I sat down at the table and Mum told me they were talking about the play they'd seen last night. I'd been asleep when she came in.

'To be fair,' said Brian, talking precisely as if he were picking insects from his food, 'the ending was good. It meant we got to go home.'

Mum flashed him a brilliant smile. 'That's right,' she said. 'And the seats,' she said, 'those little hard seats!'

'We should go to the pantomime next time,' Brian said, 'I bet you get a comfy seat there.'

Mum started talking about how she'd never been to the theatre until she was seventeen – 'It was *Death of a Salesman*,' she said. 'I just sat there, gripped' – and how she'd hardly been since because she had no one to go with.

'You've never invited me,' I said.

'That's because you wouldn't like it.'

She looked at me absent-mindedly and then directed her attention back to Brian. 'She'd fidget, like her dad. I took him to see *The Silver Darlings* once and he fidgeted the whole time. He only perked up when I bought him a Cornetto at the interval.'

Brian started talking about his ex-wife, the one Mum told me about who had tried to poison him and phoned him up late at night to screech at him. He didn't look the kind of man anyone would screech down the phone at. There was something well tended and carefully refined about him – his fine black sweater, gold-rimmed glasses, the considered smile on his face. A certain amount of woody aftershave floated around him and got up my nose.

Mum made us bacon and eggs for lunch. It took her ten minutes to notice I hadn't touched my bacon.

'What's wrong with it?' she said. 'Why aren't you eating?'

'You've given me all the fatty bits,' I said, looking down at my plate and pushing the bacon around with my fork.

'Don't be ridiculous,' she said.

I was angry and more upset than the situation warranted. I sat staring at the table until Mum cleared the plates away and said that it was up to me if I didn't want to eat it.

'Missing a meal won't kill you,' she said.

I never saw Brian after that, although Mum went out with him at night. He waited for her in his car, the engine purring. They still went hill-walking on Saturdays, and during the week there were poetry readings, plays, the foreign cinema, folk-singing evenings at the Scotia bar.

'Why don't you go along?' I said to Dad one night. He was sitting in the living room, reading the paper. Mum was getting changed in the bedroom.

'It's not really my cup of tea,' he said. 'I just get bored at that kind of thing.'

'You might like it,' I said. 'You won't know if you never go.'

'Who'd look after you?' he said, and I said I could look after myself. I wanted to say something about Brian, although I didn't know what. I didn't know how to say it.

'Do you want to try and beat me at chess?' Dad said.

'No thanks.'

'Scared I'll thrash you,' he said, tugging me gently on the arm. I was angry at him suddenly, angry because he seemed so piteous, so clumsy and needy in his affection.

'I just don't feel like it,' I said, and left the room.

During this period – I remember it as a few weeks, although it was probably longer – Mum was positively incandescent. She laughed all the time, she acted silly, thrilled at her own silliness, and spoke constantly about what she'd seen and done, and who said what to whom. She didn't speak about the old house any more, she said moving to Glasgow was the best decision she'd ever made. 'This is my renaissance,' she was fond of saying. She enrolled for an Open University course in English literature after the summer, and read through the brochures during dinner.

'Don't get your hopes up,' Dad said. 'You might find it too difficult. It's been years since you've had to write an essay.'

'I'll manage,' said Mum serenely. She was as untouched by him recently as a Buddha is untouched by worldly possessions. She ate her dinner, enchanted with whatever she was thinking about. When Dad told her about his day, she didn't even feign interest.

One night she never returned home. We'd bought my school uniform that afternoon. It was a week till the end of the school holidays. I'd woken up because Dad had fallen against the Welsh dresser, which banged off the wall.

'Is Mum not home yet?' I said, rubbing my eyes.

Dad shrugged and let his hands fall into his lap. 'She's old enough to look after herself,' he said. 'She'll be back.'

I stood at the window and looked out at the street. It was two in the morning. The street was empty and all the lights in the houses were off.

'Phone her friends,' I said, turning round to Dad. 'Ask them if they've seen her.'

'At least she has friends,' said Dad. He was holding his head in his hands as if it were a piece of precious, over-ripe fruit. 'You don't know what it's like,' he said. 'Loneliness. Having no one care about you. They say, they say you can't name things you can't see, but try loneliness. You can't see it but it's there. It's in me.'

He patted his chest and shut his eyes very slowly and then opened them again.

'Try the soul,' he said.

I went through to the kitchen to look for her address book, but I couldn't find it. When I went back into the living room Dad was snoring. I emptied his vodka into the sink, and then stood at the window again. Still nothing. At some point I must have fallen asleep. I woke up on the couch the next morning. It took me a few minutes to remember something was wrong, and then I ran through the house, checking all the rooms. All her clothes were still there, everything she owned still there. I woke up Dad. He phoned the hospitals, police stations, all the people they knew in Dorset, Gran and Grandpa. No one knew anything. We couldn't find any numbers for the hill-walking group.

'We'll just have to wait,' said Dad.

A letter came for me the next day. I knew right away it was Mum's writing. Dad read it after me. He didn't say a word. Then he put his arms around me and said, 'I'm sorry, I'm so sorry.' I pushed him away and shouted that it was all his fault. I ripped the letter up, but later Dad Sellotaped it together and brought it up to my room.

'You might want to keep it,' he said, and put it down on my desk. And in the end, I did.

A few days later I was with Barbara. We were straddling the roof of a tenement flat, having climbed up the scaffolding on Barbara's insistence. It was windy and I grabbed onto the edge, terrified.

'I've not seen you for a while,' she said. She was hardly holding on at all. I shrugged and looked over the rooftops.

'I'm going to jump,' she said. She slid down the roof on her bum and disappeared. I shouted her name, but there was no reply. My voice echoed into the silence. I kept shouting, expecting her to reappear, but she didn't. I was scared to move and had to force myself to slide down. There was a narrow row of steel stairs scaling the building, and I went down them gingerly, my hands sweating.

She was lying on the pavement, one arm flung out behind her head. I was crouched over her, screaming, when her eyes flew open and she began to laugh.

'Got you,' she said.

'That's not funny,' I said, walking away. I was still shaking.

'As if you'd care,' she said, 'if I was dead.' She looked at me out of the corners of her eyes as if she had asked me a question and was waiting for a reply.

'I would care,' I said, 'and so would your mum.'

'Shows how much you know,' said Barbara. She started walking alongside me.

'Would your mum care?' she asked me. She spoke in her usual flat voice, but she was looking at me slyly.

'Yeah, of course,' I said.

'Hmm,' said Barbara. 'I thought friends were meant to tell each other everything,' she said.

I stopped and stared at her. 'Well, you're not my friend,' I said. 'And I don't want to know your stupid secrets anyway. I don't want to go to your smelly house, and look at your smelly mum's photographs.'

'At least my mum doesn't abandon me,' Barbara shouted. 'Shows how much she loves you.'

'She does. I mean, she's not. Abandoned me, she's not.'

'Everyone knows. *Everyone*,' said Barbara in a quieter voice.

And the next thing I knew, I was hitting her as hard as I could. I gave her a black eye, but the next day she came to my door and acted as if nothing had happened.

'You okay?' she said.

'Yeah,' I said. 'You?'

'Yeah. Want to go to Superdrug?' she said, and I said okay.

For years I looked for her. In the street, on buses, in shops. I felt she would look exactly the same as she did when I was twelve. Even when I was almost definite it wasn't her, I had to check. Always a strange tugging of my heart when it wasn't her.

She moved to Nice with Brian, and wrote me letters that I didn't reply to. She remained, remains, colossal.

I graduated with a good maths degree. Dad and Peter, my boyfriend, came to the graduation. Dad stood in the middle of the aisle and took my picture. And then again, outside in the quadrangles, drinking complimentary Bucks Fizz, laughing, toasting the end of my university days. Even then, throughout the whole time, I could hear Mum say, in her tone of tender and complicated disappointment, 'Anyone can be a counter, Cara.'

AFTER A LIFE

Yiyun Li

Yiyun Li (b. 1972) is a Chinese American author. Her debut short story collection, *A Thousand Years of Good Prayers*, won the 2005 Frank O'Connor International Short Story Award, and her second collection, *Gold Boy, Emerald Girl*, was shortlisted for the same award. Her debut novel, *The Vagrants*, was shortlisted for the 2011 IMPAC Dublin Literary Award. She is an editor of the Brooklyn-based literary magazine, *A Public Space*.

Mr. and Mrs. Su are finishing breakfast when the telephone rings. Neither moves to pick it up at first. Not many people know their number; fewer use it. Their son, Jian, a sophomore in college now, calls them once a month to report his well-being. He spends most of his holidays and school breaks with his friends' families, not offering even the most superficial excuses. Mr. and Mrs. Su do not have the heart to complain and remind Jian of their wish to see him more often. Their two-bedroom flat, small and cramped as it is, is filled with Beibei's screaming when she is not napping, and a foul smell when she dirties the cloth sheets beneath her. Jian grew up sleeping in a cot in the foyer and hiding from his friends the existence of an elder sister born with severe mental retardation and cerebral palsy. Mr. and Mrs. Su sensed their son's elation when he finally moved into his college dorm. They have held on to the secret wish that after Beibei dies – she is not destined for longevity, after all – they will reclaim their lost son, though neither says anything to the other, both ashamed by the mere thought of the wish.

The ringing stops for a short moment and starts again. Mr. Su walks to the telephone and puts a hand on the receiver. "Do you want to take it?" he asks his wife.

"So early it must be Mr. Fong," Mrs. Su says.

"Mr. Fong is a man of courtesy. He won't disturb other people's breakfast," Mr. Su says. Still, he picks up the receiver, and his expression relaxes. "Ah, yes, Mrs. Fong. My wife, she is right here," he says, and signals to Mrs. Su.

Mrs. Su does not take the call immediately. She goes into Beibei's bedroom and checks on her, even though it is not time for her to wake up yet. Mrs. Su strokes the hair, light brown and baby-soft, on Beibei's forehead. Beibei is twenty-eight going on twenty-nine; she is so large it takes both her parents to turn her over and clean her; she screams for hours when she is awake, but for Mrs. Su, it takes a wisp of hair to forget all the imperfections.

When she returns to the living room, her husband is still holding the receiver for her, one hand covering the mouthpiece. "She's in a bad mood," he whispers.

Mrs. Su sighs and takes the receiver. "Yes, Mrs. Fong, how are you today?"

"As bad as it can be. My legs are killing me. Listen, my husband just left. He said he was meeting your husband for breakfast and they were going to the stockbrokerage afterward. Tell me it was a lie."

Mrs. Su watches her husband go into Beibei's bedroom. He sits with Beibei often; she does, too, though never at the same time as he does. "My husband is putting on his jacket so he must be going out to meet Mr. Fong now," Mrs. Su says. "Do you want me to check with him?"

"Ask him," Mrs. Fong says.

Mrs. Su walks to Beibei's room and stops at the door. Her husband is sitting on the chair by the bed, his eyes closed for a quick rest. It's eight o'clock, early still, but for an aging man, morning, like everything else, means less than it used to. Mrs. Su goes back to the telephone and says, "Mrs. Fong? Yes, my husband is meeting your husband for breakfast."

"Are you sure? Do me a favor. Follow him and see if he's lying to you. You can never trust men."

Mrs. Su hesitates, and says, "But I'm busy."

"What are you busy with? Listen, my legs are hurting me. I would've gone after him myself otherwise."

"I don't think it looks good for husbands to be followed," Mrs. Su says.

"If your husband goes out every morning and comes home with

another woman's scent, why should you care about what looks
good or bad?"

It is not her husband who is having an affair, Mrs. Su retorts
in her mind, but she doesn't want to point out the illogic. Her
husband is indeed often used as a cover for Mr. Fong's affair, and
Mrs. Su feels guilty toward Mrs. Fong. "Mrs. Fong, I would help
on another day, but today is bad."

"Whatever you say."

"I'm sorry," Mrs. Su says.

Mrs. Fong complains for another minute, of the untrustworthi-
ness of husbands and friends in general, and hangs up. Mrs. Su
knocks on the door of Beibei's room and her husband jerks awake,
quickly wiping the corner of his mouth. "Mrs. Fong wanted to
know if you were meeting Mr. Fong," she says.

"Tell her yes."

"I did."

Mr. Su nods and tucks the blanket tight beneath Beibei's soft,
shapeless chin. It bothers Mrs. Su when her husband touches Beibei
for any reason, but it must be ridiculous for her to think so. Being
jealous of a daughter who understands nothing and a husband
who loves the daughter despite that! She will become a crazier
woman than Mrs. Fong if she doesn't watch out for her sanity,
Mrs. Su thinks, but still, seeing her husband smooth Beibei's hair
or rub her cheeks upsets Mrs. Su. She goes back to the kitchen and
washes the dishes, while her husband gets ready to leave. When he
says farewell, she answers politely without turning to look at him.

At eight-thirty Mr. Su leaves the apartment, right on time for the
half-hour walk to the stockbrokerage. Most of the time he is there
only to study the market; sometimes he buys and sells, executing
the transactions with extraordinary prudence, as the money in his
account does not belong to him. Mr. Fong has offered the ten-
thousand yuan as a loan, and has made it clear many times that
he is not in any urgent need of the money. It is not a big sum at all
for Mr. Fong, a retired senior officer from a military factory, but
Mr. Su believes that *for each drop of water one received, one has
to repay with a well*. The market and the economy haven't helped
him much in returning Mr. Fong's generosity. Mr. Su, however, is

not discouraged. A retired mathematics teacher at sixty-five, Mr. Su believes in exercising one's body and mind – both provided by his daily trip to the stockbrokerage – and being patient.

Mr. Su met Mr. Fong a year ago at the stockbrokerage. Mr. Fong, a year senior to Mr. Su, took a seat by him, and conversation started between the two men. He was there out of curiosity, Mr. Fong said; he asked Mr. Su if indeed the stock system would work for the country, and if that was the case, how Marxist political economics could be adapted for this new, clearly capitalistic, situation. Mr. Fong's question, obsolete and naive as it was, moved Mr. Su. With almost everyone in the country going crazy about money, and money alone, it was rare to meet someone who was nostalgic about the old but also earnest in his effort to understand the new. "You are on the wrong floor to ask the question," Mr. Su replied. "Those who would make a difference are in the VIP lounges upstairs."

The stockbrokerage, like most of the brokerage firms in Beijing, rented space from bankrupted state-run factories. The one Mr. Su visited used to manufacture color TVs, a profitable factory until it lost a price war to a monopolizing corporation. The laid-off workers were among the ones who frequented the ground floor of the brokerage, opening accounts with their limited means and hoping for good luck. Others on the floor were retirees, men and women of Mr. Su's age who dreamed of making their money grow instead of letting the money die in banks, which offered very low interest rates.

"What are these people doing here if they don't matter to the economy?" Mr. Fong asked.

"*Thousands of sand grains make a tower,*" Mr. Su said. "Together their investments help a lot of factories run."

"But will they make money from the stock market?"

Mr. Su shook his head. He lowered his voice and said, "Most of them don't. Look at that woman there in the first row, the one with the hairnet. She buys and sells according to what the newspapers and television say. She'll never earn money that way. And there, the old man – eighty-two he is, a very fun and healthy oldster but not a wise investor."

Mr. Fong looked at the people Mr. Su pointed out, every one an example of bad investing. "And you, are you making money?" Mr. Fong asked.

"I'm the worst of all," Mr. Su said with a smile. "I don't even have money to get started." Mr. Su had been observing the market for some time. With an imaginary fund, he had practiced trading, dutifully writing down all the transactions in a notebook; he had bought secondhand books on trading and developed his own theories. His prospects of earning money from the market were not bleak at all, he concluded after a year of practice. His pension, however, was small. With a son going to college, a wife and a daughter totally dependent on him, he had not the courage to risk a penny on his personal hobby.

Very quickly, Mr. Fong and Mr. Su became close friends. They sat at teahouses or restaurants, exchanging opinions about the world, from prehistorical times to present day. They were eager to back up each other's views, and at the first sign of disagreement, they changed topics. It surprised Mr. Su that he would make a friend at his age. He was a quiet and lonely man all his life, and most people he knew in his adult life were mere acquaintances. But perhaps this was what made old age a second childhood – friendship came out of companionship easily, with less self-interest, fewer social judgments.

After a month or so, at dinner, Mr. Fong confessed to Mr. Su that he was in a painful situation. Mr. Su poured a cup of rice wine for Mr. Fong, waiting for him to continue.

"I fell in love with this woman I met at a street dance party," Mr. Fong said.

Mr. Su nodded. Mr. Fong had once told him about attending a class to learn ballroom dancing, and had discussed the advantages: good exercise, a great chance to meet people when they were in a pleasant mood, and an aesthetic experience. Mr. Su had thought of teasing Mr. Fong about his surrendering to Western influences, but seeing Mr. Fong's sincerity, Mr. Su had given up the idea.

"The problem is, she is a younger woman," Mr. Fong said.

"How much younger?" Mr. Su asked.

"In her early forties."

"Age should not be a barrier to happiness," Mr. Su said.

"But it's not quite possible."

"Why, is she married?"

"Divorced," Mr. Fong said. "But think about it. She's my daughter's age."

Mr. Su looked Mr. Fong up and down. A soldier all his life, Mr. Fong was in good shape; except for his balding head, he looked younger than his age. "Put on a wig and people will think you are fifty," Mr. Su said. "Quite a decent bridegroom, no?"

"Old Su, don't make fun of me," Mr. Fong said, not concealing a smile. It vanished right away. "It's a futile love, I know."

"Chairman Mao said, *One can achieve anything as long as he dares to imagine it.*"

Mr. Fong shook his head and sullenly sipped his wine. Mr. Su looked at his friend, distressed by love. He downed a cup of wine and felt he was back in his teenage years, consulting his best friend about girls, being consulted. "You know something?" he said. "My wife and I are first cousins. Everybody opposed the marriage, but we got married anyway. You just do it."

"That's quite a courageous thing," Mr. Fong said. "No wonder I've always had the feeling that you're not an ordinary person. You have to introduce me to your wife. Why don't I come to visit you tomorrow at your home? I need to pay respect to her."

Mr. Su felt a pang of panic. He had not invited a guest to his flat for decades. "Please don't trouble yourself," he said finally. "A wife is just the same old woman after a lifelong marriage, no?" It was a bad joke, and he regretted it right away.

Mr. Fong sighed. "You've got it right, Old Su. But the thing is, a wife is a wife and you can't ditch her like a worn shirt after a life."

It was the first time Mr. Fong mentioned a wife. Mr. Su had thought Mr. Fong a widower, the way he talked only about his children and their families. "You mean, your wife's well and" – Mr. Su thought carefully and said – "she still lives with you?"

"She's in prison," Mr. Fong said and sighed again. He went on to tell the story of his wife. She had been the Party secretary of an import-export branch for the Agriculture Department, and naturally, there had been money coming from subdivisions and companies that needed her approval on paperwork. The usual cash-for-signature transactions, Mr. Fong explained, but someone told on her. She received a *within-the-Party* disciplinary reprimand

and was retired. "Fair enough, no? She's never harmed a soul in her life," Mr. Fong said. But unfortunately, right at the time of her retirement, the president issued an order that for corrupt officials who had taken more than a hundred and seventy thousand yuan, the government would seek heavy punishments. "A hundred and seventy thousand is nothing compared to what he's taken!" Mr. Fong hit the table with a fist. In a lower voice, he said, "Believe me, Old Su, only the smaller fish pay for the government's face-lift. The big ones – they just become bigger and fatter."

Mr. Su nodded. A hundred and seventy thousand yuan was more than he could imagine, but Mr. Fong must be right that it was not a horrific crime. "So she had a case with that number?"

"Right over the limit, and she got a sentence of seven years."

"Seven years!" Mr. Su said. "How awful, and unfair."

Mr. Fong shook his head. "In a word, Old Su, how can I abandon her now?"

"No," Mr. Su said. "That's not right."

They were silent for a moment, and both drank wine as they pondered the dilemma. After a while, Mr. Fong said, "I've been thinking: before my wife comes home, we – the woman I love and I – maybe we can have a temporary family. No contract, no obligation. Better than those, you know what they call, one night of something?"

"One-night stands?" Mr. Su blurted out, and then was embarrassed to have shown familiarity with such improper, modern vocabularies. He had learned the term from tabloids the women brought to the brokerage; he had even paid attention to those tales, though he would never admit it.

"Yes. I thought ours could be better than that. A *dew marriage before the sunrise.*"

"What will happen when your wife comes back?" Mr. Su asked.

"Seven years is a long time," Mr. Fong said. "Who knows what will become of me in seven years? I may be resting with Marx and Engels in heaven then."

"Don't say that, Mr. Fong," Mr. Su said, saddened by the eventual parting that they could not avoid.

"You're a good friend, Old Su. Thank you for listening to me. All the other people we were friends with – they left us right after my wife's sentence, as if our bad luck would contaminate them. Some of them used to come to our door and beg to entertain us!" Mr. Fong said, and then, out of the blue, he brought out the suggestion of loaning Mr. Su some money for investing.

"Definitely not!" Mr. Su said. "I'm your friend not because of your money."

"Ah, how can you think of it that way?" Mr. Fong said. "Let's look at it this way: it's a good experiment for an old Marxist like me. If you make a profit, great; if not, good for my belief, no?"

Mr. Su thought Mr. Fong was drunk, but a few days later, Mr. Fong mentioned the loan again, and Mr. Su found it hard to reject the offer.

Mrs. Fong calls again two hours later. "I have a great idea," she says when Mrs. Su picks up the phone. "I'll hire a private detective to find out whom my husband is seeing."

"Private detective?"

"Why? You think I can't find the woman? Let me be honest with you – I don't trust that husband of yours at all. I think he lies to you about my husband's whereabouts."

Mrs. Su panics. She didn't know there were private detectives available. It sounds foreign and dangerous. She wonders if they could do some harm to her husband, his being Mr. Fong's accomplice in the affair. "Are you sure you'll find a reliable person?" she says.

"People will do anything if you have the money. Wait till I get the solid evidence," Mrs. Fong says. "The reason I'm calling you is this: if your husband, like you said, is spending every day away from home, wouldn't you be suspicious? Don't you think it possible that they are both having affairs, and are covering up for each other?"

"No, it's impossible."

"How can you be so sure? I'll hire a private detective for both of us if you like."

"Ah, please no," Mrs. Su says.

"You don't have to pay."

"I trust my husband," Mrs. Su says, her legs weakened by sudden fear. Of all the people in the world, a private detective will certainly be the one to find out about Beibei.

"Fine," Mrs. Fong says. "If you say so, I'll spare you the truth."

Mrs. Su has never met Mrs. Fong, who was recently released from prison because of health problems after serving a year of her sentence. A few days into her parole, she called Su's number – it being the only unfamiliar number in Mr. Fong's list of contacts – and grilled Mrs. Su about her relationship with Mr. Fong. Mrs. Su tried her best to convince Mrs. Fong that she had nothing to do with Mr. Fong, nor was there a younger suspect in her household – their only child was a son, Mrs. Su lied. Since then, Mrs. Fong has made Mrs. Su a confidante, calling her several times a day. Life must be hard for Mrs. Fong now, with a criminal record, all her old friends turning their backs on her, and a husband in love with a younger woman. Mrs. Su was not particularly sympathetic with Mrs. Fong when she first learned of the sentence – one hundred and seventy thousand yuan was an astronomical number to her – but now she does not have the heart to refuse Mrs. Fong's friendship. Her husband is surely having a secret affair, Mrs. Fong confesses to Mrs. Su over the phone. He has developed some alarming and annoying habits – flossing his teeth after every meal, doing sit-ups at night, tucking his shirts in more carefully, rubbing hair-growing ointment on his head. "As if he has another forty years to live," Mrs. Fong says. He goes out and meets Mr. Su every day, but what good reason is there for two men to see each other so often?

The stock market, Mrs. Su explains unconvincingly. Mrs. Fong's calls exhaust Mrs. Su, but sometimes, after a quiet morning, she feels anxious for the phone to ring.

Mrs. Su has lived most of her married life within the apartment walls, caring for her children and waiting for them to leave in one way or another. Beyond everyday greetings, she does not talk much with the neighbors when she goes out for groceries. When Mr. and Mrs. Su first moved in, the neighbors tried to pry information from her with questions about the source of all the noises from the apartment. Mrs. Su refused to satisfy their curiosity, and in turn, they were enraged by the denial of their right to know Su's secret. Once when Jian was four or five, a few women trapped him in the building entrance and grilled him for answers; later Mrs. Su found him on the stairs in tears, his lips tightly shut.

Mrs. Su walks to Beibei's bedroom door, which she shut tightly so that Mrs. Fong would not hear Beibei. She listens for a moment to Beibei's screaming before she enters the room. Beibei is behaving quite agitatedly today, the noises she makes shriller and more impatient. Mrs. Su sits by the bed and strokes Beibei's eyebrows; it fails to soothe her into her usual whimpering self. Mrs. Su tries to feed Beibei a few spoonfuls of gruel, but she sputters it all out onto Mrs. Su's face.

Mrs. Su gets up for a towel to clean them both. The thought of a private detective frightens her. She imagines a ghostlike man tagging along after Mr. Fong and recording his daily activities. Would the detective also investigate her own husband if Mrs. Fong, out of curiosity or boredom, spends a little more money to find out other people's secrets? Mrs. Su shudders. She looks around the bedroom and wonders if a private detective, despite the curtains and the window that are kept closed day and night, will be able to see Beibei through a crack in the wall. Mrs. Su studies Beibei and imagines how she looks to a stranger: a mountain of flesh that has never seen the sunshine, white like porcelain. Age has left no mark on Beibei's body and face; she is still a newborn, soft and tender, wrapped up in an oversized pink robe.

Beibei screeches and the flesh on her cheeks trembles. Mrs. Su cups Beibei's plump hand in her own and sings in a whisper, "The little mouse climbs onto the counter. The little mouse drinks the cooking oil. The little mouse gets too full to move. Meow, meow, the cat is coming and the little mouse gets caught."

It was Beibei's favorite song, and Mrs. Su believes there is a reason for that. Beibei was born against the warning of all the relatives, who had not agreed with the marriage between the cousins in the first place. At Beibei's birth, the doctors said that she would probably die before age ten; it would be a miracle if she lived to twenty. They suggested the couple give up the newborn as a specimen for the medical college. She was useless, after all, for any other reason. Mr. and Mrs. Su shuddered, at the image of their baby soaked in a jar of formaldehyde, and never brought Beibei back to the hospital after mother and baby were released. Being in love, the couple were undaunted by the calamity. They moved to a different district, away from their families and old neighbors, he changing his job, she giving up working altogether to care for Beibei. They did not invite guests to their home; after a while, they stopped having friends. They applauded when Beibei started making sounds to express her need for comfort and company; they watched her grow up into a bigger version of herself. It was a hard life, but their love for each other, and for the daughter, made it the perfect life Mrs. Su had dreamed of since she had fallen in love at twelve, when her cousin, a year older and already a lanky young man, had handed her a book of poems as a present.

The young cousin has become the stooping husband. The perfect life has turned out less so. The year Beibei reached ten – a miracle worth celebrating, by all means – her husband brought up the idea of a second baby. Why? she asked, and he talked about a healthier marriage, a more complete family. She did not understand his reasoning, and she knew, even when Jian was growing in her belly, that they would get a good baby and that it would do nothing to save them from what had been destroyed. They had built a world around Beibei, but her husband decided to turn away from it in search of a family more like other people's. Mrs. Su found it hard to understand, but then, wasn't there an old saying about men always being interested in change, and women in preservation? A woman accepted anything from life and made it the best; a man bargained for the better but also the less perfect.

Mrs. Su sighs, and looks at Beibei's shapeless features. So offensive she must be to other people's eyes that Mrs. Su wishes she could shrink Beibei back to the size that she once carried in her arms into this room; she wishes she could sneak Beibei into the next world without attracting anybody's attention. Beibei screams louder, white foam dripping by the corner of her mouth. Mrs. Su cleans her with a towel, and for a moment, when her hand stops over Beibei's mouth and muffles the cry, Mrs. Su feels a desire to keep the hand there. Three minutes longer and Beibei could be spared all the struggles and humiliations death has in store for every living creature, Mrs. Su thinks, but at the first sign of blushing in Beibe's pale face, she removes the towel. Beibei breathes heavily. It amazes and saddens Mrs. Su that Beibei's life is so tenacious that it has outlived the love that once made it.

With one finger, Mr. Su types in his password – a combination of Beibei's and Jian's birthdays – at a terminal booth. He is still clumsy in his operation of the computer, but people on the floor, aging and slow as most of them are, are patient with one another. The software dutifully produces graphs and numbers, but Mr. Su finds it hard to concentrate today. After a while, he quits to make room for a woman waiting for a booth. He goes back to the seating area and looks for a good chair to take a rest. The brokerage, in the recent years of a downward economy, has slackened in maintenance, and a lot of chairs are missing orange plastic seats. Mr. Su fmally finds a good one among homemade cotton cushions, and sits down by a group of old housewives. The women, in their late fifties or early sixties, are the happiest and chattiest people on the floor. Most of them have money locked into stocks that they have no other choice but to keep for now, and perhaps forever; the only reason for them to come every day is companionship. They talk about their children and grandchildren, unbearable in-laws, soap operas from the night before, stories from tabloids that must be discussed and analyzed at length.

Mr. Su watches the rolling numbers on the big screen. The PA is tuned in to a financial radio station, but the host's analysis is drowned by the women's stories. Most of the time, Mr. Su finds them annoyingly noisy, but today he feels tenderness, almost endearment, toward the women. His wife, quiet and pensive, will never become one of these chatty old hens, but he wishes, for a moment, that one of them were his wife, cheered up by the most mundane matters, mindlessly happy.

After taking note of the numbers concerning him, Mr. Su sighs. Despite all the research he had done, his investment does not show any sign more positive than the old women's. Life goes wrong for the same reason that people miscalculate. Husband and wife promise each other a lifelong love that turns out shorter than a life; people buy stocks with good calculations, but they do not take into consideration life's own preference for, despite the laws of probability, the unlikely. Mr. Su fell in love with his wife at thirteen, and she loved him back. What were the odds for first lovers to end up in a family? Against both families' wills, they married each other, and against everybody's warning, they decided to have a baby. Mr. Su, younger and more arrogant then, calculated and concluded that the odds for a problematic baby were very low, so

low that fate was almost on their side. Almost, but not quite, and
as a blunt and mean joke, Beibei was born with major problems in
her brain and spinal cord. It would not be much of a misfortune
except when his wife started to hide herself and the baby from the
world; Beibei must have reminded his wife every day that their
marriage was less legitimate. There's nothing to be ashamed of, Mr.
Su thought of telling her, but he did not have the heart. It was he
who suggested another baby. To give them a second chance, to save
his wife from the unnecessary shame and pain that she had insisted
on living with. Secretly he also wished to challenge fate again. The
odds of having another calamity were low, very low, he tried to
convince his wife; if only they could have a normal baby, and a
normal family! The new baby's birth proved his calculation right
– Jian was born healthy, and he grew up into a very handsome
and bright boy, as if his parents were awarded doubly for what
had been taken away the first time – but who would've thought
that such a success, instead of making their marriage a happier
one, would turn his wife away from him? How arrogant he was to
make the same mistake a second time, thinking he could outsmart
life. What had survived the birth of Beibei did not survive Jian's
birth, as if his wife, against all common wisdom, could share
misfortune with him but not happiness. For twenty years, they
have avoided arguments carefully; they have been loving parents,
dutiful spouses, but something that had made them crazy for each
other as young cousins has abandoned them, leaving them in
unshareable pain.

A finger taps Mr. Su's shoulder. He opens his eyes and realizes
that he has fallen asleep. "I'm sorry," he says to the woman.

"You were snoring," she says with a reproachful smile.

Mr. Su apologizes again. The woman nods and returns to the
conversation with her companions. Mr. Su looks at the clock on the
screen, too early for lunch still, but he brings out a bag of instant
noodles and a mug from his bag anyway, soaking the noodles with
boiling water from the drinking stand. The noodles soften and
swell. Mr. Su takes a sip of soup and shakes his head. He thinks of
going home and talking to his wife, asking her a few questions he
has never gathered enough courage to ask, but then decides that
things unsaid had better remain so. Life is not much different from

the stock market – you invest in a stock and you stick, and are stuck, to the choice, despite all the possibilities of other mistakes.

At noon, the restaurant commissioned by the stockbrokerage delivers the lunch boxes to the VIP lounges, and the traders on the floor heat lunches in the microwave or make instant noodles. Mr. Su, who is always cheered up by the mixed smells of leftovers from other dinner tables, goes into a terminal booth in a hopeful mood. Someday, he thinks, when his wife is freed from taking care of Beibei, he'll ask her to accompany him to the stockbrokerage. He wants her to see other people's lives, full of meaningless but happy trivialities.

Mr. Su leaves the brokerage promptly at five o'clock. Outside the building, he sees Mr. Fong, sitting on the curb and looking up at him like a sad, deserted child.

"Mr. Fong," Mr. Su says. "Are you all right? Why didn't you come in and find me?"

Mr. Fong suggests they go for a drink, and then holds out a hand and lets Mr. Su pull him to his feet. They find a small roadside diner, and Mr. Fong orders a few cold plates and a bottle of strong yam wine. "Don't you sometimes wish a marriage doesn't go as long as our lives last?" Mr. Fong says over the drink.

"Is there anything wrong?" Mr. Su asks.

"Nothing's right with the wife after she's released," Mr. Fong says.

"Are you going to divorce her?"

Mr. Fong downs a cup of wine. "I wish I could," he says and starts to sob. "I wish I didn't love her at all so I could just pack up and leave."

By late afternoon Mrs. Su is convinced that Beibei is having problems. Her eyes, usually clear and empty, glisten with a strange light, as if she is conscious of her pain. Mrs. Su tries in vain to calm her down, and when all the other ways have failed, she takes out a bottle of sleeping pills. She puts two pills into a small porcelain mortar, and then, after a moment of hesitation, adds two more. Over the years she has fed the syrup with the pill powder to Beibei so that the family can have nights for undisturbed sleep.

Calmed by the syrup, Beibei stops screaming for a short moment, and then starts again. Mrs. Su strokes Beibei's forehead and waits for the medicine to take over her limited consciousness. When the telephone rings, Mrs. Su does not move. Later, when it rings for the fifth time, she checks Beibei's eyes, half closed in drowsiness, and then closes the bedroom door before picking up the receiver.

"Why didn't you answer the phone? Are you tired of me, too?" Mrs. Fong says.

Mrs. Su tries to find excuses, but Mrs. Fong, uninterested in any of them, cuts her off. "I know who the woman is now."

"How much did it cost you to find out?"

"Zero. Listen, the husband – shameless old man – he confessed himself."

Mrs. Su feels relieved. "So the worst is over, Mrs. Fong."

"Over? Not at all. Guess what he said to me this afternoon? He asked me if we could all three of us live together in peace. He said it as if he was thinking on my behalf. 'We have plenty of rooms. It doesn't hurt to give her a room and a bed. She is a good woman, she'll take good care of us both.' Taking care of his *thing*, for sure."

Mrs. Su blushes. "Does she want to live with you?"

"Guess what? She's been laid off. Ha ha, not a surprise, right? I'm sure she wants to move in. Free meals. Free bed. Free man. What comes better? Maybe she's even set her eyes on our inheritance. Imagine what the husband suggested? He said I should think of her as a daughter. He said she lost her father at five and did not have a man good to her until she met him. So I said, Is she looking for a husband, or a stepfather? She's *honey-mouthing him*, you see? But the blind-man! He even begged me to feel for her pain. Why didn't he ask her to feel for me?"

Something hits the door with a heavy thump, and then the door swings open. Mrs. Su turns and sees an old man leaning on the door, supported by her husband. "Mr. Fong's drunk," her husband whispers to her.

"Are you there?" Mrs. Fong says.

"Ah, yes, Mrs. Fong, something's come up and I have to go."

"Not yet. I haven't finished the story."

Mrs. Su watches the two men stumble into the bathroom. After a moment, she hears the sounds of vomiting and the running of tap water, her husband's low comforting words, Mr. Fong's weeping.

"So I said, Over my dead body, and he cried and begged and said all these ridiculous things about opening one's mind. Many households have two women and one man living in peace now, he said. It's the marriage revolution, he said. Revolution? I said. It's retrogression. You think yourself a good Marxist, I said, but Marx didn't teach you bigamy. Chairman Mao didn't tell you to have a concubine."

Mr. Su helps Mr. Fong lie down on the couch and he closes his eyes. Mrs. Su watches the old man's tear-smeared face twitch in pain. Soon Mrs. Fong's angry words blend with Mr. Fong's snoring.

With Mr. Fong fast asleep, Mr. Su stands up and walks into Beibei's room. One moment later, he comes out and looks at Mrs. Su with a sad and calm expression that makes her heart tremble. She lets go of the receiver with Mrs. Fong's blabbering and walks to Beibei's bedroom. There she finds Beibei resting undisturbed, the signs of pain gone from her face, porcelain white, with a bluish hue. Mrs. Su kneels by the bed and holds Beibei's hand, still plump and soft, in her own. Her husband comes close and strokes her hair, gray and thin now, but his touch, gentle and timid, is the same one from a lifetime ago, when they were children playing in their grandparents' garden, where the pomegranate blossoms, fire-hued and in the shape of bells, kept the bees busy and happy.

SORRY?

Helen Simpson

Helen Simpson (b. 1959) is a British novelist and short story writer. She worked at *Vogue* for five years before becoming a writer full-time. Her first collection, *Four Bare Legs in a Bed and Other Stories*, won the Sunday Times Young Writer of the Year award, and her second, *Hey Yeah Right Get A Life*, won the Hawthornden Prize. In 1993 she was selected as one of *Granta*'s top twenty novelists under the age of forty.

'Sorry?' said Patrick. 'I didn't quite catch that.'

'Soup of the day is wild mushroom,' bellowed the waiter.

'No need to shout,' said Patrick, putting his hand to his troublesome ear.

The new gadget shrieked in protest.

'They take a bit of getting used to,' grimaced Matthew Herring, the deaf chap he'd been fixed up with for a morale-boosting lunch.

'You don't say,' he replied.

Some weeks ago Patrick had woken up to find he had gone deaf in his right ear – not just a bit deaf but profoundly deaf. There was nothing to be done, it seemed. It had probably been caused by a tiny flake of matter dislodged by wear-and-tear change in the vertebrae, the doctor had said, shrugging. He had turned his head on his pillow, in all likelihood, sometimes that was all it took. This neck movement would have shifted a minuscule scrap of detritus into the river of blood running towards the brain, a fragment that must have finished by blocking the very narrowest bit of the entire arterial system, the ultra-fine pipe leading to the inner ear. Bad luck.

'I don't hear perfectly,' said Matthew Herring now. 'It's not magic, a digital hearing aid, it doesn't turn your hearing into perfect hearing.'

'Mine's not working properly yet,' said Patrick. 'I've got an appointment after lunch to get it seen to.'

'Mind you, it's better than the old one,' continued Matthew comfortably. 'You used to be able to hear me wherever I went with the analogue one, it used to go before me, screeching like a steam train.'

He chuckled at the memory.

Patrick did not smile at this cosy reference to engine whistles. He had been astonished at the storm of head noise that had arrived with deafness, the whistles and screeches over a powerful cloud of hissing just like the noise from Elizabeth's old pressure cooker. His brain was generating sound to compensate for the loss of hearing, he had been told. Apparently that was part and parcel of the deafness, as well as dizzy episodes. Ha! Thanks to the vertigo which had sent him arse over tip several times since the start of all this, he was having to stay with his daughter Rachel for a while.

'Two girls,' he said tersely in answer to a question from his tedious lunch companion. He and Elizabeth had wished for boys, but there you were. Rachel was the only one so far to have provided him with grandchildren. The other daughter, Ruth, had decamped to Australia some time ago. Who knew what she was up to, but she was still out there so presumably she had managed to make a go of it, something that she had signally failed to do in England.

'I used to love music,' Matthew Herring was saying, nothing daunted. 'But it's not the same now I'm so deaf. Now it tires me out; in fact, I don't listen any more. I deliberately avoid it. The loss of it is a grief, I must admit.'

'Oh well, music means nothing to me,' said Patrick. 'Never has. So I shan't miss *that*.'

He wasn't about to confide in Matthew Herring, but of all his symptoms it had been the auditory hallucinations produced by the hearing aid which had been the most disturbing for him. The low violent stream of nonsense issuing from the general direction of his firstborn had become insupportable in the last week, and he had had to turn the damned thing off.

At his after-lunch appointment with the audiologist, he found himself curiously unable to describe the hallucinatory problem.

'I seem to be picking up extra noise,' he said eventually. 'It's difficult to describe.'

'Sounds go into your hearing aid where they are processed electronically,' she intoned, 'then played back to you over a tiny loudspeaker.'

'Yes, I know that,' he snapped. 'I am aware of that, thank you. What I'm asking is, might one of the various settings you programmed be capable of, er, amplifying sounds that would normally remain unheard?'

'Let's see, shall we,' she said, still talking to him as though he were a child or a halfwit. 'I wonder whether you've been picking up extra stuff on the Loop.'

'The Loop?'

'It works a bit like Wi-Fi,' she said. 'Electromagnetic fields. If you're in an area that's on the Loop, you can pick up on it with your hearing aid when you turn on the T-setting.'

'The T-setting?'

'That little extra bit of kit there,' she said, pointing at it. 'I didn't mention it before, I didn't want to confuse you while you were getting used to the basics. You must have turned it on by mistake from what you're saying.'

'But what *sort* of extra sounds does it pick up?' he persisted.

Rachel's lips had not been moving during that initial weird diatribe a week ago, he was sure of it, nor during the battery of bitter little remarks he'd had to endure since then.

'Well, it can be quite embarrassing,' she said, laughing merrily. 'Walls don't block the magnetic waves from a Loop signal, so you might well be able to listen in to confidential conversations if neighbouring rooms are also on it.'

'Hmm,' he said, 'I'm not sure that quite explains this particular problem. But I suppose it might have something to do with it.'

'Look, I've turned off the T-setting,' she said. 'If you want to test what it does, simply turn it on again and see what happens.'

'Or hear,' he said. 'Hear what happens.'

'You're right!' she declared, with more merry laughter.

He really couldn't see what was so amusing, and said so.

*

Back at Rachel's, he made his way to the armchair in the little bay window and whiled away the minutes until six o'clock by rereading the *Telegraph*. The trouble with this house was that it had been knocked through, so you were all in it hugger-mugger together. He could not himself see the advantage of being forced to witness every domestic detail. Frankly, it was bedlam, with the spin cycle going and Rachel's twins squawking and Rachel washing her hands at the kitchen sink yet again like Lady Macbeth. Now she was doing that thing she did with the brown paper bag, blowing into it and goggling her eyes, which seemed to amuse the twins at least.

Small children were undoubtedly tiresome, but the way she indulged hers made them ten times worse. Like so many of her generation she seemed to be making a huge song and dance about the whole business. She was ridiculous with them, ludicrously over-indulgent and lacking in any sort of authority. It was when he had commented on this in passing that the auditory hallucinations had begun.

'I don't want to do to them what you did to me, you old beast,' the voice had growled, guttural and shocking, although her lips had not been moving. 'I don't want to hand on the misery. I don't want that horrible Larkin poem to be true.' He had glared at her, amazed, and yet it had been quite obvious she was blissfully unaware of what he had heard. Or thought he had heard.

He must have been hearing things.

Now he held up his wrist and tapped his watch at her. She waved back at him, giving one last puff into the paper bag before scurrying to the fridge for the ice and lemon. As he watched her prepare his first drink of the evening, he decided to test out the audiologist's theory.

'Sit with me,' he ordered, taking the clinking glass.

'I'd love to, Dad, but the twins ...' she said.

'Nonsense,' he said. 'Look at them, you can see them from here, they're all right for now.'

She perched on the arm of the chair opposite his and started twisting a strand of her lank brown hair.

'Tell me about your day,' he commanded.

'My day?' she said. 'Are you sure? Nothing very much happened. I took the twins to Tumbletots, then we went round Asda ...'

'Keep talking,' he said, fiddling with his hearing aid. 'I want to test this gadget out.'

'... then I had to queue at the post office, and I wasn't very popular with the double buggy,' she droned on.

He flicked the switch to the T-setting.

'... never good enough for you, you old beast, you never had any time for me, you never listened to anything I said,' came the low growling voice he remembered from before. 'You cold old beast, Ruth says you're emotionally autistic, definitely somewhere on the autistic spectrum anyway, that's why she went to the other side of the world, but she says she still can't get away from it there, your lack of interest, you blanked us, you blotted us out, you don't even know the names of your grandchildren let alone their birthdays ...'

He flicked the switch back.

'... after their nap, then I put the washing on and peeled some potatoes for tonight's dinner while they watched CBeebies ...' she continued in her toneless everyday voice.

'That's enough for now, thanks,' he said crisply. He took a big gulp of his drink, and then another. 'Scarlett and, er, Mia. You'd better see what they're up to.'

'Are you OK, Dad?'

'Fine,' he snapped. 'You go off and do whatever it is you want to do.' He closed his eyes. He needed Elizabeth now. She'd taken no nonsense from the girls. He had left them to her, which was the way she'd wanted it. All this hysteria! Elizabeth had known how to deal with them.

He sensed he was in for another bad night, and he was right. He lay rigid as a stone knight on a tomb, claustrophobic in his partially closed-down head and its frantic brain noise. The deafer he got the louder it became; that was how it was, that was the deal. He grimaced at the future, his other ear gone, reduced to the company of Matthew Herring and his like, a shoal of old boys mouthing at each other.

The thing was, he had been the breadwinner. Children needed their mothers. It was true he hadn't been very interested in them, but then, frankly, they hadn't been very interesting. Was he supposed to pretend? Neither of them had amounted to much. And he had had his own life to get on with.

He'd seen the way they were with their children these days – 'Oh, that's wonderful, darling! You *are* clever' and 'Love you!' at the end of every exchange, with the young fathers behaving like old women, cooing and planting big sloppy kisses on their babies as if they were in a Disney film. The whole culture had gone soft, it gave him the creeps; opening up to your feminine side! He shuddered in his pyjamas.

Elizabeth was dead. That was what he really couldn't bear.

The noise inside his head was going wild, colossal hooting and zooming and pressure-cooker hiss; he needed to distract his brain with – what had the doctor called it? – 'sound enrichment'. Give it some competition, fight fire with fire: that was the idea. Fiddling with the radio's tuning wheel in the dark, he swore viciously and wondered why it was you could never find the World Service when you needed it. He wanted talk but there was only music, which would have to do. Nothing but a meaningless racket to him, though at least it was a different *sort* of racket; that was the theory.

No, that was no better. If anything, it was worse.

Wasn't the hearing aid supposed to help cancel tinnitus? So the doctor had suggested. Maybe the T-setting would come into its own in this sort of situation. He turned on the tiny gadget, made the necessary adjustments, and poked it into his ear.

It was like blood returning to a dead leg, but in his head and chest. What an extraordinary sensation! It was completely new to him. Music was stealing hotly, pleasurably through his veins for the first time in his life, unspeakably delicious. He heard himself moan aloud. The waves of sound were announcing bliss and at the same time they brought cruel pain. He'd done his best, hadn't he? He didn't know what the girls expected from him. He'd given them full financial support until they were eighteen, which was more than many fathers could say. What was it exactly that he was supposed not to have done?

Lifting him on a dark upsurge into the night, the music also felled him with inklings of what he did not know and had not known, intimations of things lovely beyond imagination which would never now be his as death was next. A tear crept down his face.

He hadn't cried since he was a baby. Appalling! At this rate he'd be wetting himself. When his mother had died, he and his sisters had been called into the front room and given a handkerchief each and told to go to their bedrooms until teatime. Under the carpet. Into thin air.

The music was so astonishingly beautiful, that was the trouble. Waves of entrancing sound were threatening to breach the sea wall. Now he was coughing dry sobs.

This was not on. Frankly he preferred any combination of troublesome symptoms to getting in this state. He fumbled with the hearing aid and at last managed to turn the damned thing *off*. Half-unhinged, he tottered to the bathroom and ran a basin of water over it, submerged the beastly little gadget, drowned it. Then he fished it out and flushed it down the lavatory. Best place for it.

No more funny business, he vowed. That was that. From now on he would put up and shut up, he swore it on Elizabeth's grave. Back in bed, he once again lowered his head onto the pillow.

Straight away the infernal noise factory started up; he was staggering along beat by beat in a heavy shower of noise and howling.

'It's not real,' he whispered to himself in the dark. 'Compensatory brain activity, that's what this is.'

Inside his skull all hell had broken loose. He had never heard anything like it.

UP AT A VILLA

Helen Simpson

Helen Simpson (b. 1959) is a British novelist and short story writer. She worked at *Vogue* for five years before becoming a writer full-time. Her first collection, *Four Bare Legs in a Bed and Other Stories*, won the Sunday Times Young Writer of the Year award, and her second, *Hey Yeah Right Get A Life*, won the Hawthornden Prize. In 1993 she was selected as one of *Granta*'s top twenty novelists under the age of forty.

They were woken by the deep-chested bawling of an angry baby. Wrenched from wine-dark slumber, the four of them sat up, flustered, hair stuck with pine needles, gulping awake with little light breaths of concentration. They weren't supposed to be here, they remembered that.

They could see the baby by the side of the pool, not twenty yards away, a furious geranium in its parasol-shaded buggy, and the large pale woman sagging above it in her bikini. Half an hour ago they had been masters of that pool, racing topless and tipsy round its borders, lithe Nick chasing sinewy Tina and wrestling her, an equal match, grunting, snaky, toppling, crashing down into the turquoise depths together. Neither of them would let go underwater. They came up fighting in a chlorinated spume of diamonds. Joe, envious, had tried a timid imitation grapple, but Charlotte was having none of it.

'Get off!' she snorted, kind, mocking, and slipped neatly into the pool via a dive that barely broke the water's skin. Joe, seeing he was last as usual, gave a foolish bellow and launched his heavy self into the air, his aimless belly slapping down disastrously like an explosion.

After that, the sun had dried them off in about a minute, they had devoured their picnic of *pissaladière* and peaches, downed the bottles of pink wine and gone to doze in the shade behind the ornamental changing screen.

Now they were stuck. Their clothes and money were heaped under a bush of lavender at the other end of the pool.

'Look,' whispered Tina as a man came walking towards the baby and its mother. 'Look, they're English. He's wearing socks.'

'What's the matter with her now,' said the man, glaring at the baby.

'How should I know,' said the woman. 'I mean, she's been fed. She's got a new nappy.'

'Oh, plug her on again,' said the man crossly, and wandered off towards a cushioned sun-lounger. 'That noise goes straight through my skull.'

The woman muttered something they couldn't hear, and shrugged herself out of her bikini top. They gasped and gaped in fascination as she uncovered huge brown nipples on breasts like wheels of Camembert.

'Oh gross!' whispered Tina, drawing her lips back from her teeth in a horrified smirk.

'Be quiet,' hissed Nick as they all of them heaved with giggles and snorts and their light eyes popped, over-emphatic in faces baked to the colour of flowerpots.

They had crept into the grounds of this holiday villa, one of a dozen or more on this hillside, at slippery Nick's suggestion, since everything was *fermé le lundi* down in the town and they had no money left for entrance to hotel pools or even to beaches. Anyway they had fallen out of love over the last week with the warm soup of the Mediterranean, its filmy surface bobbing with polystyrene shards and other unsavoury orts.

'Harvey,' called the woman, sagging on the stone bench with the baby at her breast. 'Harvey, I wish you'd …'

'Now what is it,' said Harvey testily, making a great noise with his two-day-old copy of *The Times*.

'Some company,' she said with wounded pathos. 'That's all.'

'Company,' he sighed. 'I thought the idea was to get away from it all.'

'I thought we'd have a chance to talk on holiday,' said the woman.

'All right, all right,' said Harvey, scrumpling up *The Times* and exchanging his sun-lounger for a place on the stone bench beside her. 'All right. So what do you want to talk about?'

'Us,' said the woman.

'Right,' said Harvey. 'Can I have a swim first?' And he was off, diving clumsily into the pool, losing his poise at the last moment so that he met the water like a flung cat.

'She's hideous,' whispered Tina. 'Look at that gross stomach, it's all in folds.' She glanced down superstitiously at her own body, the high breasts like halved apples, the handspan waist.

'He's quite fat too,' said Charlotte. 'Love handles, anyroad.'

'I'm never going to have children,' breathed Tina. 'Not in a million years.'

'Shush,' said Joe, straining forward for the next instalment. The husband was back from his swim, shaking himself like a Labrador in front of the nursing mother.

'"Us"', he said humorously, wiggling a finger inside each ear, then drubbing his hair with the flats of his hands. 'Fire away then.'

She started immediately, as if she knew she only had two or three minutes of his attention, and soon the air was thick with phrases like Once she's on solids, and You'd rather be reading the paper, and Is it because you wanted a boy? He looked dull but resigned, silent except for once protesting, What's so special about bathtime. She talked on, but like a loser, for she was failing to find the appropriate register, flailing around, pulling clichés from the branches. At some subliminal level each of the eavesdropping quartet recognised their own mother's voice in hers, and glazed over.

'You've never moaned on like this before,' marvelled Harvey at last. 'You were always so independent. Organised.'

'You think I'm a mess,' she said. 'A failure as a mother.'

'Well, you're obviously not coping,' he said. 'At home all day and you can't even keep the waste bins down.'

Nick and Tina were laughing with silent violence behind the screen, staggering against each other, tears running down their faces. Joe was mesmerised by the spectacle of lactation. As for Charlotte, she was remembering another unwitting act of voyeurism, a framed picture from a childhood camping holiday.

It had been early morning, she'd gone off on her own to the village for their breakfast baguettes, and the village had been on a hill like in a fairy-tale, full of steep little flights of steps which she was climbing for fun. The light was sweet and glittering and as she looked down over the rooftops she saw very clearly one particular open window, so near that she could have lobbed in a ten-franc piece, and through the window she could see a woman dropping kisses onto a man's face and neck and chest. He was lying naked in bed and she was kissing him lovingly and gracefully, her breasts dipping down over him like silvery peonies. Charlotte had never mentioned this to anyone, keeping the picture to herself, a secret snapshot protected from outside sniggerings.

'The loss of romance,' bleated the woman, starting afresh.

'We haven't changed,' said Harvey stoutly.

'Yes, we have! Of course we have!'

'Rubbish.'

'But we're supposed to change, it's all different now, the baby's got to come first.'

'I don't see why,' said Harvey. 'Mustn't let them rule your life.'

The baby had finished at last, and was asleep; the woman gingerly detached her from her body and placed her in the buggy.

'Cheer up,' said Harvey, preparing for another dip. 'Once you've lost a bit of weight, it'll all be back to normal. Romance et cetera. Get yourself in shape.'

'You don't fancy me any more,' she wailed in a last-ditch attempt to hold him.

'No, no, of course I do,' he said, eyeing the water. 'It's just a bit … different from before. Now that you've gone all, you know, sort of floppy.'

That did it. At the same moment as the woman unloosed a howl of grief, Nick and Tina released a semi-hysterical screech of laughter. Then – 'Run!' said Joe – and they all shot off round the opposite side of the pool, snatching up their clothes and shoes and purses at the other end. Harvey was meanwhile shouting, 'Hoi! Hoi! What the hell d'you think you're playing at!' while his wife stopped crying and his daughter started.

The four of them ran like wild deer, leaping low bushes of lavender and thyme, whooping with panicky delight, lean and light and half-naked – or, more accurately, nine-tenths naked – through the pine trees and *après-midi* dappling. They ran on winged feet, and their laughter looped the air behind them like chains of bubbles in translucent water.

High up on the swimming-pool terrace the little family, frozen together for a photographic instant, watched their flight open-mouthed, like the ghosts of summers past; or, indeed, of summers yet to come.

PLUNDER

Edna O'Brien

Edna O'Brien (b. 1930) is an Irish novelist, playwright, poet and short story writer. Her first novel, *The Country Girls*, is often credited with breaking silence on sexual matters and social issues in Ireland following World War II. Due to the controversy caused by the book, O'Brien left Ireland for London where she has remained. She has written over twenty works of fiction and received the Irish PEN Lifetime Achievement Award in 2001.

One morning we wakened to find that there was no border – we had been annexed to the fatherland. Of course we did not hear of it straightaway as we live in the wilds, but a workman who comes to gather wood and fallen boughs told us that soldiers had swarmed the town and occupied the one hotel. He said they drank there, got paralytic, demanded lavish suppers, and terrorised the maids. The townspeople hid, not knowing which to fear most, the rampaging soldiers or their huge dogs that ran loose without muzzles. He said they had a device for examining the underneath of cars – a mirror on wheels to save themselves the inconvenience of stooping. They were lazy bastards.

The morning we sighted one of them by the broken wall in the back avenue we had reason to shudder. His camouflage was perfect, green and khaki and brown, the very colours of this mucky landscape. Why they should come to these parts baffled us and we were sure that very soon they would scoot it. Our mother herded us all into one bedroom, believing we would be safer that way – there would be no danger of one of us straying and we could keep turns at the watch. As luck had it, only the week before we had gathered nuts and apples and stored them on wooden trays for the winter. Our mother worried about our cow, said that by not being milked her poor udder would be pierced with pain, said the milk would drip all over the grass. We could have used that cow's milk.

Our father was not here, our father had disappeared long before.

On the third morning they came and shouted our mother's name – Rosanna. It sounded different, pronounced in their tongue, and we wondered how they knew it. They were utter hooligans. Two of them roughed her out, and the elder tugged on the long plait of her hair.

Our mother embraced each of us and said she would be back presently. She was not. We waited, and after a fearful interval we tiptoed downstairs but could not gain entry to the kitchen because the door between it and the hall was barricaded with stacked chairs. Eventually we forced our way through, and the sight was grisly. Her apron, her clothes, and her underclothes were strewn all over the floor, and so were hairpins and her two side combs. An old motorcar seat was raised onto a wooden trough in which long ago she used to put the feed for hens and chickens. We looked in vain through the window, thinking we might see her in the back avenue or better still coming up the path, shattered, but restored to us. There was one soldier down there, his rifle cocked. Where was she? What had they done to her? When would she be back? The strange thing is that none of us cried and none of us broke down. With a bit of effort we carried the stinking car seat out and threw it down the three steps that led from the back door. It was all we could do to defy our enemies. Then we went up to the room and waited. Our cow had stopped moaning, and we realised that she too had been taken and most likely slaughtered. The empty field was ghost-like, despite the crows and jackdaws making their usual commotion at evening time. We could guess the hours roughly by the changing light and changing sky. Later the placid moon looked in on us. We thought, if only the workman would come back and give us news. The sound of his chainsaw used to jar on us, but now we would have welcomed it as it meant a return to the old times, the safe times, before our mother and our cow were taken. Our brother's wooden flute lay in the fire grate, as he had not the heart to play a tune, even though we begged for it.

On the fifth morning we found some reason to jubilate. The sentry was gone from his post, and no one came to stand behind that bit of broken wall. We read this as deliverance. Our mother would come back. We spoke of things that we would do for her.

We got her clean clothes out of the wardrobe and lay them neatly on the bed. Her lisle stockings hanging down, shimmered pink in a shaft of sunlight, and we could imagine her legs inside them. We told each other that the worst was over. We bit on apples and pelted each other with the butts for fun. Our teeth cracked with a vengeance on the hazelnuts and the walnuts, and picking out the tasty, fleshy particles, we shared them with one another like true friends, like true family. Our brother played a tune. It was about the sun setting on a place called 'Boulevouge'.

Our buoyancy was shortlived. By evening we heard gunshot again, and a soldier had returned to the broken bit of wall, a shadowy presence. Sleep was impossible and so we watched and we prayed. We did that for two whole days and nights, and what with not eating and not sleeping, our nerves got the better of us and, becoming hysterical, we had to slap each other's faces, slap them smartly, to bring common sense into that room.

The hooligans in their camouflage have returned. They have come by a back route, through the dense woods and not up the front avenue as we expected.

They are in the kitchen, laughing and shouting in their barbarous tongues. Fear starts to seep out of us, like blood seeping. If we are taken all together, we might muster some courage, but from the previous evidence it is likely that we will be taken separately. We stand, each in our corner, mute, petrified, like little effigies, our eyes fastened to the knob of the door, our ears straining beyond it, to gauge which step of stairs they are already stomping on.

How beautiful it would be if one of us could step forward and volunteer to become the warrior for the others. What a firmament of love ours would be.

A deathly emptiness to the whole world, to the fields and the sacked farmyards and the tumbledown shacks. Not a soul in sight. Not an animal. Not a bird. Here and there mauled carcasses and bits of torn skins where animals must have fought each other in their last frenzied hungers. I almost got away. I was walking towards somewhere that I didn't know, somewhere safe. There had been no soldiers for weeks. They'd killed each other off. It was hard to know which side was which, because they swapped sides the way they swapped uniforms. My mother and later my brother and my two sisters had been taken. I was out foraging and when I came back our house was a hulk of smoke. Black ugly smoke. I only had the clothes I stood up in, a streelish green dress and a fur coat that was given to my mother once. It used to keep us warm in bed, and sometimes when it slipped onto the floor I would get out to pick it up. It felt luxurious, the hairs soft and tickling on bare feet. That was the old world, the other world, before the barbarians came. Why they came here at all is a mystery, as there was no booty, no gold mines, no silver mines – only the woods, the tangly woods, and in some parts tillage, small patches of oats or barley. Even to think of corn, first green and then a ripening yellow, or the rows of cabbage, or any growing thing, was pure heartbreak. Maybe my brother and sisters are across the border or maybe they are dead. I moved at dusk and early night, bunched inside the fur coat. I wanted to look old, to look a hag. They did not fancy the older women; they wanted young women and the younger the better, like wild strawberries. It was crossing a field that I heard the sound of a vehicle, and I ran, not knowing there was such swiftness in me. They were coming, nearer and nearer, the wheels slurping over the ridged earth that bordered the wood that I was heading into. The one who jumped out picked me up and tossed me to the Head Man. They spluttered with glee. He sat me on his lap, wedged my mouth open, wanting me to say swear words back to him. His eyes were hard as steel and the whites a yellowy gristle. Their faces were daubed with paint and they all had puce tattoos. The one that drove was called Gypsy. That drive was frantic. Me screaming, screaming, and the Head Man slapping me like mad and opening me up as though I was a mess of potage. They stopped at a disused lime kiln. He was first. When he splayed me apart I thought I was dead, except that I wasn't. You don't die when you think you do. The subordinates used their hands as stirrups. When I was turned over I bit on the cold lime floor to clean my mouth of them. Their shouts, their weight, their tongues, their slobber, the way they bore through me, wanting to get up into my head, to the God particle. That's what an old woman in the village used to call it, that last cranny where you say prayers and confide in yourself the truth of what you feel about everything and everyone. They couldn't get to it. I had stopped screaming. The screams were stifled. Through the open roof I saw a buzzard glide in a universe of blue. It was waiting for another to be with it, and after a time that other came that was its comrade and they glided off into those crystalline nether-reaches. Putting on their trousers, they kept telling each other to hurry the fuck up. The Head Man stood above me, straddled, the fur coat over his shoulders, and he looked spiteful, angry. The blood was pouring out of me and the ground beneath was warm. I saw him through the slit in my nearly shut eyes. For a minute I thought he might kill me and then he turned away as if it wasn't worth the bother, the mess. The engine had already started when Gypsy ran back and placed a cigarette across my upper lip. I expect he was trying to tell me something. As children we were told that why we have a dent in our upper lip is because when we are born an angel comes and places a forefinger there for silence, for secrecy. By degrees I came back. Little things, the air sidling through that small clammy enclosure and the blood drying on me, like resin. Long ago, we had an aluminium alarm clock with the back fallen off, that worked on a single battery, but batteries were scarce. Our mother would take out the battery and we'd guess the time by the failing light, by the dusk, by the cockcrow and the one cow, the one faithful cow that stood, lowing, at the paling, waiting to be milked. One of us would go out with a bucket and the milking stool. When she put the battery back the silver needle would start up and then the two hands, like two soft black insects, crept over each other in their faithful circuit. The lime-green dress that I clung to, that I clutched, that I dug my fingernails into, is splotched with flowers, blood-red and prodigal, like poppies. Soon as I can walk I will set out. To find another, like me. We will recognise each other by the rosary of poppies and the speech of our eyes. We, the defiled ones, in our thousands, scattered, trudging over the land, the petrified land, in search of a safe haven, if such a place exists.

Many and terrible are the roads to home.

AUNT TELEPHONE

Edith Pearlman

Edith Pearlman (b. 1936) is an American short story writer. She has published more than 250 works of short fiction and non-fiction in national magazines, literary journals, anthologies and online publications. She was awarded the PEN/Malamud Award in 2011, and her latest collection, *Binocular Vision*, won the 2012 National Book Critics Circle Award.

I got my first taste of raw flesh when I was nine years old. I had been taken to an adult party. My father was out of town at an investors' conference and my brother was spending the night at a friend's; and my babysitter got sick at the last minute, or said she did. What was my mother to do – stay home? So she brought me along. The affair was cocktails and a buffet featuring beef tartare on pumpernickel rounds and a bowl of icy seviche – this was thirty years ago, before such delicacies had been declared lethal. The party was given by the Plunkets, family therapists: two fatties who dressed in similar sloppy clothing as if to demonstrate that glamour was not a prerequisite for rambunctious sex.

My mother and I and Milo walked over to the party in the glowing September afternoon. Our house and Milo's and the Plunkets' all lay within a mile of each other in Godolphin, a leafy wedge of Boston, as did the homes of most of the other guests – the psychiatrists and clinical psychologists and social workers who made up this crowd. They were all friends, they referred patients to one another, they distributed themselves into peer-supervision subsets – a collegial, talkative crew, their envy vigorously tamped down. Their kids were friends, too – some as close as cousins. I already hated groups, but I was willy-nilly part of the bunch.

Among the adults, Milo was first among peers. He produced paper after acclaimed paper: case histories of children with symptoms like elective mutism and terror of automobiles and willful constipation lasting ten days. I longed to become one of his fascinating patients, but I knew to my sadness that therapists rarely treated their friends' children no matter how sick and I knew, also, that I wasn't sick anyway, just ornery and self-centered. In his published work Milo gave the young sufferers false first names and surname initials. "What would you call *me*?" I asked him once, still hoping for immortality.

"Well, Susan, what would you like to be called?"

"Catamarina M."

He warmed me with his brown gaze. ("The eyes," Dr. Lenore once remarked to my mother, "thoroughly compensate for the absence of chin.")

Milo said: "Catamarina is your name forever."

So I had an appellation if not symptoms. All I had to do was stop talking or moving my bowels. Alas, nature proved too strong for me.

Milo's colleagues respected his peaceable bachelordom: they recognized asexuality as an unpathological human preference, also as a boon to society. He had been born in cosmopolitan Budapest, which gave him further cachet. His liberal parents, who were in the bibelot business, had gotten out just before World War II. So Milo was brought up in New York by a pair of Hungarians, penniless at first, soon rich again. He inherited a notable collection of ancient Chinese figurines.

On the day of that party Milo was wearing his standard costume: flannel slacks, turtleneck sweater, tweed jacket. He was then almost fifty, a bit older than my parents and their friends. His hair, prematurely gray, rose high and thick from a narrow forehead. It swung at his nape like a soft broom. He was very tall and very thin.

Dr. Will Plunket gave me beef tartare in a hamburger bun. But the Plunket boys wouldn't let me join their game of Dungeons and Dragons. So, munching my feral sandwich, I wandered in the fall garden still brightened by a glossy sun. On a chaise on the flagstone terrace sat a woman I didn't know. She looked sulky and bored. Dr. Judah joined me for a while and wondered aloud if fairies nested under the chrysanthemums. I frowned at him, but when he went inside I knelt and peered under the mums. Nothing. After a while

Milo found me. In his soft voice he talked about the greenery near the stone wall – basil was rumored to cure melancholy, marjoram headaches, ground ivy conjunctivitis. He bent, picked up a handful of the ivy, stood, and crushed a few leaves into my palm. "Not to be taken internally." Then he, too, went in.

I drifted toward the terrace. "How lucky you are," drawled the woman on the chaise, and she drank some of her cocktail.

"Yes. Why?"

"To have such an attentive aunt," she said, and drank some more.

"My aunt lives in Michigan."

"She's here on a visit?"

"She's in Europe this month."

"I mean the aunt you were just talking to."

"Milo?"

"Her name is Milo?"

I raced into the house. I found my mother standing with Dr. Margaret and Dr. Judah. "You'll never believe it, that patient on the terrace, she thought Milo was my aunt!" My mother gave me a ferocious stare. "My *aunt*," I heedlessly repeated to Dr. Margaret, and then turned to Dr. Judah. "My—" but I couldn't finish because my mother was yanking me out of the room.

"Stop talking, Susan, stop right now, do not say that again. It would hurt Milo's feelings dreadfully." She let go of me and folded her arms. "There's dirt on your knees," she said, though dirt was not usually denigrated in this circle. "Filth."

"Garden soil," I corrected.

My mother sighed. "The woman on the terrace is Dr. Will's sister."

"I wish Milo *was* my aunt."

"Were."

"Were? Why?"

"Condition contrary to fact." As our conversation slid into the safe area of grammar, we returned to the party. Milo was now listening to Dr. Will. It didn't seem to me that Milo's longish hair was more feminine than Dr. Will's black smock. But this once I would obey my mother. I would not again relate the error of the woman on the terrace. I hoped that Milo hadn't heard my earlier exclamation. Not for the world would I hurt his feelings; or so I thought.

Milo celebrated thanksgiving here, Passover there, Christmas twice in one day, first at the Collinses and then at the Shapiros. He smoked his after-dinner cigar in everybody's backyard. He came to our annual New Year's Day open house, which I was required to attend for fifteen minutes. I spent that quarter hour behind a lamp. My parents, shoulder to shoulder, greeted their guests. Sometimes my mother slipped her hand into my father's pocket, like a horse nuzzling for sugar.

Milo went to piano recitals and bar mitzvahs and graduations. In August he visited four different families, one each week. He *was* an aunt, my aunt, aunt to many children born into our therapeutic set, if an aunt is someone always ready to talk on the telephone to worried parents – especially to mothers, who do most of the worrying. Those mothers of ours, full of understanding for their patients, were helpless when their own offspring gave them trouble. Then they became frantic kid sisters, reaching for the phone. Bad report cards, primitive behavior on the playground, sass, lying, staying out all night, playing hooky – for all such troubles Milo was ready with advice and consolation. He knew, also, when a child needed outside help – strangling the cat was a sure indication. Usually, though, it was the parent who required an interpretation and also a recommendation to back off. "No, a joint today is not a crack pipe tomorrow," he memorably assured Dr. Lenore. Dr. Lenore's daughter was, of course, listening on the extension. We were all masters of domestic wiretapping – slipping a forefinger between receiver and the button on which it rested, lifting the receiver to our ear, releasing the button with the caution of a surgeon until a connection was soundlessly established.

The July I was twelve I ran away from overnight camp. The day after I arrived home, surly and triumphant, I eavesdropped on Milo and my mother. Milo was suggesting that my mother praise me for taking the bus rather than hitchhiking on the highway.

"She stole the bus money from her counselor," my mother said.

"Borrowed, I think. Encourage her to return the money by mail."

"Shouldn't she be encouraged to return herself to camp?"

Milo said: "To the hated place?" There was a talcum pause as he drew on his cigar. "To the place she had the resourcefulness to escape from?"

"It's difficult to have her home," my mother said, with a little sob.

"Yes, Ann, I can imagine," said Milo. And then: "It is her home, too."

There was a silence – Milo's the silence of someone who has delivered a truth and my mother's the silence of someone who has received it. And a third silence, a silence within a silence: mine. "It is her home, too," I heard. The gentle living room. The kitchen whose window looked out on birds and squirrels and sometimes a pheasant that had strayed from the more suburban part of Godolphin. The attached office where my mother saw patients during the day. The bedroom where in the evenings she received those patients' panicky calls and where she herself called Milo. My brother's room with his construction projects in various stages of completion – though a year younger than I, he was already an adept mechanic. My own room: posters, books, toys outgrown but not discarded, clothing pooled on the floor and draped on lamps. A long window led from my room onto a little balcony. My mother had once planted impatiens in boxes on the balcony but I let the flowers die. Without recrimination she had watched me neglect – desecrate, even – a generous space in the house. The house that was hers, too.

For the remainder of July I babysat for the kids next door, treating them with a pretend affection I ended up feeling. ("Hypocrisy is the first step toward sincerity," Milo had written.) I made a small effort to straighten my room. ("A token is a cheap coin, but it is not counterfeit" – same source.) In August we went to Cape Cod.

Our determinedly modest bungalow faced the sea; there was no sandy beach, but we had become used to lying on our strip of shingle. The house had four small bedrooms. The walls were thin, providing perfect acoustics. There was a grille and an outdoor shower. Sometimes my father grilled fish; sometimes he and my mother prepared meals together in the inconvenient kitchen, where they bumped into each other and laughed.

As always Milo came for the third week. I could hear him, too, turning over in bed or splashing in the bathroom, just as I could hear my parents' soft conversations, my brother's indiscriminate farting. The small family – still too large a group for me. "I want to work in a private office," I said one morning.

"You could be a psychiatrist," said my unimaginative brother.

"Private! By myself! Nobody comes in."

"Ah. You could be a bank president," Milo said. "They are rarely interrupted."

"Or a hotel housekeeper," my mother said. "Just you and piles of linen."

"Or an astronomer, alone with her telescope," my father said. That was the best offer. "The work requires a bit of math," he added, mildly.

Later that day Milo took my brother and me to Bosky's Wild Animal Preserve. We visited Bosky's once or twice each summer. The wildest animals there were a pair of foxes. Foxes are devoted parents while their offspring require care. Then they separate, and next season they find new partners. But Bosky's two downcast specimens were stuck with each other year after year. The male peacock didn't seem to have much fun, either. His occasional halfhearted display revealed gaps in his feathers. A pichi, a female rock snake, a few monkeys chattering nonsense – these were our wild animals. But beyond the pathetic cages was a large working farm, with chickens and turkeys and an apple orchard and a field of corn. A pony in a straw hat dragged a cart around the cornfield. Two other chapeaued ponies could be ridden around a ring, though not independently: you had to endure, walking beside you, one of the local teenagers who worked at Bosky's. These louts did not hide their contempt for nag and rider.

The rock snake was fed a live white mouse every two weeks. This public meal was unadvertised but word got around. When we got to Bosky's that day with Milo, there were a dozen small children already gathered in front of the snake's cage. Their parents, wearing doubtful expressions, milled at a distance. My brother went off to the ponies. Milo and I were tall enough to see over the children's heads, so we two and the kids viewed the entire performance – the lowering of the mouse into the cage by Mr. Bosky, the terrified paralysis of the rodent, the expert constriction by the snake, and then the mouse's slow incorporation into the snake's hinged mouth. She fed herself the mouse, whose bones were all broken but who still presumably breathed. In it went, farther in, still farther, until all we could see was its tiny rump and then only its thin white tail.

The little kids, bored once the tail had disappeared, drifted toward their pained parents. One skinny mother vomited into a beach bag. Milo looked at her with sympathy. Not I, though.

"A recovering bulimic," I told him as we moved away.

"Giving herself a thrill?" he wondered. "Could be," he said, generously admitting me into the company of interpreters.

I love you, Milo, I might have said if we said that sort of thing.

In the fall I began to attend school regularly, forcing myself to tolerate groups at least for a classroom hour. I had to choose a sport so I went out for track, the least interpersonal of activities. I did my homework in most subjects. I made up the math I had flunked the year before.

My mother needed to call Milo less often.

I even achieved a kind of intimacy. My best friend – almost my only one, really, unless you counted Dr. Judah's daughter and Dr. Lenore's daughter and the younger Plunket boy, who were all in my grade – was an extra-tall girl with an extra-long neck. Her parents had been born in India. They both practiced radiology. Their daughter planned a career in medicine, too, as casually as a child of other parents might look forward to taking over the family store. Anjali – such a beautiful name – was plain and dark, with drooping lids and wide nostrils. Her last name was Nezhukumatathil – "Where my father comes from, the equivalent of Smith."

She lived a few blocks from us. She and I walked home along the same streets every day, rarely bothering to talk. Our route took us past the stretch of row houses that included Milo's, past his small, low-maintenance garden: a dogwood tree, a cast iron white love seat below it, pachysandra around it. Milo's front door had two bells, one for the living quarters, one for the office and playroom. He was always working in the late afternoon, and so I didn't tell Anjali that I knew the owner of that particular narrow house.

But one May at five o'clock there he was on the lacy bench, he and his cigar. A patient had canceled, I immediately understood. There was an exchange of hellos and an introduction; and then – after Milo had poked the cigar into a tin of sand beside the love seat – we were inside; and Milo was telling Anjali the provenance of some of his figurines and showing her his needlepoint utensils. How had he guessed that this mute camel liked small things and delicate handiwork? If I'd been walking with Sarah – another girl I sometimes made myself pal around with, a very good runner – he'd have known to put "Hair" on the stereo and discuss stretching exercises. Ah, it was his business. I sipped a can of Coke. You might guess that it tasted like wormwood, that I was full of jealousy – but no: I was full of admiration for Milo, performing his familial role for this schoolgirl, comfortably limited by the imminent arrival of the next patient; within ten minutes he'd give us the gate. And he did, first looking with a rueful expression at his watch. "Good-bye, Anjali," he said at the door. "See you soon, Susan. Thank you for bringing your friend," as if I had done it on purpose to display my hard-won sociability.

A block or so later Anjali made a rare disclosure – she'd like to live like Milo.

"In what way?" I asked, expecting mention of the figurines, the needlepoint, even the dogwood.

"Alone."

Me, too! I wanted to confide. But the confidence would have been false. I already guessed that someday I would marry and produce annoying children. I was not as bold as Milo, as Anjali. Nature would again prove too strong for me.

August: just before senior year. I ran every morning; it was no longer an obligation but a pleasure. The third week Anjali came to the Cape to visit me, and one of my brother's friends came to visit him, and Milo came to visit the family. He swam and baked blueberry pies and treated us to impromptu lectures on this and that – the nature of hurricanes; stars, though I had already dismissed astronomy as a career; the town of Scheveningen, where, at the age of four, he had spent the summer. He liked to recall an ancient Dutch waiter who had brought him lemonade every afternoon and talked about his years as a circus acrobat. "Lies, beautiful lies, essential to amour propre."

"To the waiter's amour propre?" I asked.

"And to mine. Taking lies seriously, it's a necessary skill."

In bathing briefs, muscular and tanned, Milo could not be mistaken for a woman. But my brother's friend, whose schoolteacher parents were not part of our exalted circle, told my brother that Milo was so fucking helpful he was probably some cast-off queen. My brother didn't hesitate to repeat the evaluation to me. "A queen!"

"There's filth on your knees," I snapped, but of course he didn't get the reference. I was furious with all three of them: the unappreciative guest, my unfeeling brother, and Milo, who had brought the accusation on himself with his pies and his reminiscences. He'd encouraged the taciturn Anjali to talk about ancient artifacts, too. Apparently they were her prime interest nowadays. Apparently Anjali and Milo had run into each other at the museum during the spring – some dumb exhibition, pre-Columbian telephones, maybe. Afterward he had treated her to tea.

On Thursday of that week Milo and I drove Anjali through a light rain to the bus station – she had to get back to town for a family party. She jumped out of the backseat and threw her traveling sack, studded with tiny mirrors, over her bony shoulder. "Thanks," she said in her toneless voice. (She had properly thanked my mother back in the bungalow.) She slammed the door and strode toward the bus.

Milo opened his window and stuck his head into the drizzle. "There's a netsuke exhibition in October," he called.

She stopped and turned, and smiled at him, a smile that lasted several seconds too long. Then she boarded the bus.

We watched the vehicle pull out.

"Shall we take a run to Bosky's?" Milo said.

"The place is swarming with ants," I said. "Bosky's fornicates," I showed off. Milo was silent. "Sure," I relented. It was his vacation, too.

On that damp day Milo paid his usual serious attention to the wild animals: the foxes forced into monogamy, the impotent peacock, the dislocated monkeys. He glanced at the languid snake, still digesting last week's meal. He stopped for an irritatingly long while at the cage of an animal new to the preserve, an agouti from Belize that was (an ill-painted sign mentioned) a species of rodent. "Among Belizeans he's considered a tasty meal," Milo told me; he knew more than the sign painter. "The agouti himself is herbivorous. A sociable little fellow. He shares a common burrow system with others of his kind."

"Does he. Like you."

He gave me his interested stare. "I eat meat— "

"I shouldn't have said that," I muttered.

" – though it's true that I have lost my taste for beef tartare. It wasn't a terrible thing to say, Catamarina M. We all do live, your parents and I and our friends, in a kind of mutual burrow, and the telephone makes it even more intimate, especially when one of you children sneaks onto the line – it's like a hiccup, I listen for it. In what way did you insult me?"

"I suggested you were a rat," I said, confessing to the lesser sin. What I had suggested, as I feared he knew, was that he was an inquisitive dependent animal, exchanging advice for friendship; that for all his intuition and clinical wisdom he did not know firsthand the rage that flared between individuals, the urge to eat each other up. Strong emotions were not part of his repertoire. But they had become part of mine during Anjali's visit as I watched her unfold under his radiant friendship – envy, hatred, fury ... *Once I saved you from ridicule, you ridiculous man.*

"A rat," he echoed. "Nevertheless, you are my favorite ... niece."

"I'm supposed to take that lie seriously? Up your goulash, Milo."

"Susan—"

"Go home." I took several steps away from him and his friend the agouti. Then I whirled and began to run. I ran past the pichi and the monkeys and into the farm area, scattering hens and chickens and little kids. "Hey!" yelled Mr. Bosky. I vaulted the railing of the ponies' riding ring and ran around it and vaulted back. "She's crazy," remarked one of the local boys, in surprised admiration. Perhaps I could sneak out one night and meet him in a haystack. I ran straight into the corn, between stag lines of stalks.

Past the corn was another field where lettuce grew close to the ground. I skirted it – I had no wish to do damage to Bosky's. I ran, faster still, enjoying one of those spurts our track coach taught us to take advantage of – a coach who, without concern for feelings or individuality, made us into athletes. I slowed down when I reached the woods, and padded through it like a fox free of her partner; I slithered, like a snake who has to catch her own mouse. On the other side of the woods was the highway. I crossed it carefully – I had no wish to grieve my parents, either. Another narrow road led to the rocky beach, a couple of miles from our house. I walked the rest of the way. My brother and his friend were sitting on the porch, amiably talking with Milo – Aunt Milo, Queen Milo, Dr. Milo, who so evenly distributed his favors. He and I waved to each other, and I went around to the outside shower and turned it on and stood under it, with all my clothes on.

As I had noticed, my mother was calling Milo less frequently. By that last year in high school, it seemed, she didn't call him at all except to remind him of the New Year's party.

And later, talking with children of the other therapists when we were home from college, or, still later, when we ran into each other in New York or San Francisco, I learned that all of our mothers eventually stopped consulting Milo. Partly, I think, they had less need for his advice. We kids were at last growing up. And our parents had incorporated and so no longer needed to hear Milo's primary rule about offspring – "They owe you and society a minimal courtesy. Everything else is their business" – just as they had incorporated his earlier observation about physical punishment: "It's addictive. Rather than strike your child, light up a cigar."

And perhaps, too, they had to flee their older sibling, the one who had seen their wounds.

A few of them may have even believed the rumor about Milo: that he was paying so much attention to Anjali N., a high school girl, that her parents had to warn him off. That fable had been astonishingly easy to launch. I merely related it to Dr. Margaret's daughter – two years younger than I, grateful for my attention. Then I swore her to secrecy.

At any rate, we grown offspring discovered from each other that Milo himself began to initiate the telephone calls, eager to know the progress of the patients, the anecdotes from the latest trips, the news of the children – especially the news of the children.

"Nosy," said Dr. Lenore's daughter.

"Avaricious," said Benjy Plunket, who had practically lived at Milo's house during his parents' divorce. "When I was in college he wanted to study everything I was studying – he even bought himself a copy of my molecular biology textbook, stuff new since his time."

"He managed to tag along on the Apfels' Las Vegas trip," said Dr. Lenore's daughter.

"People outlive their usefulness," Dr. Judah's daughter summed up.

"It's sad," we all agreed, with offhand malice.

My mother still answered when Milo called (machines allowed other old friends to screen him out) and she tolerated his increasingly discursive monologues. And she kept inviting him to our Cape Cod house, and when he joined our family on a cruise to Scandinavia it was because she and my father enthusiastically insisted. Others were less generous. The Apfels, who had lost heavily in Las Vegas, broke with him entirely.

We are adults now. We prefer e-mail to the telephone. Many of us still live in Godolphin. None of us has entered the mental-health professions. Even Anjali failed to follow her parents into medicine. She teaches art history in Chicago, and has three daughters. Nature proved too strong for her, too.

Some of our children have problems. But though the aged Milo is still working – is esteemed adviser to an inner-city child-guidance center, has done pioneering work with juvenile offenders – we don't consult him. He reminds us too much of our collective childhood in that all-knowing burrow; and of our anxious mothers; and of the unnerving power of empathy. We're a different generation: the tough love crowd. And there's always Ritalin.

I do keep in touch with Milo. It's not a burden: my husband and I are both linguists, and Milo is interested in language. "There is a striving for design in the utterances even of the schizophrenic," he has written.

I inherited the Cape Cod house, and Milo comes to visit every summer. He and I and my two sons always pay a visit to Bosky's. The wild-animal preserve has dwindled to one desperate moose, one raccoon, and those poor foxes, or some other pair. The snake has retired and the agouti is gone, too. But the farm in back continues to flourish, and the ponies get new straw hats every season. My kids have outgrown the place but they understand that old Milo is to be indulged.

A white mustache coats Milo's upper lip. His hair, also white, is still long. His hairline has receded considerably, and he's subject to squamous carcinomas on the exposed brow. Advised by his dermatologist, he covers his head. In the winter he sports a beret, in the summer a cloth hat with a soft brim.

Today, wearing the summer hat and a pair of oversize cargo pants that look like a split skirt, he is riding one of the ponies. That saddle must be punishing his elderly bones. Maybe he's trying to amuse my sons. Certainly they are entertained. When he reaches the far side of the ring they release unseemly snickers. "Granny Wild West," snorts one. "Madame Cowpoke," returns the other. Meanwhile Milo is bending toward the kid who's leading his pony – eliciting a wretched story, no doubt; offering a suggestion that may change the boy's life or at least make his afternoon a little better.

I'd like to smack both my sons and *also* smoke a cigar. Instead I inform them that Milo represents an evolved form of human life that they might someday emulate or even adopt. That sobers them. So I don't mention that he was once valued and then exploited and then betrayed and finally discarded; that, like his displaced parents, he adjusted gracefully to new circumstances.

We stand there, elbows on the railing, as Milo on his pony plods toward us. We smile at him. Within the rim of his bonnet, his face creases; below the soapy mustache his lips part to reveal brown teeth. He is grinning back at us as if he shared our mild mockery of his performance: as if it were his joke, too.

VANITAS

Emma Donoghue

> Emma Donoghue (b. 1969) is an Irish-born playwright, literary historian and novelist. She has published seven novels, eleven plays and four collections of short stories. Her 2010 novel, *Room*, was a finalist for the Man Booker Prize.

This afternoon I was so stone bored, I wrote something on a scrap of paper and put it in a medicine bottle, sealed it up with the stub of a candle. I was sitting on the levee; I tossed the bottle as far as I could (since I throw better than girls should) and the Mississippi took it, lazily. If you got in a boat here by the Duparc-Locoul Plantation, and didn't even row or raise a sail, the current would take you down fifty miles of slow curves to New Orleans in the end. That's if you didn't get tangled up in weed.

What I wrote on the scrap was *Au secours!* Then I put the date, *3 juillet 1839*. The Americans if drowning or in other trouble call out, *Help!* which doesn't capture the attention near as much, it's more like a little sound a puppy would make. The bottle was green glass with *Poison* down one side. I wonder who'll fish it out of the brown water, and what will that man or woman or child make of my message? Or will the medicine bottle float right through the city, out into the Gulf of Mexico, and my scribble go unread till the end of time?

It was a foolish message, and a childish thing to do. I know that; I'm fifteen, which is old enough that I know when I'm being a child. But I ask you, how's a girl to pass an afternoon as long and scalding as this one? I stare at the river in hopes of seeing a boat go by, or a black gum tree with muddy roots. A week ago I saw a blue heron swallow down a wriggling snake. Once in a while a boat will have a letter for us, a boy attaches it to the line of a very long fishing rod and flicks it over to our pier. I'm supposed to call a nègre to untie the letter and bring it in; Maman hates when I do it myself. She says I'm a gateur de nègres, like Papa, we spoil them with soft handling. She always beats them when they steal things, which they call only *taking*.

I go up the pecan alley toward the Maison, and through the gate in the high fence that's meant to keep the animals out. Passers-by always know a Creole house by the yellow and red, not like the glaring white American ones. Everything on our Plantation is yellow and red – not just the houses but the stables, the hospital, and the seventy slave cabins that stretch back like a village for three miles, with their vegetable gardens and chicken pens.

I go in the Maison now, not because I want to, just to get away from the bam-bam-bam of the sun on the back of my neck. I step quietly past Tante Fanny's room, because if she hears me she might call me in for some more lessons. My parents are away in New Orleans doing business; they never take me. I've never been anywhere, truth to tell. My brother, Emile, has been in the Lycee Militaire in Bordeaux for five years already, and when he graduates, Maman says perhaps we will all go on a voyage to France. By all, I don't mean Tante Fanny, because she never leaves her room, nor her husband, Oncle Louis, who lives in New Orleans and does business for us, nor Oncle Flagy and Tante Marcelite, quiet sorts who prefer to stay here always and see to the nègres, the field ones and the house ones. It will be just Maman and Papa and I who go to meet Emile in France. Maman is the head of the famille ever since Grandmère Nannette Prud'Homme retired; we Creoles hand the reins to the smartest child, male or female (unlike the Americans, whose women are too feeble to run things). But Maman never really wanted to oversee the family enterprise, she says if her brothers Louis and Flagy were more useful she and Papa could have gone back to la belle France and stayed there. And then I would have been born a French mademoiselle. "Creole" means born of French stock, here in Louisiana, but Maman prefers to call us French. She says France is like nowhere else in the world, it's all things gracious and fine and civilized, and no sacrés nègres about the place.

I pass Millie on the stairs, she's my maid and sleeps on the floor of my room but she has to help with everything else as well. She's one of Pa Philippe's children, he's very old (for a nègre), and has

VPD branded on both cheeks from when he used to run away, that stands for Veuve Prud'Homme Duparc. It makes me shudder a little to look at the marks. Pa Philippe can whittle anything out of cypress with his little knife: spoons, needles, pipes. Since Maman started our breeding program, we have more small nègres than we know what to do with, but Millie's the only one as old as me. "Allo, Millie," I say, and she says, "Mam'zelle Aimée," and grins back but forgets to curtsy.

"Aimée" means beloved. I've never liked it as a name. It seems it should belong to a different kind of girl.

Where I am bound today is the attic. Though it's hotter than the cellars, it's the one place nobody else goes. I can lie on the floor and chew my nails and fall into a sort of dream. But today the dust keeps making me sneeze. I'm restless, I can't settle. I try a trick my brother, Emile, once taught me, to make yourself faint. You breathe in and out very fast while you count to a hundred, then stand against the wall and press as hard as you can between your ribs. Today I do it twice, and I feel odd, but that's all; I've never managed to faint as girls do in novels.

I poke through some wooden boxes but they hold nothing except old letters, tedious details of imports and taxes and engagements and deaths of people I never heard of. At the back there's an old-fashioned sheepskin trunk, I've tried to open it before. Today I give it a real wrench and the top comes up. Ah, now here's something worth looking at. Real silk, I'd say, as yellow as butter, with layers of tulle underneath, and an embroidered girdle. The sleeves are huge and puffy, like sacks of rice. I slip off my dull blue frock and try it on over my shift. The skirt hovers, the sleeves bear me up so I seem to float over the splinters and dust of the floorboards. If only I had a looking glass up here. I know I'm short and homely, with a fat throat, and my hands and feet are too big, but in this sun-colored dress I feel halfway to beautiful. Grandmere Nannette, who lives in her Maison de Reprise across the yard and is descended from Louis XV's own physician, once said that like her I was pas jolie but at least we had our skin, un teint de roses. Maman turns furious if I go out without my sunhat or a parasol, she says if I get freckled like some Cajun farm girl, how is she supposed to find me a good match? My stomach gets tight at the thought of a husband, but it won't happen before I'm sixteen, at least. I haven't even become a woman yet, Maman says, though I'm not sure what she means.

I dig in the trunk. A handful of books; the collected poetry of Lord Byron, and a novel by Victor Hugo called *Notre-Dame de Paris*. More dresses – a light violet, a pale peach – and light shawls like spiders' webs, and, in a heavy traveling case, some strings of pearls, with rings rolled up in a piece of black velvet. The bottom of the case lifts up, and there I find the strangest thing. It must be from France. It's a sort of bracelet – a thin gold chain – with trinkets dangling from it. I've never seen such perfect little oddities. There's a tiny silver locket that refuses to open, a gold cross, a monkey (grimacing), a minute kneeling angel, a pair of ballet slippers. A tiny tower of some sort, a snake, a crouching tiger (I recognize his toothy roar from the encyclopedia), and a machine with miniature wheels that go round and round; I think this must be a locomotive, like we use to haul cane to our sugar mill. But the one I like best, I don't know why, is a gold key. It's so tiny, I can't imagine what door or drawer or box in the world it might open.

Through the window, I see the shadows are getting longer; I must go down and show myself, or there'll be a fuss. I pack the dresses back into the trunk, but I can't bear to give up the bracelet. I manage to open its narrow catch, and fasten the chain around my left arm above the elbow, where no one will see it under my sleeve. I mustn't show it off, but I'll know it's there; I can feel the little charms moving against my skin, pricking me.

"*Vanitas*," says Tante Fanny. "The Latin word for— ?"

"Vanity," I guess.

"A word with two meanings. Can you supply them?"

"A, a desire to be pretty, or finely dressed," I begin.

She nods, but corrects me: "Self-conceit. The holding of too high an opinion of one's beauty, charms or talents. But it also means futility," she says, very crisp. "Worthlessness. What is done *in vain*. Vanitas paintings illustrate the vanity of all human wishes. Are you familiar with Ecclesiastes, chapter one, verse two?"

I hesitate. I scratch my arm through my sleeve, to feel the little gold charms.

My aunt purses her wide mouth. Though she is past fifty now, with the sallow look of someone who never sees the sun, and always wears black, you can tell that she was once a beauty. "*Vanity of vanities, saith the Preacher, vanity of vanities*," she quotes; "*all is vanity.*"

That's Cousine Eliza on the wall behind her mother's chair, in dark oils. In the picture she looks much older than sixteen to me. She is sitting in a chair with something in her left hand, I think perhaps a handkerchief; has she been crying? Her white dress has enormous sleeves, like clouds; above them, her shoulders slope prettily. Her face is creamy and perfectly oval, her eyes are dark, her hair is coiled on top of her head like a strange plum cake. Her lips are together, it's a perfect mouth, but it looks so sad. Why does she look so sad?

"In this print here," says Tante Fanny, tapping the portfolio in her lap with one long nail (I don't believe she ever cuts them), "what does the hourglass represent?"

I bend to look at it again. A grim man in seventeenth-century robes, his desk piled with objects. "Time?" I hazard.

"And the skull?"

"Death."

"Très bien, Aimée."

I was only eight when my uncle and aunt came back from France, with – among their copious baggage – Cousine Eliza in a lead coffin. She'd died of a fever. Papa came back from Paris right away, with the bad news, but the girl's parents stayed on till the end of the year, which I thought strange. I was not allowed to go to the funeral, though the cemetery of St. James is only ten miles upriver. After the funeral was the last time I saw my Oncle Louis. He's never come back to the Plantation since, and for seven years Tante Fanny hasn't left her room. She's shut up like a saint; she spends hours kneeling at her little prie-dieu, clutching her beads, thumping her chest. Millie brings all her meals on trays, covered to keep off the rain or the flies. Tante Fanny also sews and writes to her old friends and relations in France and Germany. And, of course, she teaches me. Art and music, French literature and handwriting, religion and etiquette (or, as she calls it, les convenances and comme il faut). She can't supervise my piano practice, as the instrument is in the salon at the other end of the house, but she leaves her door open, when I'm playing, and strains her ears to catch my mistakes.

This morning instead of practicing I was up in the attic again, and I saw a ghost, or at least I thought I did. I'd taken all the dresses out of the old sheepskin trunk, to admire and hold against myself; I'd remembered to bring my hand mirror up from my bedroom, and if I held it at arm's length, I could see myself from the waist up, at least. I danced like a gypsy, like the girl in *Notre-Dame de Paris*, whose beauty wins the heart of the hideous hunchback.

When I pulled out the last dress – a vast white one that crinkled like paper – what was revealed was a face. I think I cried out; I know I jumped away from the trunk. When I made myself go nearer, the face turned out to be made of something hard and white, like chalk. It was not a bust, like the one downstairs of poor Marie Antoinette. This had no neck, no head; it was only the smooth, pitiless mask of a girl, lying among a jumble of silks.

I didn't recognize her at first; I can be slow. My heart was beating loudly in a sort of horror. Only when I'd sat for some time, staring at those pristine, lidded eyes, did I realize that the face was the same as the one in the portrait of Cousine Eliza, and the white dress I was holding was the dress she wore in the painting. These were all her clothes that I was playing with, it came to me, and the little gold bracelet around my arm had to be hers too. I tried to take it off and return it to the trunk, but my fingers were so slippery I couldn't undo the catch. I wrenched at it, and there was a red line around my arm; the little charms spun.

Tante Fanny's room is stuffy; I can smell the breakfast tray that waits for Millie to take it away. "Tante Fanny," I say now, without preparation, "why does Cousine Eliza look so sad?"

My aunt's eyes widen violently. Her head snaps.

I hear my own words too late. What an idiot, to make it sound as if her daughter's ghost was in the room with us! "In the picture," I stammer, "I mean in the picture, she looks sad."

Tante Fanny doesn't look round at the portrait. "She was dead," she says, rather hoarse.

This can't be right. I look past her. "But her eyes are open."

My aunt lets out a sharp sigh and snaps her book shut. "Do you know the meaning of the word 'posthumous'?"

"Eh ..."

"After death. The portrait was commissioned and painted in Paris in the months following my daughter's demise."

I stare at it again. But how? Did the painter prop her up somehow? She doesn't look dead, only sorrowful, in her enormous, ice-white silk gown.

"Eliza did not model for it," my aunt goes on, as if explaining something to a cretin. "For the face, the artist worked from a death mask." She must see the confusion in my eyes. "A sculptor pastes wet plaster over the features of a corpse. When it hardens he uses it as a mold, to make a perfect simulacrum of the face."

That's it. That's what scared me, up in the attic this morning: Eliza's death mask. When I look back at my aunt, there's been a metamorphosis. Tears are chasing down her papery cheeks. "Tante Fanny—"

"Enough," she says, her voice like mud. "Leave me."

I don't believe my cousin – my only cousin, the beautiful Eliza, just sixteen years old – died of a fever. Louisiana is a hellhole for fevers of all kinds, that's why my parents sent Emile away to Bordeaux. It's good for making money, but not for living, that's why Napoleon sold it so cheap to the Americans thirty-six years ago. So how could it have happened that Eliza grew up here on the Duparc-Locoul Plantation, safe and well, and on her trip to Paris – that pearly city, that apex of civilization – she succumbed to a fever? I won't believe it, it smells like a lie.

I'm up in the attic again, but this time I've brought the Bible. My brother, Emile, before he went away to France, taught me how to tell fortunes with the Book and Key. In those days we used an ugly old key we'd found in the cellars, but now I have a better one; the little gold one that hangs on my bracelet. (Eliza's bracelet, I should say.) What you do is, you open the Bible to the Song of Solomon, pick any verse you like, and read it aloud. If the key goes clockwise, it's saying yes to the verse, and vice versa. Fortune-telling is a sin when gypsies or conjurers do it, like the nègres making their nasty gris-gris to put curses on each other, but it can't be wrong if you use the Good Book. The Song of Solomon is the most puzzling bit of the Bible but it's my favorite. Sometimes it seems to be a man speaking, and sometimes a woman; she says *I am black but comely*, but she can't be a nègre, surely. They adore each other, but at some points it sounds as if they are brother and sister.

My first question for the Book today is, did Cousine Eliza die a natural death? I pull the bracelet down to my wrist, and I hold all the other little charms still, letting only the key dangle. I shake my hand as I recite the verse I've chosen, one that reminds me of Eliza: *Thy cheeks are comely with rows of jewels, thy neck with chains of gold*. When my hand stops moving, the key swings, most definitely anticlockwise. I feel a thrill all the way down in my belly. So! Not a natural death; as I suspected.

What shall I ask next? I cross my legs, to get more comfortable on the bare boards, and study the Book. A verse gives me an idea. Was she – is it possible – she was murdered? Not a night goes by in a great city without a cry in the dark, I know that much. *The watchmen that went about the city found me*, I whisper, *they smote me, they wounded me*. I shake my wrist, and the key dances, but every which way; I can't tell what the answer is. I search for another verse. Here's one: *Every man hath his sword upon his thigh because of fear in the night*. What if ... I rack my imagination. What if two young Parisian gallants fought a duel over her, after glimpsing her at the opera, and Eliza died of the shock? I chant the verse, my voice rising now, because no one will hear me up here. I wave my hand in the air, and when I stop moving, the key continues to swing, counterclockwise. No duel, then; that's clear.

But what if she had a lover, a favorite among all the gentlemen of France who were vying for the hand of the exquisite Creole maiden? What if he was mad with jealousy and strangled her, locking his hands around her long pale neck rather than let Tante Fanny and Oncle Louis take her back to Louisiana? *For love is strong as death; jealousy is cruel as the grave*, I croon, and my heart is thumping, I can feel the wet break out under my arms, in the secret curls there. I've forgotten to wave my hand. When I do it, the key swings straight back and forward, like the clapper of a bell. Like the thunderous bells in the high cathedral of Notre-Dame de Paris. Is that an answer? Not jealousy, then, or not exactly; some other strange passion? Somebody killed Eliza, whether they meant to or not, I remind myself; somebody is to blame for the sad eyes in that portrait. For Tante Fanny walled up in her stifling room, and Oncle Louis who never comes home.

I can't think of any more questions about Eliza; my brain is fuzzy. Did she suffer terribly? I can't find a verse to ask that. How can I investigate a death that happened eight years ago, all the way across the ocean, when I'm only a freckled girl who's never left the Plantation? Who'll listen to my questions, who'll tell me anything?

I finish by asking the Book something for myself. Will I ever be pretty, like Eliza? Will these dull and round features ever bloom into perfect conjunction? Will I grow a face that will take me to France, that will win me the love of a French gentleman? Or will I be stuck here for the rest of my life, my mother's harried assistant and perhaps her successor, running the Plantation and the wine business and the many complex enterprises that make up the wealth of the Famille Duparc-Locoul? That's too many questions. Concentrate, Aimée. Will I be pretty when I grow up? *Behold, thou art fair, my love*, I murmur, as if to make it so; *behold, thou art fair*. But then something stops me from shaking my hand, making the key swing. Because what if the answer is no?

I stoop over the trunk and take out the death mask, as I now know it's called. I hold it very carefully in my arms, and I lie down beside the trunk. I look into the perfect white oval of my cousin's face, and lay it beside mine. *Eliza, Eliza*. I whisper my apologies for disturbing her things, for borrowing her bracelet, with all its little gold and silver trinkets. I tell her I only want to know the truth of how she died so her spirit can be at rest. My cheek is against her cool cheek, my nose aligns itself with hers. The plaster smells of nothing. I set my dry lips to her smooth ones.

"Millie," I ask, when she's buttoning up my dress this morning, "you remember my Cousine Eliza?"

The girl makes a little humming sound that could mean yes, no, or maybe. That's one of her irritating habits. "You must," I say. "My beautiful cousin who went away to Paris. They say she died of a fever."

This time the sound she makes is more like *hmph*.

I catch her eye, its milky roll. Excitement rises in my throat. "Millie," I say, too loud, "have you ever heard anything about that?"

"What would I hear, Mam'zelle Aimée?"

"Oh, go on! I know you house nègres are always gossiping. Did you ever hear tell of anything strange about my cousin's death?"

Millie's glance slides to the door. I step over there and shut it. "Go on. You can speak freely."

She shakes her head, very slowly.

"I know you know something," I say, and it comes out too fierce. Governing the nègres is an art, and I don't have it; I'm too familiar, and then too cross. Today, watching Millie's purple mouth purse, I resort to a bribe. "I tell you what, I might give you a present. What about one of these little charms?" Through my sleeve, I tug the gold bracelet down to my wrist. I make the little jewels shake and spin in front of Millie's eyes. "What about the tiger, would you like that one?" I point him out, because how would she know what a tiger looks like? "Or maybe these dance slippers. Or the golden cross, which Jesus died on?" I don't mention the key, because that's my own favorite.

Millie looks hungry with delight. She's come closer; her fingers are inches away from the dancing trinkets.

I tuck the bracelet back under my wrist ruffle. "Tell me!"

She crosses her arms and leans in close to my ear. She smells a little ripe, but not too bad. "Your cousine?"

"Yes."

"Your oncle and tante killed her."

I shove the girl away, the flat of my hand against her collarbone. "How dare you!"

She gives a luxurious shrug. "All I say is what I hear."

"Hear from whom?" I demand. "Your Pa Philippe, or your Ma?" Millie's mother works the hoe-gang, she's strong as a man. "What would they know of my family's affairs?"

Millie is grinning as she shakes her head. "From your tante."

"Tante Marcelite? She'd never say such a thing."

"No, no. From your Tante Fanny."

I'm so staggered I have to sit down. "Millie, you know it's the blackest of sins to lie," I remind her. "I think you must have made up this story. You're saying that my Tante Fanny told you – you – that she and Oncle Louis murdered Eliza?"

Millie's looking sullen now. "I don't make up nothing. I go in and out of that dusty old room five times a day with trays, and sometimes your tante is praying or talking to herself, and I hear her."

"But this is ridiculous." My voice is shaking. "Why would – what reason could they possibly have had for killing their own daughter?" I run through the plots I invented up in the attic. Did Eliza have a French lover? Did she *give herself* to him and fall into ruin? Could my uncle and aunt have murdered her, to save the Famille from shame? "I won't hear any more of such stuff."

The nègre has the gall to put her hand out, cupped for her reward.

"You may go now," I tell her, stepping into my shoes.

Next morning, I wake up in a foul temper. My head starts hammering as soon as I lift it off the pillow. Maman is expected back from New Orleans today. I reach for my bracelet on the little table beside my bed and it's gone.

"Millie?" But she's not there, on the pallet at the foot of my bed; she's up already. She's taken my bracelet. I never mentioned giving her more than one little trinket; she couldn't have misunderstood me. Damn her for a thieving little nègre.

I could track her down in the kitchen behind the house, or in the sewing room with Tante Marcelite, working on the slave clothes, or wherever she may be, but no. For once, I'll see to it that the girl gets punished for her outrageous impudence.

I bide my time; I do my lessons with Tante Fanny all morning. My skin feels greasy, I've a bouton coming out on my chin; I'm a martyr to pimples. This little drum keeps banging away in the back of my head. And a queasiness, too; a faraway aching. What could I have eaten to put me in such a state?

When the boat arrives I don't rush down to the pier; my mother hates such displays. I sit in the shady gallery and wait. When Maman comes to find me, I kiss her on both cheeks. "Perfectly well," I reply. (She doesn't like to hear of symptoms, unless one is seriously ill.) "But that dreadful brat Millie has stolen a bracelet from my room." As I say it, I feel a pang, but only a little one. Such a story for her to make up, calling my aunt and uncle murderers of their own flesh! The least the girl deserves is a whipping.

"Which bracelet?"

Of course, my mother knows every bit of jewelry I own; it's her memory for detail that's allowed her to improve the family fortunes so much. "A, a gold chain, with trinkets on it," I say, with only a small hesitation. If Eliza got it in Paris, as she must have done, my mother won't ever have seen it on her. "I found it."

"Found it?" she repeats, her eyebrows soaring.

I'm sweating. "It was stoppered up in a bottle," I improvise; "it washed up on the levee."

"How peculiar."

"But it's mine," I repeat. "And Millie took it off my table while I was sleeping!"

Maman nods judiciously and turns away. "Do tidy yourself up before dinner, Aimée, won't you?"

We often have a guest to dinner; Creoles never refuse our hospitality to anyone who needs a meal or a bed for the night, unless he's a beggar. Today it's a slave trader who comes up and down the River Road several times a year; he has a long beard that gets things caught in it. Millie and two other house nègres carry in the dishes, lukewarm as always, since the kitchen is so far behind the house. Millie's face shows nothing; she can't have been punished yet. I avoid her eyes. I pick at the edges of my food; I've no appetite today, though I usually like poule d'eau – a duck that eats nothing but fish, so the Church allows it on Fridays. I listen to the trader and Maman discuss the cost of living, and sip my glass of claret. (Papa brings in ten thousand bottles a year from his estates at Chateau Bon-Air; our Famille is the greatest wine distributor in Louisiana.) The trader offers us our pick of the three males he has with him, fresh from the auction block at New Orleans, but Maman says with considerable pride that we breed all we need, and more.

After dinner I'm practicing piano in the salon – stumbling repeatedly over a tricky phrase of Beethoven's – when my mother comes in. "If you can't manage this piece, Aimée, perhaps you could try one of your Schubert's?" Very dry.

"Certainly, Maman."

"Here's your bracelet. A charming thing, if eccentric. Don't make a habit of fishing things out of the river, will you?"

"No, Maman." Gleeful, I fiddle with the catch, fitting it around my wrist.

"The girl claimed you'd given it to her as a present."

Guilt, like a lump of gristle in my throat.

"They always claim that, strangely enough," remarks my mother, walking away. "One would think they might come up with something more plausible."

The next day I'm in Tante Fanny's room, at my lessons. There was no sign of Millie this morning, and I had to dress myself; the girl must be sulking. I'm supposed to be improving my spelling of verbs in the subjunctive mode, but my stomach is a rat's nest, my dress is too tight, my head's fit to split. I gaze out the window to the yard, where the trader's saddling his mules. He has four nègres with him, their hands lashed to their saddles.

"Do sit down, child."

"Just a minute, Tante—"

"Aimée, come back here!"

But I'm thudding along the gallery, down the stairs. I trip over my hem, and catch the railing. I'm in the yard, and the sun is piercing my eyes. "Maman!"

She turns, frowning. "Where is your sunhat, Aimée?"

I ignore that. "But Millie – what's happening?"

"I suggest you use your powers of deduction."

I throw a desperate look at the girl, bundled up on the last mule, her mute face striped with tears. "Have you sold her? She didn't do anything so very bad. I have the bracelet back safe. Maybe she only meant to borrow it."

My mother sighs. "I won't stand for thieving, or back-answers, and Millie has been guilty of both."

"But Pa Philippe, and her mother – you can't part her from them—"

Maman draws me aside, her arm like a cage around my back. "Aimée, I won't stoop to dispute my methods with an impudent and sentimental girl, especially in front of strangers. Go back to your lesson."

I open my mouth, to tell her that Millie didn't steal the bracelet, exactly; that she thought I had promised it to her. But that would call for too much explanation, and what if Maman found out that I've been interrogating the nègres about private family business? I shut my mouth again. I don't look at Millie; I can't bear it. The trader whistles to his mules to start walking. I go back into the house. My head's bursting from the sun; I have to keep my eyes squeezed shut.

"What is it, child?" asks Tante Fanny when I open the door. Her anger has turned to concern; it must be my face.

"I feel … weak."

"Sit down on this sofa, then. Shall I ring for a glass of wine?"

Next thing I know, I'm flat on my back, choking. I feel so sick. I push Tante Fanny's hand away. She stoppers her smelling salts. "My dear."

"What—"

"You fainted."

I feel oddly disappointed. I always thought it would be a luxuriant feeling – a surrendering of the spirit – but it turns out that fainting is just a sick sensation, and then you wake up.

"It's very natural," she says, with the ghost of a smile. "I believe you have become a woman today."

I stare down at myself, but my shape hasn't changed.

"Your petticoat's a little stained," she whispers, showing me the spots – some brown, some fresh scarlet – and suddenly I understand. "You should go to your room and ask Millie to show you what to do."

At the mention of Millie, I put my hands over my face.

"Where did you get that?" asks Tante Fanny, in a changed voice. She reaches out to touch the bracelet that's slipped out from beneath my sleeve. I flinch. "Aimée, where did you get that?"

"It was in a trunk, in the attic," I confess. "I know it was Eliza's. Can I ask you, how did she die?" My words astonish me as they spill out.

My aunt's face contorts. I think perhaps she's going to strike me. After a long minute, she says, "We killed her. Your uncle and I."

My God. So Millie told the truth, and in return I've had her sold, banished from the sight of every face she knows in the world.

"Your cousin died for our pride, for our greed." Tante Fanny puts her fingers around her throat. "She was perfect, but we couldn't see it, because of the mote in our eyes."

What is she talking about?

"You see, Aimée, when my darling daughter was about your age she developed some boutons."

Pimples? What can pimples have to do with anything?

My aunt's face is a mask of creases. "They weren't so very bad, but they were the only defect in such a lovely face, they stood out terribly. I was going to take her to the local root doctor for an ointment, but your papa happened to know a famous skin specialist in Paris. I think he was glad of the excuse for a trip to his native country. And we knew that nothing in Louisiana could compare to France. So your papa accompanied us – Eliza and myself and your Oncle Louis – on the long voyage, and he introduced us to this doctor. For eight days" – Tante Fanny's tone has taken on a biblical timbre – "the doctor gave the girl injections, and she bore it bravely. We waited for her face to become perfectly clear again – but instead she took a fever. We knew the doctor must have made some terrible mistake with his medicines. When Eliza died—" Here the voice cracks, and Tante Fanny lets out a sort of barking sob. "Your oncle wanted to kill the doctor; he drew his sword to run him through. But your papa, the peacemaker, persuaded us that it must have been the cholera or some other contagion. We tried to believe that; we each assured each other that we believed it. But when I looked at my lovely daughter in her coffin, at sixteen years old, I knew the truth as if God had spoken in my heart."

She's weeping so much now, her words are muffled. I wish I had a handkerchief for her.

"I knew that Eliza had died for a handful of pimples. Because in our vanity, our dreadful pride, we couldn't accept the least defect in our daughter. We were ungrateful, and she was taken from us, and all the years since, and all the years ahead allotted to me, will be expiation."

The bracelet seems to burn me. I've managed to undo the catch. I pull it off, the little gold charms tinkling.

Tante Fanny wipes her eyes with the back of her hand. "Throw that away. My curse on it, and on all glittering vanities," she says hoarsely. "Get rid of it, Aimée, and thank God you'll never be beautiful."

Her words are like a blow to the ribs. But a moment later, I'm glad she said it. It's better to know these things. Who'd want to spend a whole life hankering?

I go out of the room without a word. I can feel the blood welling, sticky on my thighs. But first I must do this. I fetch an old bottle from the kitchen, and a candle stub. I seal up the bracelet in its green translucent tomb, and go to the top of the levee, and throw it as far as I can into the Mississippi.

GRAVEL

Alice Munro

> Alice Munro (b. 1931) is a Canadian short story writer
> and winner of the 2009 Man Booker International Prize,
> which honours her complete body of work. She has been
> awarded Canada's Governor General's Award for fiction
> three times, the Giller Prize twice and is a perennial
> contender for the Nobel Prize for Fiction. She was awarded
> the National Book Critics Circle Award in 1998 for her
> collection, *The Love of a Good Woman*.

At that time we were living beside a gravel pit. Not a large one,
hollowed out by monster machinery, just a minor pit that a farmer
must have made some money from years before. In fact, the pit was
shallow enough to lead you to think that there might have been
some other intention for it – foundations for a house, maybe, that
never made it any further.

My mother was the one who insisted on calling attention to it.
"We live by the old gravel pit out the service-station road," she'd
tell people, and laugh, because she was so happy to have shed
everything connected with the house, the street – the husband –
with the life she'd had before.

I barely remember that life. That is, I remember some parts of
it clearly, but without the links you need to form a proper picture.
All that I retain in my head of the house in town is the wallpaper
with teddy bears in my old room. In this new house, which was
really a trailer, my sister, Caro, and I had narrow cots, stacked
one above the other. When we first moved there, Caro talked to
me a lot about our old house, trying to get me to remember this
or that. It was when we were in bed that she talked like this, and
generally the conversation ended with me failing to remember and
her getting cross. Sometimes I thought I did remember, but out of
contrariness or fear of getting things wrong I pretended not to.

It was summer when we moved to the trailer. We had our

dog with us. Blitzee. "Blitzee loves it here," my mother said, and it was true. What dog wouldn't love to exchange a town street, even one with spacious lawns and big houses, for the wide-open countryside? She took to barking at every car that went past, as if she owned the road, and now and then she brought home a squirrel or a groundhog she'd killed. At first Caro was quite upset by this, and Neal would have a talk with her, explaining about a dog's nature and the chain of life in which some things had to eat other things.

"She gets her dog food," Caro argued, but Neal said, "Suppose she didn't? Suppose someday we all disappeared and she had to fend for herself?"

"I'm not going to," Caro said. "I'm not going to disappear, and I'm always going to look after her."

"You think so?" Neal said, and our mother stepped in to deflect him. Neal was always ready to get on the subject of the Americans and the atomic bomb, and our mother didn't think we were ready for that yet. She didn't know that when he brought it up I thought he was talking about an atomic bun. I knew that there was something wrong with this interpretation, but I wasn't about to ask questions and get laughed at.

Neal was an actor. In town there was a professional summer theater, a new thing at the time, which some people were enthusiastic about and others worried about, fearing that it would bring in riffraff. My mother and father had been among those in favor, my mother more actively so, because she had more time. My father was an insurance agent and travelled a lot. My mother had got busy with various fund-raising schemes for the theater and donated her services as an usher. She was good-looking and young enough to be mistaken for an actress. She'd begun to dress like an actress too, in shawls and long skirts and dangling necklaces. She'd let her hair go wild and stopped wearing makeup. Of course, I had not understood or even particularly noticed these changes at the time. My mother was my mother. But no doubt Caro had noticed. And my father must have. Though, from all that I know of his nature and his feelings for my mother, I think he may have been proud to see how good she looked in these liberating styles and how well she fit in with the theater people. When he spoke about this time, later on, he said that he had always approved of the arts. I can imagine now how embarrassed my mother would have been, cringing and laughing to cover up her cringing, if he'd made this declaration in front of her theater friends.

Well, then came a development that could have been foreseen and probably was, but not by my father. I don't know if it happened to any of the other volunteers. I do know, though I don't remember it, that my father wept and for a whole day followed my mother around the house, not letting her out of his sight and refusing to believe her. And, instead of telling him anything to make him feel better, she told him something that made him feel worse.

She told him that the baby was Neal's.

Was she sure?

Absolutely. She had been keeping track.

What happened then?

My father gave up weeping. He had to get back to work. My mother packed up our things and took us to live with Neal in the trailer he had found, out in the country. She said afterwards that she had wept too. But she said also that she had felt alive. Maybe for the first time in her life, truly alive. She felt as if she had been given a chance; she had started her life all over again. She'd walked out on her silver and her china and her decorating scheme and her flower garden and even on the books in her bookcase. She would live now, not read. She'd left her clothes hanging in the closet and her high-heeled shoes in their shoe trees. Her diamond ring and her wedding ring on the dresser. Her silk nightdresses in their drawer. She meant to go around naked at least some of the time in the country, as long as the weather stayed warm.

That didn't work out, because when she tried it Caro went and hid in her cot and even Neal said he wasn't crazy about the idea.

What did he think of all this? Neal. His philosophy, as he put it later, was to welcome whatever happened. Everything is a gift. We give and we take.

I am suspicious of people who talk like this, but I can't say that I have a right to be.

He was not really an actor. He had got into acting, he said, as an experiment. To see what he could find out about himself. In college, before he dropped out, he had performed as part of the Chorus in *Oedipus Rex*. He had liked that – the giving yourself over, blending with others. Then one day, on the street in Toronto, he ran into a friend who was on his way to try out for a summer job with a new small-town theater company. He went along, having nothing better to do, and ended up getting the job, while the other fellow didn't. He would play Banquo. Sometimes they make Banquo's Ghost visible, sometimes not. This time they wanted a visible version and Neal was the right size. An excellent size. A solid ghost.

He had been thinking of wintering in our town anyway, before my mother sprang her surprise. He had already spotted the trailer. He had enough carpentry experience to pick up work renovating the theater, which would see him through till spring. That was as far ahead as he liked to think.

Caro didn't even have to change schools. She was picked up by the school bus at the end of the short lane that ran alongside the gravel pit. She had to make friends with the country children, and perhaps explain some things to the town children who had been her friends the year before, but if she had any difficulty with that I never heard about it.

Blitzee was always waiting by the road for her to come home.

I didn't go to kindergarten, because my mother didn't have a car. But I didn't mind doing without other children. Caro, when she got home, was enough for me. And my mother was often in a playful mood. As soon as it snowed that winter she and I built a snowman and she asked, "Shall we call it Neal?" I said okay, and we stuck various things on it to make it funny. Then we decided that I would run out of the house when his car came and say, Here's Neal, here's Neal, but be pointing up at the snowman. Which I did, but Neal got out of the car mad and yelled that he could have run me over.

That was one of the few times that I saw him act like a father.

Those short winter days must have seemed strange to me – in town, the lights came on at dusk. But children get used to changes. Sometimes I wondered about our other house. I didn't exactly miss it or want to live there again – I just wondered where it had gone.

My mother's good times with Neal went on into the night. If I woke up and had to go to the bathroom, I'd call for her. She would come happily but not in any hurry, with some piece of cloth or a scarf wrapped around her – also a smell that I associated with candlelight and music. And love.

Something did happen that was not so reassuring, but I didn't try to make much sense of it at the time. Blitzee, our dog, was not very big, but she didn't seem small enough to fit under Caro's coat. I don't know how Caro managed to do it. Not once but twice. She hid the dog under her coat on the school bus, and then, instead of going straight to school, she took Blitzee back to our old house in town, which was less than a block away. That was where my father found the dog, on the winter porch, which was not locked, when he came home for his solitary lunch. There was great surprise that she had got there, found her way home like a dog in a story. Caro made the biggest fuss, and claimed not to have seen the dog at all that morning. But then she made the mistake of trying it again, maybe a week later, and this time, though nobody on the bus or at school suspected her, our mother did.

I can't remember if our father brought Blitzee back to us. I can't imagine him in the trailer or at the door of the trailer or even on the road to it. Maybe Neal went to the house in town and picked her up. Not that that's any easier to imagine.

If I've made it sound as though Caro was unhappy or scheming all the time, that isn't the truth. As I've said, she did try to make me talk about things, at night in bed, but she wasn't constantly airing grievances. It wasn't her nature to be sulky. She was far too keen on making a good impression. She liked people to like her; she liked to stir up the air in a room with the promise of something you could even call merriment. She thought more about that than I did.

She was the one who most took after our mother, I think now.

There must have been some probing about what she'd done with the dog. I think I can remember some of it. "I did it for a trick."

"Do you want to go and live with your father?"

I believe that was asked, and I believe she said no.

I didn't ask her anything. What she had done didn't seem strange to me. That's probably how it is with younger children – nothing that the strangely powerful older child does seems out of the ordinary.

Our mail was deposited in a tin box on a post, down by the road. My mother and I would walk there every day, unless it was particularly stormy, to see what had been left for us. We did this after I got up from my nap. Sometimes it was the only time we went outside all day. In the morning, we watched children's television shows – or she read while I watched. (She had not given up reading for very long.) We heated up some canned soup for lunch, then I went down for my nap while she read some more. She was quite big with the baby now and it stirred around in her stomach, so that I could feel it. Its name was going to be Brandy – already was Brandy – whether it was a boy or a girl.

One day when we were going down the lane for the mail, and were in fact not far from the box, my mother stopped and stood quite still.

"Quiet," she said to me, though I hadn't said a word and wasn't even playing the shuffling game with my boots in the snow.

"I was being quiet," I said.

"Shush. Turn around."

"But we didn't get the mail."

"Never mind. Just walk."

Then I noticed that Blitzee, who was always with us, just behind or ahead of us, wasn't there anymore. Another dog was, on the opposite side of the road, a few feet from the mailbox.

My mother phoned the theater as soon as we got home and let in Blitzee, who was waiting for us. Nobody answered. She phoned the school and asked someone to tell the bus driver to drive Caro up to the door. It turned out that the driver couldn't do that, because it had snowed since Neal last plowed the lane, but he – the driver – did watch until she got to the house. There was no wolf to be seen by that time.

Neal was of the opinion that there never had been one. And if there had been, he said, it would have been no danger to us, weak as it was probably from hibernation.

Caro said that wolves did not hibernate. "We learned about them in school."

Our mother wanted Neal to get a gun.

"You think I'm going to get a gun and go and shoot a goddam poor mother wolf who has probably got a bunch of babies back in the bush and is just trying to protect them, the way you're trying to protect yours?" he said quietly.

Caro said, "Only two. They only have two at a time."

"Okay, okay. I'm talking to your mother."

"You don't know that," my mother said. "You don't know if it's got hungry cubs or anything."

I had never thought she'd talk to him like that.

He said, "Easy. Easy. Let's just think a bit. Guns are a terrible thing. If I went and got a gun, then what would I be saying? That Vietnam was okay? That I might as well have gone to Vietnam?"

"You're not an American."

"You're not going to rile me."

This is more or less what they said, and it ended up with Neal not having to get a gun. We never saw the wolf again, if it was a wolf. I think my mother stopped going to get the mail, but she may have become too big to be comfortable doing that anyway.

The snow dwindled magically. The trees were still bare of leaves and my mother made Caro wear her coat in the mornings, but she came home after school dragging it behind her.

My mother said that the baby had got to be twins, but the doctor said it wasn't.

"Great. Great," Neal said, all in favor of the twins idea. "What do doctors know."

The gravel pit had filled to its brim with melted snow and rain, so that Caro had to edge around it on her way to catch the school bus. It was a little lake, still and dazzling under the clear sky. Caro asked with not much hope if we could play in it.

Our mother said not to be crazy. "It must be twenty feet deep," she said.

Neal said, "Maybe ten."

Caro said, "Right around the edge it wouldn't be."

Our mother said yes it was. "It just drops off," she said. "It's not like going in at the beach, for fuck's sake. Just stay away from it."

She had started saying "fuck" quite a lot, perhaps more than Neal did, and in a more exasperated tone of voice.

"Should we keep the dog away from it, too?" she asked him.

Neal said that that wasn't a problem. "Dogs can swim."

*

A Saturday. Caro watched *The Friendly Giant* with me and made comments that spoiled it. Neal was lying on the couch, which unfolded into his and my mother's bed. He was smoking his kind of cigarettes, which could not be smoked at work so had to be made the most of on weekends. Caro sometimes bothered him, asking to try one. Once he had let her, but told her not to tell our mother.

I was there, though, so I told.

There was alarm, though not quite a row.

"You know he'd have those kids out of here like a shot," our mother said. "Never again."

"Never again," Neal said agreeably. "So what if he feeds them poison Rice Krispies crap?"

In the beginning, we hadn't seen our father at all. Then, after Christmas, a plan had been worked out for Saturdays. Our mother always asked afterwards if we had had a good time. I always said yes, and meant it, because I thought that if you went to a movie or to look at Lake Huron, or ate in a restaurant, that meant that you had had a good time. Caro said yes, too, but in a tone of voice that suggested that it was none of our mother's business. Then my father went on a winter holiday to Cuba (my mother remarked on this with some surprise and maybe approval) and came back with a lingering sort of flu that caused the visits to lapse. They were supposed to resume in the spring, but so far they hadn't.

After the television was turned off, Caro and I were sent outside to run around, as our mother said, and get some fresh air. We took the dog with us.

When we got outside, the first thing we did was loosen and let trail the scarves our mother had wrapped around our necks. (The fact was, though we may not have put the two things together, the deeper she got into her pregnancy the more she slipped back into behaving like an ordinary mother, at least when it was a matter of scarves we didn't need or regular meals. There was not so much championing of wild ways as there had been in the fall.) Caro asked me what I wanted to do, and I said I didn't know. This was a formality on her part but the honest truth on mine. We let the dog lead us, anyway, and Blitzee's idea was to go and look at the gravel pit. The wind was whipping the water up into little waves, and very soon we got cold, so we wound our scarves back around our necks.

I don't know how much time we spent just wandering around the water's edge, knowing that we couldn't be seen from the trailer. After a while, I realized that I was being given instructions.

I was to go back to the trailer and tell Neal and our mother something.

That the dog had fallen into the water.

The dog had fallen into the water and Caro was afraid she'd be drowned.

Blitzee. Drownded.

Drowned.

But Blitzee wasn't in the water.

She could be. And Caro could jump in to save her.

I believe I still put up some argument, along the lines of she hasn't, you haven't, it could happen but it hasn't. I also remembered that Neal had said dogs didn't drown.

Caro instructed me to do as I was told.

Why?

I may have said that, or I may have just stood there not obeying and trying to work up another argument.

In my mind I can see her picking up Blitzee and tossing her, though Blitzee was trying to hang on to her coat. Then backing up, Caro backing up to take a run at the water. Running, jumping, all of a sudden hurling herself at the water. But I can't recall the sound of the splashes as they, one after the other, hit the water. Not a little splash or a big one. Perhaps I had turned towards the trailer by then – I must have done so.

When I dream of this, I am always running. And in my dreams I am running not towards the trailer but back towards the gravel pit. I can see Blitzee floundering around and Caro swimming towards her, swimming strongly, on the way to rescue her. I see her light-brown checked coat and her plaid scarf and her proud successful face and reddish hair darkened at the end of its curls by the water. All I have to do is watch and be happy – nothing required of me, after all.

What I really did was make my way up the little incline towards the trailer. And when I got there I sat down. Just as if there had been a porch or a bench, though in fact the trailer had neither of these things. I sat down and waited for the next thing to happen.

I know this because it's a fact. I don't know, however, what my plan was or what I was thinking. I was waiting, maybe, for the next act in Caro's drama. Or in the dog's.

I don't know if I sat there for five minutes. More? Less? It wasn't too cold.

I went to see a professional person about this once and she convinced me – for a time, she convinced me – that I must have tried the door of the trailer and found it locked. Locked because my mother and Neal were having sex and had locked it against interruptions. If I'd banged on the door they would have been angry. The counsellor was satisfied to bring me to this conclusion, and I was satisfied, too. For a while. But I no longer think that was true. I don't think they would have locked the door, because I know that once they didn't and Caro walked in and they laughed at the look on her face.

Maybe I remembered that Neal had said that dogs did not drown, which meant that Caro's rescue of Blitzee would not be necessary. Therefore she herself wouldn't be able to carry out her game. So many games, with Caro.

Did I think she could swim? At nine, many children can. And in fact it turned out that she'd had one lesson the summer before, but then we had moved to the trailer and she hadn't taken any more. She may have thought she could manage well enough. And I may indeed have thought that she could do anything she wanted to.

The counsellor did not suggest that I might have been sick of carrying out Caro's orders, but the thought did occur to me. It doesn't quite seem right, though. If I'd been older, maybe. At the time, I still expected her to fill my world.

How long did I sit there? Likely not long. And it's possible that I did knock. After a while. After a minute or two. In any case, my mother did, at some point, open the door, for no reason. A presentiment.

Next thing, I am inside. My mother is yelling at Neal and trying to make him understand something. He is getting to his feet and standing there speaking to her, touching her, with such mildness and gentleness and consolation. But that is not what my mother wants at all and she tears herself away from him and runs out the door. He shakes his head and looks down at his bare feet. His big helpless-looking toes.

I think he says something to me with a singsong sadness in his voice. Strange.

Beyond that I have no details.

My mother didn't throw herself into the water. She didn't go into labor from the shock. My brother, Brent, was not born until a week or ten days after the funeral, and he was a full-term infant. Where she was while she waited for the birth to happen I do not know. Perhaps she was kept in the hospital and sedated as much as possible under the circumstances.

I remember the day of the funeral quite well. A very pleasant and comfortable woman I didn't know – her name was Josie – took me on an expedition. We visited some swings and a sort of dollhouse that was large enough for me to go inside, and we ate a lunch of my favorite treats, but not enough to make me sick. Josie was somebody I got to know very well later on. She was a friend my father had made in Cuba, and after the divorce she became my stepmother, his second wife.

My mother recovered. She had to. There was Brent to look after and, most of the time, me. I believe I stayed with my father and Josie while she got settled in the house that she planned to live in for the rest of her life. I don't remember being there with Brent until he was big enough to sit up in his high chair.

My mother went back to her old duties at the theater. At first she may have worked as she had before, as a volunteer usher, but by the time I was in school she had a real job, with pay, and year-round responsibilities. She was the business manager. The theater survived, through various ups and downs, and is still going now.

Neal didn't believe in funerals, so he didn't attend Caro's. He never saw Brent. He wrote a letter – I found this out much later – saying that since he did not intend to act as a father it would be better for him to bow out at the start. I never mentioned him to Brent, because I thought it would upset my mother. Also because Brent showed so little sign of being like him – like Neal – and seemed, in fact, so much more like my father that I really wondered about what was going on around the time he was conceived. My father has never said anything about this and never would. He treats Brent just as he treats me, but he is the kind of man who would do that anyway.

He and Josie have not had any children of their own, but I don't think that bothers them. Josie is the only person who ever talks about Caro, and even she doesn't do it often. She does say that my father doesn't hold my mother responsible. He has also said that he must have been sort of a stick-in-the-mud when my mother wanted more excitement in her life. He needed a shaking-up, and he got one. There's no use being sorry about it. Without the shaking-up, he would never have found Josie and the two of them would not have been so happy now.

"Which two?" I might say, just to derail him, and he would staunchly say, "Josie. Josie, of course."

My mother cannot be made to recall any of those times, and I don't bother her with them. I know that she has driven down the lane we lived on, and found it quite changed, with the sort of trendy houses you see now, put up on unproductive land. She mentioned this with the slight scorn that such houses evoke in her. I went down the lane myself but did not tell anyone. All the eviscerating that is done in families these days strikes me as a mistake.

Even where the gravel pit was a house now stands, the ground beneath it levelled.

I have a partner, Ruthann, who is younger than I am but, I think, somewhat wiser. Or at least more optimistic about what she calls routing out my demons. I would never have got in touch with Neal if it had not been for her urging. Of course, for a long time I had no way, just as I had no thought, of getting in touch. It was he who finally wrote to me. A brief note of congratulations, he said, after seeing my picture in the *Alumni Gazette*. What he was doing looking through the *Alumni Gazette* I have no idea. I had received one of those academic honors that mean something in a restricted circle and little anywhere else.

He was living hardly fifty miles away from where I teach, which also happens to be where I went to college. I wondered if he had been there at that time. So close. Had he become a scholar?

At first I had no intention of replying to the note, but I told Ruthann and she said that I should think about writing back. So the upshot was that I sent him an e-mail, and arrangements were made. I was to meet him in his town, in the unthreatening surroundings of a university cafeteria. I told myself that if he looked unbearable – I did not quite know what I meant by this – I could just walk on through.

He was shorter than he used to be, as adults we remember from childhood usually are. His hair was thin, and trimmed close to his head. He got me a cup of tea. He was drinking tea himself.

What did he do for a living?

He said that he tutored students in preparation for exams. Also, he helped them write their essays. Sometimes, you might say, he wrote those essays. Of course, he charged.

"It's no way to get to be a millionaire, I can tell you."

He lived in a dump. Or a semi-respectable dump. He liked it. He looked for clothes at the Sally Ann. That was okay too.

"Suits my principles."

I did not congratulate him on any of this, but, to tell the truth, I doubt that he expected me to.

"Anyway, I don't think my lifestyle is so interesting. I think you might want to know how it happened."

I could not figure out how to speak.

"I was stoned," he said. "And, furthermore, I'm not a swimmer. Not many swimming pools around where I grew up. I'd have drowned, too. Is that what you wanted to know?"

I said that he was not really the one that I was wondering about.

Then he became the third person I'd asked, "What do you think Caro had in mind?"

The counsellor had said that we couldn't know. "Likely she herself didn't know what she wanted. Attention? I don't think she meant to drown herself. Attention to how bad she was feeling?"

Ruthann had said, "To make your mother do what she wanted? Make her smarten up and see that she had to go back to your father?"

Neal said, "It doesn't matter. Maybe she thought she could paddle better than she could. Maybe she didn't know how heavy winter clothes can get. Or that there wasn't anybody in a position to help her."

He said to me, "Don't waste your time. You're not thinking what if you had hurried up and told, are you? Not trying to get in on the guilt?"

I said that I had considered what he was saying, but no.

"The thing is to be happy," he said. "No matter what. Just try that. You can. It gets to be easier and easier. It's nothing to do with circumstances. You wouldn't believe how good it is. Accept everything and then tragedy disappears. Or tragedy lightens, anyway, and you're just there, going along easy in the world."

Now, good-bye.

I see what he meant. It really is the right thing to do. But, in my mind, Caro keeps running at the water and throwing herself in, as if in triumph, and I'm still caught, waiting for her to explain to me, waiting for the splash.

THE EYE

Alice Munro

Alice Munro (b. 1931) is a Canadian short story writer and winner of the 2009 Man Booker International Prize, which honours her complete body of work. She has been awarded Canada's Governor General's Award for fiction three times, the Giller Prize twice and is a perennial contender for the Nobel Prize for Fiction. She was awarded the National Book Critics Circle Award in 1998 for her collection, *The Love of a Good Woman*.

When I was five years old my parents all of a sudden produced a baby boy, which my mother said was what I had always wanted. Where she got this idea I did not know. She did quite a bit of elaborating on it, all fictitious but hard to counter.

Then a year later a baby girl appeared, and there was another fuss but more subdued than with the first one.

Up until the time of the first baby I had not been aware of ever feeling different from the way my mother said I felt. And up until that time the whole house was full of my mother, of her footsteps her voice her powdery yet ominous smell that inhabited all the rooms; even when she wasn't in them.

Why do I say ominous? I didn't feel frightened. It wasn't that my mother actually told me what I was to feel about things. She was an authority on that without having to question a thing. Not just in the case of a baby brother but in the matter of Red River cereal which was good for me and so I must be fond of it. And in my interpretation of the picture that hung at the foot of my bed, showing Jesus suffering the little children to come unto him. Suffering meant something different in those days, but that was not what we concentrated on. My mother pointed out the little girl half hiding round a corner because she wanted to come to Jesus but was too shy. That was me, my mother said, and I supposed it was though I wouldn't have figured it out without her telling me and I rather wished it wasn't so.

The thing I really felt miserable about was Alice in Wonderland huge and trapped in the rabbit hole, but I laughed because my mother seemed delighted.

It was with my brother's coming, though, and the endless carryings-on about how he was some sort of present for me, that I began to accept how largely my mother's notions about me might differ from my own.

I suppose all this was making me ready for Sadie when she came to work for us. My mother had shrunk to whatever territory she had with the babies. With her not around so much, I could think about what was true and what wasn't. I knew enough not to speak about this to anybody.

The most unusual thing about Sadie – though it was not a thing stressed in our house – was that she was a celebrity. Our town had a radio station where she played her guitar and sang the opening welcome song which was her own composition.

"Hello, hello, hello, everybody—"

And half an hour later it was, "Good-bye, good-bye, good-bye, everybody." In between she sang songs that were requested, as well as some she picked out herself. The more sophisticated people in town tended to joke about her songs and about the whole station which was said to be the smallest one in Canada. Those people listened to a Toronto station that broadcast popular songs of the day – three little fishes and a momma fishy too – and Jim Hunter hollering out the desperate war news. But people on the farms liked the local station and the kind of songs Sadie sang. Her voice was strong and sad and she sang about loneliness and grief.

> Leanin' on the old top rail,
> In a big corral.
> Lookin' down the twilight trail
> For my long lost pal –

Most of the farms in our part of the country had been cleared and settled around a hundred and fifty years ago, and you could look out from almost any farmhouse and see another farmhouse only a few fields away. Yet the songs the farmers wanted were all about lone cowhands, the lure and disappointment of far-off places, the bitter crimes that led to criminals dying with their mothers' names on their lips, or God's.

This was what Sadie sang with such sorrow in a full-throated alto, but in her job with us she was full of energy and confidence, happy to talk and mostly to talk about herself. There was usually nobody to talk to but me. Her jobs and my mother's kept them divided most of the time and somehow I don't think they would have enjoyed talking together anyway. My mother was a serious person as I have indicated, one who used to teach school before she taught me. She maybe would have liked Sadie to be somebody she could help, teaching her not to say "youse." But Sadie did not give much indication that she wanted the help anybody could offer, or to speak in any way that was different from how she had always spoken.

After dinner, which was the noon meal, Sadie and I were alone in the kitchen. My mother took time off for a nap and if she was lucky the babies napped too. When she got up she put on a different sort of dress as if she expected a leisurely afternoon, even though there would certainly be more diapers to change and also some of that unseemly business that I tried never to catch sight of, when the littlest one guzzled at a breast.

My father took a nap too – maybe fifteen minutes on the porch with the *Saturday Evening Post* over his face, before he went back to the barn.

Sadie heated water on the stove and washed the dishes with me helping and the blinds down to keep out the heat. When we were finished she mopped the floor and I dried it, by a method I had invented – skating around and around it on rags. Then we took down the coils of sticky yellow flypaper that had been put up after breakfast and were already heavy with dead or buzzing nearly dead black flies, and hung up the fresh coils which would be full of newly dead ones by suppertime. All this while Sadie was telling me about her life.

I didn't make easy judgments about ages then. People were either children or grown-ups and I thought her a grown-up. Maybe she was sixteen, maybe eighteen or twenty. Whatever her age, she announced more than once that she was not in any hurry to get married.

She went to dances every weekend but she went by herself. By herself and for herself, she said.

She told me about the dance halls. There was one in town, off the main street, where the curling rink was in the winter. You paid a dime for a dance, then went up and danced on a platform with people gawking all around, not that she cared. She always liked to pay her own dime, not to be beholden. But sometimes a fellow got to her first. He asked if she wanted to dance and the first thing she said was, Can you? Can you dance? she asked him bluntly. Then he would look at her funny and say yes, meaning why else would he be here? And it would turn out usually that what he meant by dance was shuffling around on two feet with his sweaty big meats of hands grabbing at her. Sometimes she just broke off and left him stranded, danced by herself – which was what she liked to do anyway. She finished up the dance that had been paid for, and if the moneymaker objected and tried to make her pay for two when it was only one, she told him that was enough out of him. They could all laugh at her dancing by herself if they liked.

The other dance hall was just out of town on the highway. You paid at the door there and it wasn't for one dance but the whole night. The place was called the Royal-T. She paid her own way there too. There was generally a better class of dancer, but she did try to get an idea of how they managed before she let them take her out on the floor. They were usually town fellows while the ones at the other place were country. Better on their feet – the town ones – but it was not always the feet you had to look out for. It was where they wanted to get hold of you. Sometimes she had to read them the riot act and tell them what she would do to them if they didn't quit it. She let them know she'd come there to dance and paid her own way to do it. Furthermore she knew where to jab them. That would straighten them out. Sometimes they were good dancers and she got to enjoy herself. Then when they played the last dance she bolted for home.

She wasn't like some, she said. She didn't mean to get caught.

Caught. When she said that, I saw a big wire net coming down, some evil little creatures wrapping it around and around you and choking you so you could never get out. Sadie must have seen something like this on my face because she said not to be scared.

"There's nothing in this world to be scared of, just look out for yourself."

"You and Sadie talk together a lot," my mother said.

I knew something was coming that I should watch for but I didn't know what.

"You like her, don't you?"

I said yes.

"Well of course you do. I do too."

I hoped that was going to be all and for a moment I thought it was.

Then, "You and I don't get so much time now we have the babies. They don't give us much time, do they?

"But we do love them, don't we?"

Quickly I said yes.

She said, "Truly?"

She wasn't going to stop till I said truly, so I said it.

My mother wanted something very badly. Was it nice friends? Women who played bridge and had husbands who went to work in suits with vests? Not quite, and no hope of that anyway. Was it me as I used to be, with my sausage curls that I didn't mind standing still for, and my expert Sunday School recitations? No time for her to manage that anymore. And something in me was turning traitorous, though she didn't know why, and I didn't know why either. I hadn't made any town friends at Sunday School. Instead, I worshipped Sadie. I heard my mother say that to my father. "She worships Sadie."

My father said Sadie was a godsend. What did that mean? He sounded cheerful. Maybe it meant he wasn't going to take anybody's side.

"I wish we had proper sidewalks for her," my mother said. "Maybe if we had proper sidewalks she could learn to roller-skate and make friends."

I did wish for roller skates. But now without any idea why, I knew that I was never going to admit it.

Then my mother said something about it being better when

school started. Something about me being better or something concerning Sadie that would be better. I didn't want to hear.

Sadie was teaching me some of her songs and I knew I wasn't very good at singing. I hoped that wasn't what had to get better or else stop. I truly did not want it to stop.

My father didn't have much to say. I was my mother's business, except for later on when I got really mouthy and had to be punished. He was waiting for my brother to get older and be his. A boy would not be so complicated.

And sure enough my brother wasn't. He would grow up to be just fine.

Now school has started. It started some weeks ago, before the leaves turned red and yellow. Now they were mostly gone. I am not wearing my school coat but my good coat, the one with the dark velvet cuffs and collar. My mother is wearing the coat she wears to church, and a turban covers most of her hair.

My mother is driving to whatever place it is that we are going to. She doesn't drive often, and her driving is always more stately and yet uncertain than my father's. She peeps her horn at any curve.

"Now," she says, but it takes a little while for her to get the car into place.

"Here we are then." Her voice seems meant to be encouraging. She touches my hand to give me a chance to hold hers, but I pretend not to notice and she takes her hand away.

The house has no driveway or even a sidewalk. It's decent but quite plain. My mother has raised her gloved hand to knock but it turns out we don't have to. The door is opened for us. My mother has just started to say something encouraging to me – something like, It will go more quickly than you think – but she doesn't get finished. The tone in which she spoke to me had been somewhat stern but slightly comforting. It changes when the door is opened into something more subdued, softened as if she was bowing her head.

The door has been opened to let some people go out, not just to let us go in. One of the women going out calls back over her shoulder in a voice that does not try to be soft at all.

"It's her that she worked for, and that little girl."

Then a woman who is rather dressed up comes and speaks to my mother and helps her off with her coat. That done, my mother takes my coat off and says to the woman that I was especially fond of Sadie. She hopes it was all right to bring me.

"Oh the dear little thing," the woman says and my mother touches me lightly to get me to say hello.

"Sadie loved children," the woman said. "She did indeed."

I notice that there are two other children there. Boys. I know them from school, one being in the first grade with me, and the other one older. They are peering out from what is likely the kitchen. The younger one is stuffing a whole cookie into his mouth in a comical way and the other, older, one is making a disgusted face. Not at the cookie stuffer, but at me. They hate me of course. Boys either ignored you if they met you somewhere that wasn't school (they ignored you there too) or they made these faces and called you horrid names. If I had to go near one I would stiffen and wonder what to do. Of course it was different if there were adults around. These boys stayed quiet but I was slightly miserable until somebody yanked the two of them into the kitchen. Then I became aware of my mother's especially gentle and sympathetic voice, more ladylike even than the yoke of the spokeswoman she was talking to, and I thought maybe the face was meant for her. Sometimes people imitated her voice when she called for me at school.

The woman she was talking to and who seemed to be in charge was leading us to a part of the room where a man and a woman sat on a sofa, looking as if they did not quite understand why they were here. My mother bent over and spoke to them very respectfully and pointed me out to them.

"She did so love Sadie," she said. I knew that I was supposed to say something then but before I could the woman sitting there let out a howl. She did not look at any of us and the sound she made seemed like a sound you might make if some animal was biting or gnawing at you. She slapped away at her arms as if to get rid of whatever it was, but it did not go away. She looked at my mother as if my mother was the person who should do something about this.

The old man told her to hush.

"She's taking it very hard," said the woman who was guiding us. "She doesn't know what she's doing." She bent down lower and said, "Now, now. You scare the little girl."

"Scare the little girl," the old man said obediently.

By the time he finished saying that, the woman was not making the noise anymore and was patting her scratched arms as if she didn't know what had happened to them.

My mother said, "Poor woman."

"An only child too," said the conducting woman. To me she said, "Don't you worry."

I was worried but not about the yelling.

I knew Sadie was somewhere and I did not want to see her. My mother had not actually said that I would have to see her but she had not said that I wouldn't have to, either.

Sadie had been killed when walking home from the Royal-T dance hall. A car had hit her just on that little bit of gravel road between the parking space belonging to the dance hall and the beginning of the proper town sidewalk. She would have been hurrying along just the way she always did, and was no doubt thinking cars could see her, or that she had as much right as they did, and perhaps the car behind her swerved or perhaps she was not quite where she thought she was. She was hit from behind. The car that hit her was getting out of the way of the car that was behind it, and that second car was looking to make the first turn onto a town street. There had been some drinking at the dance hall, though you could not buy liquor there. And there was always some honking and yelling and whipping around too fast when the dancing was over. Sadie scurrying along without even a flashlight would behave as if it was everybody's business to get out of her way.

"A girl without a boyfriend going to dances on foot," said the woman who was still being friends with my mother. She spoke quite softly and my mother murmured something regretful.

It was asking for trouble, the friendly woman said still more softly.

I had heard talk at home that I did not understand. My mother wanted something done that might have had to do with Sadie and the car that hit her, but my father said to leave it alone. We've got no business in town, he said. I did not even try to figure this out because I was trying not to think about Sadie at all, let alone about her being dead. When I had realized that we were going into Sadie's house I longed not to go, but didn't see any way to get out of it except by behaving with enormous indignity.

Now after the old woman's outburst it seemed to me we might turn around and go home. I would never have to admit the truth, which was that I was in fact desperately scared of any dead body.

Just as I thought this might be possible, I heard my mother and the woman she seemed now to be conniving with speak of what was worse than anything.

Seeing Sadie.

Yes, my mother was saying. Of course, we must see Sadie. Dead Sadie.

I had kept my eyes pretty well cast down, seeing mostly just those boys who were hardly taller than I was, and the old people who were sitting down. But now my mother was taking me by the hand in another direction.

There had been a coffin in the room all the time but I had thought it was something else. Because of my lack of experience I didn't know exactly what such a thing looked like. A shelf to put flowers on, this object we were approaching might have been, or a closed piano.

Perhaps the people being around it had somehow disguised its real size and shape and purpose. But now these people were making way respectfully and my mother spoke in a new very quiet voice.

"Come now," she said to me. Her gentleness sounded hateful to me, triumphant.

She bent to look into my face, and this, I was sure, was to prevent me from doing what had just occurred to me – keeping my eyes squeezed shut. Then she took her gaze away from me but kept my hand tightly held in hers. I did manage to lower my lids as soon as she took her eyes off me, but I did not shut them quite lest I stumble or somebody push me right where I didn't want to be. I was able to see just a blur of the stiff flowers and the sheen of polished wood.

Then I heard my mother sniffling and felt her pulling away. There was a click of her purse being opened. She had to get her hand in there, so her hold on me weakened and I was able to get myself free of her. She was weeping. It was attention to her tears and sniffles that had set me loose.

I looked straight into the coffin and saw Sadie.

The accident had spared her neck and face but I didn't see all of that at once. I just got the general impression that there was nothing about her as bad as I had been afraid of. I shut my eyes quickly but found myself unable to keep from looking again. First at the little yellow cushion that was under her neck and that also managed to cover her throat and chin and the one cheek I could easily see. The trick was in seeing a bit of her quickly, then going back to the cushion, and the next time managing a little bit more that you were not afraid of. And then it was Sadie, all of her or at least all I could reasonably see on the side that was available.

Something moved. I saw it, her eyelid on my side moved. It was not opening or halfway opening or anything like that, but lifting just such a tiny bit as would make it possible, if you were her, if you were inside her, to be able to see out through the lashes. Just to distinguish maybe what was light outside and what was dark.

I was not surprised then and not in the least scared. Instantly, this sight fell into everything I knew about Sadie and somehow, as well, into whatever special experience was owing to myself. And I did not dream of calling anybody else's attention to what was there, because it was not meant for them, it was completely for me.

My mother had taken my hand again and said that we were ready to go. There were some more exchanges, but before any time had passed, as it seemed to me, we found ourselves outside.

My mother said, "Good for you." She squeezed my hand and said, "Now then. It's over." She had to stop and speak to somebody else who was on the way to the house, and then we got into the car and began to drive home. I had an idea that she would like me to say something, or maybe even tell her something, but I didn't do it.

There was never any other appearance of that sort and in fact Sadie faded rather quickly from my mind, what with the shock of school, where I learned somehow to manage with an odd mixture of being dead scared and showing off. As a matter of fact some of her importance had faded in that first week in September when she said she had to stay home now to look after her father and mother, so she wouldn't be working for us anymore.

And then my mother had found out she was working in the creamery.

Yet for a long time when I did think of her, I never questioned what I believed had been shown to me. Long, long afterwards, when I was not at all interested in any unnatural display, I still had it in my mind that such a thing had happened. I just believed it easily, the way you might believe and in fact remember that you once had another set of teeth, now vanished but real in spite of that. Until one day, one day when I may even have been in my teens, I knew with a dim sort of hole in my insides that now I didn't believe it anymore.

BEFORE HE LEFT THE FAMILY

Carrie Tiffany

> Carrie Tiffany (b. 1965) is a British-born Australian author. Her first novel, *Everyman's Rules for Scientific Living*, was published in 2005 and made the shortlist of both the Guardian First Book Award and the Orange Prize. Her second novel, *Mateship with Birds*, won the 2013 inaugural Stella Prize and was shortlisted for the Women's Prize for Fiction.

Before he left the family, my father worked as a sales representative for a pharmaceutical company. He travelled from chemist to chemist with samples of pills and lotions and pastes in the back of his Valiant station wagon. The best sales representatives visited modern chemists in the city and suburbs. My father had to drive long distances to country chemists who had stocked the same product lines for years and weren't interested in anything new. As he drank more and more, my father called on fewer and fewer chemists, but the cardboard boxes of samples kept arriving. They no longer fitted in the back of the car, so my father stored them in the corrugated iron shed next to the house. Summer in Perth is very hot. For months and months the bitumen boiled on the roads and we had to use the ends of our t-shirts to open the iron lid of the mailbox, or risk getting burnt. The pharmaceutical samples expanded in the heat of the shed. The lotions and pastes burst their tubes and tubs and seeped through the cardboard boxes. It smelt good in the shed – sweet and clean and surgical. My brother and I went in there often and sat among the sodden boxes as we read our father's *Playboy* magazines.

In the last weeks of their marriage, our parents battled out the terms of their separation at the dinner table in between the ice-cream bowls. My mother, small and freckled, wrote lists of their possessions on a Nordette® Low Dose Oral Contraceptive notepad.

She looked like a teenage girl playing a board game. Nathan and I listened in as we watched television on the other side of the vinyl concertina doors that marked the division between the lounge room and the dining room. We watched *MASH*. Nathan sang along to the theme song, and for the first time I noticed how high and piping his voice was. And there was something creepy about his pink skin and the cowlick at the front of his fine white hair. I wondered if we hadn't created a masculine enough environment for our father. I tipped my brother out of his chair and started boxing his arms and chest. He wailed. The doors were dragged open.

'Kevin, what are you doing?' my mother said, leaning against the buckled vinyl as if she was too young to stand unsupported. I let Nathan squirm out from underneath me.

'He's a sissy,' I said. 'He sings like a girl. Tell him he's not allowed to sing.'

She looked from me to Nathan and back to me again; then she forced her eyes open wide so they boggled with exasperation.

The playmates in the *Playboy* magazines are always smiling. Or, if they aren't smiling they have a gasping, pained expression as if they've just stood on a drawing pin. None of them have someone special in their lives at this time, but with the right man they can be hot to handle. They like the feeling of silk against their bare skin, and they appreciate the outdoors and candle-lit dinners. Miss July says she likes the heat (she's from Queensland), but on the next page she says she would like to make love in the snow. This contradiction seems to have slipped past the *Playboy* editor. I wonder if this is a concern to other readers? The skin of the playmates can be matched to the samples of different timber stains that we have in woodwork class. The brunettes are teak or mahogany, the blondes are stained pine if they have a tan, or unstained pine if they are from Sweden, Finland, Denmark, or the Netherlands. The playmates don't have veins showing through their skin – it is just the one colour – like a pelt. And none of them have freckles or bits of hardened sleep in the corner of their eyes like tiny potatoes.

My father agreed to take only his personal items; his clothes, shoes, records, golf clubs, and alcohol. On the morning that he left I stood in the driveway and waved him off. My mother and brother watched from the kitchen window. My father's work shirts hung in rows down each side of the rear of the station wagon. It looked neat – like it had been designed for that purpose – like a gentleman's wardrobe on wheels. My father waved his forearm out of the window as he drove off. Just as he rounded the bend in the road and the car moved out of sight, he tooted his horn. I stood and watched for a few minutes. When I finally turned to walk away, I noticed my mother and brother were still looking out of the kitchen window; but now they were looking at me.

My father married my mother when she was eighteen, because he had made her pregnant. It was just the one time; the one date. My mother had a job interview at the shoe shop where my father was working. She didn't get the job, but my father, the junior sales clerk, asked her out. When my brother and I were little we often asked our father to tell us the story of how he met our mother. He always said the same thing. He said that our mother had the best pair of knockers he'd ever seen. For many years my brother and I believed that knockers were a brand of shoe. It was through reading the *Playboy* magazines hidden among the boxes of pharmaceutical samples in the shed that I realised my mistake. And although we never spoke of it, I believe that Nathan, who is three years younger than me, was also enlightened this way.

I heard my father's car in the driveway a few days after he left. My mother was at her bootscooting class and Nathan had gone along to watch. The Valiant was empty and I wanted to ask my father where he was living, where all his shirts were hanging now, but it felt too intrusive. My father called me over to help him load the stereo, the fan, a china dinner service that had never been out of its box, an Esky, and a bodybuilding machine into the back of his car. I knew that my mother would be angry, but I felt flattered my father had asked me for help with the lifting. No man ever refused to help another man lift.

A week later, my father came back again and tried to remove some of the boxes of pharmaceutical samples from the shed. My mother rushed out of the house as soon as she saw his car. She shrieked at him and tried to block the doorway to the shed. My father pushed past her. Nathan started to whimper. I stood near the tailgate of the Valiant – I hoped that my father would think I was trying to help him, and that my mother would think I was trying to stop him. My mother saw one of our neighbours working in his garden over the fence and she called out to him. She insisted that he help her, saying that my father was trying to steal her property. Ron looked uncomfortable, but he came and leant against the fence, holding his small soil-stained trowel in his hand.

'G'day, Ron,' my father said, cheerfully, as he carried a stack of cardboard boxes towards the car. My mother rushed at him then, and they grappled with the boxes. Some of the boxes disintegrated as my mother and father snatched at them. Ron banged his trowel against the fence palings to signal his disapproval. I was embarrassed for all of us. It was unseemly. The pieces of soft cardboard on the ground looked dirty and cheap. The value of us – the whole family enterprise – seemed to be symbolised by them.

My father never came to the house again. He took a job interstate. The telephone calls became less and less frequent, then they stopped. The first year, with the anticipation that he might write or ring on our birthdays or at Christmas, was confusing, but things settled down after that.

Because my father left Western Australia and my mother didn't know where he was working, she was unable to have any maintenance payments taken out of his wages. Money was tight. When the windscreen of the Torana shattered, my mother covered it in gladwrap and kept driving. She took a job with the local real estate agent. She didn't have her licence, so she answered the telephone and wrote down messages. On the weekends the owner of the agency let her put up directional signs in the streets surrounding houses they had listed for sale. He told her it was good experience and would help her when she sat the exam for her estate agent's licence.

One Saturday morning Nathan and I went along to help our mother with the signs. The signs were metal; they attached to a steel stake with wire. There was a rubber mallet to bang the steel stakes into the ground. The house for sale was on a recent estate behind the tip. A new road had been built to get into the estate so that the residents didn't have to go past the tip, but everyone knew it was there. In summer the tip stank as the rubbish decayed in the heat. It was better in winter when people lit fires there and the smoke was rich and fruity. We parked on the side of the road and tried to hammer the first stake into the ground. It only went in a few inches before it hit rock. We took turns. Each of us thought the other wasn't doing it right, until we had tried for ourselves. As I hit the stake with the mallet and the force reverberated, not into the ground, but back up my arm and shoulder, I knew we were no longer a family. A woman and two boys is not a family. We had no muscle. We had no way of breaking through.

It rained overnight. My mother insisted that we go back and try to erect the signs the next day, as the ground would be softer. With my father gone I had to sit next to my mother in the front seat of the car as she drove. She was wearing Nathan's old raincoat from scouts and a red gingham headscarf over her hair. I told her that it would suit her better if she tied it under her throat like the Queen.

'This way,' I said, as I turned in the seat and knotted it under her chin, 'is more dignified.' I was already a foot taller than her and I was worried someone from school might see us and think she was my girlfriend, instead of my mother. My brother sat in the back of the car while my mother swung at the stake with the mallet. The rain had muddied the surface of the ground, but barely soaked in at all. It was still hard going. It started to drizzle. I held the Lorazepam® High-Potency Benzodiazepine golf umbrella over my mother's head with my arm outstretched so I didn't have to stand too close to her. If anyone drove past and saw us I hoped they would think I was more in the role of caddy than lover.

Increasingly, when I thought about my father, my memories of him were not so much of actual events or incidents, but of the things he left behind. My father had a moustache and one of his eyes was sleepy. The sleepy eye was more noticeable in photographs than in real life. Not many adults have a sleepy eye – or perhaps it's difficult to tell because so many of them wear glasses. There was a framed photograph of my parents on their wedding day next to the telephone in the hall. My mother is wearing a too-big navy suit in the photograph. Her cheeks are uneven and she looks seasick. My father seems happier – his moustache, if not his mouth, is smiling.

His eyes are downcast though. He is looking at the most striking thing in the photograph – his massive white wrists. My father told me the story of the photograph one night when he'd been drinking and my mother wouldn't let him in the house. He climbed through my window and spent the night on the floor next to my bed. The story was this: a few months after the date with my mother, my father had another date. This date was with a girl he really liked, a girl he wanted to marry. He paid a friend who worked in a garage to give him the keys to a sports car for the evening so he could take the first rate girl out. Showing off, he took a corner too fast and crashed into a brick wall. The girl was unhurt, but my father broke both of his wrists. Because of this he was wearing plaster casts on his wrists when he married my mother a couple of months later. The casts give my father a serious and masculine appearance in the wedding photograph. The weight of them on his wrists make his arms look heavy, almost burdened, with muscle. And the thickness and hardness of the casts straining at his shirt cuffs is menacing. He doesn't look like a sales clerk, he looks like a boxer.

Underneath the photograph, in the drawer of the hall table, there are three boxes of white biros with blue writing on them – Aldactone® Spironolactone Easy To Swallow Tablets. One afternoon after school I try all of the biros on the back cover of the phone book. Out of fifty-four biros, only seven work.

Because my mother goes on a few dates with one of the real estate agents and it doesn't work out, she has to leave her job. She goes on benefits and is made to do courses. Her course at the local neighbourhood house is called 'Starting Again for the Divorced and Separated'. My mother does her homework in her *My New Life Workbook* in front of the television. When she gets up to go to the toilet during a commercial break I take a look at what she's written. Under '*What motivates me?*' she has answered, '*flowers*'.

My mother asks me and Nathan to go with her to a Parents without Partners picnic. It's at an animal nursery. I can tell that Nathan doesn't mind the sound of it, that he would like to pet the lambs and the rabbits. But I say we are too old, that it's dumb, and by holding Nathan's eye for long enough I get him to agree. My mother goes without us. She meets a man who works on prawn trawlers in the Gulf of Carpentaria. The man has a daughter whom he sees sometimes when he's in town. My mother has a lot of late-night telephone conversations with the man on the prawn trawler. She has to say 'over' when she finishes what she is saying, because he is using a radio telephone. When the prawn season finishes, my mother's new boyfriend moves in with us.

I have become so familiar with the playmates in my father's *Playboy* magazines that they don't work anymore, so I read the articles. In *Playboy* forum, men write in and describe how they meet women in ordinary places; the petrol station, the laundromat or the video library, and they have sex with them against the bowser, the dryers, or on the counter. When this happens a friend of the woman with different-coloured hair often arrives unexpectedly and has no hesitation joining in. And if the first woman at the petrol station, the laundromat, or the video library has small breasts, her friend will always have large breasts – or the other way around. After I've read all of the articles I look at the ads and the fashion pages and choose things. I choose Rigs Pants, Lord Jim Bionic Hair Tonic, Manskins jocks, Laredo heeled cowboy boots with a fancy shaft, and Aramis Devin aftershave – the world's first great sporting fragrance for men. I think I hear someone outside, but it's just a pair of dusty boxing gloves that hang from a nail on the back door of the shed. When it's windy the gloves bang into each other. I can no longer remember if the boxing gloves belonged to my father, or if they were in the shed before we came to live here.

Nathan joins the gymnastics team at school and I get a checkout job on Thursday nights and Saturday mornings. Nathan's legs are bowed and he doesn't have any strength in his upper arms. When he does his exercises his shorts ride up and his orange jocks show. The gymnastics teacher says his vaulting technique is poor. He tells me that Nathan doesn't look like he's trying to jump over the horse, more like he's trying to fuck it. He tells me this because I am standing next to my mother in the school quadrangle at open day where we are watching a display of gymnastics. I am wearing my Coles New World tie and the gymnastics teacher must think I am my mother's boyfriend. Nathan is best at the type of gymnastics where he has to throw a stick or play with a ball – a type of gymnastics that might have been invented by puppies. Because Nathan's wrists are weak he wears special white tape around them.

He brings some of the tape home – he says the gymnastics teacher gave it to him, but I doubt it. Nathan wears the tape on his wrists every day during the school holidays. When the tape gets grubby he puts more over the top until his wrists are so thick he can't hold his fork properly. When he's talking he throws his hands around in the air and watches them. This is something I've seen my mother do when she has just changed her nail polish.

By over-ringing the total on a number of small sales, it is safe to take around five dollars out of the till at work each week. It's better not to take an even amount. Four dollars thirty-nine is good. *Playboy* magazine costs two dollars. I don't buy it every month. I buy it when the cover looks like it will go with the covers of my father's magazine already in the shed.

My mother takes her wedding photograph out of the frame on the hall table and replaces it with a picture of herself and her new boyfriend on a fishing trip. The photograph shows my mother and Wayne standing on a jetty together, each holding a fishing line with a white fish dangling from it. My mother's face is puffy with the strain of holding the fish aloft. Her lips are open and stretched tight, just like the fishes' lips. If it were a group portrait you would have said my mother and the fish were related. My parents' wedding photograph is relegated to a drawer in the hall table where the envelopes and takeaway menus are kept. The photograph rises to the surface every time I search for a piece of paper to take down a message. It is crumpled now and smells of soy sauce.

There is a letter in the latest *Playboy* that I think might be from my father. In the letter a man describes an encounter he has with a woman at a bodybuilding centre. The man describes himself as well built, with a full head of hair and a moustache. He is lifting weights on his own late one night when a beautiful girl comes in to clean the equipment.

The girl is wearing a short pink cleaner's dress which fits poorly across the chest. Because her washing machine has broken down and she is poor and has no change for the laundromat, she is not wearing any underpants. The girl says hello to the man shyly and starts cleaning. The man is sweating heavily – sweat is running off his biceps like he's standing under a waterfall. The man notices that the girl is watching him. He decides to do a few rounds with the punching bag. He calls the girl (she has been bent over rubbing the weight-lifting bars with a cloth), and asks her to help him lace up his boxing gloves. As soon as the girl gets close to the man, she is intoxicated by his sweat. She ties the laces of the boxing gloves together so he is her prisoner. She tells the man to sit down on the bench press, then she takes her dress off and rides him like he's a bucking bronco.

The letter is signed, *Hot and Sweaty, Tweed Heads*. I hope that it is my father's letter. I hope the girl in the story is the same girl my father took out on a date when he broke his wrists, and when she finally takes off his boxing gloves and they hold hands, I hope they are not joined by one of her friends with different-coloured hair. I place the magazine on the top of the pile so Nathan will read it too. I hope Nathan will think that our father is happy. I want Nathan to understand that our mother was never going to make things work with our father. She was the wrong girl. And because she was the wrong girl, Nathan and I were the wrong sons. It could never have been any other way.

DIVING BELLES

Lucy Wood

Lucy Wood is a British author. She grew up in Cornwall and completed a Master's degree in Creative Writing at Exeter University. The short story collection, *Diving Belles*, is her first published work.

Iris crossed her brittle ankles and folded her hands in her lap as the diving bell creaked and juddered towards the sea. At first, she could hear Demelza shouting and cursing as she cranked the winch, but as the bell was canulevered away from the deck her voice was lost in the wind. Cold air rushed through the open bottom of the bell, bringing with it the rusty smell of *The Matriarch*'s liver-spotted flanks and the brackish damp of seaweed. The bench Iris was sitting on was narrow and every time the diving bell rocked she pressed against the footrest to steady herself. She kept imagining that she was inside a church bell and that she was the clapper about to ring out loudly into the water, announcing something. She fixed her eyes on the small window and didn't look down. There was no floor beneath her feet, just a wide open gap, and the sea peaked and spat. She lurched downwards slowly, metres away from the side of the trawler, where a layer of barnacles and mussels clung on like the survivors of a shipwreck.

She fretted with her new dress and her borrowed shoes. She tried to smooth her white hair, which turned wiry when it was close to water. The wooden bench was digging into her and the wind was rushing up her legs, snagging at the dress and exposing the map of her veins. She'd forgotten tights; she always wore trousers and knew it was a mistake to wear a dress. She'd let herself get talked into it, but had chosen brown, a small victory. She gathered the skirt up and sat on it. If this was going to be the first time she saw her husband in forty-eight years she didn't want to draw attention to the state of her legs. 'You've got to be heartbreaking as hell,' Demelza advised her customers, pointing at them with her cigarette. 'Because you've got a lot of competition down there.'

Salt and spray leapt up to meet the bell as it slapped into the sea. Cold, dark water surged upwards. Iris lifted her feet, waiting for the air pressure in the bell to level off the water underneath the footrest. She didn't want anything oily or foamy to stain Annie's shoes. She went through a checklist – Vanish, cream cleaner, a bit of bicarb – something would get it out but it would be a fuss. She pulled her cardigan sleeves down and straightened the life-jacket. Thousands of bubbles forced themselves up the sides of the diving bell, rolling over the window like marbles. She peered out but couldn't see anything beyond the disturbed water.

As she was lowered further the sea calmed and stilled. Everything was silent. She put her feet back down and looked into the disc of water below them, which was flat and thick and barely rippled. She could be looking at a lino or slate floor rather than a gap that opened into all those airless fathoms. A smudged grey shape floated past. The diving bell jolted and tipped, then righted itself and sank lower through the water.

Iris held her handbag against her chest and tried not to breathe too quickly. She had about two hours' worth of oxygen but if she panicked or became over-excited she would use it up more quickly. Her fingers laced and unlaced. 'I don't want to have to haul you back up here like a limp fish,' Demelza had told her each time she'd gone down in the bell. 'Don't go thinking you're an expert or anything. One pull on the cord to stop, another to start again. Two tugs for the net and three to come back up. Got it?' Iris had written the instructions down the first time in her thin, messy writing and put them in her bag along with tissues and mints, just in case. The pull-cord was threaded through a tube that ran alongside the chain attaching the bell to the trawler. Demelza tied her end of it to a cymbal that she'd rigged on to a tripod, so that it crashed loudly whenever someone pulled on it. The other end of the cord drooped down and brushed roughly against the top of Iris's head.

She couldn't see much out of the window; it all looked grey and endless, as if she were moving through fog rather than water. The diving bell dropped down slowly, slower, and then stopped moving altogether. The chain slackened and for a second it seemed as though the bell had been cut off and was about to float away. Then the chain straightened out and Iris rocked sideways, caught between the tension above and the bell's heavy lead rim below. She hung suspended in the mid-depths of the sea. This had happened on her second dive as well. Demelza had suddenly stopped winching, locked the handle and gone to check over her co-ordinates one last time. She wouldn't allow the diving bell to land even a foot off the target she'd set herself.

The bell swayed. Iris sat very still and tried not to imagine the weight of the water pressing in. She took a couple of rattling breaths. It was like those moments when she woke up in the middle of the night, breathless and alone, reaching across the bed and finding nothing but a heap of night-chilled pillows. She just needed to relax and wait, relax and wait. She took out a mint and crunched down hard, the grainy sugar digging into her back teeth.

After a few moments Demelza started winching again and Iris loosened her shoulders, glad to be on the move. Closer to the seabed, the water seemed to clear. Then, suddenly, there was the shipwreck, looming upwards like an unlit bonfire, all splints and beams and slumped funnels. The rusting mainframe arched and jutted. Collapsed sheets of iron were strewn across the sand. The diving bell moved between girders and cables before stopping just above the engine. The *Queen Mary*'s sign, corroded and nibbled, gazed up at Iris. Empty cupboards were scattered to her left. The cargo ship had been transporting train carriages and they were lying all over the seabed, marooned and broken, like bodies that had been weighed down with stones and buried at sea. Orange rust bloomed all over them. Green and purple seaweed drifted out through the windows. Red man's fingers and dead man's fingers pushed up from the wheel arches.

Demelza thought that this would be a good place to trawl. She'd sent Iris down to the same spot already. 'Sooner or later,' she said, 'they all come back. They stay local, you see. They might go gallivanting off for a while, but they always come back to the same spot. They're nostalgic bastards, sentimental as hell. That makes them stupid. Not like us though, eh?' she added, yanking Iris's life-jacket straps tighter.

A cuckoo wrasse weaved in and out of the ship's bones. Cuttlefish mooned about like lost old men. Iris spat on her glasses, wiped them on her cardigan, hooked them over her ears, and waited.

Over the years, she had tried to banish as many lonely moments as possible. She kept busy. She took as many shifts as she could at the hotel, and then when that stopped she became addicted to car boot sales – travelling round to different ones at the weekends, sifting through chipped plates and dolls and candelabra, never buying anything, just sifting through. She joined a pen pal company and started writing to a man in Orkney; she liked hearing about the sudden weather and the seals hauled out on the beach, his bus and his paintings. 'I am fine as always,' she would write, but stopped when he began to send dark, tormented paintings, faces almost hidden under black and red.

She knew how to keep busy most of the day and, over time, her body learned to shut down and nap during the blank gap straight after lunch. It worked almost every time, although once, unable to sleep and sick of the quiet humming of the freezer – worse than silence she often thought – she turned it off and let the food melt and drip on the floor. Later, regretting the waste, she'd spent hours cooking, turning it into pies and casseroles and refreezing it for another day.

She ate in front of films she borrowed from the library. She watched anything she could get her hands on. It was when the final credits rolled, though, when the music had stopped and the tape rewound, that her mind became treacherous and leapt towards the things she tried not to think about during the day. That was when she lay back in the chair – kicking and jolting between wakefulness and sleep as if she were thrashing about in shallow water – and let her husband swim back into the house.

Then, she relived the morning when she had woken to the smell of salt and damp and found a tiny fish in its death throes on the pillow next to her. There was only a lukewarm indent in the mattress where her husband should have been. She swung her legs out of bed and followed a trail of sand down the stairs, through the kitchen and towards the door. Her heart thumped in the soles of her bare feet. The door was open. Two green crabs high-stepped across the slates. Bladderwrack festooned the kitchen, and here and there, on the fridge, on the kettle, anemones bloomed, fat and dark as hearts. It took her all day to scrub and bleach and mop the house back into shape. By the time she'd finished he could have been anywhere. She didn't phone the police; no one ever phoned the police. No one was reported missing.

Despite the bleach, the smell lingered in cupboards and corners. Every so often, an anemone would appear overnight; she would find a translucent shrimp darting around inside an empty milk bottle. Sometimes, all the water in the house turned into brine and she lugged huge bottles of water home from the supermarket. The silence waxed and waned. Life bedded itself down again like a hermit crab in a bigger, emptier shell.

Once in a while, Annie and her husband Westy came round to see Iris. They lived on the same street and came over when Annie had something she wanted to say or if she was bored. She could smell out bad news and liked to talk about it, her own included. Westy went wherever she went. He was a vague man. He'd got his whole Scout group lost when he was twelve because he'd read the compass wrong, so he was nicknamed Westy and it stuck – everyone used it, even his wife; sometimes Iris wondered if he could even remember his real name. When Annie dies, she sometimes thought, his mind will go, just like that, and mentally she would snap her fingers, instantly regretting thinking it.

When she heard them coming up the path she would rush round the house, checking water filters, tearing thrift off the shelves. If she ever missed something, a limpet shell, a watery cluster of sea moss, Annie and Westy would look away, pretending not to notice.

Last month, they came over on a Sunday afternoon. 'I don't like Sundays,' Annie said, drinking her tea at scalding point. 'They make me feel like I'm in limbo.' She was short and spread herself out over the chair. She made Iris want to stoop over.

It was damp outside and the kitchen windows had steamed up. Annie had brought over saffron cake and Iris bit at the edges, feeling she had to but hating the chlorine taste of it. She'd told Annie that before but she kept bringing it over anyway.

'Don't forget the envelope,' Westy said.

Annie shot him a quick look. 'I'll come to that.' She glanced down at her bag. 'Have you heard about the burglaries around King's Road?'

'I read something about it,' Iris said. She crossed her arms, knowing that Annie was trying to ease into something.

'Five over two weeks. All in the middle of the day. The owners came back to stripped houses – everything gone, even library books.'

'Library books?' Iris said. She saw that Annie and Westy were wearing the same fleece in different colours – one purple, one checked red and green.

'Exactly. One of the owners said they saw a van driving away. They saw the men in there looking at them.' Annie paused, looked at Westy. 'Imagine going in there, seeing the bare walls, knowing that someone had gone through everything, valuing it.'

'Their shoes,' Westy said.

'Everything,' said Annie. 'And no chance of ever getting it back.' She stopped, waiting for Iris to speak, but Iris didn't say anything. Annie reached down into her bag and got out a blue and gold envelope and put it on the table, cleared her throat. 'Ever heard of Diving Belles?' she asked bluntly.

Iris didn't look at the envelope. 'I suppose so,' she said. She saw Annie take a deep breath – she was bad at this, had never liked giving out gifts. Iris's mind raced through ways she could steer the conversation away; she snatched at topics but couldn't fasten on to any.

'When Kayleigh Andrews did it,' Annie told her, 'it only took one go. They found her husband as quick as anything.'

Iris didn't reply. She tightened her lips and poured out more tea.

'It seems like a very lucrative business,' Annie said, pressing on. 'A good opportunity.'

'Down on the harbour,' said Westy. 'By the old lifeboat hut.'

Iris knocked crumbs into her cupped palm from the table edge and tipped them into her saucer. The clock on the fridge ticked loudly into the silence. The old anger swept back. She could break all these plates.

'A good opportunity,' Annie said again.

'For some people,' Iris replied. A fly buzzed over and she banged a plate down hard on to it.

'What you need is one of those electric swatters,' Westy told her.

'You shouldn't have gone to the trouble,' Iris said. She gripped the sides of her chair.

Annie pushed the envelope so it was right in front of her. 'The voucher's redeemable for three goes,' she said.

'It's kind of you.'

They looked around the room as if they had never seen it before, the cream walls and brown speckled tiles. A sea snail crawled over the window-sill.

'I can't swim. I won't be able to do it if I can't swim,' Iris said suddenly.

'You don't need to swim. You just sit in this bell thing and get lowered down,' Annie said. 'The voucher gives you three goes, Iris. You don't have to swim anywhere.'

Iris stood up, stacked the cups and plates, and took them to the sink. Soon Annie would say something like, 'Nothing ventured, nothing gained.' Her hands trembled slightly, the crockery clattering together like pebbles flipping over.

After they'd left, she watched the envelope out of the corner of her eye. She did small jobs that took her closer towards it: she swept the floor, straightened the chairs, the tablecloth. Later, lying in bed, she pictured it sitting there. It was very exposed in the middle of the table like that – what if somebody broke in? It would be a waste of Annie's money if the voucher was stolen. She went downstairs, picked up the envelope, brought it back upstairs and tucked it under her pillow.

The reception at Diving Belles was in an old corrugated-iron Portakabin on the edge of the harbour. Iris knocked tentatively on the door. The wind hauled itself around the town, crashing into bins and slumping into washing, jangling the rigging on the fishing boats. There were piles of nets and lobster pots and orange buoys that smelled of fish and stagnant water. No one answered the door. She stepped back to check she had the right place, then knocked again. There was a clanging above her head as a woman walked across the roof. She was wearing khaki trousers, a tight black vest and jelly shoes. Her hair was short and dyed red. She climbed down a ladder and stood in front of Iris, staring. Her hands were criss-crossed with scars and her broad shoulders and arms were covered in tattoos. Iris couldn't take her eyes off them. She watched an eel swim through a hollow black heart on the woman's bicep.

'Is it, I mean, are you Demelza?' Iris asked.

'Demelza, Demelza … Yes, I suppose I am.' Demelza looked up at the roof and stepped back as if to admire something. There was a strange contraption up there – it looked like a metal cage with lots of thick springs. 'That ought to do it,' Demelza muttered to herself.

Iris looked up. Was that a seagull sprawled inside or a plastic bag?

Demelza strode off towards the office without saying anything else. Iris hesitated, then followed her.

The office smelled like old maps and burnt coffee. Demelza sat behind a desk which had a hunting knife skewered into one corner. Iris perched on the edge of a musty deckchair. Paperwork and files mixed with rusty boat parts. There was a board on the wall with hundreds of glinting turquoise and silver scales pinned to it.

Demelza leaned back in her chair and lit a cigarette. 'These are herbal,' she said. 'Every drag is like death.' She inhaled deeply then rubbed at her knuckles, rocking back and forth on the chair's back legs.

Iris tensed her back, trying to keep straight so that her deckchair wouldn't collapse. The slats creaked. She felt too warm even though the room was cold.

'So,' Demelza barked suddenly. 'What are we dealing with here? Husband taken?'

Iris nodded.

Demelza rummaged around in the desk drawer and pulled out a form. 'How many nights ago?'

'I'm not exactly sure.'

'Spit it out. Three? Seven? If you haven't counted the nights I don't know why you're pestering me about it.'

'Seventeen thousand, six hundred and thirty-two,' Iris said.

'What the hell? There's not room for that on this form.' Demelza looked at her. Her eyes were slightly bloodshot and she didn't seem to blink.

'If it doesn't fit on the form then don't trouble yourself,' Iris said. She started to get up, relief and disappointment merging.

'Hang on, hang on.' Demelza gestured for her to sit back down. 'I didn't say I wouldn't do it. It makes more sense anyway now I come to think about it. I've never known them to be bothered by an old codger before.' She sniggered to herself.

'He was twenty-four.'

'Exactly, exactly.' Demelza scribbled something down on the form. 'But this is going to be damn tricky, you know. There's a chance he will have migrated; he could have been abandoned; he could be anywhere. You understand that?' Iris nodded again. 'Good. I need you to sign here – just a simple legal clause about safety and the like, and to confirm you know that I'm not legally obliged to produce the husband. If I can't find him it's tough titties, OK?'

Iris signed it.

'And how I track them is business secrets,' Demelza said. 'Don't bother asking me about it. I don't want competition.'

A plastic singing fish leered down at Iris from the wall. She could feel tendrils of her hair slipping from behind their pins. She always wore her hair up, but once she'd left it down and nobody in her local shop had recognised her. When she'd ventured back she'd had to pretend that she'd been away for a while. She dug a pin in deeper. Was Demelza smirking at her? She hunched down in the chair, almost wishing it would fold up around her. She shouldn't have come. She waited for Demelza to say something but she was just rocking back and forth, one leg draped over the desk.

'The weather's warming up.' Iris said eventually, although it was colder than ever.

Demelza said something through her teeth about seagulls and tourists then sighed and stood up. 'Come on,' she said. They walked to the end of the harbour. Small waves lifted up handfuls of seaweed at the bottom of the harbour wall. Demelza pointed to an old beam trawler. 'There she is.'

'There she is,' Iris said. *The Matriarch* was yellow and haggard as an old fingernail. Rust curled off the bottom. It looked like it was struggling to stay afloat. Its figurehead was a decapitated mermaid and the deck smelled of tar and sewage. None of the other boats had anchored near it.

Demelza took a deep sniff. 'Beautiful, isn't she?' Without waiting for an answer she walked up the ramp and on to the boat. The diving bell was sitting on a platform next to the wheel. It looked ancient and heavy, like a piece of armour. For the first time, Iris realised she'd be going right under the sea. Picturing herself inside, she remembered a pale bird she had once seen hanging in a cage in a shop window.

Demelza ran her hand across the metal. She explained how the diving bell worked. 'See, when it's submerged the air and the water pressure balance so the water won't come in past the bench. The oxygen gets trapped in the top. Of course, modern ones do it differently; there are pipes and things that pump oxygen down from the boat. Apparently that's "safer". They have all this crap like phones in there but they're not as beautiful as this one. This one is a real beauty. Why would you need a goddamn phone under the sea?' She looked at Iris as if she expected an answer.

Iris thought about comfort and calling for help. 'Well,' she said. 'No one likes change, do they?'

Demelza clapped her hard on the back. 'My sentiment exactly.' They walked back along the harbour. 'Give me a few days to track any signs then I'll give you a buzz,' she said.

Fifteen minutes passed inside the diving bell. It could have been seconds or hours. The hulk of the *Queen Mary* was dark and still. Iris noticed every small movement. A spider crab poked its head out of a hole. A sea slug pulsed across the keel. The seaweed swayed and rocked in small currents and, following them with her eyes, Iris rocked into a thin sleep, then jolted awake with a gasp, thinking she had fallen into the water, feeling herself hit the cold and start to sink. She hadn't slept well the night before but it was ridiculous and dangerous to fall asleep here, to come all this way and sleep. She pinched her wrist and shifted on the bench, wishing Demelza had put some sort of cushion on it.

Time passed. A ray swam up and pasted itself to the glass like a wet leaf. It had a small, angry face. Its mouth gaped. The diving bell became even darker inside and Iris couldn't see anything out of the window. 'Get away,' she said. Nothing happened. She leaned forwards and banged hard on the glass until the ray unpeeled itself and disappeared. Her heart beat fast and heavy. Every time she glimpsed a fish darting, or saw a small shadow, she thought that it was him swimming towards her. She worked herself up and then nothing happened. Her heart slowed down again.

Demelza was sure there would be a sighting. She said that she'd recorded a lot more movement around the wreck in the past few days, but to Iris it seemed as empty and lonely as ever.

Something caught her eye and she half stood on the footrest to look out. Nothing – probably seaweed. Her knees shook, not up to the task of hefting her about in such a narrow gap. She sat back down. Even if he did appear, even if she made him follow the diving bell until Demelza could reach him with the net, what would she say to him on deck? What was that phrase Annie had picked up? 'Long time no see'? She practised saying it. 'Long time no see.' It sounded odd and caught in her throat. She cleared it and tried again. 'Actually, long time lots of sea,' she joked into the hollow metal. It fell flat. She thought of all the things she wanted to tell him. There were so many things but none of them were right. They stacked up in front of her like bricks, dense and dry. She had a sudden thought and colour seeped up her neck and into her cheeks. Of course, he was going to be naked. She had forgotten about that. She'd be standing there, thinking of something to say, and Demelza would be there, and he'd be naked. It had been so long since … She didn't know whether she would … Was she a wife or a stranger? She picked at the fragile skin around her nails, tearing it to pieces.

On the first dive, Iris had got a sense of how big it all was, how vast; emptier and more echoing than she had thought possible. It made her feel giddy and sick. She had presumed that there would be something here – she didn't know what – but she hadn't imagined this nothingness stretching on and on. She shuddered, hating the cold and the murk, regretting ever picking up the envelope from the table. The silence bothered her. She didn't like to think of him somewhere so silent.

As she went deeper, small memories rose up to meet her. A fine net of flour over his dark hair; a song on his lips that went, 'My old man was a sailor, I saw him once a year'; a bee, but she didn't know what the bee was connected to.

She saw something up ahead: a small, dark shape swimming

towards her. Her stomach lurched. It had to be him – he had sensed her and was coming to meet her! She pulled on the cord, once, hard, to stop. The bell drifted down for a few moments then lurched to a halt. Iris craned her neck forwards, trying to make him out properly. She should have done this years ago.

He came closer, swimming with his arms behind him. What colour was that? His skin looked very dark; a kind of red-brown. He swam closer and her heart dropped down into her feet. It was an octopus. Its curled legs drifted out behind as it swam around the bell, its body like a bag snagged on a tree. She had thought this octopus was her husband! Shame and a sudden tiredness coursed through her. She tried to laugh but only the smallest corner of her mouth twitched, then wouldn't stop. 'You silly fool,' she told herself. 'You silly fool.' She watched its greedy eyes inspecting the bell, then pulled three times on the cord. A spasm of weariness gripped her. She told Demelza she hadn't seen anything.

'I thought you had, when you wanted to stop suddenly,' Demelza said. She took a swig from a hip flask and offered it to Iris, who sipped until her dry lips burned. 'Wouldn't have thought they'd have been mid-water like that, but still, they can be wily bastards at times.' She turned round and squinted at Iris, who was sitting very quietly with her eyes closed. 'No sea legs,' Demelza said to herself. 'You know what the best advice I heard was?' she asked loudly. 'You can't chuck them back in once they're out.' She shook her head and bit her knuckles. 'I had a woman yesterday, a regular. She comes every couple of weeks. Her husband is susceptible to them, she says. So she goes down, we net him up and lug him back on to the deck, all pale and fat, dripping salt and seaweed like a goddamn seal. And all the time I'm thinking, what the hell's the point? Leave him down there. But she's got it in her head that she can't live without him so that's that.'

'Maybe she loves him,' Iris said.

'Bah. There are plenty more fish in the sea,' Demelza said. She laughed and laughed, barking and cawing like a seagull. 'There are plenty more fish in the sea,' she said again, baring her teeth to the wind. 'Plenty, fish, sea,' she muttered over and over as she steered back to the harbour.

*

On her second dive Iris heard the beginning of a song threading through the water towards her. It was slow and deep, more of an ache in her bones than something she heard in her ears. There was a storm building up but Demelza thought it would hold off long enough to do the dive. At firsr Iris thought the sound was the wind, stoked right up and reaching down into the water – it was the same noise as the wind whistling through gaps in boats, or over the mouth of a milk bottle, but she knew that the wind wouldn't come down this far. It thrummed through the metal and into her bones, maybe just her old body complaining again, playing tricks, but she felt so light and warm. The song grew louder, slowing Iris's heart, pressing her eyes closed like kind thumbs. It felt good to have her eyes closed. The weight of the water pressed in but it was calm, inviting; it beckoned to her. She wanted to get out of the bell, just get up and slip through the gap at the bottom. She almost did it. She was lifting herself stiffly from the bench when the song stopped and slipped away like a cloud diffusing into the sky, leaving her cold and lonely inside the bell. Then the storm began, quietly thumping far away like someone moving boxes around in a dusty attic.

Iris waited, shuffling and sighing. She felt tired and uncomfortable. Her last dive. She wanted tea and a hot-water bottle. It was chilly and there were too many shapes, too many movements – she couldn't keep hold of it all at once, things moved then vanished, things shifted out of sight. She was sick and tired of half glimpsing things. It had all been a waste of time. She cursed Annie for making her think there was a chance, that it wasn't all over and done with. She would give the dress away and after a while she would see somebody else walking round in it. Her glasses dug into her nose.

She felt for the cord, ready to pull it and get Demelza to haul her back up. She had never felt so old. She stretched the skin on the backs of her hands and watched it go white, and then wrinkle up into soft pouches. Her eyes were dry and itchy. She saw a flicker of something bright over to one side of the wreck. It was red, or maybe gold; she had just seen a flash. Then a large shape moved into the collapsed hollow of the ship, followed by two more shapes. There were a group of them, all hair and muscled tails and movement. They were covered in shells and kelp and their long hair was tangled and matted into dark, wet ropes. They eddied and swirled like pieces of bright, solidified water.

Then he was there. He broke away from the group and drifted through the wreck like a pale shaft of light. Iris blinked and adjusted her glasses. The twists and turns of his body – she knew it was him straight away, although there was something different, something more muscular, more streamlined and at home in the water about his body than she had ever seen. She leaned forwards and grabbed for the cord bur then her throat tightened.

No one had told her he would be young. At no point had she thought he would be like this, unchanged since they'd gone to sleep that night all those years before. His skin! It was so thin, almost translucent, fragile and lovely with veins branching through him like blown ink. She had expected to see herself mirrored in him. She touched her own skin. His body moved effortlessly through the water. He was lithe, just as skinny, but more moulded, polished like a piece of sea glass.

He swam closer and she leaned back on the bench and held her breath, suddenly not wanting him to see her. She kept as still as possible, willing his eyes to slide past; they were huge and bright and more heavily lidded than she remembered. She leaned back further. He didn't look at the bell. Bubbles streamed out of his colourless mouth. He was so beautiful, so strange. She couldn't take her eyes off him.

There were spots on her glasses and she couldn't see him as well as she wanted to. She breathed on the lenses and wiped them quickly. Her hands shook and she fumbled with them, dropping them into the open water under the bench. They floated on the surface and she bent down to scoop them out but couldn't reach. Her hips creaked and locked; she couldn't reach down that far. One lens dipped into the water and then they sank completely. Iris blinked. Everything mixed together into a soft, light blur. She peered out, desperately trying to see him. He was still there. He was keeping close to the seabed, winging his way around the wreck, but everything about him had seeped into a smudgy paleness, like a running watercolour or an old photograph exposed to light. He was weaving in and out of the train carriages, in through a door and out through a window, threading his body through the silence and the rust. Iris tried to keep him in focus, tried to concentrate on him so that she wouldn't lose him. But she couldn't tell if he had reappeared from one of the carriages. Where was he, exactly? It was as if he were melting slowly into the sea, the water infusing his skin; his skin becoming that bit of light, that bit of movement. Iris watched and waited until she didn't know if he was there or not there, near or far away, staying or leaving.

EXTENDED COPYRIGHT